Fresh Ice

Enjoy!
SNB
10-21-2023

Sarah J. Bradley

FRESH ICE

By

Sarah J. Bradley

Sarah J. Bradley

For Tom, who introduced me to the fun of hockey, the wonder of movies, and the importance of good coffee.

ONE

I hope you're enjoying your funeral, Jason; it's the best your sister's money could buy, since you left your own family with nothing.

Izzy Marks looked around the room hoping no one read her bitter thoughts. Her eyes rested on the silver urn. Inside was what was left of her husband. Izzy tried to keep her face smooth, calm; what her sister-in-law would want. It was a losing battle. Her sense of betrayal clung to her features like stage make-up.

Cremation is best, in cases like this. That's what the mortuary told her a week earlier. It's best when all that remains is what's left after an explosion in an auto body shop. *So there's nothing left of you, like you left your wife and daughter with nothing.*

She felt justified in her anger. Izzy recalled too well the years of working and saving and paying the mortgage. She knew about the life insurance policy Jason paid on every quarter. She knew about the money in the bank. She knew about the mortgage burning party they had three years ago.

What she didn't know about until her meeting with Jason's accountant three days earlier, was the two new mortgages on the house. She didn't know every bank account was empty. Jason drained every asset they had in the span of three years.

Which made you look desperate, suicidal. And life insurance policies don't pay on suicides. This much I now know.

What did you do that was so much more important than taking care of your daughter?

It was a question she'd asked herself a thousand times in the past week.

There were so many questions for which she did not have answers, and it never bothered until now. Married at a very young age, Izzy hadn't finished high school, and never went to college after finishing her GED. By the time she was eighteen she was raising Jenna and keeping the house. Jason took care of everything else.

And before that, Daddy did. Or Mother. Or Coach.

"Hello, Izzy." Adele Grady, Izzy's sister-in-law, crossed the room and stood next to table containing her brother's urn. Mikayla, Adele's daughter, stood just behind her, tears rolling down her face. Sean, Adele's husband, stood in the background, as he always did around his loud, commanding wife.

"Hello, Adele." Izzy attempted to smile, an expression she hoped was the one Adele expected. She'd hoped the drive from Rock Harbor, just north of Green Bay, would have taken Adele and Sean longer. *I should have known better, though. Nothing would keep Adele from publicly mourning her dear baby brother.*

"Aunt Izzy, where's Jenna?" Mikayla dabbed her eyes with a tissue.

She's dealing with the loss of her father calmly, like she deals with everything that comes her way. Izzy glanced over Adele's shoulder for her daughter. "She might be in the bathroom. I know she'll be glad now that you're here, Mikayla."

Mikayla nodded and fled.

"Are you holding up?" Adele handed her a tissue.

Izzy blinked and dabbed her eyes, trying to decide how to answer Jason's overbearing sister. "I'm fine. I don't think it's sunk in yet."

Adele glanced at the group of mourners huddling near the back of the room. "Well, keep it together. A lot of people will be coming today. You don't want a scene."

Leave it to Adele to worry if I'll embarrass her with a show of emotion at my husband's funeral. "I know." Izzy sighed. "I have a lot on my mind. There's so much to do. I have to settle up the business. I have to go through his things." Izzy dabbed her eyes again and squared her shoulders. "I'm a little overwhelmed."

"Sean will take care of things at the business." Adele's voice was low, but her tone, as usual, was imperious and cold.

Izzy looked beyond Adele to Sean, who nodded. Relief washed over her and she smiled at her brother-in-law. *Is it wrong that I just want to clean out the house and let Jason fade away?*

"Izzy?"

Put on the right face, Isabella. Put on the right face and give the audience a great performance.

Izzy shook her mother's words out of her mind. *Where on earth did that come from? How long has it been since my mother said those words to me?*

Jenna, her beautiful eighteen-year-old daughter, entered the room.

Nineteen years.

"Izzy?"

Izzy focused on Adele again and forced a weak smile. "Sorry. I'm drifting today."

"Don't drift too far." Adele glared at her. "Sean and I will be here, for support, of course. We have always supported Jason, and you."

Izzy did not miss the double meaning in Adele's words.

Adele fished in her purse and pulled out a tube of lip balm. "Here, take this. It's going to be windy at the internment later. One thing you can depend on in Wisconsin in March. The weather will be awful." Adele frowned again. Izzy wasn't certain if Adele was displeased with the weather for daring to be unpleasant on the day of her dear brother's funeral, or if she blamed Izzy for the weather, as she blamed Izzy for so many other things.

It's probably me. She believes Jason killed himself because of me. Left us penniless because of me. Ended his promising professional career before it even began…because of me.

Izzy took the tube and tucked it in the pocket of her suit coat. "Thanks." She blinked back a tear and focused beyond Adele's shoulder. "Who is that?"

Adele followed Izzy's gaze to a tall man standing a few feet away in the archway. "I haven't a clue. He's not some relative, is he?"

None of my relatives would be here. Izzy blotted a tear from her cheek. "No."

"You sure?"

I think I'd remember someone like that. Izzy stared at the man. He was tall, very tall, and fit enough to be an athlete. He seemed frozen, unable to step inside the room. He scanned the room slowly, as if looking for someone or something specific. His gaze settled on Izzy for a beat. The stranger had, quite simply, the most beautiful blue eyes Izzy had ever seen. *No, they're green.*

"If he doesn't belong here, you should get rid of him."

You're right. I'm only the widow; I'll get rid of the unwanted guest. You're the one truly bereaved, you stay here and weep.

Izzy wiped her eyes again. The stranger was no longer in the doorway, but she had an overwhelming need to get away. "I need to run to the ladies' room for a minute."

Adele checked the archway. "No, not now. You can't possibly leave this line; people will want to talk to you, after they've looked at all the picture boards and signed the guest book. I can't cover for you all day, you know."

Izzy closed her eyes and inhaled deeply, something she learned to do in the years since she and Jason had escaped one angry, disapproving family unit only to join another. "Adele, if I don't go now, I'll pee in front of the mourners and that," she allowed the corners of her mouth to turn up in this tiniest of victories, "would be bad manners."

Adele's frown deepened, but she said nothing as Izzy scurried out of her reach.

Once in the lobby, Izzy breathed more evenly. *I've got to stop letting Adele have that effect on me.*

A cold fog washed over her. With Jason gone she had very few choices, and her most logical one, the safest one, the easiest one in many ways, was to move in with Adele and Sean. It was really the only option Jason left her.

She closed her eyes, inhaled deeply, and bumped into someone.

"Oh excuse me." She opened her eyes. In front of her was the stranger. *Blue-green.*

"No, pardon me. I wasn't looking where I was going."

His voice warmed her. While his accent was clearly Midwestern, there was the slightest hint of a drawl that she remembered all too well. It made her homesick, and she ached to hear him speak again.

"Is that a family member you're mourning?"

"Yes." She cleared her throat, hoping a stronger sound would come out. "Yes, my-my husband."

The man took her hand in his and patted it. "I am sorry for your loss."

"Are you...did you know my husband?"

Something, a shadow, crossed his face and his eyes darkened slightly. "No." The word came out hard, strained, as if he were denying something. The shadow left his face and he smiled, "I'm here, with friends. Some of the Milwaukee Admiral Hockey players are here to pay their respects."

"Oh yes. Jason did a lot of work for them. He rebuilt classic cars."

The man nodded. "Yes, I know." He looked beyond her. "Someone's looking for you."

Adele, no doubt. Why should I be allowed a conversation with anyone she doesn't know?

"Again, I am sorry for your loss." He dropped her hand and backed away.

She stared at her hand, his warmth lingering. *I never got his name.* She looked up, but he was already gone.

"Aunt Izzy, Mom says if you don't get your ass back in there, she's going to make you live in the garage."

Izzy smiled at Mikayla. "I'm sure she didn't say that."

"No, but what she said wasn't enough to get you to smile."

Izzy hugged her niece. "Thanks kiddo. I guess I should go in there and greet people."

"It is the tradition. Sort of barbaric, if you ask me, walking past the dead person." Mikayla put an arm around Izzy. "But I guess people need to say good-bye, right?"

Izzy walked back to her station near the urn and stared at the people gathered to say farewell to her husband. There were friends, coworkers, and people who knew Jason because he rebuilt automotive works of art for them. She could match each face with the pristine classic car they owned. *My parents aren't here. You'd think after all these years they'd forgive us. They should be here for something like this. How long am I supposed to pay for my sins? I gave up my career. I gave up my life. I lived in exile for almost twenty years. Now Jason's gone and everything we had went with him. How much more must I pay for that one night?*

TWO

Quinn Murray looked at his surroundings and sighed. Normally, he didn't mind the tiny radio studio. He guest hosted the morning sports show just often enough to get free tickets to every sporting event in Nashville, which, in turn, kept his name in the forefront of Nashville's sports scene. But after a long weekend in Milwaukee, where he watched more AHL hockey than he had when he played for the Milwaukee Admirals, Quinn wasn't ready for four hours of morning sports radio antics. What he wanted was a vodka tonic and a long nap. He wasn't allowed to have either. Serena, he knew, would see to that.

"Geez, you look like hell. I thought vacation was supposed to be relaxing."

Quinn nodded to his broadcast producer, Benny Jensen, as the round man squeezed into the studio and sat down. "It wasn't a vacation, Benny. It was a long working weekend. I went up with some of the brass over at the Predators to look at the Admirals."

"Any good prospects?"

Quinn shook his head. "Let's save that conversation for the callers. The NHL playoffs are just around the corner, I'm sure there will be plenty of questions about our AHL affiliate to the north."

"At least tell me you went to some good clubs."

"It was all hockey; all the time."

"Man, you can't lie to me. You are Quinn freakin' Murray. You are a legend!"

"Really? You wanna check my stats again, there Ben?"

Benny chuckled, setting his layers of pudginess into motion. "Okay, maybe not on the ice. But dude, off the ice, you are a rock star."

And that's exactly what got me into the situation I'm in now. Quinn nodded. There were days he ached to confide in someone, anyone, even Benny. Today was one of those days, but Benny looked far too cheerful. Quinn didn't want to ruin his mood right before the show.

"Well, you look like death. Tell me you've at least got a massive hangover, because that's how you look. You look like you drank all the beer in Milwaukee."

"That would have been a tall order, even for me." Quinn thumbed through a stack of fan emails Benny had printed out for him. "But I was the human hockey puck at an Admirals game."

"Oh see, now that's not all work all the time. Man, you get all the fun gigs." Benny glanced at the clock and stuffed the remainder of his donut into his gaping mouth.

"I had to do it. You know, breed goodwill between the Admirals and the team the Admirals wish they were."

Benny shot him a disapproving look. "Dude, that's cold."

Quinn knew his comment was harsh. Having played in Milwaukee for a few months while rehabbing a knee injury, Quinn Murray knew very well how forgiving and supportive the Milwaukee Admiral fans were, even of players who were moving on quickly. *Chalk it up to my overall terrible mood.* "Well, like I said, it was a working trip. If you don't believe me, go ask Serena. It was her idea I go."

"Boss lady doesn't give you much leash, does she?"

"She does not have me on a leash. She doesn't like hockey and she doesn't like winter, but she has a big interest in the future of the Predators. So she sent me."

"Oh please. You and Serena-" Benny let out a laugh that actually freed donut crumbs from his mouth.

"You and Serena what?" Quinn shot a sharp glance over the pile of papers.

Don't continue with this line of conversation, Benny. You won't like where it takes you.

"Oh, you know. You and Serena. Come on. Everyone knows about it."

Everyone thinks they know about it. If they really knew they'd run, screaming, into the river. "What do you actually think you know?"

"You're getting' it on, with the Boss Lady, right?" Benny started humming some sort of lascivious music which Quinn surmised was the producer's attempt at a porno movie soundtrack.

"Very funny. Don't we have work to do?"

Benny stopped humming and stared at him. "Oh my gawd! Did you meet someone in Wisconsin? Did you get some non-Boss Lady Lovin' with a Dairy State beauty?"

The very thought was so ludicrous, Quinn laughed out loud. "Okay, obviously you're not going to let anything go. Go ahead; tell me what you're thinking."

"Okay. Deny this if you can. You and Serena have been a thing for what, two, three years. She gives you zero breathing space. Am I right?"

You have no idea. "I will neither confirm nor deny anything."

"Which proves my point completely."

Quinn leaned back in his chair and studied Benny with amusement. "I'm dragged out from schmoozing the brass on two hockey teams for almost a week and you think it's because I've been, how did you put it? Getting something other than 'Boss Lady Lovin'?"

"Well, you look different which means you did something different. Look at you…you were out there, being charming with that face of yours and that air of mystery women love, and you were a whole time zone away from Serena? That's a no brainer! I want details!"

Unbidden, the image of the funeral sprang to his mind. More precisely, the image of the beautiful, petite widow sprang to his mind. *Why did I let myself do that? Why did I put myself right there in front of her?*

She hasn't changed one bit since the first time I saw her. All these years, I had to talk to her, just once.

Quinn realized Benny was still staring at him, waiting for an answer. "Well, you're not getting any details, because there are none. I did get a little ice time."

"Dude, unless that's a euphemism for sex with a cool looking chick, I'm not that interested."

"Sorry to be such a disappointment. The Admirals let me work out with them. It was a blast." Quinn checked the studio clock and noted they were on air in two minutes.

"I thought you abstained from the ice."

No, I abstain from alcohol. I abstain from normal relationships. I love the ice. "Just because I don't skate out every time the Predators need to have some sort of bobble head promotion doesn't mean I hate ice."

Benny let out another donut crumbed guffaw. "Dude, that last bobble head night was classic. 'Quinn Murray' night, and they've got the wrong numbers on them."

"Yes, Benny, I was there."

"And they had the wrong name on the back."

"Yes, Benny, I was there."

"And the bobble dude was black!"

Quinn rubbed his temples. "This is what I get for not giving you a play by play of some sexcapades that never happened? You are a complete jerk."

Benny wiped a mirthful tear from his eye. "No, I'm an overweight radio producer who is very, very lonely. And, you're on in twenty seconds." Benny pointed to the clock as he closed the studio door and seated himself behind the soundboard.

Accepting the inevitability of how long the next four hours were going to feel, given his brain-numbed mental state, Quinn put on his headphones, checked the clock, and pulled the microphone close to his mouth. "Hey there all. You've got Bruiser and Benny Sports Talk. I'm Quinn Murray, sitting in for Bruiser. And yes, we will continue the discussion about the debacle at the Superbowl a few weeks ago. But, today I want to lead off with hockey. I just got back from a trip up north to see how our AHL affiliate, the Milwaukee Admirals are doing, and I'd love to answer your questions about the Preds chances in the NHL playoffs. Benny, who's our first caller?"

***

After the show, Quinn headed upstairs and tapped lightly on Serena Shipley Chapman's office door. He closed his eyes and silently prayed that she wouldn't hear his knock, wouldn't be in the office, or wouldn't want to see him. Then he would go home where he would have a quiet day, alone to recoup from the weekend.

He could never be that lucky.

"Come in, Quinn."

Hand on the doorknob, Quinn paused to gather himself. Serena Shipley Chapman was a formidable woman. Everyone at the station feared her. Quinn Murray feared her as well, but for far different reasons than everyone else. Unlike everyone else, he didn't fear losing his job to one of her renowned temper tantrums. *She could do something so much worse.* "Hello, Serena."

"Sit down, Quinn." Serena didn't look up from the spreadsheets on her desk.

Quinn sat in the stiff chair on the opposite side of the desk. Every time he saw Serena, one thing struck him: the woman was beautiful. Tall, fit, well-coiffed dark auburn hair all fit together to make an attractive package. No one could accuse Serena Shipley Chapman of being warm, or friendly, but she had an undeniable magnetism.

Call it the magnetism of power, the aura of complete control.

"Quinn, how are you?" Serena folded the spreadsheet and sat back in her chair. "How was your vacation?"

He had to bite the inside of his mouth to keep from frowning. *You know very well it wasn't a vacation.* "Just fine."

"Successful, I assume?"

Quinn clenched his teeth before answering. "Well, the Admirals stand a good chance of winning the Calder Cup this year. I pointed out a couple of guys who could be nice additions to the Predators next year."

"You know full well I could not care less about hockey." Serena shot him an icy stare. "What about your other business? Do you have something for me?"

"No, I don't." Quinn hoped Serena didn't press him for the money he'd been sent to get from Jason. That money he'd put into a hastily purchased sympathy card for Isabella Landry, along with every other form of cash he had in his wallet including, he realized later, a Tennessee Lottery ticket he'd bought the week before. "As you know, Jason is dead."

"Yes, I got your text."

"So it's over now. There's nothing else you can do to him. He's dead."

"How can it be over? Do I have my dream back? Do I have a gold medal?" She pounded her perfectly manicured fist on her desk.

Quinn took a step back and slouched a little. *If I say one word, she might just go ahead and kill me.*

"You saw the casket, but did you see the body? Did you see his face?"

"No I did not." Quinn shook his head. "They cremated him."

"So you don't know for sure that he's dead?"

"Serena, I don't know what you think I'm hiding from you. I went to talk to him, like I always do. He had nothing left to give me. You've drained him dry. So I went back to my other job, you know, scouting for the Preds? Couple days later, I'm at the Bradley center, one of the guys on the Admirals says that the guy that rebuilt his classic 'Vette died in an explosion at the shop. Apparently Jason did a lot of work for the Admirals, because the whole team went to pay their respects. It was easy for me to go along. There was a picture of him next to the urn." Quinn called to mind the image of Jason's widow. Izzy, they called her now. Almost twenty years since he'd seen her, and Isabella Landry was every bit as lovely as she had been the last time he'd seen her skate. *I'm not sharing that with Serena either.*

"Was that little bitch there?"

Quinn shrugged, assumed an air of nonchalance. "There was a group of women standing there, and every one of them was mourning. I didn't go up and ask, 'Which one of you wrecked Serena Shipley's dreams?' There wasn't anyone there that seemed more broken up than the rest of them. Maybe they weren't even married anymore. Nineteen years is a long time for any marriage." He kept his eyes steady with hers; hoping Serena's sharp senses didn't detect his lie.

"A little sloppy with this, aren't you?" Serena frowned at him. "Have you forgotten, my dear Quinn, exactly what I did for you? What you owe me? Think again."

How could I forget what I owe you? It's something you bring up every other day. "No," his voice was chalky. "Of course I haven't forgotten what I owe you. I was just thinking…Jason's dead. If Isabella Landry did stay with him, she has nothing. And think of all the time we have, you and I, if I don't have to run anymore of these errands."

The fury faded from her eyes and she sat back in her chair. "Always the charmer. Fine, I'll do this your way for now. Let's talk about more pleasant things. How did the show go today?"

"Well, you know I always enjoy filling in."

"Yes, I do know that."

"I have some stuff I have to go do. You know, I've got that charity thing next month. And then I'm starting the plans for the big one I have in the early spring."

"Oh yes, Quinn Murray, the saint of a hockey player. The former bad boy loves to help the downtrodden." Serena gave him a hint of a smile, her voice smooth with only the vaguest echo of a Minnesota accent, and not even a breath of a Tennessee accent, though she'd lived here nearly two decades. Her accent, or lack thereof, Quinn knew, was the result of years of vocal training. *All part of a package. A very attractive, very lethal package.*

"Yeah, okay then." He stood, attempting to put as much space between Serena and himself. "You know, you might want to come with me to the event. It might give the station some good publicity. The one in the spring is going to be huge. It would be great to get some official help from the station in return for major positive publicity. It'll be for the Aubri Brown Club."

"Which charity is that? I can never keep all your good deeds straight."

"That's the foundation that helps families who have lost children. Helps pay for counseling, funeral expenses, that sort of thing."

Serena took a deep breath in, as if trying to swallow something very bitter. She folded her hands on her desk and made direct eye contact with Quinn, the light in her green eyes ice cold. "I have no interest in helping you with that, Quinn."

Quinn couldn't quite understand her reaction, but the look in her eyes unsettled him. "Okay."

She relaxed a little, the laser light softened in her eyes. "However, I'm not busy right now."

Her change of tone was all too familiar to Quinn.

"Lock the door."

Quinn turned and faced the door as he locked it. He listened as she walked around her desk to stand behind him. She reached around his broad body, her red clawed hands pawing up and down until coming to rest just below his belt. Quinn closed his eyes, trying to fight his body's inevitable response to her intimate touch. Unbidden, Isabella Landry's innocent face floated through his mind, then vanished like a whisper, drowned out by the throbbing cry blackmail and duty.

He had no other choice.

THREE

Izzy stared at the stack of cards between her and Jenna. *I don't want to open any of these. I can't look at them.*

"Come on Mom, we have to go through these cards. It's been almost two months, and Aunt Adele says we have to send thank you notes. I'll write them. All you have to do is sign them."

Izzy cringed. Sean and Adele were spending the weekend in Rock Harbor, but even from that distance, Adele tried to control her. *Of course Adele demands a thank you note. Because above all, putting on a good show is the most important thing.* In the weeks since Jason's funeral, her relationship with Adele worsened. Adele rarely spoke to her directly, choosing instead to send text messages to Jenna, who then passed on the message to her. *Once I live with her, will she still text Jenna, in Tennessee, while I'm sitting upstairs?*

"Okay, let's open them." Izzy picked up the first card and tore open the envelope. She didn't read the sympathy poem on the front and the pastel picture made no impression. Opening the card to read the signature, a check fluttered to the table.

"Mom, that's money. They put a check in the card."

Izzy read the name on the check, vaguely recognizing it to be one of Jason's customers. "I suppose people want to help out with the costs." She glanced at the pile of cards with less apathy. *Maybe I can fill the gas tank this week.*

"Mom, there are checks in all of these!" Jenna tore into the cards with abandon.

I'm about to be homeless. This is a godsend. Izzy opened a few cards, mentally thanking every person who slipped a small sum of money in. *I'll be able to drive Jenna to Nashville.*

"Mom," Jenna's voice was low, stunned. "Look at this one."
"What is it?"
"It's a thousand dollars, and a lottery ticket."
"It's what?" Izzy glanced up from her stack of cards.

Jenna held up a fist full of bills. "I counted it. It's a thousand bucks. And here," she handed Izzy a small slip of paper, "it's a lottery ticket."

"Weird. Who would put a lottery ticket into a sympathy card?"

Jenna held up the card, opened. "It's not signed. But the ticket is from Tennessee."

"How do you know that?"

"It says, 'Tennessee Cash' on it."

"Who would have put a Tennessee lottery ticket in a sympathy card?"

"Maybe one of those hockey players? Some of them have spent some time in Nashville, right?"

"Maybe. I don't remember who was there." Izzy closed her eyes and tried to picture the men from the Admirals. *I should have paid closer attention to everyone who was there that day. The only person I really remember…*

The tall man, with the beautiful eyes, and the hint of Tennessee in his voice.

Izzy took the ticket from Jenna's hands and stared at it. The name of the store where it was purchased was vaguely familiar to her, a chain of gas stations in Nashville, and the address was a downtown location. "Well, this is dated almost three months ago. It says we have 180 days to claim a prize."

"So, you want to drive down to Nashville this weekend?"

Izzy smiled. "No, that would be silly. Especially since it's probably not a winning ticket. But, when we go to take you to Vanderbilt, maybe we'll just go a few days earlier and see if it's worth anything."

Jenna nodded and returned to opening cards. "Sounds like a plan, Mom."

Izzy set the ticket aside and continued opening cards. Every few moments she stared at the ticket. *What a weird thing to put in a sympathy card.*

Especially one that's so far from where I live. At least for now. The "for sale by foreclosure" sign was in the front yard, had been for more than a month. *I really don't want to live with Adele and Sean.*

I could move back to Nashville.

Could I live there again after everything that's happened?

Izzy studied the ticket again. *It's almost as possible as this being a winning lottery ticket.*

***

Quinn drove the predawn streets of Nashville slowly. He loved this city, especially in late spring, before the weather got too hot. There was a vibrant life force in Music City he'd never found any other place. In his years as a professional hockey player, he'd lived in a lot of different places. Nashville was home.

Nashville in the early morning hours reminded him of a woman he'd once known, one of the very many littering his memories. She glittered at night, neon and music and laughter. Then, with the cool touch of dawn, she settled down to the daily routine of wife, mother, and car pools.

He'd been lucky, getting traded to the Predators after he couldn't pass the physical in Toronto. He'd been lucky to build enough of a fan base in Nashville in a short time, and because of his popularity, the team let him retire instead of cutting him outright.

Easing his car into the Waffle House parking lot, Quinn allowed himself a rueful smile. He couldn't pass the physical for the same reason he got cut from the Blackhawks and the Maple Leafs. The luckier part was landing a job that kept him close to hockey.

"WNSH, sports talk radio…" Quinn rattled off the call letters of the AM station where he worked as a color commentator covering the Predator home games mere weeks after his ignoble ouster from the league. They never sold a jersey with his name on it. He never stayed in one place long enough to make a positive enough impression.

He slammed the car door shut and headed into the Waffle House. *I really wish they'd sold jerseys with my name on them.*

Quinn checked his watch. His appearance at the charity game at Bridgestone Center wasn't scheduled until two, but he knew if he got there early, the ice crew would let him skate a while before the event started. The stolen time he had on the ice was one of the few things he held sacred. *Everything else in my life might be a weird dog and pony show, but skating, that's still real.*

"Hey there, Quinn, honey!" Tina, the toothy waitress with the nicotine voice nodded to him. "Don't ever expect to see you on a Saturday. Gonna be a nice day."

And everyone in Nashville is very, very sweet. The image of Serena flashed through his mind. "I'm in a hurry, this morning, Tina. Just a cup of coffee."

"Oh Sweetie, you're breakin' mah heart if you don't at least have a little bit of breakfast."

Quinn glanced at the clock on the wall. "Okay Tina. Have Frank whip up some scrambled eggs with mushrooms."

"And grits?"

"It's not breakfast without grits, is it?"

Tina flashed him a brilliant smile. "Well, it's not a good breakfast, anyway."

Quinn watched Tina as she went about her business in the small restaurant. *How simple is her life? Give folks a good breakfast and all is well. A good day's work done for Miss Tina. No worries, no secrets.*

No Serena.

Tina set the plate of eggs and creamy grits in front of him. "There ya go, Hun." She gave him a wide grin. "Maybe this will put a smile back on your handsome face."

If only it were that simple.

FOUR

"Mom, can we talk?"

Izzy smiled at Jenna. "We've got fourteen hours to Nashville, and Aunt Adele and Uncle Sean are, thanks to Mikayla's massive amounts of luggage, about an hour behind us. We have a ton of time together. What's on your mind?"

"Are we homeless?"

Izzy let out a nervous laugh. What the lawyers told her right after Jason's death was all too true four months later: there was no money, the house was in foreclosure, and the insurance company was not going to pay her a dime on the two million dollar policy because the police were adamant that Jason committed suicide. So, as they drove to Nashville to deposit Jenna and Mikayla at Vanderbilt for the coming school year, the house Izzy loved was being sold to the highest bidder at an auction.

Her impending move to Adele's house loomed like a heavy cloud. *I should have finished college.*

I should have gone to college. After I got my GED, I should have taken classes. Then I could have gotten a good job and I could tell Adele where to shove it.

Izzy inhaled and cleared her mind. "We are not homeless, not in the truest sense of the word. You will live at school and I will live with Aunt Adele. What else do you want to ask me?"

"Mom..." Jenna's voice lowered as if they weren't the only two people in the car. "Mom, did you love Dad?"

Izzy was surprised Jenna hadn't asked her much sooner. She never asked, and there was never a reason to tell her the truth. "Why would you ask that?"

"Mikayla told me Aunt Adele said you didn't. I thought it was a pretty shitty thing to say."

Adele, of course. Of course she would say something like that to her daughter. "Don't say 'shitty,' Jenna. It's low class. And yes, of course I loved your father."

"Well, saying something like that, it is. Low class I mean. Why wouldn't you love Dad? Everyone did. All those people who came to the funeral, they all said really great things about him. Even guys Dad did a little repair for eons ago, they came and put a card in the basket and said nice things about him."

"Your Dad was the best in his business," Izzy said softly.

"See, I told Mikayla her mom was full of beans. Aunt Adele should keep her trap shut." Jenna adjusted her seatbelt.

Yes, Adele should keep her trap shut.

"Mom?"

"Yes?"

Jenna pulled something out of her purse. "What's this?"

Izzy glanced at the medal in Jenna's hand. "Where did you find that?" She tried to keep her voice even, calm.

"When we were packing Dad's office. There's a whole box of this stuff. I didn't want to say anything, so I just put it in the storage unit with everything else. What is it?"

What can it possibly hurt now? "Well, kiddo, you found the big family secret."

"It's a figure skating medal." Jenna studied the medal in her hand.

"Yes, it is."

"There were a ton of them in that box. Why did Dad have a box of figure skating medals in his office?"

Izzy shifted in her seat, uncomfortable as images flooded her. "We wanted to wait until you were old enough to understand."

"According to the State of Wisconsin, I'm an adult." Jenna turned the medal over in her hand. "This one says 'National Championship.' What's that mean?"

"Okay. Okay." Izzy took a deep breath. "We were…we were pretty good, your father and I."

"You and dad were figure skaters?" Jenna started laughing so hard tears ran down her cheeks. "Dad?" She paused in her laughter to stare at Izzy. "Dad was a figure skater?" She covered her face with her hands and laughed more.

"Yes, he was. We were a pairs' team." Izzy waited until Jenna took a breath. "I'll go on, if you're ready to hear more?"

Jenna wiped her eyes, "I'm not sure I can take more. What's next, you're going to tell me you and Dad skated in the Olympics?"

"Well…"

"Oh come on! You two live your whole lives here in boring old Cobia, Wisconsin, where nothing ever happens. You work in a dentist office and Dad rebuilds old cars. Two of the most boring people ever. No offense."

"Right. None taken."

"Then you tell me that you and Dad were Olympic figure skaters? In what alternate universe is that even probable?"

"Listen, missy, are you going to stop howling and listen?"

Jenna took a deep breath. "Sorry." She bit her lip in an attempt to hold back another gale of laugher.

"Thank you." Izzy took a deep breath. "I was a pairs' skater, and quite a good one. But about a year before Nationals, the competition that would send my partner and me to the Olympics, my partner dropped out. Just like that. We'd been skating together for eight years and he just up and decided it wasn't for him. He wanted to go to a real high school or something. I don't even remember. I just remember one day we were practicing and all excited, and the next day he cleaned out his locker."

"Bastard!"

"Don't say bastard, Jenna, it's foul."

"Mom, I'm literally in the car on my way to college. It's not like I can say, 'oh fluffy bunnies.' Mike says I'll be mocked from one end of the campus to the other."

"Unless you're planning on having a career in the merchant marine, I'd like you to not take your verbal cues from Mikayla."

"Fine…"

"Thank you. Anyway, my parents were frantic."

"Oh so you had parents. You weren't just hatched."

"Very funny."

"Not funny. Mom, I've never known my grandparents. Dad's parents died like when I was four, and the only relatives I've ever known were Uncle Sean and Aunt Adele and Mike. That's weird. Now you're telling me you were this huge skater with parents…it's a little bit much for me to absorb."

Well then hang on to your socks, my dear. "Well, I wasn't hatched. I had parents. I had parents who poured all kinds of money into skating. A fortune, really, when you figure in tutors, traveling, costumes, all that. They were not going to let that huge financial investment go down the tubes, so they had to find me a partner."

"Is that how you and Dad got together?"

"He was part of a pairs' team from Minneapolis that was very, very good. They'd been together for a very long time, and had been to Nationals a couple of times, won it once, in a non-Olympic year. They were getting a little old, for skaters. Dad was twenty six and Serena, that was his partner, she was twenty-five."

"Ancient!"

"For skaters it is. Anyway, everyone figured this would be their last real shot at the Olympics."

"Mom, you did not steal someone's partner!"

Izzy tried to ignore the look on her daughter's face. Jenna's expression resembled too closely the horrified visages of fans when she and Jason first stepped onto the ice. *As if I'd broken up a marriage or something.* "I did not steal anything. It was a business decision. My father met with Jason and the next thing I knew, we were partners with a lot of work to do." *I always wondered what my father offered Jason to leave Serena and skate with me. It had to have been a king's ransom.*

Izzy blinked, remembering too well her parents' final words to her. *Yes, they had to have given him everything for a shot at a medal. A shot I gave up in one night.*

"What about his partner?"

Izzy shook her head. "That was the horrible part. I'd never met her personally, I'd been in a couple competitions with her, but every skater knew her and feared her. She was good. She was very, very good. She also had a reputation for having a vicious temper. I remember people talking about the epic temper tantrums she'd throw if things didn't go her way."

"They were a couple, right? Dad and this Serena?"

"Certainly in Minnesota, they were. Everyone loved Shipley and Masters. Masters was your dad's real last name." Izzy held up her hand to stop Jenna's inevitable question. "Fans loved to refer to them as a couple." Izzy shook her head. "Announcers kept pointing to their skating and saying things like 'That kind of passion on the ice obviously has its roots in their off ice relationship.' Every time they skated, people talked about how in love they must be."

"Was it true?"

Izzy shrugged. "By the time I met him, your father was certainly not in love with her. His plan, he told me, was to finish that season with her and then end the business relationship quietly."

Jenna studied the medals for a moment, as if organizing her thoughts. "So why all the mystery all these years later? Why haven't I ever met your parents? Why did Dad change his last name?"

Izzy took a deep breath and gathered herself to continue the story. "Word got out about the split between Jason and Serena, and the feedback from the skating community was not positive for us. Everyone saw Serena as the wounded, abandoned partner, thrown over for a younger model, so to speak. The first time your Dad and I skated together in public, we were booed."

"That's harsh."

"No, that's skating. There's this romantic notion that skaters have this deep romantic connection, like a marriage. Sometimes that happens, sometimes not. Jason and Serena had had a long relationship, but it was over. The fans just didn't realize it. And, if that weren't enough, the two of us were sort of an odd pair."

"Why?"

Izzy smiled. "Jason was ten years older than I."

Jenna counted mentally. "Mom, you were sixteen?"

"I was."

Jenna did more counting. "Mom..." she paled.

"Before you say one more word, let me finish." Izzy took another deep breath. "We wanted to win Nationals, which was the only way we were getting to the Olympics, because the US could send only one team that year. Jason was a strong partner. We worked very, very hard all those months."

"But you were..."

"Wait. Meanwhile, Serena had a press conference and said she could skate to the Olympics with anyone who wanted to go with her."

"That's gutsy."

"In her prime she probably could have skated with a chair and made it. But she was older, and those hours on the ice add up. She had the desire, but she'd lost a step. Jason told me their practices had gotten brutal because she would fall or lag behind and then she'd throw a tantrum."

"Did she get a partner?"

"Oh sure. They did a series of exhibition skates to huge applause. I don't even remember his name. He was just some guy that looked good in the costume and could toss her. The Twin Cities' broken hearted darling...that's what they called her."

Jenna rolled her eyes. "Blech."

"I know."

"So then when, exactly, did you and Dad...you know...fall in love?"

Could you call it falling love? Izzy ran her hand through her hair. "I don't know how it happened exactly. All I wanted was to go to the Olympics. But working together like that...and you know your father, he is...was...a very passionate man with his work." Izzy closed her eyes. *Passionate...and persuasive.*

He could have had any woman he wanted. He chose me. And I was so young, I was flattered, honored. I thought I was in love. But why did he choose me? Why seduce a teenager?

It was a question Izzy had never been able to answer for herself.

"Do I really want to hear this?" Jenna put a hand on her arm.

Izzy shook her head. "Probably not. But, it's long past the time you should understand your family history." She wiped tears from her eyes and smiled at Jenna. "Of course I developed a crush on your father. It was natural, I suppose. I was so young; he was the only male I came in contact with on a regular basis. Anyway, two months before Nationals, a few months before I turned seventeen, we made...you."

"Ew! Mom!" Jenna covered her ears with her hands in mock horror. "You can't just spring parental sex on my virginal ears! Ew!"

In spite of herself, Izzy laughed at her daughter. Jenna inherited Jason's dark hair and delicate facial features. But in Jenna's blue eyes and sense of humor Izzy saw her own image. "Sorry to damage your dainty sensibilities."

"How did you manage to skate in your delicate condition?"

"Not well. Skating is so much about reputation, and we had a lot going against us before we ever stepped onto the ice. Of course Serena spoke to anyone who would listen. She threw accusations at my coach, my parents, at your father. There was such a big age difference between us, some really unseemly rumors started to surface."

"Which apparently were true, Mom."

"Yes, which apparently were true. Everyone talked about how Serena was going to kick serious ass over us."

"Don't say 'ass' mom, it's vulgar. But seriously, how did you keep it a secret?"

"I have no idea. I was sick and terrified. So much was riding on us getting to the Olympics. Another four years and I would almost be too old, and your father, of course, would be ancient. The clock was ticking. Nationals were in the Twin Cities that year."

"Enemy territory."

"It certainly felt that way. I'd never been so scared in my life. I almost didn't get on the plane in Nashville. But my desire to go to the Olympics was stronger than any fear I had, plus, given the money involved, there was no way my parents were going to let me skip." Looking at her daughter, Izzy realized that Jenna was wrapped in the story.

"The first day, with the short program, we did very well, and we were behind Serena and her partner by a tenth of a point. But the crowd was so cold. I was miserable and I think it showed. Serena, well, this was her town, her people. Everyone, including the judges, loved her. The second day of Nationals, the long program, we were ready, or as ready as we could be, since your father and I had never performed our long program for an audience before. That was a long day. The other pairs did really well. The scores were very tight. Then Serena's turn." Izzy stared at the ceiling, as if watching the routine there. "My coach never let me watch other teams skate at a competition, so I didn't see it.

The crowd seemed to love them, though. Serena was still one of the very best. Just as he lifted her to do the throw triple loop, something happened. His shoulder snapped or something just as he was throwing her. She landed hard."

"Holy crap…I mean, holy carp."

Izzy smiled. *Something we taught her together, Jason. Using the word 'carp' instead of 'crap.' All our Southern sensibilities boiled into one word.* "Serena was fine, a little bruised, but her partner was really hurt. Oh, and the drama! There she was on one of the biggest figure skating stages, and she threw this monumental tantrum, and stormed off the ice. He just laid there, holding his arm. The paramedics had to help him off."

"So much for the Twin Cities' sweetheart."

"The mood in the room changed in that instant. By the time they got the guy off the ice, cleaned things up, the audience was actually really interested in seeing us. You could feel it. All we had to do was skate clean and we'd be fine."

"Did you?"

It was the most perfect moment I'd ever had on the ice. "Oh Jenna, it was beautiful. It was that perfect, perfect moment when two people realize they're going to do something that will bind them together forever. It was…magic. I didn't feel sick; we did every step, every element spot on. The crowd got louder and louder and by the end the place was in an uproar. Flowers…people tossed hundreds of flowers on the ice. That was rare for me, you know I'm allergic to most flowers and my fans knew not to throw them after I skated. I suppose the flowers were meant for Serena, but no one threw any after her skate. And after it was over, your dad lifted me in the air and kissed me there on the ice."

"Didn't that shock everyone?"

"Not in the audience. Skating fans love that romantic storyline, and it wasn't a super passionate kiss. But our parents, the coaches, and most importantly, the judges raised eyebrows."

"So what, then you went to the Olympics?"

"Well, we won Nationals. But I knew that by the time we got to the Olympics, I would need a maternity costume. It simply wasn't possible." Izzy glanced at Jenna, praying her daughter wouldn't ask the obvious question.

"You didn't think about getting an abortion?"

Jason begged me, my parents begged me to do it. "Sweetie, that simply wasn't an option for me."

"Mom, you gave up your dream…for me?"

"I don't think of it that way. I think, at the time, I was certain I'd have you, and then go back to skating. I was just going to take a year off. I was so young; it never really occurred to me that I wouldn't be able to come back. I tried to lay out that plan to everyone."

"And?"

"There was a major fight. My parents demanded I have an abortion. They'd put so much time and money into me…you cannot even imagine. Our coach wasn't all that excited but at least he was supportive." Izzy closed her eyes, recalling how the disappointment in Coach's eyes hurt her more than any of her parents' shouting. "Once the US Olympic committee got wind that I was pregnant…it became a legal issue, because I was a minor. Your father…well he faced some pretty stiff charges."

"What did you do?"

"We vanished. We left Nashville, got married, and changed our last name. Dad got a job working in Uncle Sean's body shop, and that turned out pretty good for him. Skating was done. I couldn't watch skating for a very long time. We certainly didn't put skates on until you got older and started going to skating parties."

Jenna smiled. "I always thought it was cool that my mom didn't crash into the walls when we skated. Everyone else's mom did. Now I know why." She chewed on her lower lip for a moment. "Did you and Dad, did you ever regret…you know…giving it up?"

Izzy shook her head. "All I have to do it look at you and I do not regret it one bit. I'm so proud of you and I love you. I wouldn't change a thing if I had to do it again."

"So I have a big dramatic family history." Jenna stared at the medals. "I think I'm glad you told me. I think it explains a lot."

A tear welled in Izzy's eye. "I thought it might."

FIVE

It was late, but after an evening in Serena's bed, Quinn needed a shower. The hot water stung him like nails, but he didn't care. More and more his evenings with Serena left him feeling dirty, and scalding water helped cleanse his body and his soul, if only a little.

Leaning against the shower wall, Quinn closed his eyes and accepted the release the water's sting gave him as he tried to erase images that ran through his mind, the images that haunted him every day.

How did I get to this place?

He knew the answer all too well. He opened his eyes and adjusted the water to make it hotter, wishing he could wash away the images burned into his memory like scars, ugly and red. Red, like the lights of the police cars and the rescue vehicles were that night.

Has it really been three years?

It didn't feel like three years. Standing in the shower, in the upscale apartment paid for by his fame, he felt as lost and as agonized as he had the night Sally died.

Don't think about that now. It's over, it's past.

Only it's really never over, is it? Every time I sleep with Serena, every time I had to go harass that poor bastard Jason, it was all there in front of me.

Sally was the stereotypical personal assistant. Young, fresh like a new rose, still tightly closed, dew rolling off the bud. Quinn's stomach churned as her face, so sweet, so trusting, crossed his memory. *She'd be twenty-four now, wouldn't she?*

No, she'd be twenty-two.

That's how it started: A simple lie on a job application. A high school graduate, too poor to afford college, looking for a job that would support her and give her a leg up, that's all it was. Though why such a sweet girl like Sally ever wanted to be a personal assistant to someone like him, Quinn never knew.

Five years ago, Quinn signed with the Predators, and was the hottest thing in town. His arrival gave a struggling team a shot of energy, and Quinn capitalized on it by giving great post game interviews. *Well, that and a hell of a lot of personal appearances.* His appearances started to overwhelm the front office, so they suggested he have a personal assistant, a suggestion the womanizing Quinn relished.

I would never have touched her. Quinn brushed water away from his face and mentally repeated the mantra he swore to whenever he thought of Sally. *Had I known she wasn't twenty-one, I would never have touched her.*

Even I have boundaries.

Age, he knew, was about the only boundary he had back then. There wasn't much female skin that didn't carry his fingerprints in those early days in Nashville. At thirty-three, after knocking around the NHL for more than a decade, he was finally where he wanted to be. Money, fame, and an endless supply of fans were all his. He was on top of the world, and everyone wanted to be near him, Sally most of all.

She was twenty-one, her application said. She was twenty-one and very happy to join him on all of his appearances. She was happy to run his little errands, to fetch him coffee, to be his personal attendant. He was the king in her world. It was his god-given right to have her, and she was entirely too willing.

Looking back, Quinn should have known. He should have read the signs and known that Sally wasn't quite everything she said she was. But he was drunk with power, drunk with lust, and just plain drunk. Everyone, everywhere, wanted to buy him a drink, and he was quite willing to accept. After all, to refuse would be to offend his adoring public.

Every night became a party for Quinn, with Sally at his side always ready to drive him home after he'd drunk himself into a stupor. It was Sally who bore his weight as he staggered into his apartment, and it was Sally who eased his shoes off and tucked him into bed with gentle hands.

It was Quinn who crossed the line.

Guilt tore through Quinn and he crossed his arms over his stomach to keep from throwing up in the shower. *It still makes me sick to think about it...what I remember of it.*

Cloudy images floated in his mind. He remembered so little of that last night, which wasn't new. He never remembered much when he was drinking. Something as simple as a couple glasses of wine could turn out the lights on his memory, and that night there was far more than a couple glasses of wine.

The party had already gone on too long, that much he remembered. Sally tried to get him to leave, begged him to leave. *But I was too busy being the huge hockey star. I couldn't leave when there were drinks being bought for me.*

And then...

And then she told me about the baby.

Suddenly Sally's face was there, in the shower with him, everywhere, in front of him. Quinn closed his eyes and crumpled to the floor of the shower, guilt burning him with every drop of water.

"Quinn, I'm pregnant."

Those three words should have sobered me up. But I was so impressed with myself. I bought a round for everyone in that damn place and announced it to the world. And what did I say, what did I insist on?

I had to drive her home. She couldn't drive in such a delicate condition, I wouldn't hear of it. So I drove.

And my drunken ego got her killed.

Now he slumped on the floor of the shower, unable to wash away the film of filth that clung to him since that night. How long he sat there, he didn't know. He didn't care. The hot water depleted and chilled, he turned off the stream and stepped into the bathroom. His robe was warm on his chilled, wet skin. Wiping the mirror clear of steam he looked at himself.

Serena saved me. She was there at the hospital before the police. She was the one who knew Sally wasn't yet twenty. She was the one who covered up the whole sordid thing so completely that even the people in the bar, even the people I bought celebratory drinks for, couldn't recall even seeing me that night. She was the one who insisted I needed medical treatment immediately, so immediately that the police didn't get a shot at a sobriety test until I was well on my way to being sober.

How she did it all so quickly, Quinn never asked, and preferred not to know.

She couldn't save my hockey career, the Preds insisted I retire. But Serena saved everything else; my reputation, my lifestyle. She gave me another avenue to fame and fortune in Nashville. All I had to do was everything she said.

Their arrangement stopped feeling sexy quickly and started feeling more like slavery. It was a trade off, as she reminded him frequently: His top shelf life in Nashville for his obedience to her.

I now live a filthy half life, doing whatever Serena wants me to do, whenever she wants me to do it.

The filthiness of his obedience to her took on a whole new meaning the day she found where her former skating partner, Jason Masters, had been hiding since the day she was humiliated at Nationals.

I had a hand in ruining the life of a man simply because he crossed Serena. And now he's dead, and his widow is destitute.

No one can save me from that.

Quinn shivered at the thought, and tied the robe more tightly around him as he left the bathroom. *A trip to Chance's place is clearly in order.*

***

An hour later, Quinn set his glass down and stared at the rows of bottles on the other side of the bar. There was something mesmerizing about the promises each bottle offered glimmering in the half-light of the bar. *How easy would it be to just sail away again?*

"You want something else, Quinn?"

Quinn tore his gaze away from the bottles. *Of course I want something else. I want to forget everything the way I used to. I want to be the life of the party. I want the last three years never to have happened* "No, no thanks, Chance. Just another ginger ale."

"Comin' up."

The music from the stage downstairs annoyed him. Quinn swirled the ice in his glass and looked over the railing. Chance's place, aptly named "Second Chances" after Chance's first bar burned to the ground in a grease fire six years earlier, was a cavernous two story affair, dance floor and stage downstairs, bar upstairs. The bar used to be called "Chance's" and when Chance ordered a new neon sign for the front window, it should have read "Second Chance's." When they came to install the mammoth neon fixture, it read, "Second Chances," without the apostrophe. Chance cursed the sign company foully for several weeks until he wore himself out and returned to his usual lackadaisical persona. Everyone knew if they wanted to get a rise out of Chance, all they had to do was mention the sign.

Quinn came because he liked Chance. They went way back, and Chance was one of the few who didn't constantly beg him to be 'his old self.' Quinn liked Chance, but he rarely liked Chance's choice of music acts. "What the hell is that, Chance?"

"Ginger ale, what you asked for. I know it's not the special brand of ginger ale your pampered ass is used to, but it's what I've got." Chance didn't look away from the television screen above the bar. Quinn was the only patron sitting at the bar. Everyone else was the responsibility of the downstairs bartender, and Chance, Quinn knew, was a man who didn't like to step in and take on more responsibility than he had to.

"It's called Vernor's, and that's not what I'm talking about. What is that infernal noise down there?"

"That, my friend, is music."

"That's what we're calling music now? Some guy sobbing on his guitar?"

Chance threw a glance over his shoulder. "Leave the guy alone. He's a local kid. Sings sad folk songs. The girls seem to like him."

Quinn held up his glass for a refill. "What girls? There's no one in here but you, me, and sad sack down there." Quinn studied the musician more closely. "And he's hardly a kid. If he's a minute younger than I am, I'll eat whatever fried mess you're calling today's special."

"He's a guy who comes in here a lot to write music. Name's Collier James. He doesn't bother anyone, and he does not have a bad voice. He and a group of guys travel around those Renaissance fairs during the summer and sing drinking songs or whatever. During his off time he comes in here and works out material."

"He's annoying me."

"You could always go someplace else." Chance turned his attention back to the ball game.

"What, and miss all this great customer service?"

"Well if you feel that strongly about it, then by all means don't be here Saturday night."

"Why not?"

"His band's my opening act. I got three on stage Saturday night and his band is first up."

"You can't be serious. You think the under aged college co-eds are going to buy your watered down drinks and listen to that guy?"

Chance frowned at him. "First of all, every person that walks through that door has proper I.D. Second, girls like this guy and they bring their boyfriends to listen to him and the boyfriends can't listen to him without drinking. It's what you might call a circle of life."

"I notice you didn't say anything about watering down the drinks."

Chance twisted his face into an expression Quinn could only assume to be a smile. "Hey, this isn't a non-profit organization."

Quinn blinked. *Not getting here before nine on Saturday.*

"You know, you could help me out in that department."

Quinn looked up from his glass. "Which department would that be? The watered down drinks, the kitchen, or the music?"

"Smart ass. No, you know you used to get up on stage with the bands and really get the crowd riled up. You were a star."

"That's the operative word, Chance. I'm not a star anymore."

"Bull. You know very well you're still one of the hottest sports figures in this town."

Quinn shook his head. "I'm not sure what you want from me, but I doubt I'm going to like it."

"It won't be that bad. Just get on the stage between acts and tell the crowd how awesome this place is."

"I'm not going near the stage if that guy is on it."

"Okay, so be here around ten. Introduce the headliner."

Quinn sighed. "Fine. I'll be here."

Provided Serena doesn't have me tied up.

He looked over the railing at the singer again and cringed. *Not sure which is worse.*

SIX

Izzy set her suitcase on the bed and looked around the room. The room felt too large. She realized she'd never had her own hotel room. She sat on one bed, then the other, feeling just the tiniest bit wicked. Outside her window Jenna and Mikayla's giggles floated as they dragged several cases into the room they were to share for a night before they could move to their dorm room the next day. Sean and Adele had the room between hers and the girls'.

Sitting on the bed, Izzy realized she was the odd wheel. For the first time since she was a child, she didn't have a partner and everyone else did. The idea was exhilarating and frightening at the same time.

Here I am, back in Nashville.

Not sure what I expected. Border guards?

She smiled at the thought. As they'd gotten closer to the city, Izzy flashed back to the night she and Jason left. *I was so scared. It felt like the world was chasing us with pitchforks and torches.*

She frowned. "Why were we so scared? Sure, my parents were furious, but Jason's parents were okay. We were out of skating, the Olympics were gone. Why did we run in the middle of the night?"

Jason woke me up. "We have to go. We have to go now." Izzy heard his voice as if he were sitting next to her in the room, not an echo two decades old.

"Where are we going?" Izzy pictured herself as she had been; sixteen, obviously pregnant, still sleepy.

"Don't worry about that. We'll change our names and we'll be safe."

Izzy blinked at the memory. "Funny. I never asked what we'd be safe from."

Why didn't I ask that?

I didn't have a choice. I let Jason take me to Wisconsin to live and work and raise a child under a name that wasn't mine. And I never asked why.

I'm not afraid to be here. I'm...home.

The feeling was unexpected, and undeniable.

"Mom?"

Izzy looked up from her reverie at Jenna, who stood in the doorway. "Oh, are you two settled?"

"Yeah. We thought we'd hit that Irish pub across the street for dinner and then go down to the District for some music. Wanna join us?"

"Sounds good to me. But I'm a little tired from the drive, so maybe I'll just come back here after dinner."

"You okay?"

Izzy forced a smile. "I'm fine, Jens, just tired."

Jenna nodded. "Is it weird, being back?"

Izzy glanced past her daughter out the door to Demonbreun Avenue. *Just down the street is the Sommet Center where I skated...but they don't call it that anymore. It's Bridgestone Center.* "Maybe. I'm sure I'll see a lot of changes this weekend."

"You excited to be moving back?"

Izzy nodded, but put her finger to her lips to quiet Jenna. "They don't know. You haven't told Mikayla, have you?"

Jenna grinned. "Oh I've told Mike. She's all for it. And no, she didn't say a word to Aunt Adele. She wanted to be there, though, when you told them."

"I'll bet."

"Yeah, apparently Aunt Adele's all hot to have you living in Mike's room now that our house is gone. She is convinced you're all packed up to move to their house. Mike says it's going to be epic."

"I'm sure Mikayla didn't just say 'epic,' but she's right. Adele really wants me to live with them." *Likes the idea of having me to boss around full time, is probably more like it.*

"Oh geez, Mom, what about the ticket?"

Izzy picked up her purse. "Do we have time before dinner? This store isn't far from here."

Jenna checked her watch. "We can make time." She leaned out of the doorway. "Mike!"

"What?"

"You wanna run downtown before dinner?"

"Hell yeah! I gotta pick up some smokes!"

"You are not picking up cigarettes, Mikayla Grady!" Adele stepped out of her room and glared at the girls.

"Oh take a pill, Mother. I don't smoke. I get my kicks getting a rise out of you." Mikayla stepped out of her room and closed the door. "So where are we going?"

"You're not going anywhere. We're having dinner at that place across the street." Adele nodded to the small row of shops and eateries. "Just as soon as your father is out of the shower."

Mikayla rolled her eyes. "You know how he is about showers when he doesn't have to pay the water bill. He could be hours." She led the way down the stairs to the sidewalk.

"Be back by six." Adele called after the retreating forms of the girls.

"This won't take long," Izzy said calmly as she locked her hotel room door and caught up with the girls. Her heart beat a little faster, as if she was escaping something.

***

It's a rare Saturday night that Serena doesn't have me in her clutches. Quinn smiled at his glass of ginger ale as it glimmered in the dim lights of Chance's bar. *And now that Mr. Sad Singer and his band of sadder misfits is off the stage maybe I can have a good time.*

With practiced eye, Quinn scanned the women on the dance floor below him. On any given night, not that long ago, he'd call it 'fishing' and he'd find a woman, or two, and have one of the waitresses bring them to him. *It was all so easy back then.*

He caught the eye of one beautiful brunette who smiled and waved flirtatious fingers at him. *It's still too easy.*

"You know she's a felony, don't you?"

Quinn broke eye contact with the girl, swung around in his seat, and glared at Chance. "I thought you said everyone in here was legal."

"I thought you said you were done with your fishing expeditions."

"I am." Quinn drained his glass and pushed it toward Chance.

"Pity. I can't lie: your parties made me money back in the day."

"I know, my bar tab sent your kids to college."

Chance refilled Quinn's glass and pushed it toward him. "Not just your bar tab. Every guy in the place turned into a big shot, trying to be you. It was good for business."

Quinn stared at his glass, wishing, not for the first time that evening, that ginger ale had the same memory erasing powers of whiskey.

"Still, the new view you have on life, it's much healthier for you, I suppose."

Quinn shook his head. "Careful, Chance. You're sounding a little nostalgic." Quinn drained the glass again. "But I made you a promise and I'm a man of my word. I'll do a little monkey dance on stage and introduce the headliner."

"You mean it?"

Quinn shrugged. "Just keep the ginger ale coming and don't hand me a bill at the end of the night."

"You're on," Chance grinned. "At the rate you're going, you'll probably drink me out of about five bucks tonight, so it's more than a fair trade off."

Chance poured Quinn another glass and set it in front of him. Quinn watched the bubbles of the carbonated beverage float around in the amber liquid. *And it'll be the high point of my week. How sad is that?*

***

"Here we are." Jenna pointed to a dubious looking gas station some six blocks from the hotel.

"This is the right address. I guess this is it." Izzy didn't move. Both girls walked into the mini mart, then walked back out.

"Mom, are you coming?"

"Aunt Iz, if this is too much for you, we can just do it. We're over eighteen, so whatever, right?"

Izzy sighed. "This is my quest." She squared her shoulders and walked in. An icy wall of air conditioning slapped them.

"Wow, what the effin ef is that smell?" Mikayla wrinkled her nose.

Izzy looked around the vast, crowded, disorganized convenience store. "Wait, there's the counter." She pointed toward the back of the store.

Careful not to touch anything, or let anything touch them, the three women moved toward the counter. The closer they got, the more clear two things became: First, the counter area was no more organized or clean than the rest of the store, but, situated closer to the rest rooms, it did smell far worse. Second, the man behind the counter may have been the owner, or he may have been a homeless person taking a nap.

"Uh, excuse me?" Izzy could barely get the words out, for fear of breathing in the fumes emitting from the rest rooms. "Excuse me?"

"Hey, buddy!" Mikayla shouted, jolting the man behind the counter awake.

"What, what do you want?"

"Look, we're so sorry to disturb…whatever it is you're doing here," Izzy looked around behind the counter and frowned. "We have a lottery ticket that was bought here and we'd like to see if it's a winner."

"Scanner's right there." The man nodded vaguely at some point on the counter to his left. "See for yourself."

"Yes, I can see you have quite a lot of work to do." Jenna took a step to her right and gingerly moved a display rack of cherry flavored cigars and silk roses to reveal a lottery ticket scanner. "Okay, Mom, go ahead."

Izzy held the ticket under the scanner and waited until a beep sounded. She looked at the display screen. "Jenna, what does that say?"

Jenna studied the blue numbers. "Uh, well, I think you have a winning ticket." She leaned closer. "Mom, I think you won some money!"

Izzy's hands trembled as she held the ticket under the scanner once more. "It says I've won…I've won five thousand dollars!"

The three women squealed and hugged each other. Counter guy leaned forward as a greasy smirk crossed his dirty face. "Now we're talkin'."

They froze in their tracks and stared at him. "You're a pig." Izzy murmured.

"That might be, but I'm the pig who gets to verify your ticket. I'm the pig who tells you how to go about collecting your winnings."

Mikayla held up the ticket. "Well, it says here, Mr. Pig, where we're supposed to go if this ticket is worth more than $600." She cast a smile at the man. "So I guess that means we don't need your skanky ass for anything."

Izzy and Jenna laughed out loud at Mikayla's brash speech and started for the door.

"Yeah, well, you won't get the full five k, ya know! They take out taxes! They take out lots of taxes right off the bat!"

"Maybe some of that tax money will go to removing this landfill!" Jenna shouted back as the women, all laughing out loud, left the store.

SEVEN

"Now that was a good meal!" Adele held the door open as the girls, Sean, and Izzy stepped out of the dark, closed space of the Irish pub and into the sticky damp of the early Nashville evening.

"Who knew you could get the best Irish food in the South?"

"Show me, Sean, where deep fried pickles are Irish food." Izzy grinned.

"Okay, you got me there. So, who's up for a stroll downtown? Maybe find a place with great live music."

"Sounds like fun. Girls, you wanna hang out with the parents a bit more?"

"I've got just the place!" Mikayla tossed her hair and laughed at her mother. "A place called 'Second Chances' Jenna, you are going to love the bands they have there and the guys are seriously hot, it's a complete meat market!"

"Oh yes, that's what a mother wants to hear from the mouth of her daughter." Adele frowned at Mikayla. "Izzy, how about you?"

Izzy glanced in the direction of the hotel. "I was thinking I'd just turn in early."

"Oh Mom, come on. Please come with us?"

Izzy looked at her daughter and smiled. "Okay. Where is this place?"

The walk to Second Chances was several blocks down to the heart of the music district. As warm rays of the sun lengthened and cooled in the settling of night, revelers filled the sidewalks and the doorways of the countless clubs and eateries. Music and neon throbbed through a haze of mouthwatering food smells. Dazzled with the color of it all, Izzy was hardly conscious of the distance they'd walked until Sean opened a door and said, "Here we are!"

The girls evaporated in a sea of dancing bodies while Sean led Adele and Izzy up the stairs to the bar, where tables lined the railing overlooking the stage.

"I'll go get the drinks, ladies, you enjoy the show!" Sean left as Adele and Izzy looked at the band on the stage.

"At least it's not a howling band." Adele toyed with the salt and pepper shakers on the table. "I can't abide howling bands or bands that are too country, you know what I mean?"

"Sure," Izzy answered vaguely, leaning on the railing to get a better look at the band.

Sean returned with drinks, and the rest of their conversation faded from Izzy's consciousness as she lost herself in thoughts of her future now that she held a winning lottery ticket. She sipped her drink and nodded politely whenever Adele glanced in her direction, but her brain was busy sorting out what she was going to do. She was so deep in thought, she wasn't aware the music stopped until she realized Adele was shoving her roughly. "What, Adele, what do you want?"

"Why does that man look familiar?"

As she focused on the tall, dark haired man on stage, Izzy took in a deep breath. The man was perfection. Under the hot lights his dark, gleaming hair just brushed his strong jaw. *I've seen him before.*

"Ladies and gents," his easy, light Tennessee accent stirred something warm and wanting deep inside Izzy. "I'd like to thank you for coming out tonight and listening to some great local bands."

"We love you Quinn!"

The unified shouts of several women startled Izzy, breaking her trancelike concentration from the man

Quinn smiled back at the audience. "I love you all, too. Most of you know I make my living talking about sports, but music has been a passion of mine for years. How about a big hand for Chance, for keeping this place open and bringing us fantastic independent music night after night?"

Here he pointed up to the balcony, where a spotlight suddenly glowed near Izzy. She didn't look toward the owner of the bar, who waved at the crowd below. Her gaze was locked with the clear, blue-green eyes of the singer. She couldn't look away and she couldn't blink. *Those are the most beautiful eyes I've ever seen.*

He's the man from the funeral.

Everything around her narrowed until all that was left was the glow of the spotlight around him. Izzy saw nothing but Quinn's eyes looking up at her. He held his gaze steady with her for a silent eternity. Everything else was dark and silent, like a protective cloud around them. There was no time, no sound, just the glow of recognition in his beautiful eyes. It didn't matter one bit that they were strangers and would probably never be closer to each other than in this dumpy space. There was a connection between them, and Izzy was lost in it.

"What are you staring at? Do you know that guy?"

Izzy blinked at the staccato blast of Adele's voice, and the connection was lost. The party below raged on as the band Quinn introduced started playing. Quinn was gone.

Izzy, too, ached to leave. "I'm sorry, Adele. I'm not good company tonight. I don't think I feel well. I'm going to go back to the hotel."

"You're not sick are you?" Adele's eyes narrowed. "We have a lot of moving to do tomorrow you know."

No room for discussion about that. "Oh, no," Izzy wiped her eyes. "It's fine. I'm fine. I just need…I need some air. I think I'll walk back to the hotel."

"What, right now? Alone?"

"Sure. It's not that late, really, and besides, you and Sean, you guys need some time alone, too. So I'll just get back."

"Are you sure?"

Izzy looked over the balcony hoping to spot Quinn, but she couldn't find him. "Oh, I'm sure. I'll be fine."

***

She's here. Quinn walked backstage and laid his guitar in its case. *Isabella Landry is here, in this building. I could reach out and touch her and it wouldn't be weird or stalkerish.*

But what could I possibly say?

Well, she seemed really interested in what I saying. I could go up and maybe thank her for coming or something. That wouldn't seem weird. Quinn rubbed his hands across his face. *That's the best reason I can muster for going up to meet a woman? Good manners? My, how the mighty lady killer has fallen.* Shaking his head at his own folly, Quinn started for the stairs.

"Quinn, dude, where ya goin'?" One of the musicians put a hand on his arm.

"I saw someone…I have to catch up with."

The musician's face creased with a lecherous grin. "It's a chick, isn't it? I spotted a couple out there I'm thinkin' of scorin' on, too."

Quinn shook off the drummer's hand, repulsed by the lecherous expression on his face. "You're a pig."

The drummer shrugged. "Yep. I'm a pig. But I'm a pig that's gonna get laid."

Quinn ignored the band members' cat calls as he ran through the back stage and up the stairs. Once in the bar, he scanned the crowded room. *She's gone.*

"Hey, Quinn!" Chance shouted over the din of conversation. "I told you, didn't I? You're good for business!"

Quinn nodded to Chance, but searched for Isabella.

"Who ya lookin' for?"

"There was a woman up here. Probably at that table where that couple is."

"Buddy, there are a thousand women here and quite a few of them are age appropriate. Take your pick."

"No, Chance, this one was…well, I'm looking for her. You don't remember if she was with that couple?"

"Quinn, are you kiddn' me? Look around! I'm workin' here! If you're so interested, go ask them if they know her."

Quinn nodded to Chance and stepped away from the bar. He studied the couple at the table and toyed with the idea of approaching them. A light tap on his arm broke his concentration. Looking to his left, he saw two women, girls really, both looking very interested in him. "Hello, ladies."

"My friend and I think you are the hottest thing in this place."

Quinn's face warmed as the two women moved close enough for him to be very aware that neither was wearing a bra…and both were young and firm enough, not to need the support. "Well, um, thank you ladies."

"So how about if we get out of here?"

Quinn closed his eyes. *How often have I turned down an offer like this?*

Never.

When was the last time anyone offered?

Sally.

The thought choked him. He couldn't breathe the air in the bar anymore.

"Oh Quinn, you must introduce me to your new little friends."

Quinn shivered at Serena's icy touch. *Of course she showed up. She'll find a way to make me regret doing something remotely fun without her.*

He looked down into her glittering green eyes and gave her a smile. *Hopefully Isabella Landry left before Serena sniffed her out.*

That would be something for the gossip reporters.

Quinn almost smiled at the thought.

"Ladies, you'll have to excuse us. Quinn has a previous engagement." Serena's eyes narrowed as she glanced at the girls.

"What, you really have to leave so soon?" The braver of the two also seemed to be the denser of the pair.

She is clearly not reading the dynamic here.

"Yes, I'm sorry, little girl. But I sure there are more age appropriate men elsewhere in this...place." Serena gave a little sniff to remind Quinn how much she hated Chance's place.

"Geez Quinn, can't your mom let you come out and play?"

Ah you brave little idiot. Quinn didn't need to see Serena's face to know exactly what she was thinking. She buried her nails deep in the skin on his forearm.

"Listen here, co-ed..." Serena's normally cool voice was a ragged snarl.

"Okay, ladies, how about we all just say good night?" Quinn freed himself from Serena's claw and put a hand on each of the girls' shoulders. His fingers dangled just close enough to their twenty-one-year-old breasts to make both the girls giggle. *I've still got it.*

I can't make use of it anymore. But at least I've still got it.

"Now my lady friend and I are going to move on, but I'm going to have my friend Chance take care of you this evening. Chance!" Quinn pointed to the two girls. "You take care of these ladies, and put it on my tab, okay?"

Chance nodded and winked at Quinn.

"There, now you two have a wonderful night on me, and thanks for coming out tonight." Mustering up every ounce of Southern charm he had, he kissed each of their hands lightly, causing them to erupt in another wave of giggles as he ushered a still seething Serena out the door.

Once outside, Quinn inhaled the humid night air. "So, that was fun, wasn't it?"

Serena's hand stung across his face before he saw her move.

"Hey! What was that for?"

"Don't you ever act like that around me again, Quinn Murray!" The light of an over head streetlamp made her sharp features seem hollow, dark. Yet her eyes glowed with rage.

"Act like what? I was trying to keep you from killing those girls."

"Why? They were horrible little bitches."

Quinn put both his hands on her shoulders. "Yes, they were horrible little bitches. Horrible little co-eds whose daddies would probably love to bring a lawsuit against you and the station if you actually did tear their eyes out."

"You weren't thinking about me. You were thinking about those girls the whole time, wondering what they'd be like."

"Serena…" he crouched slightly to look her in the eye, "when in the last two years have I not been thinking about you?" *At least that much is true. The thought of her haunts my every waking nightmare minute.*

Her jaw tightened. "Why would you even be here, on stage? You were the one who got up on stage and made them all want you, just like you used to. And I won't have it, Quinn. You belong to me now."

Her words shattered against him like glass against a stone wall.

As if I could ever forget. You won't let me replace you with other women and I won't let myself drink you away.

Isabella Landry is back in Nashville. And not even that thought can wipe out our little arrangement.

"Serena, of course I belong to you." He draped an arm around her shoulders and guided her up the street.

"Really?"

He knew this new, desirous tone, well. "Sure."

"Then let's go back to my place and you can prove it."

"Great idea," he replied with hollow enthusiasm. *Isabella Landry, the woman I've adored for two decades, is somewhere in this town, and I'm shackled to Serena.*

He pictured Isabella's face as she watched him from the balcony. Her face melded to Sally's.

And what could I possibly do to deserve anything else?

EIGHT

Izzy leaned over the railing and soaked in the sounds of the city. There was something peaceful about the sleepy silence that settled like a blanket over a district that had, as recently as four hours earlier, throbbed with music and barbeque and neon. She sipped the coffee she'd made herself in the tiny hotel coffee pot and wondered if she could truly pull herself away and go back to Wisconsin.

"Mornin' Iz." Adele stepped out of her room, still clad in her t-shirt and lounge pants. "It's really quiet this morning, isn't it?"

"I know. Like the whole city is sleeping."

"Are you feeling any better?"

Izzy rubbed her eyes, trying to wipe away the faint ache that lingered within her. Surprised by Adele's rare show of concern, Izzy was honest. "A bit. I took some Tylenol PM and pretty much just zonked out. How late was it before you guys got in?"

Adele stretched her arms over her head. "Late enough. But we should get the girls up. We've got a lot of moving in to do today."

Izzy glanced to the parking lot where the U-haul trailer attached to Sean's van waited for them. She suddenly felt exhausted, drained of any energy. "Adele, I don't think I can help today."

"What are you saying? Of course you can." The civil tone, and the concern that went with it, were gone.

"I don't think I can. I'm sorry. I'm exhausted and I need some rest."

"Fine, fine. Don't help move your own daughter into the dormitory. Sean and I will just do that, just like we'll have to move you into the house when we get home."

Izzy bit the inside of her cheek, keeping her temper in check. "I'm sorry, Adele. I'm just not feeling well."

Adele gave her a doubtful look, but said nothing more. Instead, she pounded on the girls' door and shouted, "Girls! It's moving in day! Get up!" before slamming her door.

"Holy carp, Mom, what's up her butt?" Jenna emerged from her room.

"Don't say butt, Jenna. She's actually a little put out with me. I can't help you guys move in today."

"Still not feeling well?"

"Just not feeling up to moving."

Jenna put an arm around her mother. "It's cool, Mom. You know I don't have much of anything to move in. It's Mikayla that's got all that furniture. Probably why Aunt Adele's so bent, she knows it's going to be a complete bitch to move up the stairs."

"Jenna!"

"Sorry, I know that's vulgar." Jenna grinned, reminding Izzy a little of Jason in the days when they shared little jokes. "You feel better, Mom. I'll check in with you tonight when we get home."

"Thanks honey. You're a good kid."

"I have a good mom." Jenna hugged Izzy, and returned to her room to get dressed.

Izzy returned to her room as well, turned the AC on high, curled up under some blankets and fell asleep.

**

Quinn checked the clock. *Two more hours.*

As he expected, Serena was not easily coaxed from her foul mood. Thanks to his short conversation with the two young women the night before, he'd had to do penance. Serena informed him moments after a fairly tawdry session in her bedroom, he was to fill in the Sunday afternoon spot.

She's still blaming me for those girls calling her my mother.

The good news is, no one cares what I do on a Sunday afternoon because everyone is at the Volunteers opening game of the season, and we aren't airing it. So I can rerun a Titans game from five years ago and no one is going to care.

Checking the dials to make sure the rerun game was still playing properly, Quinn leaned back in his chair and allowed himself a rare moment of reflection on his history with the woman who held his darkest secret in her dangerous hands.

Serena Shipley Chapman, former world-class figure skater, was also a world-class hellfire. Too well, he knew the story of

Serena's humiliation at the hands of Jason Masters, her long time skating partner. The fact that Serena experienced her biggest humiliation months after Jason left skating forever didn't seem to figure into her equation of hate. She blamed him for forcing her to skate as a single.

More precisely, she blames Isabella Landry for stealing Jason and forcing her to skate as a single.

Getting on the Olympic team as a single's skater was nothing more than a foot in the door for Serena; just enough of a push to get her on the plane. When the US champion shattered her ankle in practice, Serena got her golden moment.

Her story of how she was even at the event spread like wildfire. The relentless media dug up as much as they could on the strange chain of events that put Serena Shipley on Olympic ice, alone.

The short program lasted two minutes.

In all the years Quinn had known her, Serena Shipley Chapman talked endlessly about everything else surrounding her skating career. But those two minutes of her life were a silent void. It didn't take long before curiosity got the best of Quinn and he found the clip on the internet.

Even now, Quinn couldn't stop a perverse little smile from crossing his face. To say the short program was a disaster was a complete understatement. Unaccustomed to skating alone, and skating a program she'd put together on the plane ride to the Olympics, Serena's luck ran out. In two minutes, Quinn counted three outright crashes, two skipped tricks, and a triple axel that turned into an awkward single. Applause for her was lukewarm, unlike her scores, which were ice cold.

In the following days the press was merciless. Writers pointed to her age and her ego as the reasons for her failure. Stories about her backstage tantrums surfaced. Two days later, mere hours before she was to skate her long program, Serena contracted a sudden case of the flu. More rumors and commentaries flurried around her. By the time Serena flew home, every sports program and tabloid magazine mocked and reviled her.

But in true Serena fashion, she landed on her feet. Or, at least she landed on her back in the bed of someone who had enough money to put her on her feet.

For reasons no one understood completely, Serena moved to Nashville, hometown to the woman she blamed for everything; Isabella Landry. Isabella, of course, was already gone, vanished with Jason under a cloud of scandal after pregnancy rumors arose.

If Serena wanted immediate revenge, she was sorely disappointed.

Serena got a job as station manager at WNSH. That, of course, was a cover for her real intentions. She caught the eye of the aging station owner, Burkes Chapman. As the rest of the world prepared for another Winter Olympics, Serena Shipley married a very silent part owner of the Nashville Predators, and the richest man in Nashville.

She hated sitting with Burkes at the games. Quinn smiled at the thought of the lovely Serena standing in Burkes' cloud of cigar smoke and bourbon. *Old Man Chapman adored her…almost as much as his cigars and those Civil War pistols he has displayed in his owners' box at Bridgestone Center. He gave her everything she wanted.*

Except that gold medal.

The first time Quinn saw her, he was finishing his final game with the Predators. It wasn't common knowledge to the fans, but the writing was on the wall. The Preds tired quickly of his bad boy image, and wanted to trade him. Quinn didn't want a trade. He was done getting passed around the league like a bad joke. By then he'd fallen in love with Nashville.

It's not that hard, even after everything, to remember how regal she was, looking down from the owners' box. She was the queen. We were just part of her kingdom.

He must have made an impression on Serena as well, because a week after he retired, Quinn received an invitation to an owners' event. Burkes was there, jovial country boy that he was, and Serena was on his arm. A brief conversation with the two of them, and the next thing Quinn knew he was the WNSH color commentator for Predators' games.

Then Burkes died, and Serena took over.

And then Sally.

"Quinn Murray, what…the…hell are you doing here on a Sunday?"

Quinn shook himself to attention. Benny glared at him from the studio door. "I guess this should put to rest any ideas you have that I get special treatment from the boss, right?"

"Not really. I bet she's tweaked because of your moment in the spotlight last night."

Quinn smiled. "You are living proof that even a blind horse finds the gate once in a while."

"You're the horse that should have put on blinders last night, dude. I saw Serena. When are you going to get that she is never amused when other women drool on you?"

"She gave me an earful after I took her home."

"I'll bet. But dude, seriously, you could have mentioned the station at least once when you were on stage. She probably wouldn't have minded quite so much."

"I wasn't there to promote the station. I was doing a friend a favor."

"Your good deeds will kill you one day, my friend." Benny adjusted his chair. "Yeah, well, you are owned by WNSH and you aren't supposed to be going out into the public without express written permission from the headmistress. You know that."

Quinn stood and stretched his arms over his head. "I just forgot."

"At least tell me you noticed some of the prime women that were there. At least tell me you're not completely dead inside."

The image of Isabella Landry, standing in the balcony, came to his mind. The idea of someone like Benny staring at her like a piece of meat made Quinn's stomach roll. "And you wonder why you can't get a date, when you talk about women like that."

"That's a yes!" Benny raised his hand for a high five. Quinn responded with little enthusiasm. "You spotted someone and you're trying to be cool because she's classy, right? Although what a classy chick would be doing in a place like Chance's is beyond me."

"You're a pig, Benny. And it's time for you to go to work. The game I was airing is almost over." Quinn pointed to the control board as he walked out of the studio.

NINE

Izzy opened her eyes and reached for her cell phone. *Five-thirty? It's five-thirty in the afternoon? I slept all day?*

She pushed back the covers, welcoming the invigorating chill her deep freeze settings on the room AC gave her. A quick shower further brought her back to life. She studied her reflection in the mirror as she blow dried her hair. *Something's different about me.*

I look hopeful.

It's the lottery ticket. That and the first real sleep I've gotten since Jason died. I'm not worried about money so much.

It's more than that.

Quinn Murray's face flashed through her mind. *Those beautiful eyes.*

Izzy turned off the blow drier and smiled at her reflection. "And about three hundred women screaming his name. Let's move back to reality, shall we?"

Izzy blinked at her reflection. "That's right. I'm talking out loud to myself now. Clearly I need something to eat."

Her first step into the steamy Nashville afternoon ended any illusions she had about keeping her hair tidy. *How many mornings did my mother straighten my hair with that vicious iron?* She shook her head, feeling her hair curl in the humidity. *I sort of liked it curly.*

She walked downtown, and found herself standing in front of Second Chances. In the softening daylight, the place seemed entirely too quiet, so unlike the night before when the building throbbed with music. It was an energy Izzy ached to feel again. Stepping inside the dimly lit building did little to convince her that Chances was open, until she saw a sparse collection of patrons sitting at various tables near the bar upstairs.

The ambiance of the place perfectly suited Izzy. She climbed the stairs, replaying the glance she shared with Quinn, wondering what the connection was between her husband's funeral and a packed bar a thousand miles away.

She took a seat at the bar, and surveyed the place more closely. The scattered customers, as diverse as they looked to a casual glance, all had one thing in common; they were all doing something that looked work related. At one table, a woman sifted through stacks of manila files. At another, a man read a book about software design. In a far corner, Izzy saw two college students, one tutoring the other. In the darkened booth across from her...

Collier. Collier James.

It can't be.

Izzy studied the man as closely as she could without drawing attention to herself. His sandy brown hair was shoulder length and his shoulders were far broader than she remembered, but as he looked up from his stack of papers to signal the waitress, there was no mistaking his cheerful features or steel gray eyes.

Collier's father, Izzy's skating coach, paired them when they were very young. Collier wanted little to do with the world of skating, and it didn't take long before he convinced his father that skating wasn't for him. While his father paired Izzy with another boy, Collier spent his days blissfully reading books, playing his guitar, and eating whatever he wanted to eat. *How much did I envy him those long autumn afternoons when he'd take a backpack of books to the tree house in his yard, and just eat cookies, drink chocolate milk, and read until his father came home from coaching me through eight hours of compulsory figures?*

Now here she was ten feet away from her best friend. She ached to call his name. But the cold hand of reality stopped her as the bartender approached and asked what she wanted to drink.

"A glass of pinot noir, please," she murmured without looking away from Collier, "and a glass of ice."

If the bartender thought her order odd, he didn't let on to her.

Nineteen years earlier Collier was the first person who knew that she and Jason slept together. His reaction, she remembered, was the first step on the long fall from grace.

The bartender set two glasses in front of her. Izzy put an ice cube in the wine glass, and took a sip. The deep red wine could not stop the flood of memories tugging at her heart.

The last time I saw Collier, he was furious. I'd never seen him that way.

"You did what?" Even now, in a bar a lifetime away from that morning in Coach's office, the tremor of anger in his voice was vivid.

"I slept with Jason. Two nights ago. He said it would prove we loved each other and make our performance that much better."

Collier's normally peaceful face was a hot shade of red then. "So you just did it? Izzy, he's old…he's almost twice your age!"

"He's my partner."

"What does that have to do with it?"

"Jason says all partners sleep with each other. He did with that Serena."

"Oh yeah, take Jason's experience with Serena as the guide."

Izzy had been confused by the whole conversation. "What's your deal? This will help us, don't you see? It'll make us better!"

"No, it won't. It won't make you a better skating pair. It won't make you anything other than yet another teen girl who gives in to a slimy old bastard."

Izzy remembered, with shame, her petulant pout. "So what do you care?"

"Because I love you, Izzy."

He was the only one to call me Izzy back then. And he only did it when he really wanted to talk to me about something secret.

I didn't know anything about love or relationships then. I may not now. "I love you too. You're my best friend."

"I'm not talking about friends. I love you. I love you the way you think you love Jason."

I should have known how serious he was. I didn't. I was so young. I had no idea how much it hurt him. I was such a stupid, egotistical child.

"Who said I loved Jason?"

"Well, if you don't, then you're a whore."

I threw a skate guard at him for that. "Collier Braden James! You take that back."

"Take it back? What do you think people are going to say when they hear about this? You're sixteen. He's thirty."

"Twenty-six."

"Whatever. You just gave yourself away. For what?"

"To make myself a better skater! To win!"

Collier grabbed her by the shoulders then, and shook her lightly. "It's not all about skating! Some day skating is going to be gone, and you'll be left with this one decision, this one stupid, bad decision, and it will be all you have."

How could he have known so much? He was only eighteen. But he knew exactly what would happen.

Collier walked out then, walked out of the room and out of her life. He moved away to live with an aunt, so he could go to school in Memphis. Jason hustled her out of Nashville. Sipping her wine, Izzy wondered for the millionth time how different her life might have been had she stayed in Nashville, had she not slept with Jason, had she loved Collier back.

Had I been able to make different choices, would I still be sitting here right now?

She turned on her stool and stared at the nicked up bar. *I disappointed so many people and damaged so many lives because of what I did.* She drained her wine glass and set it on the bar. *I'm not ready to face any of it until I have the right words.*

She slipped off the bar stool, catching the heel of her sandal on a rung of the stool. The end result was her lying on the floor, and Collier looking down at her with a mix of amusement and concern.

"Miss, are you..." Collier squinted for a beat, looking confused. "Izzy? Izzy Landry?" He helped her up. "What on earth are you doing here?"

"I-I was having a glass of wine. Waiting for some friends." *That's it. Be as lame as you possibly can.* "They are late."

"Well look at you," he took a step back and studied her. "The years have been kind to you Izzy, that's for certain. Won't you join me until your friends arrive?" He pointed to his booth.

"I...sure." *Smooth, Izzy. Good job.*

He sat across from Izzy and studied her for a moment. "So where's Jason?"

"Dead." Izzy hoped Collier heard more emotion that she put into the single word. She doubted it, however. "He-there was an accident this spring."

"I'm sorry to hear that." His voice was soft, comforting, like she remembered. But there was something in his eyes, something less than sympathetic. "I mean, I am sorry for your loss."

"Thanks."

"He was-," Collier tapped his fingers on the stack of spiral notebooks in front of him. He seemed to be unable to find the right words. "It's been a long time."

This could not be more awkward. "It has. So, how's Coach?"

"Also dead. Had a stroke a couple years ago."

In spite of herself, Izzy laughed out loud. She shook her head, but was unable to stop laughing. "I'm so sorry, Collier." She took a deep breath. "I'm so sorry, that was so wrong of me to laugh."

Collier's smile was warm. "Take heart. We haven't seen each other in forever, and we open with a dead husband and father. We can only go up from here."

"One would seriously hope anyway."

Collier picked up a pen and toyed with it. "So what brings you to Nashville?"

Despite her misgivings, Izzy answered truthfully. "My daughter, Jenna. She's moving in to Vanderbilt this weekend. She got a volleyball scholarship." Izzy watched Collier count in his head. "Yes, the rumors were true. You were right...about pretty much everything back then."

As if she'd spoken some magic words, Collier's interest in his pen vaporized and he fixed his eyes on her. "Don't say that. Don't tell me that."

Izzy took a deep breath. "Well, you were. I don't regret Jenna. She's wonderful. But," she took a drink of her wine. *Change the subject.* "But everything else was a long time ago."

"It was." Collier's voice was soft, gentle, but his tight expression didn't ease.

Seriously, change the subject. "So what's with all the notebooks?"

The intense light in his eyes faded. Collier relaxed and smiled. "I'm a bit of a songwriter now."

"Really? That's great. I knew you'd do something creative."

"Well, writing, you know, is sort of therapeutic." He waved his hand at the stack of spiral notebooks. "I can pour my soul out and solve all sorts of problems through my songs, and get paid a little in the process."

"So what kind of music do you write?"

Collier shrugged. "I'm what you'd call a traveling minstrel."

"I'm not sure I know what that means."

Collier reached into his messenger bag and pulled out a CD. "I'm in a group that travels around and sings at Renaissance Fairs and things like that. Old sailing songs, drinking songs, whatever sounds right for the whole Renaissance thing."

Izzy took the CD from his hand and studied it. "That sounds sort of cool."

"It pays the bills, and we have fun. On our down time we get to play cover songs and some original stuff at places like this. Chance," he nodded toward the bar, "lets us play all the time. Maybe you saw us last night?"

The hopeful tone in Collier's voice tugged at Izzy's heart. "I'm sorry. I must have missed you. I was here later in the evening." She handed the CD back to him.

"No, keep it."

"Really? Thanks!"

An uncomfortable silence fell between them. *Too many years, too much to talk about and neither of us knows how to start.*

"I did see that Quinn guy get up on stage. What's his deal?"

A shadow passed over Collier's face. "I suppose you would wonder about him. Every woman does."

What could he possibly have against Quinn Murray?

"The guy's a complete hound. There aren't many women in this town who don't have his paw prints somewhere on their person."

"Oh, okay. I was just wondering, because. . ."

"Because he's hot?"

Izzy laughed out loud and this time the tension between them thawed. "Col, this is so great catching up with you. I can't believe I just wandered in here and here you are. I could talk to you all night!"

"Don't you have friends you're waiting for?"

Friends? What...oh, right. "No, don't worry about that. I-I'll just...oh whatever." She giggled.

"I have an idea." Collier laid some bills on the table. "My band's got a gig out of town tomorrow night, and I have to leave in the morning, but the night is ours. How about coming to dinner with me, Miss Izzy...Masters?"

"Marks. Izzy Marks."

"Ah. Miss Izzy Marks come on. An evening of good food, and recalling good times. Are you up to the challenge?"

Izzy took his hand and stood. "I believe I am."

Collier draped his arm over her shoulders as they left Second Chances.

***

Quinn wasn't surprised to find himself standing in the lower foyer of Second Chances. What surprised him was the cozy couple leaving as he entered.

Was that Isabella? Was that Isabella Landry leaving with a man?

Who was that guy? That looked like that sad singer from last night.

A wave of jealousy washed over him. For a heartbeat, he considered following them. Thinking the better of it, he climbed the stairs. *I've got her on the brain. That was probably nobody. I'm seeing things.*

A strong Scotch would take care of that.

But a good strong Scotch would create a lot more problems than just seeing someone who looks like Isabella Landry.

"Hey, Chance. How are ya?"

"Quinn!" Chance greeted him with an energy that made Quinn nervous. "My favorite on stage performer of the week!"

"Let's not get nuts, Chance."

"Did you see the steaming hot women crawling all over the place?"

"Every one of them in need of a decade or so of aging."

"You clearly weren't looking upstairs. Those college co-eds brought their mothers. Quinn, they brought their mothers and the mothers were hot, too!"

Oh I looked upstairs. I only saw one woman that mattered.

"Just pour me that swill you call ginger ale, and let me watch the game."

"Suit yourself. There was one I think was really hot for you. Couldn't take her eyes off you, like she was glued to you or something." Chance pointed to the spot where Isabella Landry stood two nights earlier.

"Yeah, you big dumb idiot! I came up here looking for that very woman that night! You told me you had no idea what I was talking about."

"Oh quit sulking. Look, that same woman, she was just in here." Chance nodded toward the corner booth. "She was sitting right there, not five minutes ago. I'm surprised you didn't bump into her on the stairs."

I probably did. "Was she with anyone?"

"Not when she came in. Ordered the weirdest thing. Glass of red wine and a glass of ice." Chance shook his head. "Yankees...what are you gonna do?"

Quinn remembered her accent, only lightly laced with a hint of Nashville. *She would sound Northern to everyone down here.*

"But she and the singer guy, the one you hate, had a conversation and then left."

"They left together? You're sure?"

"Yep."

Quinn drained the ginger ale wishing he could drink the image of Isabella with the folk singer out of his brain. *Why would I think she didn't have friends? She's a grown woman. It's not like she's been frozen in time. Not really.*

But did it have to be that guy?

His cell phone buzzed. *Serena.*

Of course.

***

"It's weird, having dinner with me, isn't it?"

Izzy looked up from her plate of lasagna. "Not as weird as you thinking I could eat this much food."

Collier smiled over the rim of his wine glass. "Yes, one thing about the attractions of the Old Spaghetti Factory is that they're good for boosting those who look like they could use a good meal."

"Are you saying I'm too thin?"

Collier broke off a buttery piece of garlic bread and handed it to her. "Not if you're in training for an Iron Man competition or something."

Izzy took the bread and sank her teeth into the buttery, garlicky delight. "I guess, over the years, I worked out a lot. I liked running. I had a membership to the gym. I like weight lifting, if you can believe that."

Collier reached over the table. "Put up your arm. Oh yeah, that is one massive gun you have." Collier cleared his throat, sat back and smiled. "You have a lot of questions."

"How would you know that?" *Collier always read me better than anyone else.*

"Well, it's written all over your face."

"That's spaghetti sauce." She wiped her mouth with a linen napkin and took a sip of wine. "But you're right. I have questions."

"So do I, but ladies first. Fire away."

"An easy one, for starters. How's Uncle Archie?"

Collier's face clouded and Izzy panicked. "Oh Col, don't tell me he's passed, too!"

"No, no, as far as I know he's still living in Milwaukee, still being all 'Mr. Archibald James, lawyer to the elite of the Dairy State." Collier shrugged. "We haven't spoken since my father's funeral, and we barely had contact before that. I just don't come from that sort of family."

"Okay. Let's stay away from family. Let' me try again." She studied him. In the half light of the restaurant, the years dropped away from his face. "Why folk singing?"

"Oh that's easy. While you and Dad were spending endless hours on sit spins and figures, I was in my tree house listening to folk music, writing folk music, and dreaming of the day I could wander the earth singing folk music to middle-aged housewives who put on corsets once a year and truly, in their heart of hearts, believe they should have been born during the Renaissance era because it was so darn romantic."

Izzy smiled. "And there's nothing more to it than that?"

Collier shook his head. "Not really. I didn't want a complicated life. I don't mind singing about drama, but I didn't want any real part of it." He paused for a beat. "I'm sorry. I probably shouldn't have said that."

Izzy recognized the shadow darkening his features. *He's talking about me.*

"You made the right choice."

The naked honesty of her words hung between them, a cold cloud over the warm glow of reunion.

"Hey, I think another glass of wine would be a good thing." Collier waved to the waiter.

Izzy bit her lip. *Don't talk about it. Keep it hidden.* "No."

"No?"

"No, I mean, yes another glass of wine would be very nice. But no, you shouldn't feel like you have to apologize. You made the right choice."

"I had choices to make. You never had any to make on your own."

Izzy shook her head. "I made one choice, and it brought me all the drama I could handle for a short time, and then nothing. Now I'm back in the middle of drama, probably."

The waiter filled their glasses and Izzy talked for the next ten minutes, sharing her worries about the future, her hopes for Jenna. She told Collier about the emptied bank accounts, and how there was no insurance money. As he paid the bill, she told him about the lottery ticket, and her decision to move to Nashville. "And then, today, there you were. Like a sign or something."

"There I was." Collier's voice was distant as he folded the credit card receipt and put it in his pocket. "Would you like to take a stroll along the river or something?"

"Sure." Izzy stood a little too quickly and stumbled.

Collier caught her and grinned. "So you're still 'Dizzy Izzy' aren't you?"

She smiled and accepted his arm for extra balance. Collier opened the door and the hot, sticky air of the Nashville night swathed her in a comfortable mental fog.

"Izzy?"

Adele's grating voice jolted Izzy. "Oh, hi guys."

"I thought you were too sick to help the girls move today."

Izzy flushed, hating the imperious look on Adele's face. "I am...I was. When I woke up, I decided to go for a walk. I ran into Collier, who is an old friend."

"An old friend. Yes, I'm sure he is."

"Adele..." Sean's voice held a warning note.

"Yes, I'm very sure. Tell me, Collier...is it? What do you do?"

"Collier is a musician." *Oh just pour gasoline on the flames.*

"A homeless one, from the looks of things," Adele huffed.

"Very pleased to meet you, Miss Adele," Collier bowed low in an exaggerated show of manners.

"Would I have heard any of your stuff?"

"Shut up Sean!" Adele whirled on her husband like a viper. "We are talking to Izzy about this new old friend she's found who raised her from her sick bed and took her out for dinner and...a few drinks it looks like."

"You do not need to be insulting." Izzy's eyes stung with furious tears.

"And you do not need to lie to me. If you wanted to spend the day with street people, that's your choice."

"Excuse me, ma'am?" Collier spoke in a soft, heavily Southern voice, "I really do prefer 'traveling minstrel' if you don't mind? And if you don't mind, I think your husband was taking you to dinner and I was escorting Miss Izzy back to her hotel. Good night." He gripped Izzy's arm and ushered her away from a stunned Adele.

Once out of sight of the restaurant, Izzy giggled. "I can't believe you! No one talks to Adele like that and lives to tell."

"That woman does not like you at all. Who is she?"

"She's family. She's Jason's big sister. You know, the protective big sister who believes with all her heart that I ruined her baby brother's golden dreams."

"I see." Collier put a protective arm around her shoulders. "And you and she, what, live close to each other?"

"You could say that. If I go back to Wisconsin tomorrow I'll be living with her." Izzy made a face. "If I had the lottery money right now, there would be no question. I'd just stay here." She made a worse face. "I hate to think of the big wicked scene that would get out of her, though."

Collier's laughter was gentle, much like the one armed hug he gave her. "May I say something about you moving here?"

"If you want."

"Here, sit on this bench." Collier pointed to a bench on the walk way.

Izzy sat and stared at the moonlight shining on the Cumberland River. "It's beautiful here, isn't it? I'd forgotten how pretty the river is at night."

Collier knelt in front of her. "Izzy, I'd like you to stay in Nashville."

His earnest manner surprised her. "Okay." She was uncertain about what to say further.

"I'd like you to move back, because, in a way, for me, you never left." Collier slid next to her on the bench. "You've always been right here." He put a hand over his heart.

The expression on his face took her back to the last time she saw Collier, and Izzy was suddenly uncomfortable. "Col…"

"No, let me just say this, and then you can walk right back out of my life for another couple of decades and I'll be okay. But this meeting, this weird random meeting, I can't let this moment pass by without telling you everything."

"Okay." Izzy really didn't like the intense light in his eyes, but she was unable to look away.

"Izzy, that night I left, I was shattered. I thought for sure I would never be able to put together the pieces again. And then, this song came to me. I started writing it. I wrote about lost love. I was an idiot kid, but all this stuff just poured out of me. And in the end, I had a whole stack of shattering love songs no one wanted, until I ran into some guys who wanted to round out a folk album with something other than another sailing song. Suddenly I'm making women cry at Renaissance Fairs, like I'm really a talented poet."

"Oh, but Collier, you are!"

"No, I had a broken heart I carried around with me for nearly twenty years. I've written songs for ten albums. Every single one was about a girl I knew, a girl I loved, every one of them a sad song, something that would guarantee sympathy and big tips at the fair. But I always wondered, deep down, I always wondered if I would ever be able to write a happy love song, something joyful, about you."

"Col…"

He put a finger to her lips. "I knew the night I left you would never be happy with Jason. There was just too much wrong. But Izzy, in my heart, I knew if you and I could just find each other again, I could make you happy. And now here you are, and that idiot kid inside me can't help hoping I get the chance to at least try."

Izzy was speechless. They sat, for several moments, staring at the river as other couples strolled past.

"Please say something." His voice was still, nearly a whisper.

Izzy wiped a tear from her eye and smiled. "Collier, I think that's the most beautiful thing anyone has ever said to me."

"So you'll stay here in Nashville?"

Izzy shook her head. "Col, I don't know if I'm ready for anything, you know, romantic. I think my reality might not live up to your expectations."

The smile on Collier's face was faint, but sweet. "I don't expect anything. I just needed to tell you how I feel, and you can do whatever you want with that information. You have no idea how long I've carried that around." He looked over her shoulder to the lights of the Old Spaghetti Factory. "But if I could persuade you at all, if moving in with that woman is your reality, how bad could moving back to Nashville be?"

"Okay, okay Col, you've sold me." She laughed at the stars as he swept her into his arms and spun in a full circle. Dizzy when he set her on her feet, Izzy gripped his arm. "Okay. I think I need to go home now. I have a lot to figure out before tomorrow."

"What's to figure out?"

"What I'm going to say to Adele."

Collier grimaced. "You want back up? I can bail on the guys for a day or two."

She put a hand on his arm. "No this I have to do on my own. I have a lot to do on my own." She flagged down a cab. "I will be here when you get back."

"Promise?" The single word dripped with hope and uncertainty.

"I promise."

"I'm not going to lie. That woman scares me a little." He opened the cab door for her. "Wait." He pulled a card out of his wallet. "These are all my numbers. Call me, for anything."

"Thanks." She hugged him, reveling in the feeling of home she had in his arms. "Col, I'm so glad we ran in to each other."

"Ironically, at Second Chances." He smiled, and kissed her lightly on the forehead. "I have a good feeling. You might just find the life you deserve here."

With you? Izzy stopped the train of thought. *Romance is the last thing on my mind. Learning to stand on my own two feet for the first time ever, that's my focus.*

Collier closed the cab door. She gave the cabbie the address of her hotel, and glanced out the back window. He waved at her. She waved back. *Then again, maybe there is a happy ending here for me.*

***

Quinn wandered the river walk, as he did many nights after being with Serena. It was rare, while the clubs pumped out all genres of music and liquor, that anyone else would be outside. Tonight, especially, he enjoyed the solitude.

There was something about the river, the way it was always moving, but was always there, that comforted him. Tonight, with the moonlight dancing on it like broken stars, Quinn wished he could lose himself in the shining ripples of water. *She left Chances with the sad singer. She's probably known him forever, and, she'll fall in love with him.*

Why didn't I try harder to find her the other night? Why didn't I fight through that crowd? It was my chance, and I blew it.

He jammed his hands deep in his pockets. *Really, what hope did I have? I mean, come on. She's Isabella Landry. Sure, time has passed. But she is who she is. She still has people here who know her, and probably love her. For all I know, she made this trip to meet with him.*

Her face flashed through his mind. The spotlight on her face, and her...looking at him. *No, there was something there. There was a connection.*

Why am I going over this? I was the focal point of everyone in the place, and she was probably just trying to figure out why I looked familiar. She probably realized I was the idiot at her husband's funeral, and then she put me out of her mind. There's no use trying to make that moment more than it was.

I'm hopeless.

Ahead of him, a cab pulled to the curb, and a woman paused at the door. *It's her.*

The man she was with said something to her. Then he kissed her on the forehead. She got in the cab and rolled past Quinn, who stared at the retreating cab until the tail lights turned out of his view.

He kissed on the forehead and put her in a cab? That's not quite the passion that would bring a woman back to the South.

Too bad for you, Singer Guy.

TEN

Izzy sipped her iced tea and tried to ignore the chatter floating around her like cottonwood pollen. Jenna and Mikayla carried on a loud discussion about what they would wear on the first day of classes. Izzy knew it was a hilarious conversation, simply by looking at Adele's disapproving glare. Sean, probably thinking about the long day's drive he had ahead of him in the morning, was quieter than normal, which only emphasized Izzy's own lack of participation.

I have to stay focused. I have to think of exactly the right words to somehow make this decision seem right for everyone involved, including Adele.

"Ladies, I hate to break up your chit chat," Sean pushed his chair back from the table, "but we have a long drive tomorrow and us oldsters need our sleep."

Adele looked at her watch. "Oh you are right, Sean. Okay, girls, give me a hug." She stood and held her arms out wide. Jenna and Mikayla stood and positioned themselves into her iron embrace. Izzy knew, from the girls' body language, that this hug was not soft and motherly.

If she's hard and unyielding with the girls, what's she going to be like with me when I flat out defy her?

"Come on Izzy," Adele could have been summoning a dog to her side. "Let's go."

"No."

The word was out before Izzy had time to second guess herself. It hung in the air like the glow of an unexpected bolt of lighting.

"I'm sorry. What did you say?" Adele put her hands on her hips, a fighter, waiting for the bell.

Sean and the girls froze in their positions. Only their eyes moved back and forth from Adele to Izzy.

"I said no, I'm not coming with you." Izzy struggled to keep a fearful waver out of her tone.

Adele's expression clouded. "I see. So you're having a few moments with the girls before you turn in?"

"No. I mean I'm not coming back to Wisconsin. I'm staying in Nashville."

Sean and the girls slipped back to seating positions and waited.

"You're staying here?"

"Yes."

"You're not coming back?"

"No." Izzy shook her head for emphasis.

"What do you intend to do?"

"I guess I'll do what people do. I'll find a place to live, a place to work. There's nothing for me back in Wisconsin. The house is foreclosed, my job won't support me."

"Oh, and there are so many opportunities here? What kind of job do you think you'll get here? There isn't much of a market for a former figure skater with no education and bad credit."

Adele's words stung like a slap to the face. Izzy blinked, and glanced at Jenna, whose expression of fury steeled Izzy's resolve. "My daughter is here. I have, or will have, enough money to get a modest place."

"How do you have any money?" Adele waited a beat. "Unless that man you were with paid you. Just how good are you that you can snag a dirty musician and suddenly have enough money to make a major move like this?"

"Mom!" Mikayla shouted. "You don't know what the hell you're talking about."

"No Mikayla, you don't know what you're talking about. Remember yesterday when she was so sick she couldn't help you move? Well, I found her out with a man, and they looked like they were headed to bed."

"All right Aunt Iz!" Mikayla cheered.

"Adele, shut up." Izzy kept her voice low. Fear was gone, replaced by righteous anger. "I was not headed to bed with a man. Collier was my best friend growing up. We happened to meet yesterday purely by chance. We talked, we had dinner. And then he put me in a cab and I went back to the hotel. Alone." She glanced at Jenna, who gave her an uncertain smile.

"Well at least you can't ruin him like you ruined Jason. He's already homeless."

Izzy staggered back at the force of this unexpected blow. "I didn't ruin anything for Jason."

"That's not the way I remember it."

"Adele, that's enough," Sean said quietly.

"No, Sean, this is a long time coming. My brother had everything going to him until her father bribed him to skate with her and then she trapped him with a pregnancy."

"Your brother was a grown man who got a young girl pregnant." Sean's face turned a shade of red Izzy had never seen on him.

"Yes, and had she gotten the abortion like we all told her she should, he wouldn't have been exiled in shame."

"Mother…shut the hell up!" Mikayla put her arm around Jenna. "Do you listen to anything that falls out of that gaping pie hole of yours or do you just say every damn word that comes to your head?" Mikayla eased a stunned looking Jenna out of the booth. "You are one foul bitch. For your information, Aunt Izzy won the lottery. Not a million bucks, but certainly enough to tell your queen bitch ass to go to hell."

"Mikayla! Language!"

"Whatever." Mikayla hugged Sean, who was now also standing. "Sorry Dad. Have a safe trip back. Come on Jenna."

Without another word, the girls walked out.

"Do you see what you did?" Adele turned on Izzy, her eyes blazing.

"What I did? What I did? I didn't do anything to you." Izzy took three steps toward the door.

"Everything you owe me, and this is how you repay me?"

Izzy paused, her hand hovering over the knob. The idea of owing Adele anything froze her. "What on earth could I possibly owe you?"

"If it weren't for us, you and Jason would have been on the street."

"Adele, Jason more than paid for that and you know it."

Adele whirled her viper eyes on Sean. "Shut up Sean! That was nothing! That was a pittance! We gave them a life, we gave them livelihood!"

"They paid for that. Izzy's more than paid her share."

Izzy stared at Sean, his intense glare of defiance surprising her. Sean never stood up to Adele. *What does he mean, we paid for it?*

"It wasn't enough given the years I've had to put up with this!"

Izzy's glance whipped back to Sean as she waited for a spirited rebuttal, but the look was gone, replaced by his usual slack expression of defeat. *I'm on my own against her again.* Izzy squared her shoulders. "Well, Adele, I'm so very sorry you've had to put up with me all these years. So I guess I'm taking that huge task away from you. Whatever will you do with all the time you'll have, now that you can't think up ways to blame me for everything?" She didn't wait for a response, and given the purple hue to Adele's face, it was doubtful the one she got would have been pleasant. She whipped the door open and charged through it, rage speeding her steps.

Once out on the street, the warm night air did little to calm her. She started up the street with a vague notion of tracking down Jenna. She didn't realize she was nearly running until she crashed into another pedestrian and fell down.

"Hey, where's the fire?" The tall man held out his hand.

"Thank you. I'm so sorry…oh, it's you…" Her knees went weak as she looked into the clear, beautiful eyes of the mystery man from Jason's funeral.

He smiled, and kept his hand on her arm. "Yes it is."

"I'm so sorry. I mean, you're the guy from the other night, the one who introduced the bands. Quinn…something." *Why am I blanking on his last name?*

"Yes. Yes, that's what my stage name is; Quinn Something."

Izzy brushed herself off. "I'm sorry. I'm a bit preoccupied."

"I gathered that."

"Well, anyway." She shook his hand. "Thank you for your help, Quinn Something."

"You're very welcome, Miss. Look, can I buy you a cup of coffee or something?"

Izzy looked up into Quinn's face. Again she was mesmerized by his eyes. "Are you in the habit of asking out complete strangers?"

"No, of course not. But we're not complete strangers."

"Really?"

"Really. I mean, you saw me at Chances, and we just ran into each other here. Plus, we know 25% of our combined names. We're nearly old friends."

"Ah. So what would we be if we knew each others' full names?"

"Well, this is the South. We'd be kissin' cousins." He gave her a dizzying smile.

Her knees went weak, and Izzy laughed out loud to cover her sudden flash of arousal. Her anger at Adele shed itself from her like a heavy coat. There was something about Quinn that put her at ease. Also, there were his beautiful eyes. "Say, you don't have a twin, do you?"

"No. Why do you ask?"

"Then we have met before. My name is Isabella Marks, but everyone calls me Izzy. But you must have already known that."

A shadow crossed his face. "Why do you say that?"

"You were at my husband's funeral, back in March."

Quinn was quiet for a long moment, his eyes darkened. "Yes, I was there."

Briefly Izzy wondered why admitting that fact was so difficult for him. She decided not to pursue the line of questioning.

"So they call you Izzy." He seemed happy to change the subject. "That is a properly Southern nickname."

"I grew up here."

"Okay then, Miss Izzy," he bowed low, and used an exaggerated Southern accent, "my full name is Quinn Murray. I did not grow up here, but here is where I have taken root." He took her hand and brushed his lips lightly on the tips of her fingers. "So, where would you like to go?"

"I don't suppose there's any place I could get some good coffee and grits, is there? I have a sudden urge for grits."

"Miss Izzy, this is the South. Finding grits here is like finding cheese curds in Wisconsin. And I know the perfect place for grits this time of night."

Ten minutes later, Izzy and Quinn were seated in a Waffle House, waiting for their food to arrive.

"So Mr. Murray…"

"Call me Quinn, please."

"Quinn. What are you celebrating?"

"I do some charity events at Bridgestone Center and I just got something lined up for the spring that could help a very worthy cause in a big, big way. And today I got permission to use the Center for the event. I'm pretty excited about it."

"Well that is a reason to celebrate." She set her coffee cup down. "You said some of the Admiral players were your friends. Are you a hockey player?"

Quinn took a long time stirring cream into his coffee before he answered. "I work for the Nashville Predators, that's the NHL affiliate of the Milwaukee Admirals." He took her hand in his. "Ja-Your husband seemed to be well liked. I am sorry for your loss."

There's something about his expression. He doesn't look all that sorry.

I'm imagining things.

"Thank you. It's been a big adjustment. I've just decided to move back to Nashville. My daughter is starting at Vanderbilt and I've got nothing holding me in Wisconsin." Remembering Adele's hurtful words, Izzy shook her head. "I'm celebrating moving back."

Quinn smiled at her, his clear blue-green eyes lighting up. "Well, then, I guess welcome back Izzy Marks. Welcome home."

***

Quinn lay in his bed later that night unable and unwilling to stop smiling.

Isabella Landry. Izzy Marks. Whatever she was calling herself now, she was going to live in Nashville. It was almost too good to be true. He'd loved her from afar for a lifetime, and now he'd just had a late night Waffle House meal with her.

Should I have told her I knew who she was?

Maybe. But she's obviously not going by her old name. She's trying to get a fresh start.

How much do I want to star in that new life of hers?

Quinn closed his eyes, and one last thought streamed through his conscious mind.

More than anything I've ever wanted.

***

The buzz from his cell phone woke Quinn late the next morning. He rolled over onto his side and squinted at the display.

"Serena. What, you sensed I was having a nice time with someone last night?" He set the phone on the nightstand and sat up. Stretching his arms over his head, Quinn caught a glance of his image in the full length mirrored closet doors. He studied his reflection closely for a moment.

I look happy.

The image of Izzy sprang to his mind, and his face broke into a full smile.

"I am some kind of idiot. Sitting on my bed, smiling." He got up, and reached for a shirt and his jeans.

"Okay, okay. So she's staying in Nashville. But what else do you know? Her kid's going to Vandy. That's it. You don't know where she's living; you don't know where she's working. You don't know anything about this woman, except that you've been in love with her for twenty years."

Oh yeah, and don't forget, Serena's not exactly going to be jumping up and down about you hanging out with the woman who ruined her life.

Even this dour thought, Quinn noted, didn't erase the smile from his face.

Isabella Landry is finally in my life.

ELEVEN

"Collier, no, I've told you, I'm not going to live in your apartment."

Collier sighed. "It makes no sense. You've been living in the hotel for a couple weeks. I'm on the road most of the time. You could at least just stay there until you get the lottery check and then find a place."

"I appreciate your offer, I do. But this is the first time I'm really, really on my own. I need to do things on my own or I may never grow up."

"Still you could let me help you out, you know, old friends?"

Izzy glanced at the door of her hotel room and sighed. She glanced at Collier, and there was no mistaking his expression. *How easy would it be to just fall in love with him and have him take care of me?*

Unbidden, Quinn Murray's eyes flashed through her mind.

No, no, no. I have to learn to stand on my own two feet, and everything is going to be just fine once that check from the lottery people shows up.

"Thanks, but no thanks." She unbuckled her seatbelt and climbed out of his car. "I'll see you when you get back."

"Well, the offer stands. Have fun at work tonight." Collier pulled out of the parking lot and Izzy unlocked her door.

I have a job. She smiled at the thought. Sure, Waffle House was the only place that would hire someone without a permanent address, no schooling, and few marketable skills. And when the tips weren't coming in, the pay wasn't great. But there was something gratifying about the fact that she now had a job. After another seventy-eight days, the job would include health and dental benefits for her and for Jenna. *I never realized that was a big deal until I didn't have them.*

And I get to eat all I want for three dollars a shift. Since they take the money out of my check whether I eat there or not, I may as well eat all my meals there, until I can afford something better like fresh fruit, or a vegetable.

Unable to buy herself much in the way of groceries since paying for the hotel room ate up most of the money she'd gotten from the funeral, Izzy was happy to eat grits and eggs. She closed her eyes, saying a quick prayer of thanks again that Jenna's education, housing, and needs were completely covered by her scholarship.

On her bed was her mail: A few bills, remnants of her life in Wisconsin, and one slim envelope from the Tennessee Lottery.

She opened the envelope with reverence, as if it held the secret to her entire life. A tear welled in her eye as she looked at her winnings, and realized what this money could do for her.

Living without money, without a real home, had given Izzy a new perspective on what was really important. Having the money in her hand gave her the tools to start her new, independent life.

"Tomorrow," she said out loud, "I'll get an apartment of my own."

She hopped onto the bed and stared at the check. "Tomorrow after work I'll open a bank account and call that landlord guy Jenna suggested. Tomorrow, I am a grown up."

Tonight, however, I go to work.

*** *** ***

What a lousy night to have insomnia. Quinn looked down the wet sidewalks and hugged his arms around himself. Gusty wind snapped raindrops into his face like shards of glass. *I should just go home. Go home, take a sedative, and sleep.* It was a pattern that seemed to work, mostly because he was only able to ignore phone calls from Serena when deep in a sedated sleep.

But a hunger pang reminded Quinn why he was standing in the parking lot of a Waffle House at three in the morning, in the middle of a strange monsoon. Wiping raindrops from his face, Quinn walked into the welcoming confines of the restaurant.

Shivering in his wet clothes, Quinn's senses were overcome with the heady smells of breakfast. *Good call. First, some really heavy food, then the sedative and sleep.*

"Just go ahead and sit anywhere."

Quinn looked up, suddenly alert. *Izzy!* He hung up his jacket and sat down at the empty counter. A foot away, the cook was cleaning the grill. Quinn looked over his shoulder. The only other people in the tiny eatery were a table of college aged kids who seemed to be ending a very successful evening of drinking.

"Hey, there, how are you?" Izzy smiled at him and handed him a menu. "Good grief, you're soaked!"

"I'm okay. When did you start working here?"

"Oh, couple weeks ago. Right after you and I ate here."

"Liked it so much, you decided to make a career of it?" He studied her closely. There were dark circles beneath her eyes, and she'd clearly lost some weight. *Not that she had much to spare.*

Izzy smiled, her whole face lighting up. "Something like that. Guess I just really liked the grits." A noisy conversation behind Quinn got louder and Izzy frowned. "I'll be right back." She walked around the counter to the table of revelers. "Here you go, guys. It's probably time for you to go home and get some sleep now, okay?"

The noisy teens paused in their conversation and a strained quiet seemed to settle over the room. "What you got there?"

"Your bill."

Without turning around, Quinn pictured the expression the teens wore, and he tensed at the thought of trouble.

"We ain't payin' that."

"Well, you ate the food, you're going to pay the bill." Izzy's voice never rose, never wavered. She might have been a mother speaking calmly to her own naughty child.

"We're not payin'. So what you gonna do about it?"

Without looking up from his menu, Quinn kept his ears trained on the conversation. The cook took no note of it, busy as he was with his cleaning.

"Kids, look. I don't want trouble. So tell you what, why don't you just go on home and sleep it off."

"We don't gotta listen to a Yankee in here!" One of the males slid out of the booth and stood directly behind Quinn. "So what y'all gonna do about that?"

Quinn snapped his menu on the counter and stood. He towered over the kid by at least six inches. "Listen here, you little punk," he said, ignoring the murmurs of the other kids in the booth, "you and I both know your momma raised you better than this and I'm quite sure that if she knew you were mistreating a waitress at the Waffle House, she'd probably slap you silly, wouldn't she?"

The boy blushed slightly. "Uh, yeah, I guess so."

"You guess what?"

"I guess so, sir."

Quinn nodded. "That's what I thought. Now I'm going to call a cab," he pulled out a cell phone and started dialing, "and you children are going to say thank you to the nice lady, you're going to pay your bill, you're going to leave an enormous tip, and then you're going to get your asses into that cab and go home. And you're going to hit your knees tonight and pray to God that I don't mention you and your bad manners on the radio. Got that?" Quinn turned his attention to his cell phone. "Hey Sam? It's Quinn Murray. How y'all tonight? Great, listen, I have some young friends of mine over at the Waffle House by the Target? Yeah, that's the one. They're in need of a ride. I would consider it a large personal favor if you teach them a few things about manners when you drive them home? Thanks!" He ended the call and glared at the boys.

"Are you…are you really…"

Quinn glowered at the speaker, a pock-faced thug in a high school letterman's jacket from a high school Quinn did not recognize. "Yes, I am."

"Shit man, we're sorry."

"Yeah, we are so sorry."

Quinn noted their expressions. Cockiness was gone, replaced by fear. *I've still got it.* "Don't apologize to me you little assholes. Apologize to the lady and then get your no mannered drunken butts into that cab out there. And I wasn't kidding about the tip."

The group filed out, quietly mumbling apologies to Izzy who stood, looking amazed, next to the table. Once the glass door closed behind them, she wiped a tear from her eye. "Thank you."

He smiled at her and sat back down on his stool. "Please, that was nothing."

She set a cup of coffee in front of him. "Maybe not to you." A beautiful pink blush swept across her cheerful face and she lowered her eyes. You saved my life." Her voice was soft, little more than a breathy whisper.

Quinn stirred a packet of sugar into his coffee. "I'm pretty sure you could have handled that."

"Possibly, but I'm still really new to this self sufficient stuff." She grinned at him and brushed a stray wisp of blonde hair from her eyes. "It's nice to know there are still gentlemen out there ready to step in for a lady." She made a few notes on her order pad and smiled at him again. "They seemed really afraid of you, especially after you said your name."

"I should warn you; I'm a semi celebrity around here."

"Yes, but enough of one to instill fear in the hearts of drunken college kids? What did you do before you worked for the Predators?"

"I played a little hockey."

"Professionally?"

"Yeah." He shrugged and took a long drag of coffee.

"What, like in the NHL?"

"Yeah."

Izzy grinned, and then laughed out loud. "Seriously? You're an NHL player?"

"Was. I was an NHL player. I played for the Preds for a couple years before I retired. I had a bit of a reputation."

"It must have been quite the reputation. It scared away those punks fast enough."

"Yeah…I wasn't exactly well behaved on the ice." *Or off of it.*

"Well, tell you what, breakfast is on me. A thank you for coming to my rescue. You strike me as a steak and eggs sort of guy. Scrambled with mushrooms."

"How would you…"

She laughed, a musical joyous sound, and handed the order to the cook. "I suppose I could pretend to be all psychic."

"But you're not going to do that, right?"

She poured herself a cup of coffee before coming around the counter to join him at a booth. "No, I'm thinking that wouldn't be very nice, given how kind you've been to me." She poured some cream into her coffee. "It's no big secret. There's a note in the back about certain special customers and what they like. Your mushroom consumption is actually sort of a legend here."

Quinn frowned. "Ah, the secrets of the back room at the Waffle House."

She sipped the coffee and looked at him over the brim of her cup, her eyes dancing with mirth. "You know what else is back there? A lost and found. You need to at least get out of that wet shirt."

"No, I'm okay, really."

She gave him a very parental look. "Quinn Murray, you might be the big NHL scary guy, but how scary can you be if you get a cold and have to stay in bed sneezing? What will happen to helpless night waitresses who need you to scare away drunken boys?" She ran into the back room and returned with something large and pink. "Put this on."

Quinn held up the massive pink sweatshirt. "GO LADY VOLS!" screamed across the chest. "Seriously, I think I'd rather chance the cold."

"Oh stop. I know it's not a manly color, but it's warm, and you look miserable. This air conditioning will be the death of you. Go on…go change. Breakfast will be ready in a minute."

He was not about to disobey Isabella Landry. Quinn took the shirt, and headed for the men's room. He peeled off his wet shirts and eased the soft material over his head. Even on his large frame the shirt drooped. *I look like a wrinkly pink elephant.*

At least Benny doesn't troll Waffle Houses at this hour of the night. I would never live this down.

He stepped out of the men's room, expecting the ribbing to start.

"Oh good, you look so much warmer."

He studied her honest face. There was not a trace of mockery there.

"Come on, breakfast is at the table."

Quinn sat down and surveyed the meal. He was moderately certain nothing had ever smelled so good in his life. "So what's been happening since the last time I saw you?" He noted she wasn't eating much. "You're not hungry?"

"All I eat is food from here. I'm not in the mood for it this morning I guess." She poked at her well done fried eggs. "So I got the job." She glanced up at him. "Not glamorous, but I like it. The third shift takes a bit of getting used to."

That would explain the dark circles under her eyes. "Miss Izzy, working at a Waffle House is a career much revered in these parts. You just don't remember because you've been away so long."

"Well, some things are starting to come back to me." She smiled at him. "So, what do you do, other than rescuing damsels in distress?"

"I do color commentary for the Preds, and I fill in for the morning show at WNSH when they need someone to fill the chair."

"I'll bet you do more than just fill the chair."

Quinn liked the way her cheeks colored as she realized how her words sounded. "Now you're just flattering me."

Her blush turned to a full smile. "I should think you'd have more respect for the institution of Waffle House waitresses than to question my assessment of your skills. Didn't your momma raise you with any manners?"

Quinn laughed out loud. "She tried. It didn't stick."

No customers disturbed them and they ate and talked for nearly an hour, as the first rays of morning cracked through the shutters of the restaurant.

"Is that the time?" She glanced at the clock. "I gotta go get myself presentable."

Quinn studied her top to bottom, polyester uniform, mussed hair, and eyeliner that was definitely past its prime. Yet it didn't seem to matter. She was still beautiful. "Where do you have to be so early?"

"I'm checking out an apartment."

"At the crack of dawn?"

"The landlord lives out of town, and he's just around this morning." She sighed. "I can't go looking like a homeless person and smelling like eggs and desperation."

"Where are you staying now?"

She shrugged. "Over at the Super Eight on Demonbreun. I've been there since I moved Jenna into Vanderbilt. They've been so nice, but I need a place. I can't live in a hotel room forever."

"I imagine not."

"I finally have the funds to move into an apartment, I have to meet this guy." She slid out of the booth. In spite of the nylons and sensible shoes she wore, there was no denying that her legs were still in world class shape.

Quinn idly wondered what her workout routine included. *Stop thinking! Say something that will make her keep talking to you.* "Look, if it's not too weird, I can give you a ride there."

She smiled, but there was a wary look in her eyes. "Thanks, but I have a car."

Of course you do. You're not destitute, you're just between houses.

She grabbed her purse from under the counter. "Hey, this has been nice. And thank you for rescuing me. You're sort of my hero." She put a hand on his arm. Her whispery touch warmed his skin.

Then she was out the door.

Quinn rubbed his arm where she'd touched him, his skin still warm. *She thinks I'm her hero.*

She has no idea how wrong she is about me.

Quinn grabbed his jacket and stepped outside. *I could be a hero.*

Clearly I'm sleep deprived. Time for bed. A sedative and bed. Izzy.

TWELVE

Izzy lay in her bed and stared at the ceiling. Two weeks in her new place, a two room efficiency over the coffee shop where Jenna worked three afternoons a week, and there were still only two pieces of furniture in the place: the bed, a purchase she'd made with Jenna and Mikayla's help, and a flat screen TV mounted so securely to the wall the previous tenants gave up all hope of moving it. Izzy looked at the display on her cell phone. It was Jenna requesting another trip to a second hand furniture store. Izzy grinned. Her daughter meant well, but more furniture just meant more clutter. She liked her new, clutter free life. She was free to do whatever she wanted, and she didn't have to answer to anyone.

Of course I'll need nightstands and a table. She looked at the text from Jenna. *I'll just have Jenna pick them out. She loves doing that.*

She sat up and glanced at the sunlight out her window. Looking at her clock, she realized it was two in the afternoon. *Well, it's morning to me.*

Izzy pulled a battered T-shirt over her head and headed downstairs to the coffee shop. At first she hadn't loved the idea of living over a bustling coffee shop that boasted its own bakery and live music or movie screenings nearly every night. But the obvious advantages of having fresh baked goods and coffee without any of the mess won out. *Besides, I work nights. The daytime customers aren't that noisy.*

Sitting at the counter, Izzy studied the menu board.

"Morning Izzy. What'll it be today?" Catherine Countryman, owner of Silver Screen Coffee leaned in front of Izzy. Known as Cat to her army of faithful patrons, she was a devotee of movies and great coffee. The effervescent woman, who was about ten years older than Jenna, changed her hair color based on the flavored coffee of the month. This month, she explained to Izzy, the flavor was Red Sombrero.

"Morning, Cat. How about just a plain cup of black coffee and do I smell cinnamon rolls?"

Cat nodded. "Fresh out of the oven. I'll get ya one." She reached a cup of steaming coffee over the counter to Izzy.

Sipping the coffee, Izzy glanced at the many notices and signs hung above the counter. One in particular caught her eye. "Oh Cat?" She nodded thanks to the younger woman, who set a mountainous cinnamon roll in front of her. "How long has that note been up there?"

"Which one?"

"The one with my name on it." Izzy pointed to a dog-eared piece of cardboard on which was written in the artsy script of a graphic design student:

Shhhhhhhhhh!

Izzy is our new tenant upstairs.

She works third shift.

If you are here between the hours of 7 am and 2 pm, please use your indoor voices.

Cat shrugged and laughed. "Oh you know how it is...landlord likes to be nice to his tenant."

Izzy pictured the landlord as she knew him from their one meeting. "I may not know everything, but I'm fairly certain he had nothing to do with that sign."

"Okay, fine. But before you get all grumpy, ponder this: A man came in here yesterday, ordered a blueberry kiwi smoothie, and when he read that sign, he started asking all kinds of questions about you."

Izzy took another sip of coffee. "You didn't give him my life's story, did you?"

"I don't know your life's story. Besides, I wouldn't give any stranger a word, unless he was really good looking."

"And?"

"He was spectacular!" Cat grinned wickedly.

"Let me guess," Izzy chewed on a forkful of cinnamon roll. "Perfect body, dark hair, utterly devastating eyes and a voice that would melt butter."

Cat touched her index finger to her nose. "You've met him!"

"I've met him." Izzy poured creamer into her half empty coffee cup. "He's a sports guy here in town or something. He used to play hockey for the Predators."

"Wait, are you talking about Quinn Murray?"

"Yes, that's it."

Cat clapped her hands together and gave out a little squeal. "I thought he looked familiar! Quinn Murray is looking for you? Omigod Izzy! He fills in for the sports guy on WNSH sometimes and his voice makes me all tingly in all the right places!"

So Quinn came in here and asked questions about me.

"Izzy?"

Izzy shook herself alert. "I'm sorry, Cat. What were you saying?"

"Well, I was extolling the many great talents of one Quinn Murray, but then I asked you why he'd be here, in this dumpy little college coffee shop, looking for you. You spaced to the outer limits."

"Oh, sorry. He had breakfast a couple of weeks ago in the restaurant. Maybe he saw the sign while he was having a totally normal cup of coffee here and just wondered if that was the same Izzy."

"First of all, that man has never been in here before." Cat shook her head. "Second his questions were more along the lines of a guy getting up the courage to ask a girl out on a first date."

"Like what?"

"He started with the lame stuff, do you like your job, what's your favorite coffee flavor, and he worked his way up to asking about Jenna, and what you did when you weren't working." Cat shrugged. "I'm all about customer service. I gave the man what he wanted.

Why would Quinn Murray possibly have an interest in me?

Izzy realized, as Cat continued her cheerful monologue, she rather liked the fact that he wanted to know more about her.

***

Benny stared at Quinn. "Since when are we devoting almost an hour of prime NFL discussion time to Vanderbilt volleyball? Vanderbilt women's volleyball? Why, Quinn, why?"

Because I'm insane. Quinn rubbed his eyes, knowing full well that Benny's questions were harmless compared to the grilling awaiting at Serena's hands. *I stalk Izzy all the way to her new place and ask that girl with the weird hair a bunch of questions about Jenna, and why? Just so I can spend some time talking about her on the show? Am I that desperate to have a reason to think about Izzy?*

Yes.

"I just think that we should look at the other sports in town, not just what the Titans are doing. The Titans play once a week. And the Predators just started preseason. So what if I want to spend a few minutes talking about a women's volleyball team that could win the national title?"

"Because it's women's sports, dude. It's fine if you want to give it a nod if they actually do win the national title. But you spent an hour taking questions about Vanderbilt women's volleyball."

"It wasn't a full hour. It was two calls."

"That's because those were the only two people who called in! The rest of the time it was you, reading stats and talking about a couple of the freshman players. Dude, did you hook up with a college freshman on the team and promise you'd make her a star with this show?"

"No, Benny, I did not hook up with one of the freshmen on the team." *I've worshiped the mother of one of the freshmen my entire adult life.*

The red light on the intercom flashed. Benny shook his head. "This might be the first time I do not envy you, dude. Not even a little bit."

Quinn set his headphones on the table and left the booth and headed for Serena's office.

Her door was ajar. "Don't bother knocking, Quinn, just come in here and shut the door."

He obeyed, and stood next to the closed door awaiting her next command.

"Sit."

Ever the obedient pet, he sat.

"Quinn, what the hell was that?"

"What?"

"You spent nearly an hour discussing Vanderbilt women's volleyball. Why would you spend more than thirty seconds on that topic? Tell me you're not stalking someone on the team."

"Of course not. I just thought, hey, the team looks like a contender this year, why not give them a little time?"

Serena tapped a pen to her lips. "You mentioned one name more than once. Marks…Jenna Marks. That's not any relation, is it, to Jason?" Her eyes narrowed, cat like and cold.

A chill ran through Quinn. *I never thought of that. Of course she'd make the connection. Shit.* "Or course not, Serena. Of the thousands of college kids in this town, how likely is it that I manage to find the one who just happens to be the daughter of your arch nemesis?" He hoped his smile would soften her taught features. It didn't.

"Don't mock me, Quinn. I hate to be mocked."

"I'm not mocking you, I swear. It has to be a monumental coincidence, that's all." *Make her believe it, or there's a very real possibility Jenna will be in danger, you big idiot.* "Besides, don't you remember, Jason's daughter died."

"What?"

Quinn closed his eyes, praying his fiction would sound real. "Yeah, I was there one time with Jason and he was really upset and he just blurted out that it was the anniversary of his daughter's death."

Serena's posture eased, the warning bells stopped ringing in Quinn's head. "Jason told you that?"

"Yeah. It wasn't like we ever made pleasant chit chat, but I remember he told me that."

A shadow fell away from her and Serena resumed her air of all business. "Very well. But just so I'm very clear on this; unless a women's team actually wins a championship, we stick to the sports people actually care about. Understood?"

Quinn nodded, unable to believe the storm had passed.

"Good. Now, go on. But don't go far. I may want to see you tonight."

Quinn opened the door and breathed the relatively fresh air of the outer office. "Of course." He closed the door behind him and made his escape.

THIRTEEN

Mid October always meant one thing for Quinn: the official start of the NHL season, when he spent more time away from home than at home. For the past three years, Quinn enjoyed traveling with the radio station, covering the Predators. It was an escape from Serena, and a return, if in a limited capacity, to a life he loved.

Now, however, as he strode through the Detroit airport on a gloomy Friday night, ready to board a plane headed back to Nashville, Quinn was mired in a deep well of homesickness. The Make-a-Wish event was nearing. He dreaded the day, not because he was unprepared, but because once the event was over, the Preds were slated for a ten day road trip. The thought of a ten day road trip, away from Izzy's cheerful greeting at the Waffle house darkened his mood. *Away from the only thing about my life that's good.*

Quinn marveled, as he made his way through the crowded airport, at how close he and Izzy were after two short months. He liked to think they were two lost souls who had no one else in the whole world.

Well, that's not true. Izzy has Jenna and Mikayla. She's got that girl, Cat.

I've got Benny.

Still, it hadn't taken long to become a regular fixture at her Waffle House. He liked to watch her move among the late night patrons, smiling, pouring coffee, sharing mildly funny anecdotes about being a night owl. While he nursed endless cups of coffee, and more mushroom covered eggs than one man should eat, Quinn learned more about her than he ever could have taking her out on actual dates.

When it was quiet in the restaurant, they talked. They talked about everything touching on the present and the future. Quinn learned little about Izzy's past he did not already know: She rarely spoke of Jason, and when she did, she didn't mention him by name. While she spoke quietly of mistakes in her past, she didn't elaborate, nor did she try to push Quinn to reveal much about his past. He liked that. She seemed to sense where the closed door was in his heart. Instead of trying to dig deeper, she accepted him for exactly what he was to her; a completely decent guy who could make her laugh.

I can reinvent myself with her.

They exchanged cell phone numbers the first weekend of the NHL season, when Quinn admitted that he had no emergency contact other than the radio station. It wasn't something he liked admitting. In fact, he wasn't even sure how she got that piece of information out of him.

"What, there's no one they call to sit by your hospital bed if you get hit in the face with a puck?" Her face was very serious, a rare expression for her.

"Most of the time I sit in the booth way above the ice. Someone would have to be aiming for me, and firing a puck from a T-shirt cannon to get it up where I sit."

"Still," she tore a check off her order pad and wrote her number on it. "Put this in your phone. That way, they can call me."

"You'll sit by my hospital bed?" He immediately entered the number into his phone. "Even if I'm far away, like Vancouver or something?"

"I'd have to update my passport, but sure. That's what friends do."

He chose to ignore the part about being friends. "Well, I suppose you should have my number then, too." He tried to be cool, but a surge of adrenalin rushed through him and his hand trembled as he wrote his number on a napkin. "In case you have any grit mishaps or something."

She pocketed the napkin and smiled. "You never know. Those college boys might come back."

"Not on my watch."

Her smile at his flip comment was angelic. "I believe you're right. I believe I'm safe with you around."

While he hadn't abused this new privilege of her phone number, Quinn had, in subsequent weeks, found little reasons to call her. He often used Vanderbilt's volleyball schedule as an excuse, and as an excuse to see Izzy, who made as much time as she could to watch Jenna and Mikayla play.

I didn't watch this much college volleyball in college when I was trying to score.

Isn't that sort of how it is now?

Quinn pictured Izzy, handing him a cup of coffee and a smile. *No, this is completely different.*

Reaching his gate, Quinn set his traveling case down and looked around for Benny. It was his request that Benny work on the road this season. Benny's loud personality covered Quinn's own lack of interest in any conversation that wasn't with or about Izzy.

"Quinn! Over here man!" Benny waved to him.

"Hey there, Benny. Bob. Sorry, I had to make a phone call and reception seemed spotty over here."

"What he means is that he had to call a lady friend and didn't want us overhearing. Isn't that right?" Benny nudged Quinn in the ribs.

Like I'm going to admit to you that I call Izzy to ask her about Jenna's volleyball games and what the flavor of the month is at the coffee shop just so I can talk to her for five minutes?

"No Benny, you know he and the Boss Lady are exclusive. Nope, our friend here is getting older, slower, fatter." Bob patted Quinn's flat stomach. "Happens to the best of us, buddy."

"Now that you mention it, he has been coming in smelling less like a gym and more like a Waffle House." Benny chuckled. "Here I thought finally getting on the road with Quinn Murray would mean the Benster would get some action. Just my luck, I'm on the road during his epic fast food phase."

Quinn joined in the laughter. "Benny, I swear, as long as you never call yourself the 'Benster' again, I will find you a woman."

Benny grew serious. "You're not kidding? Really? You've got a woman for me?"

The whole idea of picking up any woman for a one night stand, even for Benny, nauseated Quinn. *Those days really are over.* Quinn brushed his hair back and thought for a moment. "If I do, Benny, it won't be a hook up. It'll be something better."

Benny and Bob stared at him for a moment, and burst out laughing.

"Oh that's rich, Quinn. You, the world class womanizer, you're going to bestow a grand romance on anyone, especially on Benny?" Bob laughed. "What on earth would you know about romance?"

The image of Izzy, smiling at him in her Waffle House uniform, sprang to Quinn's mind, and he smiled. *Not much. But I'm learning.*

FOURTEEN

Izzy poured what felt like her millionth cup of coffee of the night. An icy cold snap forced the area's homeless indoors, and, by the looks of the packed booths, the shelters were full. She didn't mind. Working nights for several weeks, Izzy realized she got a great sense of satisfaction in the simple things. A hot cup of coffee, a kind word, a pat on the back, these were the things that meant so much to people with so little. The realization made Izzy feel light in a way she hadn't since her skating days.

Not a lot in the way of money, true, but at least I feel like I'm contributing something.

In spite of how busy she was, Izzy found herself thinking about Quinn. What started as a surprise meeting and a cup of coffee was now an easy friendship, one Izzy couldn't picture living without.

With Jenna and Mikayla so busy in school, and with Collier, who checked in by phone twice a week, on the road with his band all the time, Nashville was a lonely place for Izzy. Even though they really didn't talk about anything serious, Izzy looked forward to seeing Quinn in his usual seat at the counter. In private moments, Izzy felt as if he was watching over her, like some self appointed guardian angel. *And who wouldn't want a ridiculously hot guardian angel?*

She valued this unexpected bond with the former hockey player. Sometimes she considered telling Quinn her whole story, but always thought the better of it. *So many people look up to him and I'm the world's big disappointment.*

Oddly enough, though the place was packed tonight, Quinn's seat at the counter was empty. Waiting, like Izzy, for him to fill the space with his warmth.

The door opened, letting some of the sharp air in. There was a general grumble from the assembled patrons, and Izzy quietly scolded the two men at the counter. "You don't know who needs a warm spot tonight, so shush."

She set the coffee pot on the warmer and turned back to the counter. "What will it be? I'll have fresh coffee in...Quinn!" She cheered, scooting around the end of the counter and hugging him. "When did you get home?"

Quinn settled on the stool, his beautiful eyes tired, but smiling at her. "I dropped Benny at his place and came over here. I needed a cup of coffee from my favorite waitress."

"Well, give it a minute. I've got three fresh pots brewing."

"This place is packed. Are you alone here?" Quinn looked around and wrinkled his nose. "You've got some colorful folks in here tonight."

"One of the other girls couldn't make it in, but I'm not alone, Carlo's in back." Izzy shrugged and picked up a coffee pot. "It's cold out. Folks need a place to go."

"Yes, but," Quinn eyed the man next to him with some disdain, "isn't there a policy about loitering?"

Izzy bit back a scolding retort. Quinn's words were unkind, which surprised her. She knew not everyone shared her need to reach out to the rag tag group congregated around her. She was well aware, listening to Cat and others, that he did an enormous amount of charity work for children. *There's a good heart in there, don't knock it if it doesn't stretch to the homeless.* "They're nursing cups of coffee to avoid going outside. If that's loitering, I know a few people with perfectly good homes who wouldn't be able to kill a few hours in here."

She didn't have to look over her shoulder to sense the surprised shame glowing in his eyes. Bending over a table to reach a cup, she smiled.

***

Shell shocked from Izzy's soft spoken reprimand, Quinn watched her move from table to table, the smile never leaving her face. *I bet she doesn't get five bucks in tips tonight. Which means, with the restaurant paying her $2.33 an hour, and taking their $3.00 from her for her dinner, she won't make a dime after taxes for a long night of work.*

And she's as happy as anyone I've ever seen.

He drained his coffee, and watched her again. *It's so pure, and so simple, what she's doing. I need to be part of something that pure.*

He hung his jacket on the wall hook. As Izzy passed by him, he caught her by the shoulder. "What can I do to help?"

Izzy arched an eyebrow, a knowing smile on her lips. "I'm pretty sure we have a policy against civilians just helping out."

"Okay. I'm an ass. But I'm an ass who did time in diners in high school. Plus, I've eaten here so often in the past couple months, I have the menu memorized. So come on," he held his arms open.

"I won't turn away help." She handed him an apron. "Tend the counter, make sure the coffee is hot, and help Carlo if anyone orders food." She looked past him to Carlo. "And Quinn?" She lowered her voice.

"Yeah?" He bent down to hear her better.

"Don't write up any checks. Just tell Carlo the order. Got it?"

Quinn nodded, more from shock than anything else. "Got it."

The Waffle House stayed packed all night. As the first light of dawn broke through the clouds and the weary guests started to shuffle outside, Izzy gave them each an order of fries and a cup of coffee to go. By the time the morning shift came to relieve them, Quinn felt like an official Waffle House employee, right down to the smell of fried food permeating his pours.

He walked Izzy to her car. "You were good, tonight. Thanks." She nudged his arm.

Quinn scuffed his foot on the frosty pavement. "Call it penance for being a jerk."

"We can forget that. You did me a huge favor, staying. I owe you."

"I'm going to remember that," Quinn leaned against her car and crossed his arms. "It's not glamorous, what you do."

"And you're back to being an ass." She leaned next to him and grinned.

"Let me finish. It's not glamorous. But it's important, isn't it?"

"Some wouldn't think so."

Most wouldn't think so. But those are the same people who think I'm worth a truckload of money. Quinn draped an arm around her, and gave her a quick hug. "Look, you're beat, I'm beat. We both smell sort of funky. How about if I take you out for breakfast?"

She leaned into his one armed hug. "I believe I'll take you up on that. Got any place in mind?"

"No offense to Waffle House, but I hear the Silver Screen offers up some decent bakery, and the dress code isn't too tough." *Plus I'll get a chance to spend more time in your world.*

"Okay. You're on." She climbed into her car and rolled down the window. "Hey Quinn?"

He leaned on the car door. "Yeah?"

"I really do owe you for tonight. Carlo and I would never have managed it by ourselves."

"That's fine. I think I've got a way for you to pay me back."

"I'm intrigued. I'll see you at the coffee shop."

Quinn watched her drive out of the parking lot before he got into his car. He stared at the Waffle House sign for a moment, the tiniest seed of an idea planting itself in his brain.

***

Izzy waited for Quinn to park his car before walking into the coffee shop. The cold snap from the night before hadn't stopped the Silver Screen faithful from their favorite Saturday morning breakfast spot.

"Hey guys." Cat greeted them with a smile, tray in hand. "Geez, you're both a mess."

"Busy night. Quinn was a huge help."

"Whew! Is that you or did my coffee go bad?"

Izzy rolled her eyes. "Okay, I get it. I stink."

Cat took a sniff near Quinn. "You're not alone, Iz. Sorry, Quinn, but I have to ask, were you rolling in dead fish?"

"Lots of street people came in because of the cold." Quinn cast a wary glance at Izzy. "And I didn't exactly smell like flowers when I got off the plane. But hey, counter duty is sweaty work." He tried to grin, but Cat raised an eyebrow. "Okay, it's my natural man-stink."

Cat broke down and laughed. "Okay, so not what I was expecting from Mr. Nashville Metro!"

Izzy found Quinn's blush charming.

"I like being helpful more than smelling good all the time."

He's definitely learning. I knew there was a good heart in there.

"Well guys, I have a nice smelling bakery here, so you two can't stay here smelling like that. Even if you are attractive," Cat shot a lascivious grin at Quinn.

"Yeah, we're going upstairs to shower." Izzy clapped her hands over her mouth and her face warmed. "I-I mean…" She tried to ignore Cat's howls of laughter and the quirky smile on Quinn's lips. "I mean, Quinn, if you'd like to clean up before breakfast, you're welcome to use the bathroom in my apartment."

"Right. That's exactly what she meant. And after you clean up I'll bring you something delish as soon as I finish throwing baked goods at that group of idiots." Cat nodded toward the group of college guys gathered around the TV, shouting at the screen. "Remind me never to agree to a Monty Python film fest on a Saturday morning. It brings out the strangest characters. Makes those 'Rocky Horror' drips look normal and productive."

"Sounds good. Don't forget, decaf for me with ice." Izzy took a step toward the stairs, her face still flaming. *I'm an idiot.*

"Decaf for you, too, Quinn?"

"No, I've got some stuff I have to attend to today." If Quinn felt any discomfort, he didn't show it. "I'll grab my duffle out of the car. I'm pretty sure I still have something clean in there."

He ran outside. As soon as the screen door snapped closed, Cat set down her tray and put her hands on Izzy's shoulders. "Tell me you have a clue what you're doing."

"What are you talking about?"

"I was afraid of that. Gads, you are so innocent." Cat sighed and picked up her tray. "I wouldn't mind climbing around on that tall playground, that's for sure." She wistfully gazed out the window. "Do me this one favor. Boxers or briefs. That's all I want to know."

"Cat!" Izzy blushed again. "It's not like that at all."

"Oh come on! You and he are going up to your apartment. There are only two things in your apartment; a bed and a shower."

"I've got more furniture than that now."

"Yes, but you are missing my point! You have a bed, and you have a shower, and you both are going to be naked at some point. Iz, I'm a lonely girl. My biggest thrill is when the delivery guy accidentally brushed my boob the other day. I'm not kidding. It's so bad, I'm actually thinking of it as our first date. Just give me this one small crumb: boxers or briefs!"

"Shush!" Izzy giggled. "It's not like that at all."

"I bet you don't even know he's got it bad for you."

Izzy sobered. "What?"

"Oh, you think he helped out all night at a Waffle House, serving coffee to the homeless because he's a deep soul who can't help giving back to the needy?"

"Well he does a lot of…"

"Oh stop!" Cat cuffed her upside her head. "Do not be that dense. There is one reason and one reason only that a guy as in demand as Quinn would allow himself to smell that foul; he wants to get into your shower, and I'm guessing that if you're in there with him, he would not complain."

"I'm not listening to this." Izzy held up a hand.

"Fine. Fine. But if you don't answer the door on the second knock, I'm going to just assume the best." Cat grinned as Quinn returned, duffle bag in hand.

"Whatever, Cat." Izzy shook her head, hoping Quinn didn't notice her blush. She lead him upstairs. Pausing at her door, she tried to remember if she'd cleaned up her apartment before leaving for work. *Please, no underwear on the bed. No underwear on the bed.* She opened the door. *Oh good. I did manage to put the laundry away. I have to thank Jenna for forcing me to buy furniture. Dressers come in handy when trying to hide matronly undergarments.*

"So this is home sweet home?"

She set her purse on the table in the kitchenette. "It's not huge, but it's everything I need." Her phone buzzed. "Hey, Quinn, it's Jenna. I always talk to her after a shift. You wanna go first? Clean towels are in the closet."

Once she heard the hiss of water, Izzy dialed Jenna and tried to pretend there wasn't a stunningly handsome man in her shower.

***

Quinn dried off after his shower and studied the tiny bathroom. It was difficult for him to turn around without bumping into walls. There were no frilly towels or decorative soaps cluttering the shelves. There was little in the way of sprays, perfumes, and lotions. Everything was simple and tidy.

I feel more comfortable here than at my own place. Even if I can practically touch both ends of the whole place by standing in the middle.

Putting on his jeans was enough contortionism for him. Shirtless, he opened the door. "It's all yours." He set his duffle on the table and pulled out a pair of clean socks.

Izzy ended her phone conversation and shook her head. "You didn't have a shirt in your duffle?"

Quinn studied her. *She looked at the menu board downstairs with more enthusiasm.* "Hey, don't blame me. There isn't room in there for me to put a shirt on." *Am I feeling unappreciated because she's not falling into a pool of drool over my pecs?*

"Don't get defensive." She grabbed some clothes from the edge of her bed. "I didn't say I didn't like it."

I'm ridiculous. He could not, however, deny the tiny flicker of relief he felt.

His relief was short lived. She closed the bathroom door and the sounds of the shower didn't drown out her giggles.

"You don't do much for a guy's ego, you know," he shouted at the bathroom door. Izzy's giggles turned into full blown laughter.

He pulled on his socks. He always loved the feel of clean socks after a shower. When he gave up drinking, he found smaller ways to make himself comfortable. *Old jeans and new socks. Most comfortable things in life.*

Except for this apartment. A table, two chairs, two nightstands, a killer TV, and a big, soft bed. That's all anyone really needs to be happy, as long as they have a life they like, right?

So what's my defect? My life is a mess. Why can't I let go of what's not working?

He lay on the bed, his feet dangling near the floor. His eyes closed, he tried to picture a world where he could be as at peace as he was in this still moment and still keep the trappings of his glory days. *That place doesn't exist. It's a world where Izzy knows what I really am and she still lets me shower in her tiny bathroom and lie on her massive bed and be at peace.*

A knock on the door jolted Quinn out of his reverie. "Coming!" He pulled on his other sock and opened the door. "Hey, Cat."

Cat stared at him for a beat. "Oh come on!" She shouted, shoving a tray of food at him and storming down the hall. "You cannot be serious!"

"Wait, wait…" Quinn juggled the tray a bit before setting it on the table. "Cat!" He stuck his head out the door. "Cat?"

"What's all the yelling?" Izzy, dressed in soft sweatpants and a long sleeved thermal shirt walked out of the bathroom. "Oh good, food. Ooh, cinnamon rolls."

"What's up with her?" Quinn liked how she looked. Her hair, still damp, trailed onto her shoulders. Her face was clean and smooth. He'd never seen her look prettier.

Izzy looked at him. "Did you answer the door like that?"

"Like what?"

"Shirtless and muscley." She picked up the mug marked 'decaf' and dumped in three ice cubes. "At least she didn't spill the ice."

"So, a guy can't take his shirt off around here?"

Izzy bit deep into a cinnamon roll. "No, most guys can. I'm sure those Monty Python guys downstairs, they could strip naked and Cat probably wouldn't make a big deal about it." She licked a bit of frosting off her fingers, a move that stirred something in his gut. "But have you seen yourself?"

Quinn couldn't stop the faint shiver that ran up his spine. *I'm not even going to pretend I don't like that she thinks I'm good looking.* "Fine, fine. I'll put on a shirt."

"Don't get huffy, think of it from another point of view. Cat is a lonely, lonely, lonely woman. And you, you're like guy on the cover of a romance novel. Guys like you can't just wander around without a shirt; you have no idea what sort of trigger sequence you're launching."

Quinn laughed out loud as he pulled a long sleeved t-shirt over his head. "I don't think I've ever heard a woman equate arousal with launch sequences."

She picked up her coffee cup, walked past him, and sat cross legged on her bed. "I used to watch a lot of the History Channel. My husband liked it." A veil of melancholy passed over her face.

"Anyway…" she drank more coffee, seemingly unaware she'd stopped talking.

Eager to bring the light mood back, Quinn sat on the edge of the bed, coffee cup in hand. "So why the ice cubes in the coffee?"

Izzy shook herself out of her thoughts. "I don't know. I do it with wine and coffee. I've done it for years. I don't even remember when I started drinking coffee."

"Or wine?"

"Oh wine!" She chuckled and set her empty coffee cup on the nightstand. "No, that I remember really well. Col and I…"

"I'm sorry, who's Col?" *Don't be Singer Guy.*

She leaned against the pillows. "Collier James."

Damn. They do have a history.

"He was my very best friend growing up. We used to sneak into his father's office and one night he had this bottle of cherry wine."

Quinn set his cup on the opposite night stand and slid next to her. "How old were you?"

"Fourteen. Col was sixteen, and way more rebellious than I. We drank the whole bottle. I got so sick." She laughed at the memory. "That was my first kiss." Her smile faded slightly and she looked at Quinn. "I'd forgotten that part."

Oh, good move, Murray. You're finally on a bed with the woman and you've got her thinking about kissing someone else.

"How about you? What was your first experience with demon liquor?"

"Demon liquor?"

Izzy shrugged. "History Channel."

"I was young, too. I think my brothers snuck me into some party when I was in high school. I was older though."

"Well, things were sort of in fast forward for me." She sat up and hugged her knees to her chest. "You say you wanted to take me up on that favor. I'm guessing a hot shower and some breakfast won't quite cover it?"

Quinn adjusted to her conversational gear shift. "You see…I've got this charity thing in a few days. It's for the Make-a-Wish Foundation. Some little boy here in Nashville wanted to skate with real NHL players. It's not a huge deal, but my assistant sort of bailed on me last minute. I could use someone to, you know, maybe greet people at the door, hand out gift bags. Maybe skate a little in a scrimmage, if one comes up?" He studied her face to see if his request sparked anything in her.

"Skating?"

"Can you skate?" He felt stupid asking the question.

"Oh a little. I used to go to skate parties with Jenna." She hugged her knees tighter. "I won't crash into the wall, if that's what you're worried about."

Crashing into the wall? I'm more worried about falling to pieces if you really start to skate. "So it's a yes?"

She was quiet for a moment. Then, as if she'd finished some internal battle, she relaxed and lay back on the pillow. "Before I say yes, answer a question for me."

"Okay, I'll try." *And I'll try harder to not take you in my arms right now.*

"You're not that old, why did you retire from hockey?" Her dark blue eyes pierced through the protective layers he'd wrapped around himself.

I could tell you, but you wouldn't sleep for a month. "Bad knees. But I don't miss it that much. I've got the radio station thing and I'm on the road with the Preds a lot."

Her eyelids drooped. "Oh, okay. I was just curious."

"That it? Now you'll help with the event?" He brushed a damp strand of hair away from her face. Completely relaxed, her face looked like porcelain. He brushed his fingertips lightly on her cheek, unable to keep from touching her.

"Sure." Her voice was far away, dreamy.

Watching her drift to sleep, her face a perfect image of an angel, Quinn thought about her words. *How can I tell her I'm in a prison of my own making because I can't picture living as simply as she does?*

I could if Izzy could forgive my past.

But that is very unlikely.

His cell buzzed in his pocket. He eased off the bed. Wrapping a quilt around Izzy, he made sure she was safe and warm. *Serena summons. Time to go pay the rent.*

FIFTEEN

"So, ya had the hottest guy in town in your bed this morning and you, what do you do? You order decaf and you fall asleep!" Writing the next day's specials on the menu board, Cat flicked a small piece of pink chalk at Izzy. "And don't sit there and be all innocent and try and tell me that 'it's not that way' between you two. The man met me at the door without his shirt on. I don't even like hockey players, and I would have 'been like that with him' right there in the hall!"

"Is that true, Mom? Was Quinn in your room?"

Izzy picked at her cranberry scone and sighed. "As I told you this morning, Cat, Quinn and I are friends. It's a friendship I really, really treasure."

"Oh effin ef Aunt Iz!" Mikayla emerged from the kitchen where she'd been washing dishes. "You're not forty yet. And he's ridiculously smokin' hot. He was up in your room. Naked. And you fell asleep?"

"For the hundredth time, he was not naked in my room. He was naked in my bathroom while he took a shower, which is completely normal."

"Given the size of your apartment and the paper thin quality of the doors in this building, I would say there isn't that much difference, Mom."

"Proximal nudity is what it is."

Mikayla laughed so hard at Cat's statement, she leaned against the doorframe and slid to the floor. "Proximal nudity? Is that even a thing?"

"It is when you haven't had a date in six months and you're living vicariously through the only woman in the world not turned on by Quinn Murray." Cat grinned at Izzy. "Come on, spill it. When are you and Mr. Hockey going to take this thing to the next level?"

"Next level?" Izzy rubbed her eyes. "I don't even know what that means."

"Give me one good reason why you two aren't doing the tangled sheet tango."

"Cat, I'll give you the best one yet: Have you seen him? No one who looks like that is ever going to be interested in me."

"Well at least we know you're not blind." Cat grinned.

The four women laughed together. Their laughter annoyed the few remaining Monty Python film fest fans, who made rude noises in their general direction.

"Oh shove off you geeks!" Cat shouted at the small group. "Why don't you pull yourselves away from that rubbish and go kiss a girl or something?"

Izzy watched as the sorry collection of men and boys filed out of the coffee shop. "Cat, I'm not sure if you were scolding them or flirting with them. And since when are you British?"

"I've had to listen to the entire collected works of 'Monty Python' all bloomin' day. I love 'Holy Grail' and give me credit, I served Spam for lunch. But fifteen hours of it is more than I can stand." Cat sank into a nearby arm chair. "But don't change the subject. Admit you wouldn't mind a steamy throw down with Quinn."

Izzy closed her eyes. "Well, of course, there's an attraction. I'm not an idiot."

"Whooo hooo!" Cat and Mikayla jumped up and down, hooting and howling. Jenna, a little more reserved, patted Izzy's arm.

"Are you three done?"

"Oh come on. This is huge! You can't expect to drop a bomb like that and then have no reaction!" Mikayla clapped her hands.

"What bomb? I like Quinn. He's got a good heart. He's been very kind to me."

"He's like butter melting on a stack of pancakes. Yummy and, if you play your cards right, sticky." Cat high fived Mikayla.

"Would you two stop it?"

"Jenna, your mom is in total denial about this." Mikayla picked up her duffle bag. "Unfortunately, we have mid terms, so you and I can't hang out here and wait for the previews of next week's episode of 'Geriatrics in Love.' Come on roomie."

Jenna followed Mikayla. "Mom, could we go shopping next weekend?"

"Oh, wait," Izzy hopped off her stool and followed Jenna outside. "I won't be able to do anything next weekend. I'm helping Quinn with his Make-a-Wish event."

"Oh yeah, some of the kids at school were talking about it. I guess the older brother of the kid it's for is in my psych class. But it's a skating thing, right?"

"Yeah."

"You gonna be okay? I mean, you haven't told anyone about who you are. Mikayla doesn't even know the whole story."

Am I risking everything by helping Quinn? "I know. It's going to be fine. I can skate without, you know, skating. I fooled the moms in your school easily enough."

Jenna hugged her one last time, and slid into the passenger seat of Mikayla's ancient Chevy Monza. "Okay Mom. I'll talk to you later."

Izzy waved as the car pulled away from the curb, turned the corner and vanished from her sight. She walked toward the darkened coffee shop, replaying the events of the morning in her mind. *A real relationship with Quinn? With any man? What would I know about that?*

Might not be terrible to find out.

***

Quinn picked his T-shirt off the floor and pulled it over his head. *The last time I put on this shirt, I felt so clean. And now I'm filthy.*

"Where are you going?" Serena nudged his leg with a bare toe.

Quinn studied her. She was glossy, like a magazine cover. From the rumpled satin sheets to the negligee she wore, everything about her was slick and shiny. Closing his eyes, Quinn pictured Izzy's bed, with its soft comforter and fluffy pillows. Then he pictured Izzy's clean, honest face. *How can I even think about her right now?*

"I said," Serena ran her toes up his spine, "where are you going?"

Quinn stood and tucked in his shirt. "Serena, I've been up for at least thirty-six hours. I'm exhausted. And I thought, since you were...done with me...I'd go home and get some rest."

"Who said I was done with you?" She crawled across the satin sheets and threw her arms around his neck. "It's not my fault you decided to read a book at a Waffle House all night. You're supposed to come here when you get back from a trip."

Her heavy perfume choked him. "I'm sorry. I had a lot on my mind. You know I have that Make-a-Wish thing going on next week."

"That's not my problem. What you insist on doing when we aren't together isn't my problem. You know the rules, Quinn."

Quinn nodded, trying not to breath in her scent. *How is it I've never noticed this before?* "I forgot. Sorry."

She released him and sat back on the bed. "I suppose I got everything I'm getting out of you today."

Quinn sat in a nearby chair and pulled on his socks. "I think you're right."

"It's just as well." She waved him away with a dismissive hand. "I have to fly to Montreal tomorrow for a league owners' meeting."

"You're going?" Quinn was surprised. "You never go to those."

"True, but you've got half the team's owners tied up with your charity thing, so someone's got to go protect the team's assets. Who knows what the league is going to try to make us do now. These new safety measures are ruining the game."

"Yes, we wouldn't want the players to be safe and healthy."

Serena arched an eyebrow. "Says you, who once caught a puck in the throat. Didn't stop you, did it? You played the whole game."

Most likely because my blood alcohol level was high enough to dull the pain. "Yes, but I wound up retiring a lot earlier than maybe I could have."

"Getting hit in the throat had nothing to do with that and you know it."

I sometimes wonder.

"Well anyway, if we protect the players from serious injury, they will play longer. Having familiar names out there is good for the game. Fans are more interested in players they know. Why do you think everyone knows Brett Favre's name, even though he's been retired for a few years?"

Serena wrinkled her nose. "You know I don't follow baseball."

"It's football, but whatever. The man played more games than most guys do in three lifetimes. People grew up watching him. A whole generation of players grew up watching him and then got to play with him. His jersey is still hugely popular." *He sold jerseys for three different teams. Lucky bastard.*

"You're boring me now. You'll be driving me to the airport tomorrow morning early, and then I'll be gone for a week."

"A week for an owners' meeting?"

Serena heaved a bored sigh. "I need a few days off."

And if I'm lucky, I'll be back on the road when she returns. If I play this right, it could be three weeks before I have to see her again.

"What on earth are you grinning about?"

Quinn blinked. "Sorry, I was thinking about…something."

"Well stop. It's creepy. No go get your precious beauty sleep. And be here at five tomorrow to take me to the airport." She rolled to her side and turned off the lamp.

Driving home in the twilight, Quinn marveled at this unexpected reprieve from Serena's demands. His spirits rose as high as Nashville's neon skyline.

SIXTEEN

Izzy opened the box and stared at the contents. The last time she was on the ice, she wore rented skates and pretended to have trouble making corners at the local rink. *Even then, after so many years, it was like I'd never been off the ice. It was so hard to keep from letting loose and landing some jumps.* She smiled at the idea. *What would those other moms have thought? They already hated me because I looked so young.*

She pulled out her competition skates. *I always loved these skates.*

They were my glass slippers. When I wore them, I was a princess.

A light knock shook her out of her reverie. "Come in."

"Izzy, how are ya?"

"Collier!" Izzy hopped up and hugged him. "I can't believe you're back. I thought you were going to be gone for another week."

"Oh, I'm not really here. I have to catch up with the guys in a couple hours. But our booking agent called me about a charity event, said the guy organizing it wanted to bring in as many local celebrities as possible, I wanted to get the details before I signed the band up for something we might hate. Here," he handed her a small package. "A present for you."

She tore off the paper. "Oh, Col, it's your CD!"

"Hot off the presses. It's the first copy of a couple songs I wrote on my own. My plan is to send it to this recording studio up in Wisconsin. It's a real independent studio. Here," he handed her another CD. "Listen to this when you have a minute, tell me what you think."

"'Teacher's Pet?' Hm. Well, the lead singer isn't nearly as good looking as you are, so there's that."

"Very funny."

"Orphans and Runaways Records? That's the name of the company?"

"Founded by Shara Brandt, who is supposed to have one of the best ears for talent in the country. Fingers crossed I get up the guts to actually send her this."

Izzy crossed her fingers and waved her hands at him. "So, the charity thing…it's not a Make-a-Wish thing is it?"

Collier shook his head. "No, something else in the early spring. From what I understand, it's going to be big…" he caught sight of the skates, "although not quite as big as Isabella Landry putting on her competition skates. What's going on here?"

"Have a seat," Izzy pointed to the bed. "I'm supposed to help with this Make-a-Wish thing later today. It's a skating event. Apparently, the child wants to scrimmage with some NHL players. So my friend…he's a former NHL player…"

"Quinn Murray?"

"How'd you know?"

Collier shook his head. "Two reasons: first, Quinn does more charity work in this town than anyone. Second, you've had an eye on him since the day you got back to Nashville, and don't you even dare deny it."

"What are you talking about?" The icy edge in Collier's voice made Izzy defensive. "We're friends."

Collier's laugh was loud and mocking. "I wasn't aware he was in the friendship business when it came to women."

Izzy rolled her eyes. "I swear, why is it so hard to believe he and I can have a completely platonic friendship?"

"Because he has never had a completely platonic friendship with any woman," Collier put his hand on her shoulder.

"Yes, well, we're friends. He asked for some help, and I'm going to help him."

"Does he know who you are?"

Izzy focused her attention to a microscopic spot of dust on her skate blade. "Of course he knows who I am."

"Oh, so you've shared with him your impressive skating credentials, and that's why he wants your help?"

"Not exactly…" Izzy rubbed the skate blade with her thumb, wishing Collier would stop staring at her with his steel gray eyes. "Okay, no. He knows I'm a mom, and a widow, and he knows I'm from Wisconsin. He knows I work at Waffle House, and he knows I give free coffee to homeless people when it's cold outside. He's been to a couple Vanderbilt games with me."

"Tell me again how you don't think you two are dating."

"I swear, first Cat, now you. We are friends. If we were more than that, which we are not, I might share more with him, but we are not, so I will not."

"Hey you don't have to defend yourself to me." Collier held up his hands. "You can tell people or not. We can let it be our secret. I sort of like having a secret with you. It's like we were kids again. Only maybe," his voice had a wistful tone, "maybe we get it right this time." He shook his head. "So when is this event?"

Izzy checked her watch. "He's supposed to pick me up in half an hour."

"Can you still skate?" Collier's eyes twinkled. "I mean, it has been a lifetime."

"I can skate rings around you, Collier James." She grinned. "I've kept myself in shape. I might not be able to pull off a long program, but I can skate a few laps with some hockey players."

Collier laughed again. "There's my girl! Pop always said you were the best natural talent he'd ever seen. He'd say that to your parents all the time."

Izzy tried to ignore Collier's mention of her parents and hoped he didn't see the flush warming her face.

"Tell me you've contacted your parents."

Izzy shook her head. "I haven't had the guts. I keep telling myself I want to wait until I've done something. I'm this huge failure right now and I don't want them seeing me this way."

"Who says you're a failure?" Collier slid off the bed and sat on the floor next to her. "Do you feel like a failure?"

Izzy looked around her apartment. *I love my life right now.* "No."

"Are you happy?"

"I'm very happy."

"So what's the problem?"

Izzy rubbed her skate blade again. "You tell me. I've managed to work myself up to a waitress who lives in an efficiency apartment over a coffee shop."

"Yeah, true. They probably wouldn't appreciate the finer points of your new life. They were always sort of high strung."

"That's an understatement."

"Still, you need to talk to them, even if just to introduce them to Jenna. I mean, it might be okay."

Izzy studied Collier's face, not understanding the shadow darkening his normally expressive features. "It might be okay. And it might be horrible."

"That's true, too. But you are never going to know until you know."

They do have to love their granddaughter, right? Izzy closed her eyes, her father's final words ringing in her ears. *No, they don't have to love anyone. They didn't have to love me. They just had to pay the bills until I won a gold medal.* "Fine. Fine, I'll do it. I'll go this next weekend. Happy?"

"Happy-ish. It would make me happier if you came on the road with me right now, instead of hanging out with Captain Grab Ass and his band of hockey misfits. That would make me happy, and I would make you forget all this talk about being a failure."

"Very tempting." Izzy laughed out loud and punched his shoulder lightly. "But, I gave my word."

Collier let out an exaggerated sigh and looked at his watch. "In that case, you should get going."

"Yes, but first, I need coffee." She set the skate in the box and closed the latch.

Collier reached the bottom of the stairs. "About your parents: I sort of hate that I brought it up and I won't be there. I could rearrange a couple things. Do you want me to stick around for moral support?"

"Since when are you moral?"Izzy playfully shoved him. "Thanks, but I think I'll be okay."

"Collier James as I live and breathe. When did you get here?" Cat looked up from her book, a delighted smile lit her face.

"Cat Countryman. You get prettier every time I see you." Collier hugged Cat. "Let me guess. Blue Pirate is the flavor of the month?"

Cat tossed her head and laughed. "What brings you here?"

"Oh, I…" Collier shot a glance at Izzy.

"He came to see me. Collier and I went to school together. You know, when I was growing up."

A sharp expression flashed across Cat's features. "Oh yeah, you grew up here."

"Yeah, so he stopped by to say hi. How do you know each other?"

"Oh I used to play here all the time. Cat was good enough to give me an audience when I was just starting out."

"Yes, but now you're Mr. Big Time, aren't you? Too good for our little coffee shop." Cat punched his shoulder.

"What is it with you women and punching today?" Collier pretended her punch hurt. "I don't know, I might have an opening in my schedule. Fair season is about over and I think I need some time at home." He let his gaze settle on Izzy for a beat too long. "But now I should go." He hugged both women before leaving through the back door.

As the screen door slapped closed, Cat frowned. "You have to move out. Now."

"What?" Izzy was shocked.

"You've got some kind of voodoo workin' over all the eligible men around here."

"I have no idea what you're talking about, Cat. Collier and I are just friends."

"Right, just friends. I've heard that before. Meanwhile, Collier's willing to come and sing in this dumpy coffee shop after filling places like Second Chances. And there's Quinn pulling up outside. Now what could possibly bring two such talented, busy, hot single guys here?"

Izzy shrugged. "Your cinnamon rolls are world famous."

Cat laughed and smacked her rear with a tray. "It's a good thing I like you. Otherwise, I would have to hate you so bad."

Izzy watched Quinn get out of his car, and smiled. "Well, I'm glad you like me. Quinn's just here to pick me up for his charity event."

"Charity event? That is the worst euphemism for sex ever."

"Cat! Stop."

"You still owe me an image, Izzy Marks. Boxers or briefs. You owe me!" Cat called over her shoulder as she returned to her duties.

"You owe her what?"

Izzy blushed, thankful Quinn hadn't heard the entire exchange. "I…uh…I owe her for my monthly coffee tab. You know, getting to be the end of the month."

"Okay don't tell me. Are you ready?"

"Yeah. Let's go."

"You've got your skates, right?"

"Right here." She took them out of the box and draped them over her shoulder.

He nodded. "I was half afraid you'd chicken out on me."

"Of course I'm not chicken."

Quinn walked her to the car. "Wait until you meet this kid. He's so sweet. It's almost hard to believe he loves hockey as much as he does."

Quinn continued talking all the way to the rink. What he said, Izzy had no idea. Her focus was on the skates in her lap. The feel of them, the familiar cold of the blades, whisked her back to her childhood. Her father, rattling on about something, as they drove to Coach's rink. Her skates in her lap, just as they were now.

Maybe Collier's right. Maybe I should tell Quinn about my past.

She glanced at Quinn, who continued his monologue about the event as if she were an active participant. His face was alive, more animated than it normally was. *He's such a hero for those kids.*

He's been my hero, too.

Maybe he could be more.

***

On the ice, Quinn's heart was always light. But today it floated as he watched Izzy move around in the small group assembled at the rink. Her warm smile made everyone feel welcome, and, though he'd done dozens of events larger than this one, Quinn wondered more than once how he'd managed to do any of them without her.

It was easy to love her. It was almost easy to forget the sight of Collier James emerging from her building as he pulled up to get her.

Almost.

Trying not to obsess about what Collier meant to Izzy, Quinn spent the afternoon trying to catch her eye as she helped someone lace their skates. He wondered what memories stirred in her mind. Her royal blue eyes sparkled, but gave away nothing. *If she's nervous about anything, she's not showing it.*

The event involved a young boy who dreamed of playing hockey in the NHL. Quinn knew, from his conversations with the parents, that it was unlikely the child would reach his mid-teens. So today, with the help of many of Quinn's former teammates and the boy's own hockey team, they were going to scrimmage on the perfect ice of the Bridgestone center. He would then be the honorary captain at the evening's Predator's game.

It was a great day, though days like these were always bittersweet for Quinn. *This kid wants nothing more than a tiny piece of the life I've lived. He'll never see it, given his prognosis. He's dying to live one minute of the life I threw away with both hands.*

This dark thought threatened to sour his mood, but a quick glance toward Izzy, who was showing some very young girls how to skate backward, cheered him. *If she was trying to hide her true identity, she's not trying terribly hard.*

Maybe she's ready to be honest about her past.

Am I ready to be honest about mine?

A puck whizzed past his ear, and the buzzer signaled a goal. The boys from the youth hockey team celebrated, but Quinn's teammates scowled at him as they skated by.

"Geez, Quinn, at least look like you're into this. Otherwise, I swear I'll take over as goalie."

"Guys, come on, it's for the kids." Quinn followed them to the bench for a break.

"Yeah, but you're at least supposed to try." One of the guys elbowed him. "Then again, that little blonde is a distraction, isn't she?"

"She looks familiar," someone noted. "What did you say her name was?"

"Izzy Marks." Quinn nodded at her as she waved to the bench. "She skated some in college, I think."

"Is she in town with the Ice Capades?"

"If she's with Quinn, she's already had an Ice Capade or two, right Quinn?"

Quinn let the general good natured ribbing pass by him without more than a nod and a weak smile. *Even here, among friends, my reputation is too much to ignore.*

Why on earth would someone as kind and perfect as Izzy want me in her life?

SEVENTEEN

The day was over far too soon. Everything about the event gave Izzy joy, and she felt a certain twinge of loss when the last child gave her a parting hug.

Not everything had been easy. The urge to fly over such perfect ice was difficult to ignore. She kept up a deluge of cheerful chatter with the parents and an impromptu skating lesson for the siblings of the youth hockey team, hoping to drive the ache in her heart away. She skated slowly, trying to calm the nervous energy in her legs. *I might as well try to reign in wild horses.*

She'd never seen Quinn as comfortable as he was on the ice, with his friends and the kids. The cloud that always seemed to follow him lifted. His smiles held no echo of sadness. *Funny, I never thought of him as sad until I saw how different he is today.*

What fascinated her most was his easy rapport with everyone. So often, when they talked at the Waffle House, he seemed distant, as if some huge space lay between him and everyone around him. *But here, on the ice, he's present and connected.*

He's not looking over his shoulder.

Briefly she wondered what past spirit haunted him.

Now, sitting on the bench, staring absently at the empty ice, Izzy envisioned herself skating as she once had. *Had I known I was going to give it up forever, would I have made a different decision? Would I have slept with Jason?*

She knew the answer. Sleeping with Jason lead to Jenna, and Jenna was the one thing in Izzy's life she never regretted.

"You look a million miles away."

Izzy startled at Quinn's touch on her shoulder. "I was just remembering when Jenna was little. I'd take her to skating parties and school outings. It's been a long time."

"You were pretty awesome with those kids. I owe you."

"No, I think we're even."

He sat down and nudged her shoulder with his. "Nope, see, I forgot that there would be all these little kids, with nothing to do. You saved the day. I owe you big."

"I'll keep that in mind. Having Quinn Murray owe me a favor might come in handy at some point."

He checked his watch. "Look, we've got a couple hours before the ice crew comes in. I usually just spend the time skating. I don't get the opportunity too often. You don't mind hanging around for a bit, do you?"

"No, not at all." Her heart beat a bit faster. *Some free time on the ice?*

"You could join me." His beautiful eyes glowed hopefully. *Calm down. He's just being nice.* "What, like be the goalie?"

Quinn smiled, mischief glowing in his eyes. "That would be great for my ego!"

"Oh, you think I'd be a push over?"

"I think I'd score on you easily. Oh wait…that didn't come out right, did it?" His cheeks reddened, something Izzy found endearing.

Izzy laughed. "Not really. But I like a challenge."
Cat would be so proud of me.

***

"Give me a minute, okay? I'll be right back." Quinn started up the stairs to the announcer's booth. Behind him, he heard the smooth swish of blades on ice and knew that Izzy was skating slowly around the rink. "Nick, good, you're still here." Quinn greeted the young music coordinator who was locking the announcer's booth.

"I gotta lock up Mr. Murray. You and your friend should probably get going."

"Nick, do you know who that is?"

Nick squinted at Izzy's small form on the distant ice. "Nope. She's a decent skater though. Is she with the Ice Capades?"

Probably best not to let him in on it just yet. There's a reason she's hiding. "I'm not sure. But look, Nick, I'd really like to spend a little time with her, on the ice. Okay?"

"Oh, I don't know. I'm supposed to get everyone out of here. The ice crew is coming in a couple hours to get the rink ready for the Preds game tonight."

"Look, Nick, how about this: I have two keys in my pocket. One is for the owner's luxury box. The other is for the bar in the owner's luxury box." Quinn watched Nick's expression transition from doubt to interest to glee. "I'm sure a guy like you has a friend you'd like to maybe impress for an hour or so?"

"You have no idea!" Nick clapped his hands together. "Won't the owners get mad?"

Only if we get caught. "It'll be fine. Just be sure you leave everything the way you found it."

"Oh, I will!"

"How about if you return my keys in an hour?"

"I can do that."

"And Nick?"

"Yes, sir?"

"Keep the curtains in the box closed. Neither of us wants an audience."

Nick nodded. "You want the lights up?"

Quinn glanced at the shadowy ice and shook his head. "No, I like it dim. Oh, you could put some music on, something mellow?"

"I'm not sure what I have." Nick rifled through a stack of CD's. "Oh, wait, how about this?" He held up a CD marked, 'Boring 80's tunes chicks dig.' "I think the guy who used to have my job used it, you know… to get chicks."

"Where's he now?"

Nick shrugged. "I'm pretty sure he got caught with a girl in one the Preds' cushy locker room chairs. They fired him."

"So let's not get caught." Quinn spoke more to himself than to Nick. Leaving the booth, Quinn heard the first strains of Toto's "Won't Hold You Back" and smiled. *It's like it's meant to be.*

He sat on a bench and tightened his laces, watching as Izzy moved to the music that would have won her a gold medal. She was hesitant, at first, as if only vaguely recalling the steps. As the music continued, she moved more confidently, her body floating over the ice. Her motions and jumps, though simplified, were clean, effortless. The years melted away. There were moments in the routine where Jason would have lifted her or sent her whirling into some fluttering, perfectly landed, throw element. Only because he'd memorized the routine did Quinn miss the elements. Anyone else would have thought her footwork was part of the routine.

She's still breathtaking.

The song faded and another started to play. Quinn skated out to center ice where Izzy stood very still.

He put his hands on her shoulders. "That was spectacular…Miss Landry."

She shuddered as if waking from a trance. "How?" Her voice was light and breathy from the exertion. Her eyes darkened. "How long have you known?"

Don't freak her out by telling her you've stalked her. "Call it a suspicion I've had for a while. The bigger question," he circled her, "is why you've kept it a secret."

"I haven't been really ready to talk about it. It's been a long time."

He didn't miss her hesitation. "I understand if you don't want to share with me."

"It's not you." She leaned against the boards. "Jenna's the only one I've told, and Collier, well we grew up together. My hus—Jason always said we'd be safe if we didn't talk about it. I got out of the habit of thinking about…my past. Until recently."

That explains her connection to Singer Guy. Childhood buddies. I can work with that. "Look, I'm sorry if I brought up bad memories. That wasn't my intention."

She smiled, and in that smile was more forgiveness than Quinn thought he deserved. "Don't be. I mean, it's actually sort of a charge, skating again. I've missed it." She started skating backwards, still facing him. "I guess you can never completely escape who you are, right?"

I've been trying to do that for years.

"Don't beat yourself up. It might be good to talk to someone. At least you get it. You understand what it's like to be away from the ice when you still love it." She put a hand on his chest. "Our secret?"

I get to share a secret only a select few know? I'm in. "Our secret." He watched her skate away from him. "On a completely different note, you'd make a great defenseman."

"How so?"

"You skate backwards faster than most guys I've seen in the league."

"Sorry," she slowed her speed and smiled. "On that same note, you'd be a pretty good pairs' partner."

Their easy give and take was restored. Relieved, Quinn laughed out loud and sped up to skate next to her. "Doubtful."

"No, honestly. You're tall, and strong. Those are key points. Plus, you know how to skate."

"No, you skate. I move around."

"Oh, shut up. False modesty doesn't work on you."

"Did the First Lady of Pairs' Skating just tell me to shut up?" It was his turn to skate backwards.

"Oh, that's where we're going, seriously?" Izzy shoved him. "Monster Mash Murray is calling me names?"

"Obviously we've found each other's Wikipedia page."

"Obviously." She slowed and skated next to him.

Emboldened by her nearness, Quinn softened his tone. "Show me some moves."

The request surprised her. "What, now?"

"Sure, why not? We have world class ice right here."

She frowned. "What did you do to make everyone in the place just leave?"

Quinn nodded to the faint light in the glowing from one luxury box. "I have a lot of charm and a couple of very important keys for rooms in this place."

"How much time do we have?"

Quinn checked his watch. "An hour, give or take."

Izzy skated a few paces ahead of him, then turned and skated backwards. She seemed to assess him more like a side of beef than a skater.

"A spin and a jump would take way too long, plus you really can't spin in those." She pointed to his hockey skates.

Quinn shook his head. "I always thought a death spiral would be cool."

"No, those are way more complicated than they look, and you," she looked him up and down with a practiced eye, "don't look ready for something like that. But," she reached her hand to him, "you could do a throw."

Quinn took her hand willingly, but was not amused at her suggestion. "I'm sorry, a throw? Not a chance."

"A throw is probably the simplest thing I could teach you. I would have a bit more control over the end result of a throw than I would a lift."

Quinn pictured himself lifting Izzy over his head, and the image ended with her crashing more than six feet down, slicing his face open with her skates in the process. "Okay, a throw it is."

"Now a lot of people debate over what the easiest one to do is, but I like the throw double Salchow." She sidled up to him. "It's almost romantic and I'm fairly sure I can stick a landing on a double without killing us both."

"Oh, well, that sounds so easy. Sign me up."

"Oh, come on!" She put a hand on his arm. "Just give it a try. I'll admit, I'm sort of interested to see if I can still do it."

"What do I need to do?"

Izzy's eyes glowed in the dim light. "Okay, the first thing you have to know is that if you're going to be a pairs' skater, you have to trust your partner."

"Got it. Trust." *Simple word. Impossible concept.*

As Izzy explained a few things, her whole body quivered with an energy Quinn hadn't seen in her before. *How much magic did the skating world lose because they pushed her out?*

"Now, put your hand here on my waist and one here on my shoulder. Now skate."

He obeyed her command and they skated over the full oval of the ice. He held her, but Izzy lead them both. Her body was taut, tense, like a guitar string. He marveled at how easily she moved, and how natural it was to have his hands on her.

"Now, you're going to throw me."

"Now?" His feelings of comfort abandoned him.

She slowed and skated backwards in front of him. "Don't sweat it. All you have to do is put your hands here, and hold my hand here. When I say go, just fling, sort of a like a Frisbee."

"Frisbees don't have arms and legs that break."

"You're not chickening out on me, are you?"

"No, of course not." Quinn held her, tense, waiting for her command.

"Now!"

He spun and let her go. All he could do was watch as she twirled in the air twice, and fumbled to a wobbly landing. She regained her footing quickly, and shot a dazzling smile at him. "You did it!" She glided to a stop and leaned against the boards.

He caught up to her. "Are you okay, though? That landing looked awkward."

She waved a hand in the air. "Please. No ice on the butt, no problem."

"In that case that was incredible!" He caught her in his arms and whirled her around. "I can't believe I just did that!" He set her back on her feet and studied her flushed, smiling face. "Izzy…" he breathed on her cheek before sealing his lips to hers.

In that moment the weight of Quinn's past fell away from him. One kiss, one perfect first kiss, and every other woman washed out of his memory. His senses filled with her, the sweet taste and smell of her surrounded him, wrapping him in a blanket of warmth. Here, on the ice, was a place of safety. Here he was strong.

He was a hero again.

***

Heat flowed from his kiss through her body. *I've never been kissed this way.*

It was the only conscious thought she had for several moments. Her knees weakened and every nerve in her body woke to wild sensation as he pulled her closer. She steadied herself, her hands on his broad chest, her finger tips throbbing to the beat of his heart.

They broke apart breathlessly, fighting a force neither could see. Izzy glided backward a few feet on wobbly legs as she watched emotions spark in Quinn's eyes.

"Um…okay then." She was horrified at the sound of her own voice.

Quinn reached out a hand, an apologetic gesture. "Hey, I'm …"

"No, no." She stopped skating away from him and put a hand on his chest. "No, it's…it's okay. I, think…yeah. It's all good."

It's all good? Oh please someone stop me from saying stupid things!

"How about if we try that again?" She put a hand over her mouth. *What is wrong with me?* "The, uh, the throw, you know."

"Oh, yeah, right."

It took Izzy two full trips around the rink before she was ready to shout, "Now!"

This time Quinn was confident. He lifted and released her with power and direction. She did a double and landed perfectly. She cheered again, this time jumping up and down like a child. "That was awesome!"

***

As she skated toward him there was a light in Izzy's eyes, a vibration to her whole being Quinn couldn't miss. She was as connected to the ice as he was. She had been exiled, not from Nashville, not from her friends and family, but from the ice, for almost twenty years. Now that she was back, now that she'd felt that rush beneath her skates again, Quinn knew, she couldn't give it up

"Quinn," she put her hands on his shoulders, "I had no idea how much I missed this. I'd forgotten. Thank you." She hugged him.

This time, Quinn was more ready, and in control as his lips claimed hers. His hands roamed over her, sensitive to her responses. No longer shy or surprised, Quinn sought to pull her spirit in to his own. He tightened his arm around her, protective and possessive She melded to him, her defenses down. He traced the length of her back to her hip, then down her thigh. Even through the soft denim of her jeans, Quinn felt her body warm to his touch. Her scent, the taste of her lips, swirled around and into him, intoxicating him. He grasped her thigh, and pulled her closer, tight against him, aching to lose himself in her closeness.

A flash of warning fired through him. *Not like this!*

He broke away, the separation was jagged, burning. His heart pounded as he circled away from her. *What am I doing?*

I'm doing the right thing.

If this is the right thing, why can't I look at her right now?

"Quinn?" Izzy's voice seemed very far away. He was surprised, as he turned, to see her right behind him. "Are you...okay?"

He took a deep breath. "Yeah, yeah. I just…I mean, you know…" he couldn't find the words to answer the question in her dark blue eyes. "This isn't what I envisioned. I've got my skates on." His stammering clearly did little to ease her confused frown. Quinn picked a focal point beyond her right shoulder. "Look. Are you hungry?"

She blinked as if trying to switch gears. "I could eat, I guess."

He tensed, and skated backwards. *How am I making this so weird?* "You don't have to work tonight, right?"

"No, I'm free." Izzy smiled uncertainly. "But don't you have to be here for the game? You know, for that kid?"

Crap! I forgot about the kid.

Steamy kissing will tend to wipe out charity obligations.

"Right, the kid. Yeah, I have to be here at least for a while."

"Are you sure you're okay?" She seemed to be struggling to suppress a giggle as she circled him smoothly.

Get it together, Murray! "I'd like to ask you out on a proper date. Later. Tonight."

She stopped short, a small cloud of spray firing from her skate blades. "You're asking me on a date?"

"I am." Quinn's face heated.

Izzy cleared her throat. "Just so I understand. This would be a romantic date?"

"Yes." The word fell from him in a wave of choking relief.

She nodded. "Okay."

Quinn liked that it was now her turn to be completely off balance. "I could pick you up at your place, say around ten?"

"Right. Ten."

Quinn skated to the bench and sat down. Now that he'd actually said the words out loud, he was weak with relief. He unlaced his skates as she sat down. "So ten's not too late?"

Her hair fell forward, hiding her face from him. "Ten is fine." Her laugh was a nervous giggle.

"What's so funny?"

"I'm picturing you, pulling up to the coffee shop, all formal and flowers." She sat up and nudged her shoulder against his.

All of the tension in Quinn's body eased, and he felt like himself again. He grinned and ruffled her hair. "I wouldn't bring you flowers."

She arched an eyebrow. "And why not?"

"Because you're allergic."

Izzy bit her lip and this time it was her cheeks that colored warmly. "Is that on my Wikipedia page too?"

"Nope, I knew that. I think Cat told me, or Jenna." Confidence flowing through him again, Quinn picked up his gym bag and guided her out of the arena. *I know a lot of things about Isabella Landry. Maybe tonight I'll get to know Izzy Marks a little better.*

Her kiss still warmed his lips. *Maybe a lot better.*

They walked in silence to the front doors. "Okay, so ten?"

"Ten." She walked to her car.

Quinn checked his watch. He had two hours before the game to create a romantic evening. *An evening worthy of Isabella Landry.*

No.

An evening worthy of Izzy Marks.

EIGHTEEN

After driving up and down the streets of Nashville, trying to make sense of the afternoon, Izzy pulled into her parking space at the coffee shop and turned off the car. It was only then that she acknowledged that her knees were still wobbly from the kiss.

What have I just gotten myself into?

The skating? The kissing? Now I'm going on a date with Quinn?

What does he think I'm expecting? What should I be expecting?

Oh lord, he probably thinks I'm expecting sex.

She rolled the thoughts in her head as she walked into the coffee shop.

"Hey, Mom. How was Quinn's charity thing?" Jenna looked up from a text book.

"Well, I just did something I haven't done in a long time."

"What haven't ya done in a long time?" Cat met her at the foot of the stairs. "Sex? Did you have sex? I want details! Oooh, did he wear skates? How sexy would that be?"

"Ewwwwww! Cat shut up!" Jenna shouted.

"Yes, Cat, shut up. I'm not sharing the details of my sex life with my daughter."

"That means you have a sex life, and it has to be with Quinn!"

Izzy scurried up the stairs, thankful that no other customers were in the shop to witness this fresh humiliation. "I am not going to share the intimate details."

"Hey, Jen? When your mom says 'intimate details,' she means sex!"

"Eww!"

Izzy shouted over her shoulder. "I'm not sharing anything with the two of you until you both grow up!" She slammed her door for good measure.

She counted to five, and, as if on cue, a light knock was followed by, "We're sorry."

Izzy opened the door. "Can I help you girls?"

She laughed out loud at the comically sad faces they both wore. "Okay, come on in. I do have news and I don't think I have enough time."

"Time for what, Mom?"

"Sit down, and help me pick out something to wear. I am going on a date."

Both younger women sat on Izzy's bed. Jenna looked confused.

"Does Quinn know you're going out with someone?"

"What are you talking about? The date is with Quinn."

"Mom, haven't you two been going out for awhile?"

Cat tapped her chin. "No, remember, Jens, your mother insists she and Quinn are just friends. So tonight is a new level for them, and they are calling it dating."

"So, this is a date, and then, what, Quinn asks Mom to go steady?"

Cat and Jenna fell on Izzy's bed laughing.

Lord, grant me patience. "Will one of you find something appropriate in my closet?"

Jenna frowned. "What would be appropriate for a first date between two people who have been a total couple for at least a month?"

"Oh, if only we had a Hepburn here." Cat hopped off the bed. "Audrey or Kate…both fashion icons. They would know what to do at a platonic date."

"For your information," Izzy shouted from the bathroom, "this is a romantic date."

"What?" Both women continued laughing uproariously.

"Yes, well," Izzy donned her fuzzy pink robe and sat down in the armchair, "we did have one…no, two, amazing kisses."

"Where did he kiss you?"

"On the ice."

"On the ice? Geez Iz, I mean, he's a great skater, but isn't that sort of dangerous? I mean, you slip and fall and drag him down, and then it's all blades and bruises, which some would find sexy, but you two don't really strike me as that sort of couple."

"You're wrong there, Cat," Jenna shook her head. "Mom's a great skater. She would've gone to the Olympics. Why are you waving your arms at me, Mom?"

Izzy stopped frantically waving her hands at Jenna. "Jenna, dear, you know I haven't told anyone about that."

"Mom, Cat's practically a member of the family. She's helping you pick out sexy underwear. Tell her."

"Tell me what?" Cat held up a pair of Izzy's 'granny panties.' "If you're going to tell me that you have zero date appropriate dainties, don't bother. I figured that out."

"No, Cat, I think Mom here should tell you."

"So you kissed a guy on the ice. Very 'Ice Castles,' minus the blindness. Oh, but how cool would it be if you were a figure skater, right? 'Cause he's a hockey player, then you could totally be like "The Cutting Edge" which a lot of people dismiss, but it's such a good...wait a minute." Cat took a breath and stared at Izzy. "Izzy? 'Izzy' could be short for...no way. Jenna, what did you say your dad's name was?"

"Jason."

"Jason, as in maybe Jason Masters, pairs' figure skating god from when I was like seven. And that would make you Isabella Landry?"

"Yes." Izzy blushed and nodded. "Guilty as charged."

Cat dropped the underwear on the floor and clapped her hands over her face. "Oh. My. Gawd! Jenna, did you know this? Did you know Izzy was Isabella Landry?"

Jenna grinned. "Yeah, I'm recently aware of it."

"Izzy? I can't believe it! I'm standing like, in the presence of greatness!"

"I wouldn't go that far, Cat." Izzy slumped in the chair and rubbed her temples.

"Jenna, has she ever showed you the routine?"

Jenna shot a sharp look to Izzy. "My parents sort of kept a low key about their skating."

"Jason Masters and Belle Landry. Jason was the sexiest skater, I didn't even know what sexy was until I saw him skate. I was totally jazzed when he dumped that bitch Serena Shipley. I thought for sure he'd find me, little-nine-year-old me, and make me his new partner. But then he paired up with Isabella Landry...with you!"

"Okay, Cat, we all know the story." *And now is hardly the time to relive it.*

"True, but I would love to have seen the routine, Mom."

Cat jumped up and down. "I have it on tape! I totally have it on tape!"

Cat raced out of the room, leaving Jenna and Izzy gaping at each other. She returned in a minute, waving an ancient VHS tape over her head. The tape was marked USA FIGURE SKATING: LANDRY AND MASTERS BEST NATIONALS EVER.

"My mom was such a fan. We would sit there and watch every minute of every figure skating program we could find. And Jenna, your mother, well, she was like some little fairy flitting all over the ice. She had this one partner he was okay. But then your mom paired up with, well, you dad. It was magic. And it was a little scandalous, right, because your mom was so young and your dad was so not. And bigger scandal, your dad was supposedly in a big romantic thing with Serena Shipley and that blew up big time when he went to skate with your ma. And then there were stories about Serena having Jason's baby and all that, but by that time, your parents were gone."

"Cat, the tape?" *No need to go that far down that road.*

Cat took a breath. "Sure, sure. My mom was so heartbroken after your parents passed on goin' to the Olympics, 'cause they would have totally won because the only competition that year was some snaggle toothed Korean couple that completely died during the short program…"

"Cat! The tape already!" Jenna pointed to the VHS player under Izzy's TV. "I'd love to see it. Mom, are you okay with this?"

Izzy turned a blank gaze to her daughter. "Yeah, go ahead." She blinked. *Secret baby? It was all tabloid silliness. That's what Jason always said.*

And Jason never lied, right?

Izzy tried to shove the thought away as the opening bars of the music rose.

"Okay, so this is Serena Shipley and her partner. Wanna see her temper tantrum?"

"No, that's not really necessary."

"Mom, I'd like to see it. I mean, why not, it sort of made what you guys did that much better, right?"

Cat grinned. "Cool. You would not believe this. There's Serena. You know she lives in Nashville now. Married some super rich guy, he died and now she travels a lot."

Good thing Nashville is a big town. Izzy studied the pair on the tape and realized she'd never actually seen Serena Shipley up close. *Coach never allowed me to watch anyone in a competition, and he never let me watch tape on other teams. Funny, I never realized her hair was so red.*

"Wait for it….wait for it…<u>and bam</u>!" Cat cheered as Serena's partner hit the ice, clearly injured. "Now go ahead, feel sorry for the guy, but watch Serena's reaction. Priceless."

"You can almost read her lips."

"Almost nothing, Jenna. The mouth on that woman!" Cat doubled up laughing.

"Is the crowd actually booing?"

Did they boo? I don't remember. I was so nervous.

"Geez, Mom, look at you!" Jenna breathed. "You're both so young!"

The three of them sat, entranced, for four minutes. Tears sprang to Izzy's eyes, remembering the feeling of complete connection she felt with Jason that night it was a feeling she never felt again with another person.

Until this afternoon.

"Mom?"

"Yeah, Jen?"

"You and Dad, you were really good. I'm so-so sorry." Jenna bit her lip.

"You have nothing to be sorry for." Izzy hugged Jenna and tears welled.

"Wait, if you're going to have a big cry fest, I want in." Cat wrapped her arms around them both. "Okay, so we have got to get you ready for the big date. And now that I know what I'm working with, I'll be right back!"

Left alone to wipe her daughter's tears, Izzy smiled. "You know no matter what, your father loved you. He stayed with me because he loved you."

"I know, it's just so hard seeing the two of you so connected on the ice like that. Skating was so much a part of you."

"You were a bigger part." Izzy hugged her. "Never forget that, okay?"

"I won't." Jenna wiped a tear from her eye then stared at the screen. "Mom, look at that crowd shot. Look at that tall guy in the back. Is that...?"

Izzy rewound the tape a few frames and watched. "Look at that. Quinn Murray."

"Holy carp Mom. He's hot! I mean he was back when this was taped."

"No, Jens, he's still hot. You're just too young to appreciate a slow simmered hotness like that." Cat trotted back into the room carrying a garment bag. "Yep, aged to perfection. That's him in a nutshell."

I agree. "Why on earth would he be there, watching figure skating?"

"Well, where was this? The Twin Cities? So okay, he's there because the Preds are playin' a game the next night or something."

"No, he wasn't in the league that far back. He would still have been in college."

"Where did he go to college?"

"North Dakota State."

"So, then, why is he at the Nationals in the Twin Cities?"

Just add it to the list of mysteries I have to solve.

"Okay, Izzy, I'm back and I have the outfit for you. It's classy. It says, 'I'm someone you should know,' but it's subtle like, 'you should know me but if you don't, that's cool because I'm not here to be a celebrity.' But, and here's the kicker about this outfit, it also says, 'I want you to treat me like a lady...and wait until we're at your place for a nightcap to completely ravish me.'"

Izzy sighed and got off the bed. "An outfit that says that much, what will be left for me to say?" She took the garment bag from Cat. A moment later she emerged from the bathroom, wearing a very chic knee length midnight blue sheath that moved with her in all the right places. "I don't know what to say, Cat. This is gorgeous!"

"You like it? Yeah, someone left the garment bag here last week. I'd put it in the lost and found, but usually if anyone leaves stuff here, it's left for good. Here are the shoes to match. They aren't super matchy-match like some kind of 1980's prom dress, so you're good. Oh, do you need nylons?"

Izzy looked at herself in the mirror. "What do you think, Jenna?"

"I think it might be wrong that my mom has such great legs. No to the nylons."

"Okay," Cat looked at her watch. "What time is he picking you up?"

"Ten."

"That gives us three hours. I just hope we have enough time. Jenna, go to my room and get my make up kit. Not the little one, the big one, with the industrial paints and what not. Izzy, get yourself into the shower. We don't want you smelling like the Waffle House."

"Very funny!" Izzy shouted, as she slammed the bathroom door and turned on the shower. The hiss of the water did nothing to drown out the jumbled thoughts in her head, and hot steam on her skin only conjured the feel of Quinn's lips on hers.

I was so young when Jason and I got together. I never went on a date. My first real kiss, my first everything, happened that night with Jason.

Izzy rinsed her hair and let the water cascade around her face. *Now I'm going on my very first date. I'm thirty-six and I'm going on my first date.*

By the time Cat and Jenna were done with her, Izzy barely recognized herself. She stared at her reflection in the mirror. "Are you sure about this?"

"This is exactly what Audrey Hepburn would do with her hair, if she were about to go on a date with a hockey player, if she was wearing that dress."

"You look great, Mom. The hair is amazing!"

Izzy eyed herself critically. "The hair seems a little tall."

Cat signed. "It's a Nashville thing, honey. It has to be big or it's not special."

"But the make up?"

"It's night. You're going on a romantic date with a man, I should probably tell you, who has been out with a lot of women. He's come to expect a certain look."

No pressure there. Izzy sighed again.

The back door bell downstairs jangled and all three women jumped.

"You look amazing." Jenna hugged her. "I'll go answer the door."

Izzy turned to Cat. "Do I really look okay?"

Cat smiled gently. "Iz, you are my best friend. I would never lie to you." She frowned. "So I can tell you, that make-up makes you look like a clown streetwalker."

"You put it on me! You're telling me this now?"

"Oh, stop with the panic. Let me just dab here and brush there." Cat wiped brushes and cotton balls on her face. "Okay. Now, you're perfect."

Izzy glanced in the mirror. Except for the big hair, she did look more like herself. "I think I'm ready."

"No, go forth and get some!" Cat shouted as Izzy walked down the stairs.

***

Quinn tapped his toe on the concrete step. He didn't want to walk into the coffee shop. For some reason, though he'd walked through the door a hundred times, tonight he wanted to wait out on the back stoop. *What am I, sixteen, borrowing the old man's car?*

When was the last time I took a woman out on an actual date?

Which brings us back to being sixteen, borrowing the old man's car.

"Hi, Quinn."

"Oh, hello, Jenna."

"So, you're taking my mom out?"

Quinn smiled. "I guess that's what I'm doing."

"You know…my mom…she's…my mom." Jenna grinned, and for the first time Quinn saw Izzy in her face. "I don't think you and I need to have a talk about what she means to me, do we?"

Quinn laughed. "I haven't had a predate talk since I was younger than you!"

Jenna giggled, another trait she'd inherited from her mother. "Well, I guess I wanted you to know; Mom hasn't gone out a lot."

Quinn nodded, matching her serious turn of mood. "Jenna, on my honor, I will be a gentleman tonight."

A wail emitted from the upstairs. Quinn tried to see if someone was watching them from the upstairs window, but saw no one. "What was that?"

Jenna grinned. "That was a very naughty, very nosy Cat."

Quinn sensed there was a double meaning in her words, but chose to ignore it. The screen door creaked and there Izzy was, standing in front of him. Slim and perfect in a midnight blue dress just short enough to show off her amazing legs. Legs that carried her smoothly over the ice. Legs that, if everything went well, could be wrapped…

Stop it! What did I just promise this woman's daughter? I'm going to be the perfect gentleman. Even though I've wanted her my entire life.

Be fair. It wasn't my entire life. Just in college. And the last several weeks. And at her husband's funeral.

"Quinn?"

Quinn shook himself out of his internal argument. "You look amazing."

She struck a pose and grinned. "Lost and found wins again."

"Okay. Well, then, my car is right there." He moved to one side and let her glide down the steps to the back lot.

"I see that." She scuffed her shoe against the pavement.

This was so much easier when we both had skates on and no one was watching.

Izzy cleared her throat. "We have some very interested children watching us."

"Well, then let's get out of here." He took her hand and walked her to the car, then opened the door and waited as she slid into the seat. There was a slit in the skirt that rode up just a tiny bit as she shifted in the seat…

Do I really need another cold shower? He ran around the front of the car and got in. "So, I did some thinking, and I hope you don't mind, but I have a dinner arranged at my place. I thought it would be nicer than going to a restaurant so late."

If it bothered her, Izzy didn't let it show. "I don't think I've ever been to a dinner that's been arranged. It sounds mysterious."

"I mean, normally I would cook for you. But with the game…"

"Quinn, dinner at your place sounds great."

"I can cook, you know."

"I'm sure it will be very nice."

After this brilliant exchange, they drove in silence for several minutes, the lights of Nashville washing over Quinn's car as they cruised.

"That's my building." Quinn pointed.

"Wow, you are right downtown, aren't you?"

"At the heart of it all. It seemed like a great idea to live so close to the arena, you know, walk to practice, that sort of thing. Turns out, it was just more of a necessity."

"What do you mean by that?"

Quinn pulled into the parking garage and eased the car into his assigned spot. *Let's not open with the worst part of my history.* "Oh, nothing."

He ushered Izzy to the elevator where he pushed his floor number and stood opposite from her as the doors slid closed. *Cripes, if we were complete strangers, we wouldn't be this awkward.*

This was the last thought he had before she stood on her toes and kissed him.

It wasn't a long kiss, but it was enough to reset something in his brain, and Quinn relaxed. "What was that for?"

"I was just checking."

"For?"

"Well, see, I know this cool guy. His name is Quinn. Quinn eats at Waffle House and does really awesome stuff for kids. Sort of a fair hockey player."

"Just fair?"

"And see, he's a really good friend of mine. I think I'm standing next to him, but he's all weird around me."

"Maybe he's nervous?"

"No, he's a pretty fearless guy. I'm thinking it might have something to do," she pulled her hair away from her face and banded it in a smooth pony tail, "with this hair."

"How did you…where were you hiding…?"

Izzy laughed. "A skater is never without a pony tail band. Trust me."

"Well you still look fantastic. But now you look like you."

"I'll take that as a good thing."

Quinn looked at her up and down again. "Oh, it is, trust me."

"Good, because today, my friend sort of acted like he might be interested in more than friendship." She nudged him with her hip. "There was some fairly awesome kissing involved."

"But he might be a complete moron, if he risks a stellar friendship for a couple kisses, no matter how awesome."

"Maybe I'm a little nervous about that, too." She settled against his arm and cleared her throat. "Maybe that's why I thought, 'If I kiss this person who looks like Quinn, then maybe, just maybe, the real Quinn will emerge and we can have a conversation.'"

"About the kissing?"

Izzy laughed as the elevator doors slid open. "If that's what you'd like to discuss." She took a step into his apartment. "But first, let's talk about the fact that the elevator opens right into your place!"

"Hey, your door opens right into your bedroom." Quinn followed her. "At least I have the decency to have a living room before introducing my guests to the love den."

"Oh, love den, that's what we're calling my efficiency over the coffee shop?"

"Mr. Murray, drinks are served on the balcony." A young man in a stiff white shirt greeted them.

"Thank you. I'll have the ginger ale and Izzy, what would you like?"

"The same, thanks." Izzy stared at the waiter. When he walked away, she turned her stare to Quinn.

Her amazement made him smile. "Now, if you'd like to follow me, I'll show you a view of Nashville that will blow your socks off."

"Would it disappoint you to know I'm not wearing socks?"

She's regained her humor quickly. Quinn slid the glass door open and watched her step onto the balcony. "Doubtful, since a woman's socks have never held much interest for me. Now, if you were to tell me what else you aren't wearing, I might be interested." He gave her a lecherous grin.

"There's the real Quinn. Wow, this is amazing!" Izzy leaned on the steel railing. "You get to see this every day?"

"I doubt I appreciate it as much as I should. Sometimes the scene down there seems cheap. Some of the romance of the Music City has worn off, for me."

Izzy turned and faced him. "Sounds like we have some talkin' to do, my friend."

"If you're up for it." Quinn stepped aside so the waiter could set down two glasses of ginger ale. "But first, a toast."

Izzy took her glass. "Okay, how about this: To seeing things differently."

"That's a loaded sentence." Quinn took a sip. "So you want to hang out here, or should I send the help home early?"

Izzy laughed, nearly spewing ginger ale through her nose. "Send the help home early? Isn't that a little pretentious?"

"I always thought it would be cool to say that. You know, if I had a beautiful woman up to my place to look at the lights. Maybe I'd nuzzle her hair," Quinn wrapped an arm around her waist and pulled her to him. The warm scent of honey met him as he kissed the top of her head. "And I'd say, 'How about if I send the help home early?' And it would be very, very cool."

Izzy leaned into his embrace. "It is very, very cool. Let's send the help home."

"Give me five minutes."

The look in her eyes left no doubt about her sincerity. "I'm not going any place."

He stepped inside quickly. *Before she changes her mind...or comes to her senses.*

NINETEEN

Izzy couldn't hear what Quinn said to the waiter and his two helpers, but within moments they cleared everything out of the kitchen and left. She watched as if riveted to a silent movie, and sipped the ginger ale. It wasn't like the normal ginger ale, it was a deeper color, and had a very pleasing bite.

Probably better I'm drinking this than wine. I have to keep a clear head.

Am I really going to go through with this?

I haven't been with a man since Jason.

I hadn't been with a man before Jason.

"There, everyone is gone, and dinner is served." Quinn opened the sliding door and ushered her back into the apartment. "I hope you like surf and turf. Somehow it seemed appropriate for the two of us."

He pulled a chair out for her and Izzy sat down to an elegantly set table. Candle light sparkled off the perfectly placed silverware and crystal glasses. "This is beautiful."

"Surprised?" He sat across from her.

"Maybe a little. I mean, I rarely see you outside Waffle House."

"I never struck you as a crystal/candle/silverware owning sort of guy. I suppose that's fair. My mom sort of set me up when I moved here."

"Really?"

"Oh yeah. My mom was one of those women who just knew how things should be, you know? She made sure I always had the right clothes, that sort of thing. Now my dad, well, he's a beer and brawling guy. He loves that I played hockey. He hates that I like wine with dinner. Speaking of which..." he nodded to the ice bucket which held two green cans, "If the Vernor's isn't to your liking, I do have some wine."

"Only if you're having some."

"Don't touch it anymore."

Izzy did not miss the change in his tone. "Sounds like something to add to the list of things we should talk about?"

Quinn shrugged. "It's an old story. Young idiot gets a truck load of money to play hockey. Young idiot spends several years being a young idiot on the party scene. Eventually, he stops being young, and realizes he has to stop being an idiot."

"I'll stick with the Vernor's. I've never had it before. It's good."

"Ah, you're not from Michigan then."

Izzy shook her head. "No, Tennessee born and raised, until I moved to Wisconsin with… Jason."

"It's okay to say his name, you know."

She fidgeted with a napkin. "I know. It seems strange. I haven't…I haven't talked about him since I moved here."

"Do you want to talk about him now?"

"No." She lifted her glass to the light. "Tell me about Vernor's."

Quinn filled her crystal glass with the fizzy beverage. "Best and only ginger ale worth drinking. I actually have this shipped in from Detroit. I'm a Michigan boy, except for my college years, and as far as I'm concerned, buying it anyplace but in Michigan makes it taste funny."

"A purist." Izzy sipped her drink and smiled.

Quinn filled his own glass and raised it to her. "A toast."

"Another toast?"

"Sure, why not? How about a toast to bridges."

"Bridges?"

Quinn's eyes sparkled with mischief, "Building them, maybe crossing them."

"To bridges."

Quinn stood, "Now, you just stay put and I'll bring in dinner."

A minute later he set a plate in front of her. "Wow, this looks amazing."

"Well, maybe I'm buttering you up for something."

Izzy stared at him, her fork frozen halfway between her plate and her mouth. *He's going to ask me to…do it…over dinner?*

"Wow, do you look weird all of a sudden." He sat down. "You look like you think I'm going to ask you to hand over your first-born."

"Good luck. She's pretty tough. She'll definitely put up a fight."

Quinn laughed. "Yeah, I can picture that. She's got her mother's determination."

"So, what is it you're buttering me up for with this amazing dinner?"

He chewed his food slowly before answering. "I've got this charity event this spring. It's going to be huge. I've gotten commitments from NHL players, from all kinds of local celebrities. I'm hoping to raise a hundred thousand dollars for the Aubri Brown Foundation."

"That's a ton of money." Izzy blinked. "That's the hockey player who lost a child, right? They raise money to help families who lose children and need counseling or other things."

Quinn nodded. "How did you know?"

"Don't look surprised. You've mentioned the charity a couple times."

"I'm not used to people listening when I talk about my charities, I guess. Anyway, I've got some local bands, some hockey people, even a few college figure skaters, but I don't have that one sure draw. I need something, someone really, really good, and really unexpected." He paused. "I could really use the Queen of Nashville Ice on my team."

Izzy's fork clattered to the floor. "I'm so sorry." She bent down and picked it up, her face flushed. "Quinn...I...."

"Before you say no, hear me out. The Browns, they are a great family. But charity isn't as big as it could be. I've wanted to do this one sort of mega event for a long time. I am trying to call in every favor I have coming and I'm making up several along the way. But today, when you were skating, I was blown away by the idea. If you agree to skate, even a little bit, I'm thinking we could do something like record the performance and sell the DVD. It would go a long way to hitting the goal."

"I don't know what to say. I mean, I haven't been on the ice in so long."

"You looked amazing today."

She sipped her ginger ale thoughtfully. "So, let me understand something. All of this," she waved around the room, "and that business this afternoon with the music and the skating...the throw...and ..."

"The amazing kissing?"

"Yeah, that. That was all so I would agree to skate at your charity event?" Something inside her deflated. *So much for romance, I guess.*

The light in his eyes changed. "That's what you think? Crap, I knew I was going to get this all wrong." He left his chair and knelt next to her. "Let me try it another way. Yes, the skating, the music, was to nudge you into wanting to skate again. But I could have asked you to help me this afternoon at the rink."

"When, before you tricked me into skating, or while you were kissing me?"

She was surprised at the anger in her voice. *Why do I feel like he's using me suddenly?*

He took her hands in his. "The two things have nothing to do with each other. I'm asking you to skate at the charity event because I think you'd do wonders for a really good cause. I asked you here because…because…"

Her anger passed, and she smiled at his awkwardness. "Because maybe the kissing was so spectacular, you thought a good meal might lead to more kissing?"

"Maybe."

"Mr. Murray, are you blushing?" She laughed out loud and rumpled his hair. "I'll say maybe. I'm not doing this alone. I'm a pairs' skater. You'd have to skate with me." She shook her head, surprised at her own eagerness to return to the ice.

"What? No, I…"

"That's the deal. I can't even think about it unless you agree to skate with me."

"How am I supposed to learn figure skating in three months?"

"I'm going to leave that up to you."

Quinn sat on his haunches and studied her. "You're driving a very hard bargain."

"Figure skating isn't that hard. It's all about knowing and trusting your partner. There are a lot of things I don't know about you, Quinn." She finished her dinner. "But how you feel about being on the ice isn't one of them. And you already know a ton about me," she stood and grinned at him, "more than I realized when I got up this morning."

"Okay, let's just table the idea for now. Tonight I'd like to get to know you, the real you, a bit better." Quinn cleared the table. "If you're up for it."

"I believe I am."

"You're not too tired?"

Too tired to get to know more about you? "Not at all."

"You want to sit out on the balcony?"

"Sure."

"Coffee?"

"Absolutely."

"Great, go get comfy, I'll be out in a minute. Oh, take that blanket there," he pointed to a basket near the patio door. "It's a little chilly."

She stepped out and inhaled the clear, crisp air. She slipped off her shoes and curled up on the padded two seat glider, wrapped in the blanket like a huge cape. The lights of Nashville glittered across the night sky like miles and miles of neon stars. Izzy closed her eyes and let her other senses absorb the setting.

"You're not falling asleep on me, are you?"

Izzy opened her eyes and smiled. "Not a chance. Thanks," she took a steaming mug from him. "The view is just a lot to absorb."

"I know what you mean." He stood in the archway of the door, looking at her. "I need to be honest about something."

"Sounds ominous. Do you want to sit down?"

"Not until I see how you feel about what I'm going to tell you."

She didn't miss the pained expression on his face. "Whatever it is, you can tell me. It'll be okay. I promise."

"I've known who you were since Jason's funeral. I was in town with the Admirals, and I heard about his passing and I had to see you. And when you bumped into me on the street, I knew who you were right away."

We changed our names. How would he have known whose funeral it was? Izzy stared at him, waiting for him to speak. "So are we going to dance around the phlegm wad you just dropped? Or are you going to be just a tiny bit more honest with me?"

The haunted expression vanished and Quinn laughed out loud. "Phlegm wad?"

"I have this very odd feeling, suddenly, like I've just walked into a movie where I'm the star, and I'm the only one without a script." She bit her lip, not liking her sharp tone. "How about maybe you tell me why you're a face in the crowd during the two biggest awful moments of my life?"

She again waited for an answer, but Quinn kept his gaze fixed on the Nashville skyline. "Okay. Let me simplify the question: Why were you in the crowd at Nationals?"

"Nationals?" Quinn drank deep from his coffee and shifted the weight on his feet. "How would you know that?" He set the coffee cup on the side table.

What is he hiding? "Cat, it turns out, is not just a walking movie trivia encyclopedia. She is also a maniac for US figure skating. Today she put together the puzzle that is my life, and she lost her mind. Especially when I told her I was going on a date with you."

A faint smile crossed his face and he relaxed slightly. "Let me guess, there was a reference to 'The Cutting Edge?'"

"Oh yes. But the best part is, she has a tape of Nationals. So she, Jenna and I watched the routine."

"I'll bet that was interesting." He kept his gaze away from her.

Izzy shook her head. "It was like traveling back in the worst time machine ever."

"Why would you say that?"

"At the time I thought it was the start of something so huge and beautiful." She shrugged. "And it wasn't. It was the end of my skating career. It was the end of my life in Nashville. It was the end of my girlish ideals about romance and love." She realized she spoke without emotion, simply relaying facts. "I sat there watching that tape today and all I wanted to do was scream at myself."

He sat next to her then, as if some defense shield vanished, enabling him to move again. His arm was light around her shoulders. "If you don't want to talk about this…"

Izzy shook her head. "It wasn't like I was watching me. I was watching some girl, some stupid, misguided girl who listened to some very bad advice." She nestled into the crook of his arm. "Anyway, watching the routine was not nearly as interesting as the crowd shots between performances. I have to say, you looked really good with the longer hair. You've got a head made for a mullet."

"Oh lord." Quinn laughed, pushing the glider back and forth with his foot. "I'd like to forget how dedicated I was to 'hockey hair.'"

"Which brings me back to my question. You were still in college, in North Dakota. What were you doing at a Figure Skating Nationals in the Twin Cities?" Izzy sat up as the glider came to a halt. Quinn seemed very far away. "Quinn?"

"You want the truth?"

"Yes, of course."

Quinn turned to face her and took both her hands in his. "I'd seen you on TV a few times, and the way you skated, I connected with it. Watching you was like watching something really delicate and magical. I had to see you skate live. I didn't tell anyone where I was going, I would never have lived it down with the guys on the team, you know." He paused and looked deep into her eyes, the glow in his own eyes melting the icy edges of Izzy's heart. "You left me breathless. I fell in love with you. At least, I fell in love with my idea of what you'd be like."

"Quinn…"

"So at the funeral, I really needed to see if you were still, you know, you. And you were, just maybe a more fragile, more delicate version."

"But how…"

He touched her lips gently. "If I don't tell you this now, I might not ever. When I saw you at Second Chances, I was suddenly that stupid college kid again. The last few years I've started carrying so much garbage around, I barely recognize myself. But seeing you in the balcony, you made me feel like I was a kid again, anything was possible. I went to look for you later, but you were gone. I'd lost you again. When we ran into each other on the street that night, you were like a bird trying to escape a cage. We had this amazing meal together, I felt like there was this connection, and then I lost you again. Then one horrible rainy morning, I walk into my favorite Waffle House, and you're there! It was a gift I was not going to lose again. I got to be your friend, I got to know you, who you are, and I find out that you are the kindest, most thoughtful person I have ever met." He squeezed her hands and took a deep breath. "And then, god, watching you skate today. You still left me breathless."

Izzy bit her lip, a single question tugging in her brain. "How did you know Jason and I were...us? I mean, we changed our names. I didn't think anyone knew."

A shadow darkened his face and cleared so quickly, Izzy thought she imagined it. "I don't know. One of the guys must have told me. Jason must have said something."

Who would Jason have trusted enough to tell?

Sean probably said something to one of the players.

Izzy shook her head, and focused on Quinn. His expression was unguarded, unlike any he'd worn around her. "Why didn't you say anything before this? We've known each other for months, you never said a word."

He drew her hands up in his and kissed them both. "I was sort of...afraid."

"Afraid of what?"

"Most people never have to handle half the life changing things you got fired at you in a few months. At first I thought I was just hanging around to keep an eye on you. Make sure you were okay. You bring out the protector in me. I liked feeling that way."

"Well, I do have that sort of helpless maiden quality." She smiled at him, hoping he would hear the humor in her voice.

He smiled back, but there was little joy in the smile. "Once I got to know you, I realized I was getting more from you than you were from me. You gave me something I thought I'd lost. You made me feel like a good person, like I could be a good person."

"You are."

He kissed her hands again. "No. I'm not. I'm a very bad person who does some good stuff on occasion."

Izzy hunched to look up at his face. "But you're so wrong."

"It's nice that you think so." Quinn sat up and shrugged. "Before I saw you at Nationals, I was failing school, I was an idiot. You inspired me to get my act together. I went back to school, got my grades up, played the best hockey of my life, and managed to get drafted by Detroit. My dreams came true."

Izzy smiled, and tried to lighten the mood. "You're welcome for that." She snuggled back into the warm space beneath his shoulder. "I'm still not buying the idea that you're a bad guy."

"Just wait, I'm not done." Quinn shook his head. "You weren't skating anymore, and that inspiration vanished. One by one, I ruined the things that should have mattered most. The first, my liver. I've done my best over the years to just destroy the bastard. The second...let's just say that where there's alcohol and professional athletes, there will also be women. Those two things had a very big hand in ruining my relationships with my three brothers, and my sister, who won't ever talk to me. I ruined my reputation in the league. I could have been something special. I had all the tools. What I didn't have was the discipline. Detroit traded me to Chicago. Chicago traded me to San Jose. San Jose outright cut me after a lousy season and an incident involving three airline attendants and a very large bottle of mescal. After San Jose, I spent some time in Toronto. I liked it up there. Close to home, I started to mend my ways. Then I got hurt, and they put me on waivers. That's when Nashville picked me up in a trade. I spent some time playing in Milwaukee, with the Admirals, rehabbing the knee. Then I came here. Everything was great, I was back on top. Big fish, medium sized pond. And all my old habits started coming back. And then..." he stopped.

And then what? Izzy waited a few heartbeats for him to continue talking. All she heard was the rhythmic beat of his heart. *For all the honesty, there's a part of the story he's not ready to tell.*

"And then you showed up in my life. You were my own personal angel. Every time I saw you, talked to you, I felt lighter like a weight was lifted. So I didn't tell you I knew who you were because I was afraid you'd run away."

Izzy sat up straight and brushed his hair away from his face. "How on earth could I run from you?" She kissed his forehead, "You're my hero."

Quinn started to laugh. "I've never been thought of as any kind of hero."

"Are you kidding me? Today...that kid...you are totally his hero. You've been mine since the first time we ran into each other."

"Now I know you're kidding."

"I am being completely serious. I was scared to death to move here. But then it turned out okay." She closed her eyes. *How could I not have thought of this before? How did I not put this together?* "There were cards at the funeral. People put money in them." She peered up at his face. His jaw tightened and he didn't meet her look. "There was one card, it was unsigned, so I never knew whom to thank."

"Sometimes people don't want to be thanked for something like that. They just want to know it's going to be okay."

"It was more generous, I think, than that giver ever knew. There was quite a lot of cash and a lottery ticket."

"Really." His voice was soft, far away.

"That ticket was a winner. Enough for me to escape Adele and move here."

"Enough for you to live the glamorous life of a night waitress living in an efficiency? Not exactly the safety net a real hero would provide."

"My hero isn't just about doling out rent money. Sometimes he gets rowdy college boys to be polite."

"You would have been fine."

"That's where you're wrong. I had a hundred different scenarios running through my head and all of them ended with the day waitress coming in and finding my dead body on table three. But there you were, you said a few words and they were gone. Every time I saw you in the restaurant, I felt less anxious about working there. As long as you're around, I feel safe. No, I won't be running away." She shivered, the chilly air working its way through the blanket.

"It's getting cold out here." Quinn hopped up immediately. "What say, we get you indoors and out of that dress?"

"What?" She blushed.

"Oh, sorry." He gave her an endearingly sheepish grin. "I mean, I've got some warm clothes you might be more comfortable in. I can warm up the coffee, and get the fireplace going. We maybe could hang out?" He held out his hand and she stepped into the apartment. He flipped a switch and blue and yellow flames glowed in the fireplace. "There, that's cozy. Let me just grab something for you to slip into…" he strode into his bedroom and returned a moment later, holding a large wad of pink material. "Here ya go, you can change in the bedroom if you'd like. I've got the fireplace going in there as well, so you're not cold."

"I can't believe you still have this!" She held up the massive pink sweatshirt he'd worn that first rainy morning in the Waffle House. "Why on earth did you keep it?"

"Very weird thing. I wore it home, and I was going to return it to your lost and found because, who knows when a very well endowed college co-ed was going to come looking for her school spirit shirt. But for some reason I kept forgetting it." He flashed a wicked grin. "I like to imagine holding onto a woman that would fill out that shirt."

"Now that's not something a hero would ever say!" She laughed.

"Clearly you are not familiar with the concept of the bad boy hero." Quinn's smile was genuine, the first really relaxed expression she'd seen on his face in an hour. "So go get changed, I'll warm up the coffee."

"Can't do it." *I'm not putting this thing on. I don't care if I freeze to death.*

"Why not? You'll be way more comfortable in that. I set some sweat pants on the bed. They'll be a little long, but warm."

"I'm not wearing this when you're still in your proper date clothes."

"You want me out of my clothes? Not a problem!" Quinn slipped off his suit coat, tossed it into his bedroom and pulled his dress shirt over his head in one smooth motion. He stood before her, shirtless, perfect, and obviously aware of the affect he had on her.

The sweatshirt fell from her hands to the floor. *Holy carp, he's beautiful.* "Um, yes, yes, that looks far more comfortable." She swallowed.

"I could get more comfortable you know," He slipped off his shoes and kicked them towards the kitchen. "You just tell me when I'm comfortable enough for you."

"Hey, you know, get as comfortable as…I mean it's your house…you can wear…or not wear…whatever you want to…or not." *Who is saying these things?*

Quinn leaned against the doorframe, hands on his waist, "Miss Izzy?"

"Um, yes?" She couldn't take her eyes off of him.

"It's not polite to stare. A good Southern girl like you should know that."

Good grief, am I actually salivating? She cleared her throat, set the sweatshirt on the sectional sofa and took a step closer. "A good Southern girl knows to appreciate a work of art." She didn't recognize the throaty tone coming out of her mouth.

A slow smile crossed Quinn's face. "So you're appreciating me?"

His expression called to something deep within her. "Yes. I mean..." she inhaled and tried to regulate her breathing as she took another step. *Come on, Izzy!*

This is the most beautiful man I've ever seen in my life.

"You know," he crossed the space between them and towered over her, "most people get close to a work of art to appreciate it."

"Most people don't need a step ladder." Izzy's attempt to ease the sexual tension failed as her voice oozed thick and heavy with desire.

He picked her up as if she weighed nothing. Izzy closed her eyes, reveling in the iron strength of his arms. He set her on her feet, on the bed, and stood before her. "Is this better?"

Face to face, she lost herself in his perfect eyes. She traced the lines of his jaw. *What am I doing, touching him like this?*

She rested her hands on his shoulders, and stared at the floor. He touched her chin, raising her gaze to his eye level. "It's okay," he whispered, so softly, she wasn't positive she'd heard him. "It's okay."

His grip on her waist steadied her, and the glow in his eyes encouraged her inexperienced touch. She retraced his jaw and leaned closer, close enough to breath in his scent.

He captured her lips in a kiss that began as a slow heat flowing from the point of contact through the rest of her body. There was nothing cold, or automatic, or judgmental in the kiss. Reveling in the heady warmth of it, Izzy closed her eyes and tried to remember the last time a kiss felt so completely good.

Never.

The taste of him, the scent of him, everything swirled around her in a warm, sensual wave. Dizzy, floating, she leaned against his solid support. He wrapped one arm around her waist, a firm embrace keeping her close. His other hand traveled upward, resting at the nape of her neck. He toyed with the zipper tab of her dress. Izzy inhaled, waiting for him to free her of the dress, the only barrier between her and the broad expanse of his bare chest.

A spark of desire flashed in his eyes and ignited a heat between. Izzy melted at his touch as he unzipped her dress and slid the straps off her shoulders. He kissed her throat, following a line from her chin to the front closure of her bra. Without hesitation, he opened it, and her breasts responded instantly to his worshipful kisses.

Wait. Stop.

The thoughts came from nowhere, but the damage was done. She stopped kissing Quinn and froze, motionless.

"Izzy?" His voice was low, far away.

She didn't want to meet his eyes.

"Izzy, look at me."

Unwilling to admit her sudden hesitation, and unable to give in to the desire warming her, Izzy stepped back, closed her bra and slid her dress straps back in place. She sat on bed.

He sat next to her. "What's wrong?"

Nothing is wrong. Everything is very, very right. And it scares me to death.

He seemed to read her thoughts. He leaned forward and wrapped his arms around her waist. "I have made a career out of treating women like objects." He planted a lingering kiss on her neck then broke away from her. "I don't want you to think that's the way I feel about you."

"Quinn, I've had no experience with this." She rested her head on his shoulder. "I need to take it slow." She closed her eyes and prayed she didn't sound stupid. *Why can't I find the right words for this situation?*

Because I've never been in this situation.

He kissed her lightly on the head, the brushed some hair from her eyes. The simple caress sparked something them and his lips found hers again. Izzy closed her eyes, and tried to will her misgivings away.

As if sensing her tension, Quinn pulled away from her with a groan. "Obviously this is not going to be easy." He stood and reached his hand to her. She turned and let him zip up her dress. "I have to take you home before I convince you to do something you're not ready to do."

His expression was hard, resolute. Izzy ached to smooth the lines of his face, but knew, if she touched him now, there would be no going back. She picked up the sweatshirt and slid it over her head. It was her protective shell against a desire she was not ready to admit. She glanced at the clock on his nightstand. "It's late."

"You're right." His voice was soft, husky. "I'll take you home."

TWENTY

They drove to the coffee shop in silence. Quinn ached to know what Izzy was thinking. He was all too aware that she had no experience other than Jason. *This is the right thing. It's the right thing to do. So why do I feel so lousy?*

I have no experience in doing the right thing.

The coffee shop was dark as Quinn eased his car into the back parking lot. "You know that I'm okay with whatever you want to do. Or not do." *I'm an idiot.*

She unbuckled her seat belt and shifted in her seat. "I appreciate that."

He unbuckled, but stared straight ahead. "I have not been terribly decent when it came to women. But you..." he reached out. Her hand was there, waiting for his. "I have a chance to do things the right way. I really want that." *Almost as much as I want you.*

Izzy covered his hand with both of hers. "Thank you. I appreciate that you don't mind taking whatever this is very, very slowly."

"You didn't have to add that second 'very' you know." Quinn smiled.

"Maybe not. But it is nice to know you're listening."

Quinn's cell buzzed. *Who is calling me after two in the morning?* He pulled his cell out of his left coat pocket. *Benny?*

Shit. I forgot. We're leaving for San Jose in an hour and a half.

"Is anything wrong?"

Quinn chuckled. "Nothing is wrong. I completely forgot I have to go to San Jose."

"When?"

"Pretty much now."

Izzy stared at him for a moment, and her face broke into a smile. "How do you forget you have to travel across the country?"

"You want the truth?"

"Of course."

"Spending today, this evening, with you, put every other thought out of my head." He opened his door, got out, and rounded the car to open the door for her. "I'll at least walk you to your door."

He held her hand as they crossed the gravel lot. Reaching the stoop, she climbed up two steps and looked him in the eye. "I had a really lovely time tonight." She kissed him lightly on the cheek and turned to unlock the door.

"I'll see you next week." He watched her unlock the door and turned to go back to his car.

He took two steps. *What am I doing?*

"Izzy, wait, I…" he turned and saw her standing on the step, watching him. Without hesitation, he flew to her, pressing her close as he kissed her. She wrapped her arms around his neck and returned his kiss with an enthusiasm that sent his mind spinning.

Stop it! Behave yourself!

Groaning, Quinn broke their embrace. This time he saw his own desire reflected in her heavy lidded eyes. Too well he recognized the look. *She wouldn't think I was forcing her to do anything. And she would hate me in the morning.*

He took a step toward his car, but he knew she was still standing there, waiting. He spun around and wrapped her in his arms again.

His cell phone buzzed in his pocket.

"You have to go," she whispered, her words warm in his ear.

"I know. I know." He backed away.

"So go."

He stopped moving. Something in her expression changed. She didn't seem uncertain. *Is she daring me?*

"You are not making this easy for me."

Her laughter filled the night sky. "You're the one who started something and now you have to go away for a week. So go."

"I don't want to go." *I will give everything I have for one more kiss on this stoop.*

If I kiss you one more time, Izzy Marks, I may not be able to let go.

"I'll be here when you get back."

Her words were a cool balm on the gaping hole left by his burning desire. His step light, Quinn made it back to his car and drove away.

***

My timing could not suck more. Quinn sat in the narrow plane seat next to Benny and cursed himself, again, for the events of the previous night. *I knew I was leaving on this trip. I knew it and I went ahead and opened that door anyway.*

Now I have a week away from her. A lifetime.

"So you told me weeks ago that you were going to find a woman for me." Benny drained the last of his diet cola. "Yet, here we sit, another trip, and you have come up with exactly no one and nothing. I'm starting to doubt your abilities in the romance department, my friend."

You're not the only one.

Quinn closed his eyes and felt Izzy against him, felt the heat of her soft skin. He tasted her lips.

"Hey, Quinn? Earth to Quinn? We've landed, dude."

"What?"

Benny yanked his carry on out of the overhead compartment. "Yeah, I asked about this magical woman you're supposedly fixing me up with, and you went all space cadet on me. And now, we're in San Jose."

"Oh, sorry."

"Yeah, whatever. The next time you want to just day dream about your sex life, warn me."

"What?"

Benny shook his head. "I've known you for a long time. I know your sex daydream face. And you, my friend, were daydreaming big time. So who is she? It's not Boss Lady, is it? Tell me it's not her."

"Shut up, Benny."

"Ooh, touchy. So it's <u>not</u> Boss Lady. The plot does thicken, doesn't it?"

"I'm not having this conversation."

"Not having what conversation?" Bob sidled up to them.

"Quinn was having a sex daydream about someone other than Boss Lady."

Bob laughed. "Well, we are in San Jose, which, if I'm recalling correctly, is the scene of some of your biggest conquests, Quinn."

Why would I think I could have a normal relationship with anyone? What decent woman would even allow me near them, if this is how my friends think?

He couldn't escape the image of Izzy, smiling at him. *She would. And I walked away from her.*

Without realizing it, Quinn followed Benny and Bob through the airport to the street where they were calling for him to get into a cab. Quinn stared at the pair as if seeing them for the first time. "Guys, I can't do this."

"Quinn, it's a cab. You get in, you close the door, and they drive you to a very nice hotel that will have a beautiful room service menu." Benny called.

"No, I mean, I have to go. I have to go home."

"Are you okay?"

"Yeah, yeah, Bob, I am. I'll meet you guys on Friday, in the Twin Cities. I just…I have to go."

Benny jumped out of the cab. "What the hell dude? You can't just run out. You've got two games to do before we get to the Wild game."

"Cover for me, Benny. Please?"

Benny paused and smiled. "This must be a big deal, huh?"

"The biggest."

"Okay. Okay. We'll figure out something. But be in the Twin Cities on Friday."

"I promise."

"And Quinn?'

"Find that woman for me, okay?"

Quinn laughed. "I will, I swear. But first I have to go see someone. And if she'll talk to me, I might be able to find you someone really great."

"I'm going to hold you to that." Benny got back into the cab.

"I know."

"Boss Lady is going to be pissed that you went off the grid."

"I know that, too." Quinn waved as the cab pulled away from the curb. Without another thought, he went into the airport and booked a flight home.

TWENTY-ONE

She slept most of the day. Wrapped in the sweatshirt that still held Quinn's clean scent, Izzy woke in a very pleasant mood. She lay in bed, her eyes closed, recalling the previous evening. *The way he kissed me…*

She could not suppress her giggle.

"Oh look, she's up! Jenna! Your mother's awake!"

Cat and Jenna burst into Izzy's room, a tray full of coffee, baked goods, and expectations in hand.

"Good morning girls."

"So," Cat handed her a cup of coffee. "How was it?"

"It was fine." Izzy drank the bitter brew deeply and tried to hide the blush she knew colored her cheeks.

"Oh, just fine? Jenna, take a look at your mother. She is a changed woman."

"Cat, I'm not sure I want to share my evening with my daughter."

"And, speaking as the daughter, I'm not sure I want to hear it."

Cat unwrapped a muffin and took a bite. "Oh please. Jenna, your mother rolled into the shop this morning at half past two, wearing that shirt and Quinn Murray's lips."

"Somebody was up way too late."

Cat shrugged. "The upside to my weird life is I get to see some serious post date kissin' on my back porch."

Jenna studied the sweatshirt. "Wasn't that in the lost and found at the Waffle House?"

"It was."

"Please tell me you two didn't go on a date to the Waffle House!"

"What would be wrong with that?"

Cat laughed. "I think what we really are hoping is that you didn't have the big rogerin' on one of the tables, and then don that outfit to cover your shame."

"We're British this morning again, are we, Cat?" Izzy set her cup on the nightstand.

"I'm all about Sherlock Holmes this week." Cat assumed a very proper air. "What I deduce from the state this woman is in, Watson, is that she was the victim of some very active lovin', and didn't want the rest of the world to know that she'd spent the night in the arms of a lover."

"But perhaps she was on an early morning jog, Holmes." Jenna attempted a British accent. "Which would be far more preferable to those of us who would rather not think about it."

"Quite impossible, Watson, so suck it up. You see, there, on the floor, next to her bed, is a pair of high heeled dress shoes. The very shoes, I might add she was seen wearing at a half past two when she arrived home."

"Holmes, you're a genius!"

"Holmes, you're nuts." Izzy lay back on her pillows, trying to ignore the gales of laughter from the other two. "Not that it's any of your business, but that kiss was all the active loving that happened."

"I, for one, do not believe you."

"And I, for one, am relieved to not have the image in my brain. Oh geez, I've got class." Jenna glanced at her watch. "I'd love to stay and hear all about it but, well, you're my mother so, no thanks." She hopped up and kissed Izzy. "See you later!"

Izzy waited until the door closed before hopping onto the bed. "Cat, I have to talk to you!"

"Oh so we were just playing innocent for the girl, right? The two of you are actually lovers, right?" Cat couldn't contain her giggles.

Izzy hesitated. "I don't think so."

"It's a yes or no question. Either you did the deed, or you did not."

"There's a bit more to it than that."

"I'm not following you."

"Well, you've...you know..."

Cat's mood sobered. "What, had sex? Yeah. I mean, not recently, and not with anyone as gor-ge-ous as Mr. NHL, but yeah."

"Okay, well, I've only ever been with Jason. And he was very...it was sort of ..." Izzy bit her lip. *How can I explain this? In all those years with Jason I didn't feel one tenth of what I felt in that one kiss from Quinn. How do I explain that?* "Last night, we just kissed, really. But the kissing, Cat…it was…I really can't explain it. I felt more, I was more involved, you know, than I've ever been…before."

Cat absorbed this without comment, for which Izzy was thankful.

"And then we stopped."

Cat was silent, tapping her fingers on her chin. "Quinn Murray stopped at kissing?"

Izzy shook her head. "It was me. I got nervous or something. I stopped everything. He said it was okay." Izzy sighed. "Cat, I've never had that before, that feeling of…want. I'm not entirely sure what I would have done if we hadn't stopped. I'm not what you'd call prepared for…that."

Cat patted her hand. "Well, I'd say you are the luckiest girl on the planet."

"Not the response I expected."

"I'm serious. I have yet to meet a guy who sets up a romantic date, gets the girl willing and ready with a good lip lock, and then stops without the encouragement of a swift kick to the jewels."

Izzy laughed at Cat's depiction, but something nagged in the back of her mind. "So, then what, he's not into me, so it was no big deal for him?"

"Maybe it means he is trying to be a better man with you. Do you have any idea how much control a guy like Quinn would have to exert to stop at kissing? Especially with you all dolled in that most excellent dress?"

Izzy unwrapped a muffin and took a bite. "What do you mean 'a guy like Quinn?'"

"Well look at him, for number one. For number two…"

"Wait, I know that accent! 'Cold Mountain.' That's the Renee Zellweger character. Ruby!"

Cat feigned impatience. "Anyway, secondly, he had quite the reputation during his playing days."

"He told me."

"Doubtful he told you everything. He was a real animal. Drinking, women, all the time. All the time."

"I get it, Cat."

"I mean, the man was a legend. He'd walk in to a place and half the women would want him and half the women had already had him."

Izzy grit her teeth. "I get it, Cat!"

"Sorry. Then a few years ago, he stopped everything. Quit playing for the Preds. Quit partying. He started filling in at the radio station, and he really went crazy with the charity work. Like he was rebuilding his image from scratch."

"We talked about his past a little, but he didn't say much about his life here."

"Well, when did he have time between dinner and face-sucking? I'm surprised you got any conversation in. At any rate, I think you can look at this first date as a complete success. You've hooked him. There's no keeping him away."

Izzy was unconvinced, but wasn't going to push the point. "Well, I won't be seeing him for a week. He's on the road covering the Preds. He left for San Jose this morning."

"Don't be too sure about that. A man doesn't give a girl the kind of good night kiss I witnessed and then put a country and a week between them." Cat checked the clock. "I have to get downstairs. If I'm not there at the start of the lunch rush, I know three or four regulars who will leap over the counter and clean me out!" She hopped off the bed and left the room without another word.

Izzy hugged her knees to her chin, breathing Quinn's scent from the sweatshirt. Peace and a sense of safety blanketed her. *He won't let me fall.*

TWENTY-TWO

Quinn parked his car in front of Silver Screen. Every window was full of light and he was suddenly very nervous. *What's the big deal? Just get in there and talk to her.* He squared his shoulders and walked around the building to the front entrance. It sounded as if a very loud party was going on.

Once inside, he noted an odd assembly of people gathered around the big television in the front room. Some sort of heated game seemed to be happening. At the counter, Cat read a paperback. The phone rang, and she answered it.

"Mark, you butt. I'm not going out with you again! Because you make my brain sad. Because I know that the National Anthem doesn't end with "Land of the Free." No, I'm sorry but anyone who mistakes Annette Benning with Annette Funicello is not someone I'm going to be able to date. Because one is an Oscar winning actress and one was a Mouseketeer. Oh, and that thing you do with your thumb? No, no woman likes that. Stop calling here!" She slammed the receiver into its cradle.

Wonder if I should ask her what the thumb thing is? Quinn took a cautious step toward the counter. "Wild night?"

"That? That was just some moron who thinks he can be an idiot and still get somewhere with me. And then we have the funky bunch over there." She nodded vaguely in the direction of the loud the group around the TV.

"What are they playing?"

"Oh, we just got the latest copy of that movie game 'Scene It.' This is one of the Twilight movies."

"Team Jacob!" Someone yelled over the din.

"Team Jacob sucks!"

"Vampires suck!"

"Werewolves blow!"

"Hey, you guys? If you can't keep it civil, I'm going to take it away." She returned her attention to Quinn. "If you're lookin' for Izzy, you're in the wrong place. She's working tonight." She held his gaze. "You may have already thought that might be the case."

"I guess I did."

"You're here to check the weather?"

"I'm sorry?"

"Look, you might be a very delicious chunk of yum…"

That's a new name for me.

"But you haven't been completely up front with our mutual friend." She leaned on the counter, low enough that he had to sit down to hear her, "You knew exactly who you were dealing with all along, am I right?"

"You are."

"I figured. So let me tell you something: Izzy's a world class skater who's had a sucky life." Cat shook her head. "Her sister-in-law dumped on her, I know that. I also know Jason didn't make her feel in all their years together what you did in one kiss."

Her comment surprised Quinn. He closed his eyes, remembering the feel of Izzy's fingers on his face, the thrill as she responded and returned to his kiss.

"Hey, hey!" Cat snapped her fingers in front of his face. "Focus here."

"Oh sorry."

"I saw that good night kiss. That was great theater. But dude, you dumped her off and flew to San Jose in the middle of the night? That's not romantic."

"I'm aware. That's why I came back."

"Which is a positive move. You're no saint, but you're taking some steps toward being a hero. You've got the look of one for sure. I respect you taking it slow with her. Let's face it, if a kiss sets her world on fire I can't even imagine what the full treatment from someone with your skill set would do."

Quinn nodded, unable to form words in response.

"But get this: If you go back to your wicked ways and do to Izzy what I know you've done to half this town, I will hurt you."

"I believe you would."

"So we understand each other?"

"Yes."

"Good. Now do two things for me."

"Okay?" He was not about to turn her down.

"First, get to the Waffle House and see your woman. And second…" she hesitated.

"Go ahead."

Cat picked up her book and sighed. "It's a perfectly beautiful night and I'm a perfectly lovely person. I'm sitting here giving out romantic advice, listening to the idiot patrol play a board game over there, and reading only the good parts in romance novels. If you know a guy who's not a complete moron, or just out of jail, could you send him my way?"

Quinn smiled. "I'll do what I can." He took a few steps toward the door.

"Oh one other thing?"

"Yeah?"

"He doesn't have to look like you. It would be nice, but it's not a deal breaker." Cat's smile was shy, and a little sad.

Quinn walked back to his car. Sitting behind the steering wheel, he stared at the back door of the coffee shop for several minutes. *She's right. I have to be a much better person, I have to be honest.*

Not a chance.

Quinn started the car, but didn't put it into gear. The radio started playing Toto's "I won't Hold You Back." Closing his eyes, the music carried Quinn back to the rink, to the one place where he felt good about himself, the place where Izzy was truly her most beautiful. He called to mind the feel of her skating, floating above the ice as if her skates never touched the surface. The memory of her from the night before, and that last night at Nationals, flashed before him, melding into one perfect image.

His hand on her waist, one holding her hand, twirling her, letting her go, the landing, like a flower on a still country pond, the feeling of control that flowed through him, even now, when he thought of her. Quinn tried to forget the look of her in the glow from his bedroom fireplace a halo around her lithe form.

She needs a hero.

I could be that hero. I could at least give it a good try.

He put the car in gear and drove to the Waffle House.

***

This is ridiculous. I'm standing here staring at the phone like he's going to call.

I have become every bad romantic comedy movie ever.

Cat would be so proud.

The bell on the door jangled. Izzy couldn't pull her gaze away from her cell phone display. "Just sit anyplace. I'll be with you in a minute. You want coffee?"

"Most guys wait a few days to call. I've never been a patient person, so, I thought I'd show up instead."

"Quinn!" She leaped into his arms, not caring one bit that Carlo was laughing out loud over the grill he cleaned. "I thought you had to be in San Jose?"

"I did. I do. I was standing there on a sidewalk, Benny was getting into the cab and I just couldn't, I just couldn't get into that cab. I turned around, went back into the airport, paid a ridiculous amount of money for a plane ticket, and here I am."

She didn't want to let go because none of it seemed real.

"I can't be here too long. Benny and Bob can cover for me, but I do need to get back to them by Friday. So we have a couple days to just…" he set her down on her feet and sat on a stool. "In all absolute honesty, Izzy, I have no idea what I'm doing."

Oh thank heavens! "Well, I'm glad you came back." She reached for a coffee cup.

"So am I. See, we left some unfinished business the other night."

Her cheeks heated. "What are you talking about?"

"The business about…" he lowered his voice instinctively "the charity event."

"Oh, that. I'm pretty sure I made my demands clear."

"I'm in."

The surprise on her face was well worth his misgivings. "Really?"

"Really."

"Okay, then."

Quinn set down his coffee and pulled her close to him. He glanced around the empty restaurant and smiled. "You promise?" He brushed his lips across hers lightly.

The rush of anticipation washed away any doubts, and conscious thought. "I promise." She murmured, leaning closer to him. *Just kiss me again.*

"Then we have a lot of work to do." He laid a brisk kiss on her cheek and released her. "And I need something to eat."

She took a deep breath, trying to get her heart rate back to normal. "You want grits with your eggs and mushrooms?"

"Thank you!"

Izzy gave the order to Carlo, who hadn't stopped laughing. "We do have one problem."

"No backing out. You promised."

"Yeah, well, I'm a demanding figure skater. Watch me pout."

Quinn drained his coffee and grinned. "Could you pout in front of my fireplace?"

What is this, banter? When most people learn to banter, I was learning to land on my outside edge. "Um….okay." *Oh yeah, I rock at banter.*

"So what's the problem?" Quinn picked up a fork and started in on the plate of eggs before Izzy set it down. "Sorry, I'm hungry."

"We don't have a coach."

"Can't you call up your old coach?"

"He's dead." Izzy ignored the tear welling in her eye.

He took a forkful of eggs and chewed thoughtfully. "Isn't there anyone else?"

Izzy shook her head. "No one I would trust. Plus we don't have a place to practice."

"That's not a problem. We can work out at the Bridgestone Center."

"Quinn! We can't do that."

"Why not?"

"How are you going to get permission? What, you'll hold a charity event every other day?"

"You let me worry about that. You draw on your years and years of experience and put something together that doesn't involve me breaking you in half. You can do that, easy. I mean, look at what I have to do. I have to learn to figure skate, I have to arrange training times. And what is the upside for me?" His grin was wicked.

Izzy glanced behind her to make sure Carlo wasn't listening. Carlo was out having a smoke. "You'll get to put your hands all over me?"

His voice was matter of fact. "I'll be in skates and you'll be in clothes. That doesn't count."

"Fine, how about this: I'll help with all the boring stuff, the mailing, the emails, the phone calls. I could be your secretary."

Quinn swallowed another mouthful of eggs and mushrooms. "Okay, I could use a secretary. I'll pay you a salary so you can stop working here for awhile."

Izzy bit her lip. "I don't know about that."

"I do. This is going to be a full time job. There's too much to deal with between practice and all the paperwork you're going to be slogging through."

"It's tempting, but I can't," she sighed, "I have health insurance through this job. For Jenna and me." She watched his face contort in four directions. *This has never been an issue for him.*

"Quit your job."

"What?"

"Quit your job. Come work for me."

"Quinn…"

"I'm serious. I don't just need someone for this event, I need someone full time. I'll handle your insurance, everything."

She shook her head. "You don't even know what is involved."

"No, but I know I like the idea of chasing you around the desk."

Izzy laughed out loud. "Stop. I'll keep my cushy gig here for now."

"How are you going to manage everything?"

Izzy didn't understand her reluctance, but the need to keep her job was overwhelming. "I'll manage. I'll take some day shifts. It'll be fine."

"If you say so." Quinn pushed his empty plate aside. "Let's go get to work."

Izzy laughed. "It's not even midnight. I have six hours left on my shift."

"See, if you worked for me, you wouldn't have just said that, and we'd be headed back to my place to look over entertainment contracts in front of an electronic fireplace."

"You paint a picture loaded with mixed signals."

"Don't judge me, I've been on a plane for almost twenty-four hours. I'm going to go home and fire off some emails to a few key people, letting them know I have a gold star secret weapon for this thing and they'd better come through with some massive bucks. Then, I'm going to take a shower because I'm starting to smell like a sardine rolled in jet fumes. Then, I'll probably sink into some sort of sleep deprivation coma. Then I'll come here, get you, and make breakfast for you at my place." He seemed to sense the misgivings she knew crossed her face like a banner. "And I promise; I will be as hands off as you wish." He smiled. "I think you'll find, however, that working with me on a project like this isn't quite as exciting and romantic as it sounds."

"Just wait until you start skating with me. It's nothing like it seems on TV."

"You'll probably start to hate me."

"You'll hate me more."

"Do your worst." He arched an eyebrow.

She leaned in close. "I can slice and dice parts of your body with a skate blade. What have you got?"

He shot backwards in his seat, his eyes glowing with a mix of surprise and fear.

Izzy laughed. *I'm starting to get the hang of this banter thing.*

TWENTY-THREE

Dawn broke over the Nashville skyline as Quinn rolled his car into the Waffle House parking lot. Through the window he caught her eye. She motioned to him to wait in the car, and Quinn found himself observing Izzy's work world very closely.

Two waitresses, probably those coming to relieve her, walked in. Behind them, a grimy man slunk around the side of the restaurant to the side door. Instantly alert and suspicious, Quinn studied the man's every move.

Izzy opened the side door and stepped into the man's line of sight. A hand on the car door handle, Quinn readied himself to spring to her defense.

To Quinn's surprise, Izzy greeted the man, as dirty as he was, with a smile and hug. She handed him a large covered cup, and a brown bag. The man hugged her again, and walked away, pulling strips of bacon out of the bag and eating them like potato chips.

I should be ashamed of myself.

Everyone praises me for my charity work. Meanwhile, she's the one doing the most good for the most people because she's doing it directly, quietly, and without getting anything in return.

Deep down, Quinn was far more ashamed of his reaction to the man's appearance. *I'm sure I've looked far worse, and I've never had to do without. I just assumed that because he's poor, homeless, whatever, he's also dangerous...*

Izzy approached the car, a bright smile shining for him. *I don't deserve one second of her time.*

"Hey, why so glum?" She climbed into the car.

"I was just thinking."

"Well stop because you are in danger of your face freezing that way." She pushed his shoulder.

"You're sort of amazing, you know?"

"Oh yes, you're just overwhelmed by my intoxicating scent of bacon and coffee. I'm thinking of bottling it."

"I'm serious."

Her smile faded slowly. "I wish you wouldn't be; you're sort of freaking me out."

"No, I just watched what you did right there. You know, with that guy."

"What, with Toothless Jim? Oh, he comes around every morning. We bag up the whole strips of bacon and sausages that people don't eat. It's sort of a shame to toss it and he's such a nice guy. Just a little down on his luck."

"We? So all the waitresses do it?"

Izzy lowered her eyes and blushed. "Okay. I don't know that all the girls do it. I know I do. He's between homes right now, you know?"

"No, I don't." Quinn surprised himself with his complete honesty. "I've never been in that position. And you act like it's no big deal, you just hand him some food and coffee and hug him."

"It's nothing."

"No." Quinn shook his head. "It's everything. You're the best person I know."

"Oh stop it." She nudged his shoulder again. "You do all those huge charity things, you raise all kinds of money for really great causes. You have no idea how many lives you touch. Me, I just handed a guy a bag of garbage, if you really think about it."

But you do it with a pure heart. You're not trying to buy back your soul.

"Okay, stop with that face. You promised to feed me. I have just enough energy for food, then you have to take me home and tuck me into bed."

He grinned, his good humor restored by her irresistible good mood. "And can I watch you sleep?"

"Only if you're well behaved."

Quinn looked heavenward and swore to be as well behaved as possible.

***

His apartment fairly dripped with the aroma of fresh baked goods and bacon.

"Now I know, you're thinking, 'we just came from a place where I sling eggs and bacon all night long.' I'm sure you're wondering how on earth I managed to cook this amazing meal and pick you up without leaving the stove on and risking the entire building to fire."

Izzy grinned and handed him her jacket. "I actually wasn't wondering that at all. But now that you mention it…"

He hung her jacket in the closet. "I'll tell you my big secret. My cleaning lady also cooks."

"I didn't know you had a cleaning lady."

Quinn chuckled. "Okay, you caught me. I don't have a cleaning lady. The lady next door was kind enough to check on things for me while I went to get you from work."

"Everything smells so good."

"Here, sit down please," he pulled out a chair for her and then pushed her closer to the table when she sat down. "I'll go get breakfast."

He emerged from the kitchen with the casserole. Izzy applauded. "That looks wonderful!"

"It's a recipe my mother used to make on Sundays. She put it in the oven before she herded all of us to church and then it was done by the time we got back." He cut the casserole into squares and served her a piece. "I hope you don't mind, I added the mushrooms."

She leaned over the plate and inhaled. "No, it smells heavenly. But your mother never worried about it burning or anything?"

Quinn sat across from her and grinned at the memory. "Our minister was pretty much a clockwork sort of guy. Church was fifty-seven minutes long come hell or high water. The only time it went wrong was the day we had a guest minister who got a little over zealous in his sermon."

"What happened?"

"We ate breakfast out that morning and my mother double checked the preaching schedule from then on."

Izzy laughed as Quinn poured her a glass of orange juice. "Parents, right?"

"Yeah, it's funny what you think of when you think about your parents. Like I don't think I've been in a church since the day I left home for college, but I can still remember the smell of perfume my mom wore every Sunday." He took a bite of casserole. *Oh good, it turned out.* "So what about you?"

"Well," she swallowed a bit and paused. "I've decided I'm going to see them. My parents."

Quinn sat back in his chair and waited for her to continue. She sipped some juice and set the glass on the table in slow motion. Quinn bit his lip, fighting his natural impatience. Finally, he couldn't stay silent. "Oh yeah?"

"Yeah. I've been here a few months. It's time. Well, Collier thinks it's time…"

One of these days I'm going to hunt Singer Guy down and throttle him for butting into her life like this. Why should he care a bit if she never talks to her parents again?

Why do I care if she does?

Because if she connects to her former life without me where does that leave me?

That's a very selfish way to think.

I'm putting all my energy into not bending her over this table and giving her the ravishing of her life. I've got no energy left to be a better person on any other level.

"Why open everything up like that?"

She stared at him, her expression reflecting the confusion he felt hearing his own words. *Of course she needs to see her parents. I just don't like her listening to Collier.*

"I think Jenna needs to meet her grandparents." Izzy's voice was low and tight. "I think she needs to at least connect a little bit with her family."

Quinn shook his head. "I don't see the point." *Why can't I shut up?*

"I guess you wouldn't." Her words were framed by the angry set of her jaw. "After all, when did you see anyone in your family?"

Her words halted his argumentative thinking. Okay. Stop. Back up. "So when are you going to go see them?"

"Saturday." She took a bite of casserole.

"Well I'll be back Saturday afternoon late. Would you like me to come along?"

"No. that's not necessary. This is something I have to do."

"Okay."

She set down her fork. "You know what, Quinn? I'm so sorry. I'm exhausted. Can you just take me home, please?"

Quinn chewed the inside of his cheek. "Of course."

***

He drove her home without much conversation. She huddled in the corner of the car, an empty shell of the cheery woman she usually was. For the hundredth time in the short drive, Quinn cursed Collier for even putting an unpleasant thought into Izzy's head. Then he cursed himself for arguing with her.

They pulled up to Silver Screen and Izzy climbed out of the car without waiting for him to open the door. He met her on the sidewalk. "Hey, are you okay?"

She nodded, but there was a shadow darkening her eyes. "I will be. I guess I didn't realize how much I'm dreading it, you know?"

Relief flooded him. "Believe me. Dreading family stuff is one thing I know very well." He wrapped his arms around her. "I'm really, really sorry I questioned you. Are you sure you don't want me to come along?"

"No," her denial was muffled into his chest. "This is really something Jenna and I have to do. We have to see."

"Jenna's on board with it?"

Izzy rested her head against his chest and wiped her eyes. "I'm not sure what she thinks this is going to be. I'm hoping she's not disappointed."

"Well," Quinn tightened his embrace, "from what I've seen of your daughter, she's a very strong, sensible lady, a lot like you. Whatever happens, you have each other, you have friends. You have me."

Her arms around his waist tightened very slightly, but it was enough. *I could live on that quick hug for months.*

She leaned away from his body for a moment. "Thanks."

"Don't mention it." He kissed the top of her head.

"So, when's our first practice?"

"I'm still pounding out the details on that. I was thinking Saturday, but clearly you're going to be busy, so I can shoot for Sunday if you'd like." *Maybe by Sunday I'll get permission from someone to get into the building.*

"Sounds great." She took a step away and smiled at him. "I'll see you Sunday."

It wasn't until Quinn had driven a few blocks that he realized he'd kissed her on the head. *Just like Singer Guy.*

Damn.

Trying to ignore the thought, he adjusted the rearview mirror. A white car was a block behind him. *That looks like Serena's car.*

What the…

The white car turned away and stopped following him.

I'm imagining thing, obviously.

TWENTY-FOUR

Izzy unbuckled her seat belt and sighed. Her frosty breath formed a film of steam on the steering wheel.

"Mom?"

The house looks exactly the same. Twenty years and not one thing has changed.

"Mom?"

What if nothing has changed? Am I strong enough to take it? Am I strong enough to shield Jenna from it?

Stupid Collier. If he hadn't said anything, I wouldn't be sitting here, staring at my old front door, wishing I was anyplace else in the world but here.

"Mom." Jenna poked her. "I think we need to get out of the car."

"Why?"

"Because I just saw the curtains move. I'm pretty sure they know we're here, or at least that someone is in their driveway."

Izzy inhaled deeply. "You're right. Let's go meet your grandparents." She climbed out of the car and slammed the door with a bit too much power.

Her feet grew heavy on the short walk to the front door. *Maybe they aren't home. Maybe the doorbell doesn't work.*

Jenna rang the doorbell, the sound taking Izzy back to her girlhood.

Damn.

There was a long pause, long enough, Izzy felt, that anyone in the house would have had plenty time to reach the door and open it, had there been anyone in the house. "They must not be home."

"I see someone," Jenna kept a firm hand on her shoulder. "They're in there."

"I'm not sure, Jens…" Izzy tensed, ready to turn and run, just as the door opened.

"Hello?"

Izzy blinked at the white haired woman standing behind the screen door. *Not one thing has changed.* "Hello, Mother."

***

The polite thing, the Southern thing to do, Izzy knew, was to let them in and have them sit in the front room and offer them sweet tea.

And that is exactly what Gwendolyn "Dollie" Landry did for her long lost daughter and grand-daughter. She invited them in, had them sit in the front room and offered them sweet tea, which Jenna accepted and Izzy did not.

We could be strangers for all the effort she's putting out.

Dollie fussed with the glasses for a few minutes until Izzy could no longer stand the tedium. "Mother!"

Had Izzy thrown ice water in her face, Dollie probably could not have looked more shocked. "Yes, Dear?"

"Mother, look at this young woman…this is your grand-daughter. This is Jenna. She is my daughter. You've never met her. Take a moment and look at her instead of just making sure your manners are perfectly perfect."

Dollie sat down, crumpled was a better word, as if the air had gone out of her. *Without the support of good manners, she's nothing to say or do.*

Heavy footsteps in the doorway broke the delicate silence. "Who's this?"

Izzy glanced up at her father, William Landry. There was more white in his dark hair, but his posture was as rigid as she remembered and so, Izzy guessed from the set of his jaw, was his opinion of her.

"Well Bill, look who's come to visit. It's Isabella and…and…I'm sorry, dear, what's your name?"

"My name is Jenna." Jenna stood and held out her hand to shake her grandfather's hand. "Pleased to meet you, Grandpa."

"I'm not your Grandpa."

"Daddy."

William whirled his dark blue eyes on Izzy. "Don't you, 'Daddy,' me. I told you the day you left never to come back, that you were not welcome here."

"Daddy it's been twenty years."

"Twenty years of shame. Twenty years of ruin. Twenty years of waste."

Izzy's eyes watered with rage. "You are telling me that you're still shutting me out because I made the mistake of sleeping with my skating partner twenty years ago?"

"That wasn't the mistake you made, Dear."

Dollie's thin, watery voice stilled the room, but not the tension. Izzy stared at her mother. "What do you mean that wasn't the mistake I made?"

"Dollie, be still."

Izzy glared at her mother, then her father. *What sort of weird, sick game is this?*

"No, you remember. You didn't care about them sleeping together. Well, I mean you cared, it was a little unseemly since Jason was so much older than you, Dear, but it wasn't that..."

"Dollie..." William's voice was a low, warning growl.

"No Daddy, I'd really like to hear what Mother has to say."

"Isabella, you have no idea what went on back then. You were a child."

"Well I'm an adult now, so why don't you enlighten me? Because from where I'm standing right now it sounds like my father, my parents, were totally okay with me sleeping with a guy way older than I was...and I think I'd like to know if that wasn't the huge mistake, what was."

"There's no point in talking about it." William looked up, in Jenna's general direction, for the first time.

This is all about the fact that I gave up skating instead of getting an abortion. "You know, Jenna is your grand-daughter, Daddy. Most guys would like to meet their grandchildren."

"You know our opinion. You had no reason to come here."

"Isabella, it's just that it was so very much money."

"Dollie!" William's voice was sharp, startling the older woman.

Izzy bit the inside of her cheek, "Why Jason, Mother? There must have been a million skaters out there. Why did it have to be Jason, if he was so very, very expensive?"

"Well, he did guarantee us a gold medal, didn't he?"

"Dollie!"

"Well, maybe he didn't guarantee it, but he almost did. See, Jason's other partner was demanding money from Jason, something about a baby. Anyway, Jason said he'd bring home the gold medal for us, but he needed to cover himself because he had all these expenses, with that other girl you know. He also said he'd have to work so much harder to get the gold with such a weak partner."

Izzy closed her eyes. *You really had no confidence in me as a skater, did you?* "I'm still not seeing how we got from there to this place where you won't even look at me or your grand-daughter."

"You were never supposed to get pregnant!" William barked. "If we didn't win it that year, you were young enough to get in the next time around. But you got yourself pregnant. And you insisted on keeping the thing, so we never got the return on our investment."

Izzy staggered back, as if slapped. "That thing, you're referring to, Daddy, is my daughter. She is a person. She is a lovely wonderful woman. There is nothing, no amount of money I would trade for having her. And you, the two of you, are the losers for not getting to know her."

"We don't need to listen to this."

"No I've waited and wondered for a long time. We're going to finish this conversation and then never speak again. I was a thing to you, a trained dog or something. You talk about never getting a return on an investment because I didn't win a gold medal at the Olympics? You're shutting out your only family because of money?"

"You weren't supposed to have a baby!" William's rage burst out of him like a gunshot. "You were supposed to listen to us, do what we say. But no, instead, you and Jason took every dime we had and lived the high life."

"The high life?" Izzy's let out a shocked laugh. "High life? What high life was I supposed to be living? You chased us out of here. We had nothing."

"Jason had more than fifty thousand dollars. Even if he paid all the bills he said he had, there was still plenty left over."

We lived on a shoestring budget for years, and we had nothing when Jason died.

Where did that money go, Jason? What did you do with it?

William stared at her, his face softening into something of a smile. "Apparently, Jason must not have felt the need to invest in you either."

Izzy's hand flew forward on its own accord. She wasn't even aware of the motion until she made contact with her father's face. "You son of a bitch," she hissed as she grabbed Jenna by the hand, and fled the house.

It wasn't until they were a mile away from the house that Izzy even realized she was driving. Then, shaking violently, she pulled over to the side of the road.

"Are you okay, Mom?"

Izzy turned bleary eyes to her daughter. "Jens, I'm so sorry. If I'd known it was going to be anything like that…"

"Mom, it's done. I'm fine. They were strangers to me before this morning, and they're strangers now."

Izzy eased the car back onto the road. "You know what? I don't think I'm ready to go back just yet."

"What do you want to do?"

"Well, I did promise you I'd take you to my old training place."

Jenna nodded. "That sounds great."

***

Izzy found the rink without much trouble. What troubled her was how dilapidated it looked. She eased the car up the rutted drive to the ratty, cracked parking lot. There were few cars parked around the building.

"This is where you trained?"

Izzy shared Jenna's doubt. "Yes, this is the place. I guess when Coach died, Collier sold it or something. Coach would hate how it looks."

They got out of the car and walked into the cavernous building. Once inside, memories, good memories, flooded Izzy. The feeling was as powerful as the emptiness at her childhood home had been. *Now I'm home.*

On the ice, a few children, possibly stragglers from a recently ended birthday party, slid around on wobbly legs. Izzy led Jenna to the boards where they both leaned against the worn wood and stared at the children.

"So that's how you started?"

Izzy shook her head. "No, I started out much younger. There were no parties here then, nothing like that. My parents put me into training on the ice and ballet classes off it. Every day, six days a week."

"That sounds horrible."

A tear welled in Izzy's eye as she glanced toward the door that led to Coach's office. She wiped her eyes and smiled at Jenna. "I loved it. I loved being here. This is where I belonged and I rarely felt I was missing out on a real life."

"How could you not hate it?"

Izzy turned and leaned her back against the boards. "Well, let me put this into terms you can understand. Do you hate volleyball? All the hours of practice, the traveling, the aches and pains, do you hate any of that?"

"No."

"Well, that's how I was with skating."

"But Mom, I still have a normal life. I hang out with friends, I go to school."

Izzy nodded. "When you were young, we knew you were going to be an athlete. We agreed you'd have as normal a life as possible. It was one of the few things we agreed on."

Jenna's eyes darkened. "You two really had no business getting married, did you?"

Izzy shrugged. "After a few years we fell into a routine and I didn't question it often. I wouldn't let myself think about it. I had you, and you filled my life plenty." She squinted up past the rows of bleaches to the top of the seats. "Is that Collier?"

Jenna followed Izzy's line of sight. "Looks like it. What's he doing here?"

"Guess I'll go find out." Izzy climbed the steps and met Collier halfway.

"I figured I'd find you here." Collier spoke in a low voice.

"You knew. About Jason and the money, and how everything would have been okay if only I was an obedient child?"

Collier nodded. "I'm sorry, there's no way I could just tell you that. You needed to hear it from them."

"As far as I'm concerned, Coach was the only parent I needed anyway."

"How's Jenna handling it?"

Izzy glanced at her daughter, who'd returned her attention to the children on the ice. "She's taking it like she takes everything, calmly, and in stride. We'll be okay."

Collier wrapped his arms around her. "You know I'm always here for you."

Izzy melted into his comfortable embrace, her tension easing. "I know," she murmured against his beating heart. Unbidden, the image of Quinn's face after their kiss flashed through her mind. She stiffened.

"You okay?"

Izzy broke from his arms and nodded. "Yeah, I'm okay." She looked around the arena. "So what's the deal here, Col? What happened to the old place?"

Collier shrugged. "After Pop died, I couldn't keep it up. I sold part ownership to a group who wanted to open the place to the public. You know, skating lessons, high school hockey games, birthday parties," he nodded to the small group assembled at the concession stand. "I haven't paid much attention. Obviously, it's a bit worse for wear."

"I'll say."

"Still, the ice is in good shape. Care to put on a bit of a show?" Collier's eyes twinkled.

"Tempting. Very tempting." The memory of Quinn's hands on her waist warmed her, emboldened her. "But I don't have any skates."

"Skate rental is right there. Come on. I'd love to see you skate again." He led her to the counter.

"Are you joining me?" She arched an eyebrow.

Collier laughed. "Not a chance. I haven't put on skates since the day I quit." He walked behind the counter and stared at the rows of skates. "Size seven, right?"

"Better make it six. I'm not wearing thick socks."

Collier handed her the skates. She sat on a bench and started unlacing them. "Col, I think there's something I should tell you."

He sat next to her. "What's that?"

"I agreed to do something the other day. I agreed to skate at a charity thing in the spring. The one you're playing at."

Collier nodded, his eyes narrowing. "I'm guessing your hockey player had something to do with this?"

"Apparently," she focused her attention on the ratty laces of the old skates, "he knew who I was all along."

"Not surprising. He doesn't strike me as a guy who wouldn't know the identity of every attractive woman in Nashville."

"You're upset." She finished lacing the skates and looked at him. "Be honest."

He helped her stand on the carpet and smiled. "I'm not surprised, and I'm definitely not excited at the prospect of my best girl spending quality time working up a routine for the guy, but I'm not upset."

"Not for, the guy. With, the guy. I'm skating with Quinn at the event."

Collier's expression darkened. "You're skating with him?"

Izzy stepped on the ice and waved at Jenna. "Yes. I am. Turns out, he's a good skater, and he can throw decently."

"So it's decided." There was a sense of defeat in Collier's voice. "You've already started working with him."

Izzy nodded. "I gave my word, so yeah, it's decided. You should give him a chance, Col. You might like him."

Collier shook his head, but said nothing for a beat. "Well, we should see what we're working with, shouldn't we? I think your old music is in Pop's office. Want me to go find it?"

I guess I didn't expect him to love the idea of Quinn skating with me. "That would be great."

Collier disappeared into the dark hall beyond the ice. A few moments later, "I Won't Hold you Back," floated through the speakers high above the ice. Izzy closed her eyes, took a deep breath, and started to skate. The years melted away, and with it, the shabbiness of her surroundings, until all that was left was smooth, fresh ice, and a black sky broken only by a silver spotlight on her. She had no conscious thought, she never did when she skated. She just moved as if her body was the link between the ice and the music, and her movements created the light between both.

Too soon, the music was over. The thin applause from Jenna, and the few people behind the concession counter barely reached her.

Izzy leaned against the boards, out of breath and waited for Collier's commentary. "So, what do you think?"

"I think you're insane. You've been out of this for almost twenty years. You think you can do a four minute routine with a hockey player and not be laughed off the ice?"

Izzy looked at Collier. "So what am I doing wrong?"

"You? You're perfect. Every element you do out there it's like you've been skating every minute of every day."

"Really? You're not just saying that?"

Collier shook his head. "You want my opinion? Dump the hockey player and skate a single."

The old argument. "Col, we're not going there."

"Well it's past time someone did. Pop always said you were better without a partner."

"And my parents disagreed. Vehemently."

"They paid my father to coach you and never listened to a word he said." Collier's face tightened. "Iz, think about this, because I know I have a million times over the years: If your parents had listened to my father, you and I might be living a very beautiful happily ever after."

Izzy laughed, mostly because the earnest look on Collier's face seemed comical. Then she realized he was serious, and she laughed harder, because the idea seemed even more comical. "How do you figure that?"

"I don't want to go dredging up bad memories."

Izzy waved a dismissive hand. "After what I heard today, why stop now?"

"Well since you asked; if you skated as a single, you wouldn't have a partner. You wouldn't have needed Jason. Jason wouldn't have convinced you to sleep with him. You might have left skating at some point, but you wouldn't have left Nashville. We would have stayed together long enough for me to prove to you that I'm an amazing romantic hero in spite of the fact that I don't live on the ice."

"I wouldn't have Jenna."

"Maybe you would. Maybe you'd have Jenna, only with lighter hair and my nose instead of Jason's. The point I'm making, is that if you had a crumb of self confidence, you'd be practicing on wide open ice during the day, getting ready for an exhibition that would be aired on network television instead of trying to teach a muscle head how to throw you without doing any permanent damage."

Izzy studied her friend. "You've been thinking about this a while, haven't you?"

Collier nodded. "You came back, and I'm so thankful for that. And you're skating again, which is awesome. But now I have to picture you skating with him."

"He has a name."

"Whatever. You have too much talent to waste trying to teach the unteachable."

Izzy closed her eyes, recalling the strength of Quinn's hands on her waist. "You haven't a clue what you're talking about, Col."

"Maybe not. But I'll bet he doesn't disagree with me." Collier nodded to the upper ring of seats.

Izzy looked over her shoulder. There, in the shadows, was Quinn. She blinked, and he was gone. An overwhelming sense of panic gripped her, and she started racing off the ice and up the stairs.

"Mom, what are you doing?" Jenna called from the other side of the ice.

"Izzy, you can't run in those crappy skates. You'll break something."

"Watch me!" Izzy ran up the stairs and out the main door. From where she stood, she could see the entire parking lot, but saw nothing of Quinn or his car. Just a few scattered cars, the last of the birthday partiers inside. "Quinn!" She shouted through the cold air.

"What?" He emerged from the door behind her.

"Quinn!" She threw herself into his arms, careful to keep her feet on the wood planks beneath them.

"Wow…if I thought I'd get this reaction, I wouldn't have stopped at the concession stand for a candy bar."

His arms were warm around her, secure. "I'm so sorry."

"Sorry? For what?"

She eased an inch away from his chest. "Well, for what Collier said."

"Collier? Oh, wait, Singer Guy? He said something about me?"

Izzy studied Quinn's face. "You know he's a singer?"

Quinn smiled. "I know a lot of things, Miss Izzy."

"How did you know I would be here?"

Quinn looked the tiniest bit guilty. "I stopped and talked to Cat who said you were off to see your parents. I figured that wouldn't end well, and that you'd come someplace where you really felt good about yourself. So I thought I'd try your old training facility. I didn't expect to see you in skates, but then I also didn't expect a full snack bar either. So it's a win for me." He bit into the candy bar.

"Well I am glad you're here. It's about time you and Collier met."

"I don't think I need to do that."

Izzy took his hand. "Quinn, if you and I are going to skate together, we are going to need some outside help. And that is going to include some coaching. And since my coach is no longer with us, Collier is the next best thing...he's Coach's son and he knows a lot about skating."

"And about you."

Izzy turned on him. "You two are going to get along, right?"

Quinn took another bite and chewed slowly. "I can't promise anything."

"Quinn!"

"Fine. Fine. I promise to get along."

Izzy led him to the rink where Collier and Jenna were deep in conversation.

"Collier, there's someone here I'd like you to meet."

Collier looked over his shoulder at Quinn. "Hello, Hockey Head."

"Hello, Singer Guy."

"Guys!"

Quinn's hand tightened around hers. "Come on Izzy, you can't expect us to play nicely right out of the box. Give us a few minutes."

"You know, like dogs," Jenna added with a grin.

Izzy wanted to turn the hose on both of them. "Fine whatever. Look, Quinn, we need a coach, and Collier can give us a lot of pointers. So go get some skates."

"Do you need some cash, Quinn? I know you retired guys don't always have a lot of cash on you."

Jenna burst out laughing, but Izzy was horrified. Quinn went to get some skates, and Izzy glowered at her old friend. "Can't you just be nice, for me?"

"Izzy, it's too easy. Anyone else in the world, and you know I'd be nice. But Quinn Murray? Come on! There's just too much material."

"Well, wait until you see him skate."

Collier's grin widened. "You're right. This could be fun. So much so, I think I'll offer you my rink as a place to practice."

Izzy beamed. "Do you mean it, Col?"

"They don't have hockey skates in my size." Quinn looked uncertain. "As for practicing here, I'm not sure."

"Granted, it's not NHL ice, but it was good enough to train a whole series of Olympic caliber skaters." Collier glared at Quinn. "What, you'll only skate at the Bridgestone Center?"

"No, nothing like that." Quinn looked surprised. "I'm sorry. I didn't mean to offend. I meant I didn't know if it would conflict with your other, clearly thriving business ventures for the place."

Collier followed Quinn's line of sight to the now abandoned concession stand. He chuckled. "You got me there. Look, it would be perfect. It's pretty much this dead all the time, except on Saturdays."

"Oh it would be great to practice here!" Izzy couldn't keep the smile off her face. "Collier, you're the best." She threw her arms around his neck and kissed his cheek. She didn't miss the wicked grin Collier fired at Quinn. *Whatever, you two.*

"Mom! Mom I was just sort of looking around this place and I saw the most amazing thing…" Jenna ran up to them, breathless and beaming.

"What's that?"

"There are pictures of you all over the place. It's so cool! You look so young!"

"Oh thank you. Yes, now that I'm ancient, it's nice to see what I looked like in the Dark Ages." She turned to Collier. "You never took down the pictures?"

Collier shrugged again. "I'm gone all the time. Clearly my business partners don't give two craps about much besides the concession stand and the rental skates."

"Well, whatever. Quinn, do you have your skates in the car?"

"Of course, but you know they're hockey skates."

Izzy waved her hand. "Go get them and let's practice!"

Quinn studied the ice. "How about a pass or two with the Zamboni first?"

"No way Studs McHockey." Collier held up his hand. "First show me what you've got. Then we'll decide if you deserve fresh ice or not."

TWENTY-FIVE

Letting Izzy drive to and from the rink today, Quinn decided, was pretty brilliant given how sore he was. *What is wrong with me? I am an athlete. I am used to training hard every day. But two hours a day on the ice the last two months, and I'm a corpse. A very stiff, very sore corpse.*

"Quinn, this is the best. I mean it! The best!"

It didn't help that with every practice in the past two months, Quinn felt himself falling apart while Izzy thrived. Her energy seemed boundless. *Meanwhile, everything on me hurts. Everything.*

"I could kiss you right here but I'm driving."

I think even my lips hurt. How is that possible?

"Hey are you hungry? I'm always hungry when I'm training. I remember Coach used to have to hide his lunch in a locked drawer right before big competitions because I would just sneak in there and eat it."

Does she always talk this fast? He focused on Izzy's endless stream of commentary and returned to the last thing he recalled her saying. "I could eat."

"Okay, what are you hungry for?"

Quinn stretched his arms over his head and groaned. "Nothing I have to lift."

Izzy pulled her car to a stop in front of Silver Screen. "You're sore, aren't you? I'm sorry, I thought when we added a practice this week it would be okay."

The extra practice was because Serena went on vacation to St. Maarten and with her out of the country I had some extra free time. Quinn grimaced. *Be a man! The ninety-nine pound waitress is bouncing around like she's ready for anything. No wonder Collier makes fun of me.*

"I'm a little stiff. You know, I'm used to getting smacked into the boards by a guy my size, getting up and moving again. I'm not used to being upright and graceful the whole time." He hoped his smile didn't look as painful as it felt. Quinn was very thankful Collier was out of town for a week, and couldn't revel in this new sign of weakness.

"Look, as a thank you, I'm going to go in and get us some really good coffee. Cat is brewing up something special today."

"How do you know?"

"Her hair was purple, and she was reciting something that sounded like Shakespeare. Then we'll go back to your place. You can take a long hot shower while I return some emails and then I'll rub you down with a very strong ointment."

Getting a rub down from Izzy sounds nice.

She hopped out of the car, her boundless energy surprising him again. Quinn eased the seat back and closed his eyes. *I'll just rest while she's getting the coffee. I'll picture myself skating without feeling all sorts of old man pain. It'll be like practice.*

A moment later Izzy said, "We're here. We're at your place."

Quinn opened his eyes. "What?"

"We're at your place. You fell asleep."

Quinn wrinkled his nose. "What on earth is that vile smell?"

Izzy held up a jar. "It's the ointment. I can't believe Col still had some."

"Clearly, he's a witch doctor, to have something that foul lying around. You're not rubbing that on my skin, are you?"

She got out of the car, laughing out loud. "Only if you want to feel better. Trust me. I used this all the time when I was competing."

"Right, but we aren't competing. And I'm fine. Argh!" Quinn tried to straighten up, and failed. "Okay, we'll take the stairs to the first floor and get the elevator there."

"You're going to do stairs?"

"I'm not walking past my doorman looking like this and smelling like that."

She shrugged. "Suit yourself."

It took them several minutes to get to the first floor. "I have a whole new respect for figure skaters," Quinn leaned against the elevator wall. "How is it you're not sore?"

Izzy grinned. "Well, I'm a little younger than you are." She giggled.

"Oh thanks for that."

"Plus, I'm not the one doing the lifting. How many times did we do that throw triple loop? Ten, twelve?"

"Ten or twelve hundred."

"So you're hoisting me and tossing me every time. All I have to do is fly."

"Yeah, sure, but you have to land."

The elevator doors opened. "Sure, and my knees hurt a bit."

"A bit? Hey, all I want to do is die."

Quinn started to collapse on the couch, but Izzy shoved him toward the bedroom. "Hot shower. Long hot shower. I'll make dinner."

"I think I have a bottle of ketchup and some mushrooms in the fridge."

Izzy glanced in the refrigerator. "Okay, I'll be calling for dinner. Chinese?"

He realized he was very hungry. "One of everything from Feng's."

"I'm game if you are." Izzy pulled a menu off the corkboard on the wall and started dialing. "You, shower."

She's worse than a trainer. Quinn limped into the bathroom. He studied himself in the mirror. *And damn if it isn't the best thing that's ever happened to me.*

***

Izzy ordered a ridiculous amount of food from Feng's. *At least the leftovers will make his fridge look like someone actually lives in this place.*

She kicked off her shoes and settled on the couch. Staring out the patio window, she realized she missed Coach. Collier was good at assessing their progress, but she missed Coach.

I wonder what he'd think of Quinn.

She pulled out her phone and without thinking, she dialed Collier's number.

"Hello?" Collier's voice was warm, fuzzy.

"Col, did I wake you?"

"Don't worry. What's up?"

I'm an idiot. Waking up Collier isn't going to bring Coach back.

"Izzy? Are you there? Are you okay?"

"I'm fine. Just thinking about Coach, you know?" She closed her eyes trying to hold back the sudden spring of tears. "We had a long practice today, and I started thinking about him."

Collier was quiet for a beat. "I know. I miss him, too. Sometimes I'll do something and I'll hear him yelling, 'For the love of all that's holy! Stop and do it the right way!' I used to hate it, now I wish I could hear him yell one more time."

"That's exactly what I was thinking, and then I dialed you."

"Hey, I'm always happy to take a call from you."

Izzy glanced at her watch. "Geez, it's late. I'm sorry."

"Don't worry about it. Your voice is a breath of fresh air. I can't believe the guys convinced me to play a Renaissance restaurant in New York. Worse than playing in bars, if you can believe it. But what about you. Are you really okay? How was practice?"

Izzy swallowed back the tremor in her voice. "I'm great, and practice was fine. Just a little nostalgic tonight, you know?"

"Hey, I'll be back in Nashville in a few days. We'll go down to Second Chances and get nostalgic all over the place. It'll be a mess."

Izzy smiled. "I can't wait."

"Just the two of us, though, right?"

In the short weeks since they'd been working together, it was clear Collier and Quinn saw each other as competition. Most of the off color banter fired between the two men either annoyed Izzy or made her laugh. Certain that Collier was just trying to get a rise out of her, she gave their bickering little thought. Her brain was too busy sorting out her feelings for Quinn.

"Izzy?"

"Sure Col. Just the two of us."

"Won't Puck Man be jealous?"

"No, because he won't be in town. And there's nothing to be jealous about."

"Boy do you know how to crush a guy's feelings in the middle of the night."

Izzy managed a weak smile. "Well, I try. Go back to sleep."

"You're not letting him work you too hard, right?"

"I'm the one working Quinn too hard."

"Don't know that I love the sound of that."

With a bittersweet smile, she ended the phone call. Memories of Coach rushed back. Unable to stop the spill of tears, she opened the patio door and stepped into the brisk Nashville air.

Suddenly everything hurts. My legs, my head, and my heart, and the spot where Coach should be; it all hurts.

***

Compared to the hot steam in the bathroom, the apartment was cold. Quinn shivered as he padded out to the kitchen, wearing nothing but a pair of sweat shorts. "Hey, why is it freezing…Izzy?"

She stood out on the balcony, so still, he wasn't certain she heard him. As he approached, he saw her wipe her eyes.

She's crying? He reached a hand to her shoulder. "Are you okay?"

"Me?" She turned to face him, the traces of her tears visible. "I'm great." She attempted a smile, and failed, her face broke from the strain, and she wept.

"Hey, hey, come here, you're freezing." He wrapped her in the warmest embrace he could muster, pulled her back into the apartment, and closed the door. "Come on. Let me get you warmed up." He turned on the fireplace and draped a quilt around her.

The door buzzer sounded.

"That'll be the food." She couldn't hide the quiver in her voice.

"Okay, okay. I'll get the door. I'll be back in one second." He grabbed his wallet off the table and handed his doorman a wad of bills. *I'm not counting out change when Izzy's crying on my couch.* He set the two huge bags of food on the table.

"Okay, so we'll be doing a little food therapy later." He sat down and snuggled her into the crook of his arm. "So what's up? You were all chatter and smiles before I took a shower. If this is what good personal hygiene does, count me out."

She sniffled, but laughed softly. "I'm sorry. It's so stupid."

"What's so stupid?"

"I…I called Collier."

Quinn frowned. *Not great for the ego.* "I thought he was in New York."

"He is. But I suddenly missed Coach so much and Col's my closest link."

"I get it. I think."

Izzy wiped her eyes. "Coach would like you a lot."

"Which is funny, because his son doesn't."

"No, but Coach would. He liked male skaters to be tall, and strong."

"Oh. So this has nothing to do with my winning personality."

Izzy's smile was sincere. "He'd love how tall you are. He'd hate that you skate on hockey skates, but I think he'd get over it because you're careful not to drop me or throw me too hard. He was big into making sure I didn't get hurt."

"So why the tears?"

Izzy cuddled closer under his arm. "I've been so happy, not just with the skating, but working on this whole thing. I feel like I have a purpose." She paused and sniffled. "I wish Coach was here to see it. He'd be proud, like a father."

Her voice was so thin, so lost, Quinn ached to shield her from the world. "You haven't talked about your parents since you went to see them."

"They aren't family, if they ever were. Coach was my family. I left him, just like I left everyone. I ran away. Now I can't talk to him. And I really wish I could right now."

Quinn cradled her. "Anything I can help with?" Something clicked in Quinn's brain. "Are you feeling, you know, overwhelmed? I know you're doing a lot on the administrative end of things, is it too much?"

"No-not-not at all." The catch in her voice and renewed tears belied her words.

"You know, you took on a ton of stuff with this. Plus you're still working, and you had to change your shift. It's a lot of adjustments."

"No...Quinn...I used to do stuff like this all the time, you know, when Jenna was little. I volunteered at her school."

Her tears were warm on his bare shoulder. "So what is it?" He kissed the top of her head, again at a loss for words.

"It's so stupid..." she huddled tighter and sobbed in earnest.

What do I do? A flash of panic shuddered through Quinn. "Whatever it is, whatever's bothering you, I promise I'll do whatever you want me to."

"My ankles hurt so much!"

Quinn wasn't sure what he felt more: surprise or triumph. "Your ankles hurt?"

She nodded, her hair silky on his skin. "Three workouts with you and my ankles are on fire. I'm a runner. My legs should not be in pain after a couple hours on the ice."

"Pain in the legs, we can solve that!" Quinn stood and reached for the jar of ointment. "We have this….this stuff." He wrinkled his nose. "And, if that doesn't work, I'm sure we can find other ways of easing pain." He bestowed his most wicked grin on her. "Which would you like first? Foul or fun?"

The grin had the desired effect. She laughed and threw a pillow at him. "Foul. But just the ankles."

"Just the ankles?"

She shook her head. "No…my knees…and my legs…and everything!" She hugged her legs to her and howled.

"Wait, wait, wait. Are you telling me that all that bouncing around after skating today, running in for coffee, all that chatter…that was a cover?"

"I forgot to get the coffee. I begged Cat for a fist full of aspirin." She chuckled, a throaty sound that stirred something deep in Quinn. "I didn't want to seem weak."

"Weak?" That one word brought him to his knees. "Izzy…" he knelt next to her and stroked her hair, "you are the strongest woman I have ever known."

"You're just saying that because you want me to stop crying on your couch."

"I'm saying that," he murmured against the back of her neck, "because it's the one thing I know to be true." He wrapped his arms around her, aching to meld with her.

His cell buzzed *I don't care who that is; I'm not picking that up.*

The buzzing stopped and Quinn allowed himself to inhale Izzy again.

The elevator door buzzed.

"What the hell?" Quinn glanced at the display on his phone. *Serena!*

"Are you expecting someone?"

No. And Serena's definitely not expecting anyone either. "That's probably Benny with some notes or something. Tell you what, why don't you go and get in the shower, I'll deal with him, and then we'll test this ointment and see if this really works."

"Okay." She stood and moved stiffly to the bedroom. Quinn grabbed a t-shirt from his bed and threw it on as the elevator doors opened.

"Hello, Serena." He leaned against the kitchen counter, praying he looked casual.

"Quinn."

"You're back early."

"St. Maarten was a bore. I should know better than to try and take an extended vacation." Serena waved a dismissive hand. "What the blazes is that stench?"

Quinn sniffed, as if smelling something for the first time. "Oh, well, I've got dinner here, and I just finished working out." *Chinese food and body stink...yeah, it's close to whatever is in that jar.*

"Who's in the shower?"

Quinn blinked back the panic. "Shower?"

"Your shower is running, Quinn." Her eyes narrowed. "You don't have a woman up here, do you?"

"Don't be ridiculous, Serena. You know I've never let a woman shower in my place. I was just about to get in." *Please don't be in a showering mood.* "So vacation in the island was boring, huh?"

"Awful. No one to rub sun tan lotion on me. Next time, you're coming with me."

"Then don't schedule your vacation during hockey season."

Serena rolled her eyes. "What does that leave me, three weeks a year? Anyway, I was thinking I'd have dinner with you tonight."

Oh hell no.

"But I'm not going anywhere with you smelling like that, and I don't have the time to wait for you to shower."

There is a God and He likes me just a tiny bit.

"I'm catching a flight to New York in a few hours. I feel the need to do some real shopping. What's that?"

"What's what?"

Serena locked in on Izzy's skate bag. "What is that? Are those figure skates?"

Shit. "Those? Oh some girl left those at the rink after that Make-a-Wish thing. I picked them up from the arena. She's supposed to pick them up later at the station. In fact, Benny's coming over in a bit to get them."

"Ew, Benny. Well, that would explain the ridiculous amount of food you have here." Serena made a face. "It's a good thing I'm leaving. You're a complete pig when I'm not around. I'll be back next Friday."

"Friday. Got it."

"And Quinn?"

"Yeah?"

Serena waved a hand over her nose. "Do something about that smell. I'm not coming back here until you swear to me it's gone."

I'll keep that in mind.

With one more disdainful glance Serena got into the elevator. Quinn exhaled, his shoulders sagging. He stared at the bags of take out on the table. *Not really in the mood for Chinese anymore.* He put the containers in the fridge and dialed the pizza place down the street and ordered a mushroom and sausage.

I should probably make sure she's okay with that. Without thinking twice, Quinn tapped at the bathroom door and opened it. "Izzy?"

Thick steam blurred his vision. Over the hiss of water, she responded. "Yeah?"

"I sort of changed my mind. How do you feel about pizza?" He tried very hard to keep his mental image of her clothed.

"Can we get sausage and mushroom?"

"Seriously?"

"Yeah, is that a problem?"

Stop trying to see through the steam. "It's only my favorite."

"Okay, great. I'll be out in a bit. This shower is amazing!"

Yeah, compared to yours, mine is a modern marvel. "Take your time."

Reluctantly, he closed the door. His bedroom seemed chilly after being in the bathroom, so he turned on the fireplace and the television and stretched out on the bed.

Ten minutes later, she emerged, drowning in a sweatshirt and a pair of shorts.

"You look like you feel better."

Her laughter was light and musical again. "Yeah, nothing cures a major case of the blues better than a super hot shower. I do have to say, though, if I'm going to make a habit of changing clothes here…"

"I sort of hope you might." *Was that too bold? That was too bold for someone trying to take it slow. Yep, I'm not good at taking anything slow.*

Izzy blushed, and covered her face quickly under the guise of toweling off her hair. "Anyway, I have to start just keeping a change of clothes with me. Seriously, this is the second time now I feel like some sort of tiny little cartoon character in a normal person's clothing." She reached for her comb.

"Here, let me do that." Quinn took the comb from her. "Sit right here in front of me." He combed through her wet hair with long, gentle strokes.

"I never pictured you being good at something like this."

Quinn paused. "My sister had long hair, and hated the way my mom yanked at it when it was wet. I guess I felt sorry for her, so I combed her hair out once. After that, she begged me to do it every time." He stared at the strand in his hands. "I did that until I went away to school. Funny, I haven't thought about that in ages."

The elevator buzzed. Quinn hopped up. "Stay right there. I'll get the pizza. And something for your legs that isn't quite so odiferous."

Izzy's laughter followed him all the way to the elevator. Again he handed the doorman a wad of bills. *I'm not counting change when I've got Izzy laughing in my bed.*

He set the pizza on the bed. "Now, tell me what I can get you to help with the leg pain, because I believe that we both know, as enticing as a mutual rub down sounds, we're not touching each other with that ointment."

Izzy opened the pizza box. "Fair enough. Coach had another 'cure' but only for the very worst pains." She picked up a slice and took a bite.

"As long as it doesn't involve anything vile smelling, I'm intrigued."

"Well, he'd pour half a glass of red wine, and then he'd put two ice cubes in it. 'Drink this, Bella,' he'd say. 'Drink but tell no one, for telling will cut the power of the cure in half.' He liked to pretend he was from some foreign country, he'd use this fake accent all the time."

Quinn laughed out loud. "And how old were you?"

"I think I was fifteen. It was right after Col and I drank that bottle of wine in his office, so he probably figured if I didn't die from that, I'd be okay." A wistful smile crossed Izzy's face. "Talk about not thinking of something in years."

Chance told me she puts ice cubes in her wine. "Well, I do believe that's a painkiller I can work with. Give me a minute." Quinn returned to the kitchen. *I knew that massive collection of wines I'm not drinking would come in handy.* He opened cabinet. "You said red, right?"

"Yeah. Pinot noir, if you've got it."

"You want pinot noir with ice?"

"Don't judge me. My coach got me hooked on cold wine, and one of my running partners liked pinot noir, so I just put the two together." Her giggle was infectious.

Quinn smiled. "I'm not judging. I'm thinking you probably wouldn't do well as a guest judge on some snooty food and wine tasting show, but hey, when it comes to food and wine, I say, 'whatever gets you through the meal.'"

"You say that, do you?"

"I do."

"That would explain why you camouflage everything with mushrooms. But whatever you've got, wine-wise, is fine."

Quinn stared at the wine in his cabinet. *I have four bottles of pinot noir. Four, in a sea of other wines. How in the world do I have this vast a collection of wine?* A vague memory taunted the back of his mind. *Oh yes, wine: the drink of choice for college co-eds who're trying to be classy for the older guy.*

Am I really going back to that part of my history?

No, I'm opening a bottle of wine for a completely age appropriate woman. This won't turn into anything weird. Okay, it might be weird, but it won't be sex. It definitely will not be sex.

He poured one glass and dropped two ice cubes into it. Grabbing a can of Vernors' for himself, he returned to the bed.

"Oh thank you." She took a sip from the glass and set it on the nightstand. "It's okay that I'm drinking, if you're not?"

"It's perfectly fine. Have a glass. Have three. Let's see where the night takes us." He kept his tone light to cover the sudden desire flushing his skin.

This is not how people take it slow.

This just in...I'm terrible at taking it slow.

He stretched out on the bed and cracked open the soda. "I've got my Vernor's, I'm a very happy guy."

"Okay." She took another sip of wine. "So, what's your big pain killing secret? You've got to have something good. Hockey is rough."

I have a bottle of hydrocodiene left over from my playing days but I'm not touching that, either. "Well remember, for most of my playing days I numbed my aches and pains over at Chances. Nowadays, I have the tried and true: Tylenol."

"Really?"

"Well, not just plain old Tylenol. Tylenol PM." He opened his nightstand and pulled out the bottle. "A couple of these," he opened the bottle and shook out two pills, setting them next to his can, "and I'm sound asleep in about twenty minutes."

"I'm familiar with the product, but I'll stay with the wine for now." She stretched and rolled her feet and groaned. "Did I have this much pain when I was training? I don't remember any of this hurting so much. I must be old."

"You're not old. Tell you what." Quinn finished a piece of pizza. "You keep sipping that watery cold wine, and I'll rub your legs. I used to go out with a trainer who taught me a few things."

And someday, when we aren't taking it slow, I will share those things with you. Tonight I rub your feet.

"You are way too good of a guy, Quinn Murray."

"Most people would not agree with you."

"Most people don't know you."

Most people know what a complete bastard I am.

***

She didn't miss the awkward pause. It hung between them, a void she wanted to fill, but Quinn seemed disconnected, distant. He kept his eyes locked on her foot.

"I'm serious, you know. You've been so wonderful to me."

"You make it easy." He didn't look at her. "Not everyone has your ability to bring out the best in people."

There was a note of warning in his voice, something subtle, dark. *I'm not digging any deeper.* Izzy took another sip. "So, Sports Center?"

"You want something else?"

"No, it's fine." She set the glass on the nightstand. "I need to get going anyway." *Before I decide this is just way too comfortable.*

Quinn shifted from her foot to her calf. *Okay, one more minute.* Her eyes fluttered closed. The wine and his hands had an electric effect on her. *I can't stay.*

"You don't need to leave." His voice was gentle, inviting, like his hands.

"Quinn…I…" *If I stay, he will expect something I am not ready for yet.*

He never stopped massaging her ankles, her legs. "You don't need to leave."

"I'm not…"

His voice stayed low, soothing, "I know exactly where you are, and I know I'm a hundred miles ahead of you," he lifted her foot and gave it the lightest kiss.

What is wrong with me? Izzy tried to push away her misgivings. *I'm an adult woman. He's wonderful. This is completely normal. Why am I fighting this?*

Because I'm not making the same mistakes I made before. He's my skating partner. I can't do this.

She sat up. "Quinn, you…are…wiping out the pain! How are you doing that?" She stared at him, as if seeing his hands for the first time. "My knee doesn't hurt at all."

He smiled warmly. "And I did it without using that voodoo goo you brought."

"I can't remember a time when my knee didn't ache at least a little." She glanced at the bedside clock. "It's late. I gotta go."

"Wait." Quinn set her leg on the bed and slid next to her. "Look, Izzy, you and I, we both have issues…when it comes to relationship stuff, right?"

"That is a minor understatement."

"So let me put your mind at ease," he paused, and took a drink. "I like having you here. You make this place less empty." He set the can on the nightstand. "I'd like you to stay. You could have a second glass of watered down wine, I'll keep massaging your legs. We can talk, or watch a movie, or just overdose on Sports Center until we fall asleep. And I swear, I won't…you know, unless you want me to."

She couldn't miss the hint of humor in his otherwise sincere words. "You're making fun of me."

"Not in the least. I think we're trying to build something here, but we aren't exactly traditional nine to five folks. So maybe dating means spending the night together in a completely platonic, non-naked sort of way." His grin was wicked, but the light in his eyes was honest.

Izzy yawned and stretched her arms over her head. *It would be nice not to leave when I'm this ridiculously comfortable.* She studied Quinn with a careful eye. *I can trust him. He's my partner.* She shivered. *I trusted Jason, too.*

Quinn isn't Jason. There's no hidden agenda. There aren't any parents pulling strings. There's no gold medal at the end of the rainbow. We're just two people.

"I'd really like it if you lost the argument you're currently having with yourself."

She blinked, and nodded at him. "Okay. I'll stay."

His eyes glowed. "I'll be back in a moment with another frosty glass of wine." He moved to the kitchen quickly, and returned, her glass filled, two ice cubes bobbing in the black-red liquid. "There you go," He handed her the glass.

She didn't miss his grateful, almost shy expression. "Thank you, Quinn." She sipped the wine as he returned to her leg. "And, thank you."

"For what?" He kept his gaze fixed on her calf muscle.

Izzy took another sip. "When Jason and I…he told me it would make us better skaters. I had no idea what it all meant."

"People like to think it means nothing." Quinn eased her leg upward, stretching her hamstring. "Let me know if this hurts." He leaned forward gently. "You know, they say that no matter how casual people want to be, our bodies aren't wired to believe sex is a casual thing." He backed up, set her right leg down and repeated the stretch on her left leg. "They say our bodies make promises our brains maybe aren't even aware of."

His face closer to hers, Izzy longed to believe the promise his eyes made. She exhaled as he sat back again, and let her leg rest. "They say that?"

He finished stretching her leg and slid next to her. "They say that."

"Well, I don't know what promises Jason and I made to each other. It was never like they write in books."

Quinn chuckled and draped an arm around her shoulders. "I've found it rarely is like they write in books."

Izzy thought about reaching for her glass, but was far too comfortable. "You'd be the expert in the room." She meant it as a joke, but a shadow passed over Quinn's face. "I'm sorry. I didn't mean it like that."

"No, don't worry about it. You're completely right. I never used to get why women got so worked up about it when I broke things off. I thought it was just because I was so magnificent." His grin eased her misgivings.

She wanted to say something clever, but his expression was so open, so bare, she didn't want to hurt him. "So then here we are."

"Here we are." He took her hand in his and pulled her closer. His lips brushed the top of her head lightly.

She closed her eyes, wrapped in his arms. Images of the day blinked in her brain, like grainy photos in an old picture show. The last of her tension vanished with Quinn's second kiss, brushed just above her ear. Izzy let herself float.

Candles circled the rink like a warm halo. There's no music, just the cold, smooth slice of blade against ice as she glides from one side of the rink to the other. Quinn is there, beside her, guiding her, shadowing her, but never pushing, never forcing her to go any faster than her feet will carry her.

She senses the woman before she sees her. Izzy stops short, a spray of snow flies around her feet.

The woman looks familiar. There's a glow in her eyes that strikes something deep in Izzy's soul, something cold. The candles darken, extinguished by an unseen breath. Izzy stares into the darkness, trying to see the woman better, but the woman is gone. All Izzy hears is a cold, angry hiss.

Izzy's eyes snapped open. A moment, maybe two, maybe not even that much had passed. Quinn's arms were a fortress around her. *He'd never let me fall.* Without a second thought, she reached up and brushed his cheek with her fingertips.

Surprise flashed in his eyes, replaced by the glow of desire that matched the stirring within her. Izzy laid her hand on his cheek, and brought him close enough to kiss away the whisper of uncertainty between them.

He needed no further invitation. His kisses were light, a breath of warmth on her eyelids, her cheekbones, her lips. Supporting her with his right arm, Quinn caressed her with his left hand, softly, sensually, waking a foreign heat deep within her. He brushed his lips down her throat, murmuring words distinct only to her heart. She shivered but was not chilled as he slid the shirt and shorts from her body, and let them fall next to his own smoothly removed clothes.

Skin against skin, Izzy closed her eyes, losing herself in the arousal simmering like molten gold just beneath the surface. She pressed her hands against his broad chest, his heat leaping through her fingertips straight to the deepest recesses of her being.

Vaguely she was aware of sounds; an opening drawer, tearing cellophane. The only sound that meant anything to her was Quinn's soft growl of pleasure. The ache to melt into him was strong and she wrapped herself around him, clinging to him with her legs when he tried to arch away. *Don't let go. Don't let me fall.*

"Izzy."

Quinn's voice was far away, deep in his throat. "Open your eyes."

She obeyed. He hovered over her, his eyes the only light in the room.

"I want to see you," he whispered. "Isabella."

His gaze held her, supported her as much as his body. She didn't blink and they flowed together, wrapped so tightly around each other they moved, and breathed, and soared as one being. Fire and lightening flashed through her as she saw the promise of forever deep in Quinn's eyes.

Then the heat cooled to comforting warmth, and, like the final pose of a routine, Izzy relaxed in Quinn's arms, complete and secure.

TWENTY-SIX

"My timing sucks."

Izzy grinned at Quinn, who stared at the airport security line as if he were about to join a death march. "You'll be back in a few days."

"Yes, but how can I leave you when all I can think about is…"

"Are you blushing?"

"I might be." He swept her into an embrace and kissed her, leaving her breathless. "Benny's going to have a stroke if I don't get to the gate in the next five minutes."

"Call me when you land."

His eyes bespoke volumes. "Think about me."

Like I could think about anything else. She kissed him again and let him go.

Back at her apartment, Izzy thought about getting some sleep, but realized she wasn't tired. *I'm such a cliché. I'm all energized and wide eyed after a very nice night.*

She had no interest for anything other than staring at her dark television screen and checking the clock every five minutes. *Clock watching is not going to bring him back faster. I have a million things I should be doing. I could go practice. I could send out some more invitations to the event. I could…*

I could just sit here, on this bed, and pretend Quinn is coming back in a few minutes.

Her phone buzzed. *Oh good, something to make the time go more quickly.* "Hey Col, how's New York?"

"Boring. Everyone here thinks they're so much cooler than I am."

Izzy laughed. "When you are truly the coolest of all."

There was a pause on the phone. "I thought I'd check in and see how you were. You sounded rough last night."

Izzy closed her eyes and smiled. "Nope, I'm great. Perfect."

There was another pause. "Are you sure? You still sound weird."

"I do?" She couldn't suppress a short giggle at the end of the sentence.

Collier was quiet again "Izzy…did you…"

Her giggles subsided as warning bells rang in Izzy's head. *Of course he's not going to take this well.*

"You did, didn't you?"

"Col, come on."

"How could you?"

She didn't have to imagine his face. She'd seen it before, twenty years earlier. "I didn't plan it."

"No, of course not. You didn't plan it the last time."

"There's no need to get mean. You know Quinn and I have had feelings for each other, that we've sort of been seeing each other."

"I don't know anything like that. I know he is a womanizing hound dog and you think sex is some sort of key to skating greatness."

"Collier!" She couldn't keep the anger out of her voice.

"What am I supposed to feel? Tell me that. I thought…"

"You thought what? You thought I'd fall in love with you?"

"Clearly I'd be an idiot if I said yes. Still, Izzy, I didn't think you'd be stupid enough to sleep with your skating partner… again."

"Don't be like that." Tears welled in her eyes. "Don't."

"Sorry. I don't know what you expect me to say."

"I expect you to be a grown up."

There was a pause. "Maybe when it comes to you, I'm just not."

"Collier!" Dead air met her anguished cry. Izzy ended the phone call and stared at the dark display. *I should have realized it. I just thought it was funny; their bickering back and forth. I didn't know it was real.*

She set her phone on the bed and pictured Quinn on the plane. She felt better. Then, remembering the hurt in Collier's voice, she felt worse for feeling better.

***

"Quinn! You will not believe what I just saw!"

Returning to a nearly empty airport bar after trying to make some calls, Quinn heaved a sigh. His connecting flight to Montreal was delayed and hanging out with Benny in an airport bar was the last thing he wanted to do. The first thing he wanted to do was get on the next flight to Nashville, and take Izzy back in his arms. *I'm always leaving her to go someplace I don't want to be.*

Benny's giddiness was not to be contained. "You see that guy at the bar. Doesn't he look familiar?"

Everyone in an airport bar seems familiar.

The man at the bar, however, was more than familiar. A small smile played on Quinn's lips. *Poor devil, wonder if he's writing another love song about Izzy.* Quinn couldn't suppress the quiver of triumph sparking up his spine at the memory of the previous night.

"That guy was on the phone and got into an argument with someone, a woman I think, and then when he hung up, he slammed half a dozen shots right in a row. I mean it's barely noon. I haven't seen drinking like that since you were in your prime. But then a woman comes up to him."

Quinn wanted to sink into the overstuffed leather chair and ignore Benny's chatter. He wanted to close his eyes and bring to mind every sensation from the night before. He didn't care about Collier, or Collier's drinking habits before noon on a Monday. Given Benny's expression, however, Quinn knew he couldn't ignore the conversation. "What kind of woman?"

"You would not believe it, but I could have sworn it was Boss Lady!"

Quinn's chest tightened. *She was going shopping in New York, but she flew in last night. She wouldn't still be in the airport.* "It's not possible."

"I know, right? But I could have sworn it, until she took off her scarf. She had short hair, pretty short anyway, and dark, almost like yours."

Quinn relaxed. "Well we all know how Serena is about her long, red hair."

"But how awesome would that have been, Boss Lady trying a bar pick up on that sad looking dude there? That would have made this stinkin' delay almost worth it."

"True." Glancing over his shoulder, Quinn's relief was complete. Where ever he was, Collier James was no longer ten feet from him, hanging like a cloud over Quinn's quietly euphoric thoughts. For a moment Quinn felt sorry for Collier, knowing how he'd feel if he'd lost Izzy to another man. The feeling passed quickly. He could not stifle a grin.

His cell buzzed. The airline had finally sorted out the delay. Quinn realized he wasn't going to miss the game at all.

I'm still miles away from Izzy, but at least I'm moving in the right direction.

TWENTY-SEVEN

Izzy leaned against the boards at the rink and smiled. *How great is my life all of sudden? I'm skating again. I'm back on day shifts. I'm not a walking zombie.*

I've fallen in love.

Quinn was due to return in a few hours, and Izzy ached for him. She craved his smile and voice, almost as much as she craved the weight of his body pressed against hers. She closed her eyes, recalling his good-bye kiss at the airport.

If this is what love feels like, bring it on!

She opened her eyes and took a deep breath. *I've got work to do.*

Building up some speed, she transitioned into a spin sequence, something she could never teach Quinn. Too well, she remembered Coach's constant barking when it came to spins. No one could time revolutions properly, he always said. She was too fast, and her partners were too large to move as quickly as she did. *Jason was closer than anyone, but Coach hated Jason.*

Coach's stance had always been clear: Izzy was a strong enough skater to skate solo. In the end, thanks to her parents, Izzy wound up with a partner and virtually no spins in her routines.

How different would my life be if my parents had any confidence in me?

Izzy grabbed her water bottle and drank deeply. *Doesn't matter. I would never trade Jenna for a box of gold medals.*

She set her bottle on the bench and glided to center ice. *Besides, I wouldn't even be close to appreciating the magic of skating right now, completely by myself. Just me and the guy at the concession stand.*

She whirled herself into a long sit-spin combination, not stopping until her brain was completely disoriented. She slowed and glided unsteadily to the boards, where she leaned heavily, catching her breath. *I do love to spin.*

Glancing at her watch, Izzy frowned. *Time to go already?* She checked the concession stand, which was abandoned. *He must be closing for the night.* She put on her skate guards and walked up the ramp to the locker room.

In the half-light of the locker room, Izzy removed her skates and slipped into her warm-up pants. She bent low over her shoes to snug the laces.

"You have no right to be here."

Izzy startled at the sight of the woman shadowed in the corner. She couldn't make out a face, only a slim frame, clad in black, and dark hair pulled into a sleek, short ponytail.

"I'm sorry, but I do. My friend is an owner. He said I could skate here."

"I'm sure he did." The woman stayed out of the reaches of the dim overhead light.

Izzy bit her lip. "I'm leaving. I'm going right now." She picked up her skate bag.

"Not yet." The woman moved suddenly, smoothly, like a snake. Izzy wasn't aware how close she was until her arm was in the woman's vise-like grasp.

"Look, lady, I don't know what your issue is, but I'm leaving so it's okay." Izzy attempted to pull her arm away, but the woman merely tightened her grip.

"You have no right to be here. Not in Nashville, not on the ice." The woman hissed against Izzy's cheek, her grip tightening.

Izzy swallowed and tried to remain calm. *There's no one to hear me if I yell.* "Okay, okay. I'll leave."

"Oh, that's very right you'll leave."

Izzy knew her shoulder was dislocated a heartbeat before the bolt of pain fired from her neck to her fingertips. She couldn't contain an initial screech, but tried to bite back her cries, sensing a prolonged reaction would encourage her attacker further. *Breath through it...*she closed her eyes and called up Coach's encouragement from the day she dislocated her shoulder in practice. *Breathe through it.* Anger bubbled up as Izzy tried to make out the woman's face in dim light. *There's something familiar about her.*

"You're leaving Nashville now. Before that charity event. Quinn thinks he's in love with you. I can't have that. If he's in love with anyone, it's me."

Who are you? How would you know anything about the event, or me? Izzy blinked, trying to stay conscious as wave after wave of pain wore away her resolve. "Look, I have no idea who you are, or what I did to offend you."

"Don't talk to me about offense!" The woman shoved Izzy without letting go of her dislocated arm.

Off balance, Izzy waved her free hand wildly. The woman howled as Izzy grasped her hair, pulling several strands from the woman's scalp. The woman twisted Izzy's dislocated arm, sending Izzy to her knees, weeping in pain.

Showing no mercy, the woman jerked Izzy to her feet. "You dare to talk to me about giving offense?" The women shook her.

Summoning what was left of her strength, Izzy slapped the woman as hard as she could. Her fingers curled, her nails caught a corner of the woman's cheek. Shrieking, the woman flung Izzy against the lockers.

Pain raged through her, and Izzy slid to the floor, helpless.

The woman crouched over her, a predator on its prey. "This is your only warning, Isabella Landry."

Who is she, that she knows my real name?

It was Izzy's last conscious thought.

***

Quinn paid the cabbie and stepped onto the sidewalk in front of his building. He stared up the thirty floors to where he knew, his windows looked over the city, cold and unseeing. *I should have had Izzy stay here while I was gone. Then I wouldn't have to come home to an empty apartment in the middle of the night. At least Izzy would be sleeping in my bed. And maybe she'd make some coffee.*

The simplicity of the domestic image warmed him.

His cell buzzed in his pocket. *Izzy.* "Hey there, Beautiful."

"Mr. Murray?"

His body tensed. *Why would anyone but Izzy be calling me from her phone?* Quinn tried to match the strained voice with a face. *Oh yeah, the concession stand kid at the rink.* "Chase?"

"I'm sorry to call you, but I can't get hold of Collier, and something's happened. You were listed as Miss Izzy's emergency contact."

The hair on the back of his neck prickled. "What's going on?"

"Someone…someone attacked her."

Quinn blinked, and tried to process Chase's words. "What do you mean, someone attacked her?"

"She was here really late, practicing, like Collier told me she would be. I closed everything down, then I waited at the door to let her out and she wasn't there. So I went back and did a complete search of the place. I went to the locker room, and she was here, out cold, and her arm looked weird."

Quinn's stomach churned. *There's only one person who would want to hurt her.*

But Serena had no way of knowing Izzy was even at the rink. He took a deep breath. "Okay. Did you call an ambulance?"

"I did. I'm sorry, sir. I know you wanted this lady to be a secret."

Someone obviously found out.

Chase told Quinn where they'd taken her. His jaw taut with rage, Quinn hailed a cab and headed for the hospital, dialing Izzy's friends and family as his cab tore through the predawn streets of Nashville.

Mikayla, Cat, and Jenna beat him to the waiting room. "How is she?"

Jenna wiped her eyes. "The gash in her head wasn't too deep. They're stitching her up right now. We can go see her in a few minutes."

A nurse waved at them. Quinn held up a hand. "Ladies, I know you're really eager to see her, but do you mind? I'd like a minute alone."

"The cops are in there." Mikayla pointed out.

"That's fine. I won't be a minute."

Quinn hustled down the hall and pushed the door open with more force than he intended. The door slammed open, nearly toppling a female detective.

"Quinn Murray?" The detective looked confused. "What are you doing here?"

Izzy looked like death; her arm in a broad sling, a trace of new stitches peeking out under her bangs, her skin translucent under the harsh lights. "This lady is a friend of mine." Quinn glanced quickly at the badge and credentials the detective held up.

"Detective Emerson, we want the same thing right now, so let me clear something up right away. I didn't do this."

"I didn't say you did. I heard you on the radio, calling the game. You must've gotten the world's fastest flight out of Toronto."

"I had a very good reason to come home quickly." He continued staring at Izzy's silent form. "If you don't mind, I'd like to talk to her for a moment."

"Sure. I'm done here anyway. I have hair and skin samples to get to the lab."

"Hair and skin? She wasn't..." a chilling thought stopped his heart.

"No, there's no sign of sexual assault." Detective Emerson nodded at Izzy. "She's a pretty resourceful lady. She managed to get some hair and a little bit of skin under her fingernails. It's evidence anyway." She nodded to Quinn one last time, and left.

"Izzy," Quinn flew to her side.

"Hey," she eased one eye open, and managed a weak smile. "Did the Preds win?"

Quinn ached to laugh and take her in his arms. "Yeah, they won. You look like one of the Leafs' forwards, though. What happened?"

She tried to sit up better, and failed. "It was so strange." Her voice was weak, far away. "I was in the locker room, and this woman grabbed my arm. She said some really strange things."

"Like what things?"

"She told me to leave Nashville. That I couldn't skate in the event." She paused, staring at the sling. "This is my catch arm. The last time I dislocated my shoulder it took almost two months for it to feel right. The event's in less than a month." She raised tear filled eyes. "What if I can't skate? This'll ruin everything!"

Of course she's more worried about my event than her own safety. "Don't you worry about anything than healing, you hear me? The event's not ruined. We'll just..." His voice trailed off as he suddenly understood.

Izzy can still skate. Just not with me.

Serena's warning me.

Izzy closed her eyes again. "I've been trying to think about her face. It was dark. She had dark hair, really dark, and sort of short. I saw an outline of her face. That's it."

The door opened a crack, and Jenna peered in. "Jenna and Mike and Cat are here. I'm going to let them talk to you. But I'm coming back. I'll come back and I'll take you home when they release you. Okay?"

"Okay."

Quinn kissed the top of her head. "I love you," he whispered against her forehead. He leaned closer. "Whatever else you might hear, you hold on to that, got it?" *God only knows where this is going to end.*

She nodded.

He got up and hustled outside where the sunrise promised a beautiful day. "How could you, Serena?" He hailed a cab, and gave the driver her address.

The ten minutes it took to get to Serena's apartment building were the longest in his life. The doorman tried to stop him, but withered behind his desk when Quinn shot him an icy glare. The elevator door opened immediately, and he stepped in, punching Serena's floor number with venom. *It ends now.*

He knocked on her door, which, for the first time since he'd been coming to her place, was closed. A moment, then two ticked away before she opened. "What a nice surprise. It's a bit early, but please come in." She stepped aside slowly, as if welcoming him for a casual evening.

"What the blazes did you do?"

She sat at the kitchen table, and picked up a glass of orange juice. After a slow, ponderous sip, she glanced at him innocently. "I haven't a clue what you mean. And you didn't say anything about my hair. I had it done in New York."

Really dark and short, just like Izzy said. He studied her face. *Make-up isn't hiding that scratch.* He paced in front of her, trying in vain to slow his racing heartbeat. "You attacked a woman late last night."

Reflexively, Serena touched her cheek. "Oh. That."

Her calm demeanor enraged him. "Why? Why would you attack a random woman in some crappy skating rink?"

Her eyes glittered coldly. "If she's random, why are you so upset?"

"She's the woman I met at the Make-a-Wish event. I told you about her when you were here, and you saw her skates. Nothing more than that."

"So you're in the habit of arranging secret skating sessions out of town with a woman who means nothing to you?"

Quinn shrugged, attempting to look casual. "Who said I arranged anything? It's not my rink. It's not any rink I even know. I was in Toronto, Serena. You know that. Why would you think she has any connection to me? I haven't had anything other than a business relationship with any woman since…" he couldn't say the name.

"Since Sally." Serena voice remained calm, but there was a tension in her body that hadn't been there a moment earlier. "That might have been true, before. But since Isabella Landry showed up, I'm sure all that's changed."

"What are you talking about?" Quinn swallowed hard, a weak attempt to fight the fear that was roiling up inside him. "You're being ridiculous."

"Don't treat me like I'm an idiot!" Serena slammed the juice glass on the table, shattering the glass. "Damn it! Look what you've made me do." She glared at him as she wiped the mess up with a napkin.

"I'm not treating you like you're an idiot," Quinn blinked, unable to keep his heart rate steady.

Serena stood inches from him. "I saw the security tape of the two of you leaving the Bridgestone Center."

Quinn didn't move, and dared not breathe.

"You saw her at Jason's funeral, didn't you? Is that when you fell in love with her, or was it after you brought her here?"

"I went to that funeral for you, to make sure it was your Jason. I only went for you." To his own ears, Quinn's righteous indignation sounded sincere.

The tension in Serena's face eased and she stepped away. "He was my Jason, you know. He was mine. Then he threw me over for that-that child. They were the perfect couple, and they had the perfect baby, and the perfect little life. Meanwhile, I had to scratch and claw and fight for everything."

You slept with the boss, and got everything handed to you on satin sheets. Your life story really yanks the heartstrings.

"I gave Jason everything!" The tension returned and Serena clutched her hands in fists. She started pacing. "I gave him everything he asked for. I never denied him. I gave him the abortion he wanted. He still left me for a younger model, someone who got to keep his baby." She paused, as if waiting for a reaction from Quinn.

He didn't dare breathe.

Her demeanor changed. "If only he hadn't run away from me." Her voice was soft, almost childlike. "I was on my way back from the Olympics, and I just wanted…" she wiped a tear from her eye. "I just wanted to talk to a friend, a sympathetic ear. But he was so cold. He offered me money, as if that was all I wanted from him." She bit her lip. "I didn't want to argue with him, I didn't. But he was so…it was like we'd never meant anything to each other. I got angry. I said things, horrible things. And then I felt horrible, so when I got home, I got on the first plane to Nashville and I came here to find him. I had to make things right."

Quinn watched her expression, her whole being, change as she told the story. It was if he was watching her entire life pass over her in a faint shadow.

"But he was gone. They were gone. He left me a letter, though, with his mother." Serena's face melted into a mask of remembered hope. "I held it for the longest time, it was my link to him. But then I opened it…"

"What was in the letter, Serena?" Too invested in the story, Quinn couldn't help himself.

She glared at him, her tears glittering ice. "Money. A cashier's check from Isabella's parents, made out to him, signed to me. No word, no clue where they'd gone, just the check. A pay off. Hush money. After everything we'd gone through together, it was as if everything I gave him had a price, and he could pay it with one check."

Her face settled into the hard, familiar mask. "I never cashed that check. I thought I'd save it for the day he came to his senses and came back to me. I still have it." She left her chair and walked into the bedroom. Returning a moment later, she handed him a slip of paper. "He never came back. She stole him from me."

Quinn couldn't keep the nagging question from his lips. "So, Serena, all that money you sent me for, why didn't you just cash this check? This is for way more than I ever got out of him." Quinn stared at the check and a sick thought dawned. "You didn't care about the cash…this was really all about revenge, wasn't it?"

"Revenge on him. Not on his parents. And that money there," she waved at Quinn, "none of that was his." Serena laughed, a high pitched, unsteady sound. "I spent years trying to find him, you know. He hid himself pretty well, but I found him. By that time I wanted to hurt him, like he'd hurt me. And, since money was what he cared about, I knew I had to take his money. I told him if he didn't give you the money I would tell everyone I left him because he was on steroids. It's been very chic, you know, getting Olympic level athletes to confess to steroid use. The public eats that sort of story up. Better yet, the skating community would review his wins, his medals. There would be hearings; there would be very, very public hearings. But mostly, Quinn darling, I simply told Jason if he didn't give you the money, I'd have him killed. It was a promise I'd made to him when he left me to skate with that little bitch. He knew if I could find him, I could kill him."

He felt uneasy. "You didn't need the money. When you married Burkes, you got everything you could ever dream of. Burkes loved you. Burkes gave you everything. You've reinvented yourself. You're the most powerful woman in Nashville."

"Burkes couldn't give me a gold medal." Serena hissed. The venom dripped off her words. "Burkes couldn't stop people from using my name as punch line when the topic of comical Olympic mishaps came up. Marrying Burkes couldn't give me the revenge I wanted. It only gave me the tools."

Her smile was more frightening than her words.

"So why send me to get the money? Jason could have wired it."

Serena continued to smile. The longer she did so, the more unsteady Quinn's stomach felt. "You know, Burkes taught me something very important."

"What was that?" Quinn's mouth was dry, as if he were sucking on cotton.

"He taught me never to do anything that didn't have a reason. 'In business Darlin', he'd say, 'in business, if you don't have a purpose for someone, cut 'em loose.' He must've said that a hundred times. 'With you by my side Darlin' I'm the most attractive man in Nashville.' I served his purpose. In return, he gave me everything. So he served my purposes, too." Serena sat down and poured herself another glass of orange juice. "You don't look so good, Quinn. Are you sick?"

"No, not really." His voice sounded strained.

"Well I'm sure you haven't had breakfast yet. Please, sit down and have something."

"I'm not hungry, Serena. So what kind of purpose did I serve for you?"

Serena sipped the juice and again the eerie smile crossed her face. "I had my reasons."

"Other than keeping me as a sex slave, what purpose could you possibly have?"

A shadow darkened her expression. "Don't be unpleasant Quinn."

"What was my purpose, Serena?"

"You served so much more than just my physical needs." She took a sip of juice, as if trying to rinse the sickly sweet tone from her voice. "They ruled Jason's death a suicide. His widow insists it was an accident, right?" The eerie smiled returned.

"I don't see how…" and like lightning, a thought left him breathless.

"Do you know who the last person was to see Jason Marks alive? Well, the last person anyone witnessed seeing him?" She licked a drop of orange juice from her lips. "I imagine it was someone very striking looking. Someone tall, handsome, perhaps. Someone who visited Jason at his place of business a couple times a year, but someone no one else knew. Someone Jason never talked about. A man of mystery."

She's trying to pin Jason's death on me?

"Someone stupid enough to show up at Jason's funeral. 'Who's that man?' the wives whisper to their husbands. 'Don't know, but he looks familiar,' the husbands whisper back. Then maybe there's a connection. Maybe one of the Admirals players has a quiet chat with one of the employees. The employee says, 'who was that guy, the tall one?' And, completely innocently, your name comes up. Later, the employee says, 'Wait, that's the guy that came to Jason's office. They met behind closed doors. And when he left, Jason didn't say a word. The night before he died, you talked to him, didn't you, Quinn? Probably waited for the shop to close, but someone was there. Someone saw you." She licked her lips. "And when he came to work the next morning…well, we know what happened then, don't we? Sure, you and I know Jason's death was simply the most exquisightly timed accident ever. But, to others, it might look different."

And she'd be successful. Quinn's stomach churned with the full realization of exactly how trapped he was.

"All you have to do is keep our arrangement as it is, and I'll protect you, as I always have."

Yeah, you've protected me from you. "Why are you doing this?"

Serena dabbed a napkin delicately to her mouth and set it down. "I have always hated losing. I lost everything because of Isabella Landry. It's her turn to lose." The cold light in her eyes froze Quinn's soul. "You want to save her life? You want to be her hero? Get her out of our lives."

Everything was very, very clear. "You won't get away with this." He stood.

"Shhh, Quinn." Serena stood and put a finger to his lips. "Of course I will. Of course, you'll keep your all access pass to hockey, and your status as a sports icon in this town. Nothing will change."

She can pin a murder on me. Not just an accident, a murder. All I have to do is cut Izzy completely out of my life, and I'll be safe. Quinn frowned. *Safe from what? From conviction in a murder I didn't commit. From public ridicule? None of that matters to me anymore. Izzy's all that matters.*

"You can go to hell with your threats, Serena. I'm done." Quinn took two quick steps to the door.

"That's your choice, of course." She paused. "Oh, one more thing, Quinn, dear."

"Yes?"

"I didn't kill her. Yet."

He straightened and swallowed his fear. "No, and you won't get the chance. That make up isn't covering the bit of skin you managed to leave in the locker room."

Serena laughed. "You think a little scratch is going to save your precious Izzy from me? Oh, Quinn, that's rich. I bet you think you're the only person I ever sent to harass Jason. I bet you think if you're no longer doing my dirty work for me, then no one will." She set her glass down and laughed again. "No, there's only one way you're going to be able to save Isabella Landry's life."

Her words and their sinister import hung between them like a storm cloud. Quinn swallowed back the fear that rose in him. He jerked open the door and fled the apartment.

Whatever it costs me, I will keep Izzy safe.

It will be the last act of a damned man.

TWENTY-EIGHT

He returned to his apartment and sat, unaware of the passage of time. So he was surprised when his elevator doors slid open and Izzy walked in.

"I thought you were coming right back? That was two days ago. What happened?"

Her tone was gentle. Her eyes were kind.

I don't have the strength to do this.

"Quinn? Are you okay?"

"I'm fine." He hated his gruff, angry tone.

"They let me leave without a sling." She took a couple steps closer. "I thought…I thought…"

"You thought what?" Quinn clenched his jaw and glared at her, trying to maintain a furious visage. Trying, and failing.

"Why do you look like that?"

Quinn ran his hands through his hair. *I'm doing this to save her life.* "You need to stay away from me. I mean it. I'm no good for you or anyone else."

She put a hand on his arm. He brushed it away. "What are you talking about? Of course you're good for me. You're good for a lot of people, so many people." She put her hand on his arm again, her gentle, innocent touch burning his skin. Quinn brushed her hand away again, this time with far more anger than he'd ever touched any woman.

"I'm warning you, Izzy, stay away from me." He didn't recognize his own voice. He stepped into the kitchen, the island stood as a solid barrier between them. "It's for your own good." The anger waned, leaving nothing but the echo of loss in his tone. His rage at Serena faded, and ceased to support him. He leaned on the island.

"You're being ridiculous."

"No, I'm not."

"Of course. You are a very good person." She smiled. "Look how many kids, how many families you've touched in such a wonderful, positive way. Look at this event we're working on." She took a step closer.

I have to do this. Until I figure out a better way to keep Serena from killing her, I have to do this. "You think I'm a good person."

"Yes, Quinn, yes. What it wrong with you?"

Quinn glared at her, his rage at his own impotence giving him the will to break the bond between them. "How good could I possibly be? I'm the reason you were left penniless when Jason died."

She blinked, then smiled, as if he'd just told her a joke she didn't quite understand. "What on earth are you talking about?"

"I'm the reason Jason cleaned out his bank accounts."

"That's not possible."

"I'm not the hero you think I am. I've done horrible things to those close to me. I'm the one who came to Jason's shop and I took his money."

Her eyes darkened, but she still looked unconvinced. "But...why? Why would you...how could you?"

Serena's words and her intentions flashed in Quinn's mind. "I was in Milwaukee a lot. I found out where Jason was. I told him..." the lie choked Quinn, "I told him that if he didn't pay up, I'd start making noise about the fact that he raped a minor, got her pregnant, and took her, against her parents' consent, across state lines. I told him I wouldn't stop there, that I'd start using words like 'steroids' and 'narcotics' in my sports casts when talking about skating greats of the past. I promised him I would destroy his past, present, and future if he didn't give me cash. I'm a very popular sports personality, Izzy. It would have been easy."

Izzy put a hand on the table, as if unable to keep herself steady. Her eyes were black, dead. "Why would you even care about Jason or about me?"

Quinn shrugged, attempted to be casual as, again, Serena's words came out of his mouth. "Jason had you. He had you and I wanted you more than I've ever wanted a woman."

Her face flushed. "This was all about sex?"

Quinn's stomach churned, and he ached to stop the charade and take her in his arms. "This was about destroying what stood in my way. This was about ownership." He closed his eyes, hating himself. *It's Sally all over again.* "This was about making very certain I got what I wanted. Once I found you again, I didn't let anything stand in my way. Nothing." He released this final word and he went cold.

Silence hung like a heavy curtain. Quinn leaned against the counter and stared at his shoes. *Please don't make me say one more word.*

"So what, you were at his funeral to do a victory lap? Pick up your trophy?"

He didn't respond. *Just curse me and leave. Go and be safe far away from me.*

"And the cash, the lottery ticket. That was what, to buy me?" *Damn you, Serena.*

"We lost the house, we lost everything." Her voice grew stronger, her anger heated her words. "I moved here on a prayer and a lottery ticket. Then I met you that night after I told off Adele."

Quinn squeezed his eyes tighter shut, willing the tears in. *The most beautiful coincidence in my life and it's become part of a twisted, revisionist memory.*

"I thought you were my friend. I fell for it all." Her laugh was a short, sharp bark. "Is this your idea of some sort of joke? Wait, are you drunk?"

Damn you, Serena!

"Baby, if I were drunk, you'd be a whole lot more naked and I'd be way less charming." The words stung as they left his mouth.

Her hand connected with his face so sharply, he thought she'd hit him with a tire iron. He locked eyes with her. He struggled not to wither beneath the fury in her gaze.

"I trusted you. I gave myself to you." Her voice was low. "Worse, my daughter, who loved her father, trusted you. No matter what you took from me, you took Jenna's father away from her." Izzy stormed to the elevator and punched the button. "Go to hell, Quinn Murray." She was gone.

I very well might.

***

It was quiet at Chances. *What's the use in trying to be good anymore? The only thing that mattered was Izzy, and she's out of my life for good.*

Quinn sat at the bar and stared blankly at the TV over Chance's head.

"Hey, Quinn, haven't seen you here in a while." Chance wiped the bar in front of Quinn and set a glass in front of him. "So, the usual?"

"Quiet night here, Chance."

Chance nodded and looked over the railing to the smattering of people downstairs. "It's early. I've got a band coming on at ten."

"What's he doing here?"

Chance followed Quinn's gaze. "Oh, Collier? He called me this afternoon. Said he was back from a terrible week in New York. Some Middle Ages themed restaurant or some such bull. Probably wanted to get discovered. Don't know why those indie music guys do that. This right here is Music City. This is where you come to get discovered."

"He wasn't in New York for that."

"Oh, you know him now? I wasn't aware you were friends."

"Not friends. He's my competition." *For a prize I've given up.*

Quinn dragged his gaze away from the stage and nodded toward the rows of bottles. "Make it the old usual, Chance. I'll get this party started the right way."

"Quinn, no."

Quinn glared at him. "I didn't stutter, did I?"

Chance reached for one of the bottles and set a shot glass in front of Quinn. He paused, the bottle hovering over the glass. "Are you sure about this?"

Quinn stubbed an angry finger into the scarred wood of the bar. "Set them up, Chance. It's been way too long."

Chance reluctantly poured a double bourbon. Quinn drained it with a single swallow. "Another."

Below them, Collier began to play a song on the piano. *Funny, I didn't realize he played the piano. Talented cuss.*

Quinn emptied the second glass as quickly as the first and pushed the glass toward Chance. "Another." He then turned his attention to Collier whose low, graveled voice was just loud enough to reach the upper level.

"Good evening, y'all." Collier didn't look at the audience. "My name is Collier James. I'm one third of the Terrible Troubadours."

Quinn felt a perverse pleasure that no one applauded. The third drink woke a corner of his brain long dormant. He found supreme humor in someone else's discomfort. Chance handed him a fourth, and this one Quinn carried to the balcony rail, the same spot where he'd seen Izzy that first night.

The irony was not lost on him.

"Anyway, I just got back from New York City."

Here a few of the sparse audience booed.

Collier raised a hand. "I know. I don't like that town any more than y'all do. It's dirty and it's cold. It's not like Nashville, which is home."

He's good. There are about nine people down there and he's taken them from boos to cheers.

"Anyway, while I was there, I wrote a song, and I wanted to see what the very discerning music listeners here in Nashville thought of it. My friend Chance was good enough to give me some time this evening." Collier stopped playing random chords on the piano and looked beyond the stage lights. "I hope you like it."

Quinn drank slowly, the bourbon started to melt into the corners of his brain. The lyrics of the song, framed by Collier's deep throated growl, spoke of love lost, loneliness, and the ache of longing. *Damn, he's good.*

Quinn waved his empty glass at a waitress, who wasted no time getting it filled. Sipping the drink, Quinn lost himself in the amber liquid and the song. *Good job, Collier, you nailed it right on the head. That's exactly how I feel at this precise moment. Like beautiful melodic shit.*

You, however, get to go to the coffee shop tonight where an unattached Izzy will finally be yours.

The song finished. Collier acknowledged the small audience. As he stood to leave the stage, he looked up and his gaze met Quinn's. Quinn raised his glass to Collier and nodded. *You've won by default, but you still won.*

***

Izzy stormed up the stairs and slammed her door. She fell on the bed and buried her face in the pillows. *Quinn, how could you have done this?*

How could you have been such a good liar?

Her tears burned as they wet the linen pillowcases. Her arm and shoulder ached, reminding her too much of the woman who attacked her. *I need a drink.*

She sat up, wiped the tears from her eyes, and stared out the window. "The one time in my life I want a drink. I don't have a drop in this place."

She didn't want one drink; she wanted to blot out the last two days completely.

Wait. I have the bottles of wine from Quinn's place.

She slipped off the bed and went to the cabinet where she found the three bottles of pinot noir. She pulled out the first bottle and stared at it, remembering the night they shared his bed, feeling his hands on her, his lips.

I was a fool again. I was blinded by a nice smile and good hands. Again.

She poured herself a glass. *Ice.* Her freezer held two things: a bag of pizza rolls and a large chunk of ice that had once been a bag of cubes, but, thanks to a power outage one afternoon, was now one very large cube.

Izzy grabbed a butter knife and chiseled off a handful of chips. She dropped them in the wine and drank deeply. *Here's to forgetting everything; Jason, Quinn, skating, everything, once and for all.*

***

How he got on stage, Quinn had no idea. *Why is it I can never remember anything when I'm drinking?*

Doesn't matter. This band sucks and I'm going to get them off the stage so everyone will feel like partying again. That'll make Chance happy, and since he's made me happy, I should return the favor.

The minute he stepped on stage, the crowd recognized him. The cheers were genuine. Quinn shot a bleary glance at Chance, who stared at him from the balcony with a mixture of concern and avarice.

Dance, Monkey, dance. Give the crowd what they want. Sing a song, party all night, slam that guy into the boards.

Ruin some guy's life. Help get him murdered. Screw the Boss on demand.

Give up any chance of happiness.

"Ladies and gentlemen, the band you paid to see sucks." He gave the lead singer a shove. The crowd roared in approval as the band left the stage.

Quinn stared into the blinding spotlight. "Excellent. Now we can really party."

Again the crowd roared. "Okay, now, remember, I'm not a singer, but I can do better than those jokers. Ladies, if you're very, very good, I might even take off my shirt. And guys? You're welcome."

Dance Monkey, dance.

Everything faded to black.

***

Izzy sat on her bed, staring blankly at the movie she'd stuck in the DVD player. She poured herself a third glass of wine and drank it more slowly than the first two.

A gladiator movie with lots of dead, bloody guys in it is perfect for me. If only I had a sword...something...to plunge deep into his heart. Make him feel the way I do.

Her glass emptied, Izzy climbed out of the bed and headed to the kitchenette. *One more glass and I'll go to sleep and forget...everything.*

She stared at the screen again, in a moment when the bloodied gladiator somehow became a romantic hero. *Nope, not perfect anymore.* She pushed a button on the remote and the screen went dark.

Draining her glass again, Izzy headed for the kitchen and a second bottle. She poured the wine with an unsteady hand, and an even weaker resolve. Quinn's image, his beautiful eyes pleading, flashed through her mind. *How can I possibly forget how much I love him?*

Izzy closed her eyes and heard, again, his last words, the words that explained Jason's death once and for all, the words that broke her heart. She emptied her glass quickly in a vain attempt to drown out his words, the cold tone of his voice.

How could I possibly love anyone so cruel and selfish?

She filled her glass once more and took unsteady steps to her bed. *It's too quiet.*

She pawed through her small pile of CDs and found the one Collier gave her. *Perfect. Sad sailing songs.*

She put the CD into the player, turned on the music, and floated on a river of heartbreak and pinot noir.

TWENTY-NINE

Sunlight burned through his eyelids. He eased one eye open, and closed it immediately. *How the devil did I get home?*

Summoning every bit of strength, Quinn sat up. His head spun, he was dangerously close to a serious bout of the dry heaves. A strange grinding noise in the kitchen caught the attention of his percussive brain, and he got out of bed. *Someone had no trouble stripping me naked.*

He grabbed his sweat pants and pulled them on. "Who's there?"

The noise stopped for a moment and Quinn thought he'd imagined it. Then the scraping and banging sound continued.

He lurched into the kitchen. *Serena. I should have known.*

"Good morning." She waved a plate under his nose. "I made you another breakfast, in case you're still hungry."

Bile bubbled in his throat. "Still hungry? I'm not hungry. How...how did..."

Serena set two plates of eggs on the table. "Don't you remember? Of course you don't. You don't remember anything when you're drinking."

"I don't remember you being anywhere near me."

"I suppose not. Your friend Chance called me while you were performing."

Performing what? Wait. I was singing. I got on stage and was singing.

Wonder if I was any good.

"I was really unhappy when he told me you'd been up to your old tricks again. But then I remembered you can be more fun when you're partying than when you aren't. Which is impressive, given how fun you can be sober."

Quinn's stomach churned again. *What did I think was going to happen? I had to protect Izzy. This is the trade off.*

"Oh, you sang quite the set, my dear. Brought down the house. And then you and I...well..." she nodded to the bedroom. "I'm not sure which I like better...sober Quinn who worships me, or dirty, nasty, drunk Quinn." She pulled out a chair and pointed to it. "Now, let's have breakfast. Actually, this is your second breakfast. You ate a mess of eggs and mushrooms a couple hours ago."

His stomach roiled at the smell of the eggs. "I'm not eating this."

"Suit yourself. You do have to be to the station in a couple hours, so you might want to at least drink some coffee."

Quinn rubbed his eyes. *I don't remember eating breakfast.* "Fine, I'll eat." Quinn slammed himself into a chair and stared at the plate. *This is what hell feels like.*

"Now, on today's show I'd like you to be extra complimentary to the front office of the Titans."

"Why?"

"Let's say I owe someone in that group a favor."

I can't do this. I can't do this. I can't do this. Quinn leaned back, his head pounding. "Where do I fit in your plans?"

"What do you mean?"

"Is this my next project? Say nice things on the radio so you can marry another rich old guy?"

Serena blinked, as if hearing an idea for the first time. "You're being ridiculous."

"Am I?" He poked a fork at the eggs. "Because a couple of days ago you attacked an innocent woman because she was spending time with me. Now I have to say nice things about a guy so you can land another ancient, impotent man? Am I supposed to just be shackled to you forever, while you amass a stack of dead husbands?"

"First of all, anything that happened to your little friend is your fault and you know it." Serena lifted a glass of orange juice, took a sip, and set it down carefully. "Second of all, you know you're free to go any time you want to. This has never been a prison. It's been an agreement, with a promise. You can leave me any time you'd like. Of course, there are things I am free to do as well." She smiled at him.

"Such as?"

"I can release the pictures of you and Sally and that car accident"

"And in return, I can tell the world how you blackmailed Jason Masters to torment his wife." The argument was weak, but Quinn hoped Serena would crumble if she got some push back from him. "Some might draw a line from that to his sudden death."

Serena smiled coldly. "No one can draw any lines that don't lead right to you. Besides, the footage I have from last night would be enough to destroy your good standing with the fine charitable folks who think you're so wonderful."

His heart sank. "Last night? What footage?"

"You were magnificent."

How bad could anything I did last night be? I wound up here, with Serena. He closed his eyes and saw his future with Serena. A foul taste rose in his mouth.

He sipped some coffee. *Izzy is lost to me. There's no point in protecting anything else.* The black liquid was bitter in his mouth. "Serena, you win."

"Now what are you talking about?"

Quinn stood, ignoring the pounding in his head. "I can't live like this. I can't do this anymore."

"That's not what you said last night."

His body felt filthy. He held his hands out and stared at them. *Everything is gone, except the last tiny shred of self respect.* "You don't need me anymore. Jason is dead. Izzy is..." he stopped.

Serena tapped a fork against her lips. "Isabella is what, Quinn?"

"She's not Isabella Landry anymore, that's the point. She's a waitress. She's living here because she has no place else to go, she has nothing. You ruined her completely. She's just living here and working to be close to her daughter."

The ice cold glare on Serena's face reminded Quinn he was an idiot to mention anything about Izzy and Jason's child.

"You'd like to think that, wouldn't you? You'd like for me to say you and I are over, and then you can go running back to her and then what have I gained? Then she still wins because she gets you."

"I won't be running back to her, believe me. She wants nothing to do with me. After what I told her, I'm lucky she hasn't called the police." He sighed. "You don't want me. You don't want a washed up hockey player with a terrible reputation. Did you like getting me from the bar? Was I charming and wonderful?"

I may have been. I have no idea.

"You were, until we got back here." Serena's voice was distant. "Then we got here and you opened a bottle of wine, which I thought was nice, but you kept trying to put ice in mine. Plus, you were sweating and stinking of bourbon. That wasn't pleasant."

Oh yes, I'm the romantic hero. "Serena, I'm not what you want. I was tool. One you no longer need. You've won. I'll leave Nashville. I won't make trouble for you. Izzy's no threat to you. She's nobody. I'm nobody. You win."

Serena seemed not to hear his plea. "You know, our eggs are cold and I forgot the mushrooms again. You want more of those mushrooms right?"

"Sure, I guess. Whatever."

"I have a few fresh ones left; I picked them up yesterday, right before Chance called me. See, I do remember important things about you." She took the plates away, reheated the eggs, and lightly sautéed some mushrooms. Returning, she set the plate in front of him. "Let's have one more breakfast together, for old times."

"Are these morels?"

"I know they're your favorite," she nodded. "Go ahead, eat. Then do your show."

"And then?"

"You may be right. Other than being very pretty on my arm, you can't do much for me socially. I have goals." Her eyes lost their hard glitter, and she almost looked gentle. "Maybe I should free up my schedule to find my next husband."

Quinn stared at her as he ate. The cheerful expression on her face never wavered, never faded. It made him uncomfortable. "I've finished." He held up the plate.

"Good. Now, get some clothes on. You're on the air in an hour."

Quinn dressed quickly, but not as quickly as Serena. She waited for him at the elevator. They rode downstairs in silence and walked to her car, parked in his space.

"I'll drop you off at the station."

"You're not going to the office?"

"No, not today." She sounded wistful as she turned the key in the ignition. "I have business outside the office today. But you," she faced him while the engine idled, "are on your own getting your car from Chances."

Quinn nodded, his throat tightening. "No problem."

"Quinn," she said softly as she patted his cheek with cold fingers. "We'll keep each other's secrets, won't we?"

Quinn's stomach tossed at the idea that he might actually be free. "Of course."

"I suppose then I could be gracious."

Relief washed over him. "Are you serious?"

"Yes, I'm serious. Now go. Enjoy your life." She leaned over and kissed his cheek. "What's left of it," she whispered so quietly, Quinn wasn't certain he'd heard her.

Quinn remained silent in his elation for the duration of the ride to the station. He left Serena's car without a backward glance. Inside, Benny was waiting for him.

"Geez Quinn, you look like hell. What did you and Boss Lady do last night?"

How could I look bad? I've just been freed from prison. "I actually feel pretty awesome right now, Benny. Why, what's going on?"

Benny nodded to the TV monitor in the corner of the studio. "It's all over the local gossip reports."

Quinn glared at the monitor. A cheerful female reporter chirped, "Has former NHL Bad Boy Quinn Murray returned to his partying ways? Last night, at a local club, Nashville's favorite party animal, Murray treated club goers to an impromptu serenade."

Someone had a camera phone and Serena no doubt made sure the clip got to the television station. "Turn that off."

Benny reached up to turn off the screen when images of a car crash flashed on. "What the hell?" Quinn stared at the monitor, his heart sinking.

Sally.

"Murray has been a model citizen since this car crash more than three years ago, which he survived, but in which his assistant, Sally Meyers, and the unborn child Murray was expecting with Meyers, were killed. Returning to his partying ways last night, Murray had to be helped off the stage by his longtime friend, local businesswoman Serena Shipley-Chapmen."

"I should have known it would never be over." Anger flared in Quinn's chest.

Benny turned off the TV. "Why would they mention that car crash?"

"I was responsible. I was driving the car."

"No, you weren't."

There was something in Benny's voice that broke through Quinn's anger. "I know what the official police reports said, and I know what everyone believes. But the fact is I was driving. And I…" he swallowed hard, "I was responsible for what happened to Sally and our baby."

Benny looked puzzled. "Are we talking about the same crash, or were you in one I'm not aware of?"

"What do you mean?"

Benny stared at him. "You really don't remember?"

What was there to remember? "No, I was drinking that night."

"Geez, Dude." Benny slumped in his chair. "You mean all this time you thought you were responsible for that crash? Quinn, you weren't even in the car. We were in the car behind hers when she spun out and hit those trees."

Quinn's head started spinning. He closed his eyes, trying to ward off the dizziness. "What? What are you saying to me?"

"Normally Sally was your driver. Boss Lady hand-picked her for the job. But that night you called me to come get you. You and Sally had a huge fight at Second Chances."

We had a fight?

"Sally was alone in the car."

Sally was alone in the car. Nausea washed over Quinn. "But I went to the hospital…I remember that."

Benny nodded. "Yeah, I took you there because you had be super hero guy, even in your completely blotted state. You tried getting her out of the door and got some pretty decent burns on your hands and arms."

Quinn held his hands up and stared at them as if seeing them for the first time. *I didn't get these from the accident…I was trying to save Sally?*

"And you're going to have to explain something else to me. Why does anyone think she was pregnant with your baby." Benny shook his head. "That's not even close to the truth."

"She wasn't pregnant?"

"Oh, she was pregnant, just not with your baby. Quinn, you never touched her."

"No, Benny, we had an affair."

"Quinn, you were drinking a lot back then. A lot. Do you even remember Sally?"

Quinn closed his eyes and tried to recall what the girl looked like. No face came to mind. *I can't even remember her face? What kind of monster am I?*

"The day Boss Lady hired her you said that Sally was the spitting image of your sister. 'Good,' you said, 'at least I know I won't be tempted to bang her.' Don't you remember any of that?"

The room felt off balance. Everything he knew as truth shifted. The haze cleared. "I don't…I don't remember much from those days. I certainly don't remember any of it that way."

"Sally's boyfriend got her pregnant. She told me one night that Boss Lady told her to keep quiet about it. So why would anyone know about the baby, plus think it was yours?"

Yes, Serena, why would they think that?

And why I am sweating? I'm freezing. Quinn wiped his head with his forearm. The room spun around him. "Is it cold in here?"

Benny shook his head. "Are you sick?"

Quinn closed his eyes, the spinning stopped. "No, I'm okay. But Benny, we've worked together for years. How could you not say anything?"

Benny shrugged. "Dude, you didn't want to talk about any of it. Right after that, you got sober and started having your thing with Boss Lady and no one even breathed Sally's name. It was like she never existed."

"But I wasn't in the car? And that baby wasn't mine?"

"I swear to it."

Quinn shivered, then stilled as his vision blurred. "Are you sure it's not cold in here?"

"No. Quinn? Quinn?"

The room spun out of control, then went black.

THIRTY

Sunlight brushed across Izzy's face. Gingerly, she eased her eyes open. An empty wine bottle stared at her from the nightstand. Her head pounded with a relentless beat. She struggled to sit and froze in place, waiting for the room to stop spinning. Slowly, she turned and put her feet to the floor. Certain that the floor was steady beneath her, Izzy stood and took tentative steps toward the bathroom. *How much wine did I drink?*

The empty wine bottle on the kitchen table was her silent reminder. *Oh, right.*

She searched the medicine cabinet. "How do I not have aspirin?" She rubbed her temples and tried to will away the shattering pain in her head.

Cat has some downstairs. I'll get some aspirin and maybe a roll.

Her stomach protested the thought of food.

Okay, just aspirin, and a quiet death.

Once outside her door, each step on the creaking wood floors sent tremors of agony from her feet to her brain. Her vision blurred at the top of the stairs. *Maybe I'll skip the aspirin. I'll just die here.*

Hushed voices floated on a sweet aura of coffee to her. *That sounds like Collier.*

Her curiosity was stronger than her hangover. Izzy crept down the steps to the doorway to eavesdrop.

"I can't believe what you're telling me, Cat. Geez, I was gone for a week."

"Poor Iz. You'd think Quinn could have been a bit more sympathetic. I mean, she wouldn't have been in that rink if he hadn't asked her to skate for his charity thing. Then she gets beat up and he picks that moment to ditch her."

"You sure he didn't beat her up?"

"Don't be stupid. He was in Canada. Besides, Izzy said it was some woman."

"Well, he got what he wanted out of her, so he was done with her anyway."

"What do you mean?"

"She and Quinn did it. And then he threw her over. It's what he does."

"For a poet, you sort of suck at words. They made love?"

"If you want to call it that."

"You're taking it well. I figured you'd be one to storm around."

"I did my storming around earlier." Collier cleared his throat. "I was stuck in some airport bar, waiting for my flight, and this woman comes up to me and starts talking to me. I sort of got to vent all over her."

"Ah, very Blanche Dubois of you, relying on the kindness of strangers."

"That's a movie person isn't it?"

"Geez, Col. You'd be the perfect man for me if you had one shred of interest in movies, do you realize that? Then you and I could be having a very nice post whoopee conversation in my bed instead of licking our lonely wounds here at the crack of dawn."

"And you'd be the perfect woman for me…you know."

"You know it's hopeless, right? She's in love with Quinn."

"After what I saw last night, I'm not sure she will be."

"Why?"

"Quinn was at Second Chances last night. Drinking."

"Are you sure?"

"Very. He sat in the balcony while I did my set, then he sort of, I don't know, raised a glass to me when I left the stage."

"Raised a glass?"

"Like a toast. I thought about going up and finding out what the deal was, but I wasn't ready to have polite conversation with him."

"You've been in love with her a long time, haven't you?"

"Our whole lives. I thought this time I had a chance. But then she had to go and…I said some really rotten things to her. Even with Quinn turning bastard on her, it's doubtful she'll forgive me."

"Don't crap on Quinn just yet. He's been a really stand up guy since Izzy's been around. Maybe you didn't see what you think you saw."

"I saw what I saw, Cat. He's partying again, and you know his history."

"I know what I've seen now. They had a fight. She played your weepy songs all night. I heard her chipping away at that iceberg she keeps in her freezer."

"So she was drinking wine."

"I don't expect her up any time soon, if the number of times she chiseled ice is in proportion to the number of glasses of wine she downed."

"Well surprise to you, Cat." Unable to stay out of the conversation any longer, Izzy stepped off the final stair and squinted at the light in the kitchen. "I'm up."

"Are you okay?"

Izzy managed to send a glare in Collier's general direction. "I'll be okay after a fistful of aspirin and your strongest coffee, Cat."

Cat nodded. "Sure. Go sit in a comfy chair by the TV and I'll get you something."

"Thanks." Izzy left the kitchen and went to the television room. There was no one in the room, but the huge television was on, tuned to the local news.

"Izzy," Collier followed her.

"Not now. I'm really not up to it."

"I didn't know about someone attacking you."

"How could you?" She sank into the ancient armchair closest to the television, and focused on the screen. "You were very busy feeling sorry for yourself."

"That's not fair. No one called me."

Izzy closed her eyes. "It's been sort of a hellish couple days. You'll have to excuse me if I don't feel up to being that fair to you."

"What the hell?" Collier's tone changed. "Can't this guy stay out of any minute of my life?"

"Yes, it's all about you all the time."

"Open your eyes. Quinn is on the news."

Izzy focused on the big screen where Quinn was leaning on a woman's shoulder outside Second Chances. "Turn up the sound."

" 'After performing a few songs onstage at local music club 'Second Chances' Murray had to be helped off the stage by long time friend, local businesswoman Serena Shipley-Chapman.'"

Izzy blanched. "That's the woman."

"What's the woman?" Cat set a cup of coffee on the table next to Izzy's elbow.

"Look," Collier punched the DVR button on the remote. "That woman, Izzy?"

"That's the one. That's the woman who attacked me."

"Are you sure?" Collier's voice was tight.

"Yes. That's the woman that dislocated my arm in the locker room."

"But that can't be."

Both women stared at Collier. "Why not?" Izzy didn't understand his reaction. "You look like you've seen a ghost."

"That can't be Serena Shipley Chapman."

"I thought she seemed familiar. It's got to be Serena, if that's Serena and that's the woman who attacked me."

"No, no. Serena Shipley Chapman has red hair. She's famous for it. Almost as famous for her hair as she is for anything else. That woman has…dark hair."

"She must've had it colored. The news wouldn't get something like that wrong." Cat took the remote and replayed the clip. "Why does it matter anyway what color her hair is?"

Collier stood up and paced in front of the television. "The woman…in the bar."

"And?" Cat's face blanched, confusing Izzy even more.

"I was at a bar when I called you. And I was…well, I'm sure a lot of people heard my end of the conversation." Collier paused in his pacing and set horrified eyes on Izzy. "There was a woman there, and she was so nice, so sympathetic. I told her everything."

Izzy's stomach twisted. "What do you mean, 'everything'?"

"I told her about you and about Quinn and about the charity event and how you're having this huge homecoming in Nashville. I even told her…I even told her where you were practicing." He spoke little louder than a whisper, and didn't look at her.

"You said all this to Serena Shipley-Chapman?"

Without taking his eyes away from Izzy, Collier answered Cat. "If the woman right there," he pointed to the television screen, "is truly Serena, then yes, I told Serena Shipley Chapman about you and Quinn. But that doesn't mean she's the one who attacked you, Izzy. Seriously, how would you not recognize her?"

"You sure didn't." Cat grumbled, drawing a glare from Collier. "And you saw a whole lot more clearly than Izzy did."

"She and I never really met. Coach didn't want me around her bad influence, especially after Jason…" Izzy sank deeper in the armchair. "Now I'm really confused."

Collier slumped onto the nearby sofa. "Why would she change her hair color?"

"She's talking about Quinn, idiot." Cat punched Collier's shoulder.

"At the hospital, he kissed me and said he loved me. Yesterday, he was supposed to pick me up and he didn't, so I went to his place. He told me," Izzy shook her head, "he told me he made Jason drain our bank accounts because he wanted me for himself."

"What?" Cat and Collier shouted in unison.

"I wanted to call the police."

"Why didn't you?"

"Well, because I drank a couple bottles of wine instead. But now, things just don't add up," Izzy bit her lip. "If he wanted me bad enough to destroy my husband and trick me into coming to Nashville, why would he wait until a few days ago to…you know?"

Collier grimaced. "If Quinn Murray wants the woman, he gets the woman. If he was truly willing to destroy Jason to have you, he wouldn't have waited an hour, much less almost a year."

"You know, I did have some say in it."

Cat and Collier looked at each other and laughed. "You clearly don't grasp his reputation. But let's retrace the steps: You guys have the big thing, then you're attacked by his boss, who might also be his girlfriend. Then he tells you he loves you. Then he gives you some huge story about how he's the one who made Jason give him all your money. Does anyone else see a gigantic gap in the sequence?"

"It sounds more like he realized Serena attacked you and now he's trying to protect you by keeping you as far away from him as possible."

"But why would Serena want to attack me?"

"Maybe she blames you for losing a gold medal." Collier looked at both women. "She and Jason were partners, after all. Plus, the rumors about them as a couple were pretty juicy."

"My mother mentioned that." Izzy tried to recall Dollie's words. "They had to pay him a ton of money to clear up some debts he had because of Serena."

"Now she and Quinn are together, according to the news, and you and Quinn are together, according to you. Maybe she sees this as you stealing yet something else from her." Collier blanched. "Which means…"

"Which means, genius, your little meltdown in New York sent a murderously jealous woman straight to Izzy. I'm betting Quinn made a deal with Serena, where he had to break Izzy's heart just to protect her. Well done." She patted Collier on the back.

Collier brushed away Cat's hand and knelt next to Izzy. "I'm so sorry. I had no idea. I was just so…I was so angry that you didn't choose me. Again."

Izzy's anger melted in pool of penitence in Collier's eyes. "Don't worry about, I'll mend. And as for Quinn..." Izzy looked back at the screen. "He went home with her last night, didn't he?"

Collier sat next to her. "He doesn't look that happy about it."

"He might be more than unhappy." Cat hit a few more buttons. "Look at his face as that hag lady is dragging him away. Read his lips."

Izzy stared at Quinn, at his flushed face, his dead eyes. His expression was difficult to look at, but the words he was saying were easy to read.

Where's Izzy?

Izzy stared at the screen, silent. Collier and Cat said nothing.

"Mom, you left your phone in the car." Jenna walked in, holding Izzy's cell. "You've missed like twenty calls. What's everyone looking at? Is that Quinn?"

Izzy nodded to her daughter, still numb from what she was watching on the screen. "Yes."

"I heard he put on quite the show last night at Chances."

Her phone rang. "Hello? I'm sorry, what's your name? Benny?" Izzy glanced at the others, looking for a clue as to who was calling her. Cat's eyes widened. "Benny, slow down. What? When? Okay, yes, I'll be there in fifteen minutes." She ended the call.

"Was that Benny Jensen, the producer at WNSH?" Cat asked.

Izzy nodded. "I'm Quinn's emergency contact. He collapsed at the station a couple hours ago. Benny said he was fine, then he got pale, and dizzy. He threw up and had some sort of convulsion."

Jenna jangled her keys. "I'll drive."

"Can I do anything?"

Cat grinned at Collier. "I don't know. Does Izzy have any other enemies? You could just bring them all in here at once."

"I said I was sorry."

"Stop it you two. You guys have to call the police for me." Izzy paused at the door and shook her head at Jenna who gave her a quizzical look. "Tell them to match the hair and skin they got from me against anything they have on Serena Shipley-Chapman. Collier, tell them about your conversation in New York. Ask for that Detective Emerson, the one who was with me at the hospital."

The drive across town to the hospital was endless. *Quinn has to be okay.* Izzy closed her eyes and pictured him the way she saw him last. *He said horrible things about himself, things that could not possibly be true. How could I have believed any of it?*

It was Serena who attacked me. It was probably Serena who blackmailed Jason. She thought, again, of the night so many years ago when Jason woke her, put her in a car, and drove her to Wisconsin. *He was afraid of Serena. He was trying to protect the baby and me from Serena.*

Just like Quinn did yesterday.

"Mom, here, I'll drop you off at the door. I'll park the car and catch up with you." Jenna nudged her.

Izzy climbed out of the car and walked into the emergency room. There was a stout man near the admitting desk. "I'm Izzy Marks. Are you Benny?"

"Yes, ma'am." The man looked at her with frightened eyes. "How do you know Quinn? He's never mentioned your name before."

Izzy managed a week smile. "I work at his favorite Waffle House."

Benny returned her smile. "Then you're the one."

"The one?"

"Here, sit down. They said they'd call when he was…when he could have visitors." Benny led her to the chairs. "See, I've wondered for a long time what was different about him lately. He seemed happy. He hasn't been happy since Sally died."

Sally? Who's Sally?

"I'll explain later," Benny patted her hand. "That's the longer version of the story, and we don't have time for it. You must be the one, though, that's made him happy."

"I guess. But we…we broke up yesterday."

Benny nodded. "And that would explain Chances. It's been a long time since he went on a bender. I've seen him look rough, but nothing like this morning." Benny paled at the memory. "Why did you guys break up, if you don't mind me asking?"

Izzy shook her head. "I was willing to believe something horrible about him."

"A lot of people make that mistake, Miss Izzy. Outside of being a complete party animal when he's drinking, he's a really decent guy." Benny's eyes welled.

A nurse walked up to Izzy. Her name tag read Grace Callen. "You're Mr. Murray's emergency contact?"

"Yes. Can I see him now?"

Grace shook her head. "Let's just say that in cases like this, it's best if you wait until he's a bit more presentable. How are you related to Mr. Murray?"

If I'm not family they won't let me in. "I'm his sister." She ignored Benny's surprised expression.

Grace nodded. "The doctor has some questions, family history, that sort of thing."

Why did I say I was family? I don't know anything about his family history.

Another nurse stuck her head out of the big doors. "Is this Mr. Murray's family?"

"Yes." Grace didn't look up from her chart.

"She can come in."

Izzy followed Grace through the heavy automatic doors and down the hall to yet another closed door. Grace nodded to the door, which Izzy pushed open slowly, unable to completely absorb the scene in front of her. Quinn lay motionless in a bed, machines beeping in an ominous circle around him. A breathing tube pumped air into his lungs.

"You're his sister?" A doctor stood behind her, and put a hand on her shoulder.

"Yes...I'm...Izzy Marks."

"I'm Dr. Blanche Passavant." The doctor pulled the mask off her face. "I couldn't care less who you are to him, if you can help me. You were his only emergency contact."

Izzy exhaled. "What's wrong with him?"

The woman checked the bank of monitors over Quinn's head. "I was hoping you'd be able to help me with that, Miss Marks."

"I don't...I haven't seen him since...I talked to him yesterday morning. I don't know what he's done since then."

"From what Mr. Jensen told us, and from what we saw when they brought him in, my initial diagnosis was alcohol poisoning."

"He doesn't drink."

"He did last night." Dr. Passavant studied her closely. "He presents with all the classic symptoms: Vomiting, seizures, slowed breathing, cold skin. Mr. Jensen said he seemed very confused about his recent history. Something about a Sally?"

"There's a lot of confusion about that, Doctor."

"Even so, everything fits in with alcohol poisoning. Except for one thing."

"Which is?"

"Which is a fever, When he came in with chilled skin I thought it was hypothermia, another symptom of alcohol poisoning. But he's got a hundred and four degree temperature. That's why you're here."

Izzy couldn't take her eyes off of Quinn. His chest barely moved, and there was little else about him that gave any indication of life. "What can I do?"

"If this is some other form of poison, something he maybe ate or drank in the last twelve hours or so, that's something we have to know as soon as possible."

Izzy closed her eyes. *She's going to ask the next question. I couldn't answer it when it was Jason. How can I possibly answer it now that it's Quinn?*

"Has Mr. Murray been depressed lately?"

Izzy bit her lip and recalled the last words she uttered to him. *I told him to go to hell. He told me he loved me, that I should hang on to that no matter what else I heard, and I told him to go to hell.*

"Miss Marks?"

"I'm sorry. I was thinking of the last time we spoke. We had an argument."

Doctor Passavant closed her chart. "Miss Marks, I don't have time to be coy. I know Mr. Murray was fired. The radio station had a press conference this morning. So he's out of a job and you and he had an argument. Could he be depressed about that?"

There was too much for Izzy to comprehend. "I don't know. Two days ago I would never think it possible." She watched Quinn, searching for any flickering sign of hope. "Doctor, please, can I just stay here, with him, for a minute?"

The doctor smiled empathetically. "There's a chair right there. If you're chilled, there are blankets in the cupboard there. You can stay as long as you like."

"Thank you."

"I've got nurses outside monitoring everything. If you need anything, if you think of anything, let Nurse Callen know. She'll contact me."

"Thank you." Izzy took a step toward the chair. "Oh, Doctor?"

"Yes?"

"If this was an accident, what would...do this?"

Dr. Passavant tapped her pen against her mouth. "My bet, if this was truly accidental, is something he would have ingested late last night or early this morning. If you can think of anyone who ate a meal with him that would really be good. We're running a toxicology screen on him, but those take time. Time is the one thing we just don't have."

Izzy nodded. "I can't think of anyone right now, but maybe Mr. Jensen. Let me talk to him, and I'll come right back."

She hustled down the corridor to the waiting room. "Benny!"

Benny looked up from his quiet conversation with Jenna. "Miss Izzy?"

"Who would Quinn have eaten with last night? Dinner…breakfast?"

Benny shrugged. "No clue about dinner. He was at Chances until late and Boss Lady took him home."

"What about breakfast?"

"Quinn doesn't breakfast with anyone. It's his rule. Women don't stay over." Benny lowered his eyes. "Sorry, Miss Izzy."

Geez, Southern manners! Give me some Midwestern blunt talk right now! "Benny, never mind that. Last night, would Quinn have gone anyplace after Chances?"

"Doubtful. Chances was always sort of his last stop."

"Serena took him from Chances. Dragged him, Mike said," Jenna offered.

Izzy nodded. "So would Serena have taken him home, and made him breakfast?"

"Serena Shipley Chapman? Make breakfast for anyone?" Benny almost smiled. "No, not likely. She doesn't like to get her hands dirty."

"What are you getting at, Mom?"

"They think Quinn poisoned himself. Either with alcohol, or on purpose with something else. We need to find what he's eaten in the last twelve hours."

"I could go to his apartment and look around, if you'd like?"

Izzy smiled for the first time in hours. "You can get into his apartment? I'd go, but I don't want to leave."

Benny nodded. "His doorman knows me."

"I'll go with you, Mr. Jensen."

"Please, call me Benny, Miss Jenna."

"Jenna, text me when you find anything, okay? I can't have my cell on in the room, but I'll check as often as I can."

"Okay." Jenna hugged her and followed Benny out the door.

Izzy returned to Quinn's room where nothing looked better. She inched the chair closer to the bed and slipped her hand through the bedrails. His skin was chilled, warming only where the heat of her trembling fingers brushed him. She covered his cold hand with hers and closed her eyes.

She didn't remember falling asleep, but Izzy woke to numerous alarms. Nurses raced in and shoved her to the edge of the room, where she watched, horrified and helpless, and Quinn convulsed and vomited blood. Izzy buried her face in her hands and prayed for the anguish to end. Dr. Passavant strode in, concern tightening her face. She caught Izzy's eye, but the calm empathy was gone. "Get her out of here!"

Without further word, Nurse Callen hustled her out. As the door hissed behind her, Izzy wandered down the corridor, to the waiting room. She stood, unable to focus on any point in the room.

"Miss Izzy?" It was Benny, holding a hand out to her.

"Benny. Jenna."

"Mom, what's happened?"

Izzy shook her head. "It's bad. He's convulsed again. He's vomiting blood."

Benny sank into a nearby chair. Jenna bit her lip and put an arm around Izzy's shoulders. "Mom, I don't know if this going to help, but Benny and I found this at Quinn's apartment." She held up her phone.

Izzy studied the picture for a moment. "I don't think I've ever seen anything like it before. What is it?"

"We aren't sure. Benny thought some kind of mushroom, since we found a few in a sauté pan, but these on the counter are raw. You know how Quinn is about eggs and mushrooms."

Izzy squared her shoulders. "I have to go back in there and show the doctor this. "

"Are you sure, Mom? Can you go back in there?"

"I have to." She put a hand on the door just as Grace Callen pushed it open. "Oh, Sorry, Miss Marks. I came out to give you an update on Mr. Murray."

Izzy swallowed the lump in her throat. "Okay."

"We've stabilized him, but he's unconscious."

Izzy's knees weakened, but Benny and Jenna were there on either side of her, before she fell. "Okay."

"Miss Marks, we're doing everything possible right now. It would help if we knew what he ingested."

Izzy held up the cell phone. "Do you know what this is?"

Grace frowned at the picture. "I haven't seen those since I was a girl." She squinted at the picture more closely. "No. Wait. Does Mr. Murray go mushroom hunting?"

Izzy shot at glance at Benny who shook his head vehemently. "No."

"I'll be right back." She left the three of them staring at the closing doors in stunned silence.

Jenna and Benny returned to the chairs while Izzy paced in front of them. "This has to be an accident, right? Who would want to hurt Quinn?"

The same person who carried a grudge for twenty years. "You guys didn't touch anything at Quinn's, did you?" Izzy pulled her cell phone out of her pocket and dialed.

"No, just took pictures. Looked like it was breakfast for two, which is very weird." Benny shook his head.

Izzy dialed her cell and waved a hand to quiet them. "Detective Emerson? This is Izzy Marks. I think someone tried to poison Quinn Murray, and I think it's connected to what happened to me. There's evidence in his kitchen, something I think the police should handle. The doorman will let you in. Thank you. I'll be there soon."

She ended the phone call and looked at her watch. "Jenna, you have practice."

"Mom, you cannot be serious. I mean, it's Quinn."

Izzy gave her daughter a hug. *Yes, it's Quinn. It's someone you've attached to. Someone you think of as a father maybe. Of course you don't want to go. I don't either.* "Go to practice. Fill Mikayla in on what's going on. Collier's at the police station right now, answering some questions, and they want to question me."

"Do you really have to go to the police station?"

She nodded to Benny. "If I promise you the best cup of coffee and cinnamon roll you've ever had, could you give me a lift?"

***

Detective Emerson and her partner ran out of questions for Izzy two hours later. As Izzy left the station, two very confused officers arrived carrying a large bag of kitchen garbage. Stepping into the clear evening air, Izzy glanced around the parking lot.

"I'm over here, Miss Izzy."

Benny was clearly the product of a Southern upbringing. He opened the car door for her, and waited until she was safely buckled up before closing. *Just like Quinn.* "Did the police have a lot of questions for you, Benny?"

"They wanted to know about Quinn's relationship with Boss Lady."

"What did you tell them?"

"Only what I knew for sure, which wasn't much. I did tell them about Sally, though. That interested them."

Izzy put a hand on his shoulder. "Benny, I think we have time now for the long version of the story. How about if you tell me while we go to Silver Screen Coffee? I'd like to get everyone up to speed on what's happening."

"I've heard of that place. Any good?"

"I promised you great coffee and a cinnamon roll." She gave him the address to the coffee shop. "And they've got the best of both."

Benny eased the car away from the curb. "Miss Izzy, I don't want you to feel obliged to me. I'd give you a ride anyplace, because Quinn thought so much of you."

Izzy shook her head. "Don't do that."

"Do what?"

"Don't talk about him like he's gone."

Benny nodded, and cleared his throat. "You're right. Of course he's going to pull through. He's 'Monster Mash' Murray."

"Right."

"Toughest hockey player ever. Nothing slows him down."

"Well," Izzy patted his arm, "this time he may need just a little bit of help from his friends. Now tell me about Sally."

THIRTY-ONE

Cat closed the place early, shooing out the last of the regulars with the promise of free cinnamon rolls the next day. With everyone gathered around, Izzy had Benny tell everyone about Sally. While they were digesting that, Izzy laid out her suspicions about Serena, and how she might have poisoned Quinn.

"The woman is loaded. She could buy anything or anyone she wants. Why get all hissy about you, Aunt Iz?" Mikayla stared at her coffee. "It makes zero sense."

"It's possible." Collier shook his head. "When you want something so bad and you don't get it." He shot Izzy an apologetic look. "When some idiot talks about Isabella Landry making a comeback, if you're Serena Shipley, you lose your mind."

"Wait…what?" Benny looked up from his coffee. "You're Isabella Landry?"

"You know that name?" Cat studied the newcomer.

"Isabella Landry stole Serena Shipley's partner and made Serena the laughingstock of the skating world. Best internet video ever, those two minutes of her singles routine." Benny took a large bite of cinnamon roll. "Boss Lady never got over it."

Cat leaned closer. "You like figure skating?"

Benny smiled through a mouthful of crumbs. "Not as much as I like this roll."

"Movies? Do you like movies?"

Benny directed a grin toward Cat. "I love movies."

Mikayla shook her head. "Holy effin' carp you two! Can we have a singles mixer when one of our friends isn't dying?"

Benny cleared his throat. "Right, okay. I've worked at the station nine years, and every single day for nine years, Boss Lady said she hated Isabella Landry."

"Every day, for nine years?" Jenna frowned. "Isn't that a little…crazy?"

"You don't understand skating." Izzy was more surprised by her sharp tone than anyone else.

"Your mother's right." Collier's soft drawl soothed the sudden tension in the room. "Skating at that high of a level, that's not a long span of time, especially for a woman. One day you're thirteen, skating in juniors and everyone thinks you're adorable. The next day, you're twenty-two and everyone is wondering how you manage a sit spin without a walker." He tapped a pen to his lips.

"Does Quinn know you're Isabella Landry?"

"Yes, Benny, he does." Izzy struggled to keep her voice calm. "Focus. Is Serena capable of murder?"

"She'd be capable of murdering you."

Cat stared at him. "New Guy has some insight."

"I also have a name."

"Yeah, well let's hear the insight and I'll decide if I'm going to use your name."

"Is she always this mean?"

Collier chuckled. "Not once you get through the shell."

"I'll take your word for it. Yeah, Boss Lady wants revenge. I'm betting Quinn tried to protect you from her, you know, by trying to make you believe he's responsible for your husband's death."

Everyone froze and stared at Benny, who continued chewing his cinnamon roll as if he hadn't spoken. His blue eyes twinkled. "You'll remember my name now, won't you Coffee Girl?"

"How do you know all this?"

"Quinn was never a one woman man back then, so when he and Boss Lady went exclusive, I knew something wasn't right. This morning it clicked, when that story about Sally came out. Quinn's never talked about that night, not ever. But today he told me he's been operating under the impression he was driving the car the night she died and that he was the father of her baby. So, then, who would have kept him thinking that?"

Cat jumped out of her chair. "I knew it! She had something on him. She wrapped Quinn up in this scandal so tight he couldn't get away."

Quinn has been my hero the entire time and I didn't know it.

The shop phone rang, startling them all. Cat hopped up to answer it. "Silver Screen Coffee? Yeah, yeah, of course this is Izzy Marks. Got it. Okay, thank you Detective." Cat returned and sat next to Benny as if the phone call never happened.

"Hey, Cat?'

"Yeah, Izzy?"

"What did the police just tell me?"

"Well, it turns out that tiny bit of skin under your fingernails matched that of one Serena Shipley Chapman. The mushrooms found in Quinn's garbage were false morels, a particularly poisonous and hard to identify little 'shroom. Oh, and Serena's fingerprints were all over the sauté pan and spatula."

"So she really did it. She really tried to kill the two of you?" Jenna put an arm around Izzy's shoulders.

"What are the cops going to do?"

"Well, Collier, some of them are going try and find Serena because they want to arrest her, but apparently she doesn't want to be arrested. No one's seen her today. They've started a statewide manhunt. Some are going to post guard at Quinn's hospital room. And some…" she looked out the window, "are here now to guard you, Izzy."

If Quinn dies, none of this will matter. "Guys, I hope you don't mind, I'm going to go back to the hospital."

"You want me to drive you?"

Izzy gave Collier a weary smile. "Thanks, but don't you have to leave for a fair in Baton Rouge tomorrow?"

"The guys can cover for me." Collier hugged her. "I'm not going anywhere." He shrugged. "I've got a lot of misunderstanding to atone for."

Izzy forced a weak smile for her oldest friend. "No, you don't. I should have listened to you."

Collier leaned close, his stubble tickling her ear. "About Jason, yeah. But I was way wrong about Quinn."

Izzy knew no one else in the room heard Collier's words, but it didn't matter. A weight lifted off her heart and she kissed his cheek. "Thank you."

"Miss Izzy, would you like me to go with you?"

"No, thanks. My brand new body guard is here." She nodded to the flashing lights outside the front window. "But I think Cat could use some help cleaning up."

Benny's smile was a ray of sunlight. "I'd love to help out."

"Cat?"

Cat's blush belied her feigned indifference. "Sure, I can always use an extra pair of hands."

"Mom, you're going to be okay?"

"Jens, Mike, you two get home and get some sleep. I'll keep you posted." She hugged the girls and watched as they left through the back door.

I'll be fine as long as Quinn recovers.

***

Izzy caught Grace Callen in the corridor as the nurse was finishing her shift.

"Great piece of detective work there, Miss Marks."

"Thanks, Grace, but you're the one who knew about those mushrooms."

"Well, you can go on in. There doesn't seem to be long term damage to his kidneys and liver. He's still in a coma, but Dr. Passavant is hopeful."

Quinn's room was silent and dark except for the bank of lights above his head. A respirator pumped his lungs. Izzy thought about the report Grace gave her. *His kidneys and liver aren't damaged.* Izzy marveled at the irony, recalling Quinn's comment about his efforts to destroy his liver.

Izzy pulled a chair as close as she could get it, and rested her head on the bed next to him. She covered his hand with hers, closing out the beeps and clicks of the equipment surrounding them, she strained to feel the faint tempo of his pulse.

"Don't you leave me," she whispered. "You can't let me fall. I'm depending on you." She put a hand on his chest, reassuring herself. "You have to come back to me."

The monotonous rhythm of the respirator lulled her. Exhausted, her eyes drooped. "I love you too much to let you go."

***

Quinn emerged from the fog, everything immobile, frozen. Far away, from a place deep within him, a phrase played over and over, leading him out of the fog.

You have to come back to me. I love you too much to let you go.

He struggled against the fog, willing his eyes open. Adjusting to the semi darkness of the room, he studied his surroundings without understanding.

Fresh Ice

Nothing seemed familiar. Worse, no part of his body responded to his mental commands to move. Something filled his throat. He struggled against his gag reflex. He closed his eyes, and opened them again, this time recognizing that he was in the hospital, and the tube was meant to help him. He stopped struggling and relaxed, allowing the tube to help his exhausted body take in oxygen.

I am in the hospital. Clearly, something happened.

I was at the station. I was talking to Benny.

And then…I don't remember anything.

Exhaustion took over and he floated back into the fog.

Don't you leave me.

I love you too much to let you go.

Quinn opened his eyes again. *I have to wake up. I have to…*

He opened his eyes and looked down. Blonde locks spread on the bed next to his elbow, a delicate hand covering his. *I have to…*

He tensed against the tube in his throat again, this time to break away from it, to breath for himself. *I have to protect Izzy.*

***

"Izzy?"

Izzy stirred and woke. The first thing she saw was Quinn's eyes smiling at her. "You're awake?"

"Ah, Miss Marks." Dr. Passavant strode in. "You're awake."

"You're not…you're okay?"

"They unhooked me half an hour ago." His voice was a dry whisper.

"He's not out of the woods yet." The doctor made a note in her chart.

"Kill joy," Quinn whispered, his eyes snapping mischievously.

"But you, Mr. Murray, have a great support system around you, and that's key." The doctor patted Izzy's arm. "Your sister saved your life."

"Sister?" Quinn whispered.

"Yes, I'm your sister."

Dr. Passavant wrote a few more notes in his chart, and left the room. The door floated closed behind her and Quinn smiled at Izzy. "You saved my life."

Izzy stood on tiptoe and kissed his lips softly. "You saved mine first."

Quinn shuddered. "What about Serena?"

"They're still trying to find her. But Quinn, we have each other now. It's all going to be okay."

"It will be. We're just going to have to keep each other safe." Quinn wrapped his arms around her and knew, for the first time in a long time, he spoke the truth.

THIRTY-TWO

"Izzy, you need to get some rest. You're exhausted."

Izzy opened her eyes and stared at Benny. "The event is tomorrow. Tomorrow. There are just too many last minute things to deal with."

"Benny's right. Go get some sleep." Quinn looked at her over a stack of papers.

"Oh yeah, I'm the one you're all ordering to get some rest. Meanwhile, you almost died three weeks ago, and you get to stay up late?"

Benny shrugged. "He's the Boss Man."

"Don't start, Benny." Quinn smiled in spite of his stern tone. "This is a team effort. I couldn't have gotten this together without the two of you." He nodded to Benny and Cat. The two had been nearly as inseparable as he and Izzy. *Although I'm sure they're having far more fun than we are.* It wasn't the first time he silently cursed the doctor's orders that he not exert himself.

"Izzy is the gold star secret celebrity you've been promising everyone." Cat turned off a lap top and leaned against the couch. "She needs her beauty sleep."

"Yes, but given the headlines lately, people are going to be far more interested in Quinn than in me."

"Then a lot of people will be disappointed, since the doctors don't want me to do anything. It was all I could do to get them to let me be in the building." Quinn frowned. He hated the idea of not skating at his own charity event.

"Dude, you almost died. Everyone will give you a pass. Don't sweat it."

"Still doesn't make me happy that you three had to pick up the slack."

"Shush, we loved doing this." Izzy stretched her arms over her head, and yawned.

"Go sleep in the bedroom tonight. I mean it." Because neither of them felt safe with Serena still at large, Izzy had been sleeping on his sofa since the day he came home from the hospital. Knowing she was so close was maddening. Even now, exhausted as he was, sleep was the furthest thing from Quinn's mind when he pictured her in his bed.

Blinking away the image, and the arousal that went with it, Quinn tuned in to Cat's chipper chatter.

"Speaking of romantic ice stuff, 'Cutting Edge' is on cable tonight."

"I'll make popcorn!" Benny was surprisingly quick on his feet when it came to making Cat happy.

They are a weird couple, but it works for them. "I'm assuming you think you're going to watch the movie here?"

Cat made a sad face. "Jenna and Mikayla are covering at the coffee shop this week and they promised the 'Monty Python' idiots an all night marathon. Don't make me go back there. I can't take it!" She dramatically buried her face in Benny's ample shoulder.

"Fine. Just keep the volume to a dull roar. I'm going to bed." Quinn turned off his computer. He didn't miss Cat's giddy smile.

"Don't do anything I wouldn't do!" Cat cheered as he headed toward the bedroom.

Not sure what she thinks we'd be up to. Izzy's arm is still so sore and I have my orders. Quinn smiled. *Another few days and it will be a different story.* "Just don't make a mess you can't clean up, okay?"

"Sure Dad." Benny grumbled good-naturedly, snapping Quinn out of his reverie.

"I don't like that anymore than I like Boss Man, Benny." Quinn walked into his bedroom where Izzy was already asleep on the bed.

He eased a blanket over her form and slipped next to her. He turned on the fireplace and stared at her still, angelic face in the firelight.

The only thing I regret is that I won't be able to skate with you tomorrow.

That's a lie. I can't wait to see you skate in front of a huge crowd.

No, my regret is that I didn't look for you harder that night at Chances. I should have found you, told you everything right away. We might have avoided all this mess.

Quinn turned on the television, to Sports Center. He couldn't take another news report with his face next to Serena's. Knowing she was still out there, exhausted him. He tried to focus on the positive as he stretched out on the bed.

Soon I'll be free to love this angel next to me.

***

Izzy stared at the audience and shuddered. *What was I thinking? I can't do this. I can't go out there and skate by myself. People will laugh.*

"You can do this, Izzy, you know you can."

Izzy turned to see Collier, grinning at her. "How do you know what I'm thinking?"

Collier shrugged. "You forget, we were partners, once."

"Yeah, for a minute, ages ago."

"Hey, a guy never forgets his first star lift." Collier's grin took on a lecherous quality. "Pity a hand position like that was wasted on me when I was thirteen. I'd make so much more of it now."

Izzy wanted to smack him with a skate guard. "There are so many people out there. Were we expecting this many people?"

"When I saw the guest list, I figured Quinn pulled out all the stops. People are going to show up for a celebrity list like that. Plus, having the organizer caught in the middle of Nashville's biggest scandal in a generation didn't hurt."

Izzy shook her head. "Why would people focus on that? Half of it isn't true."

"For the same reason Quinn had my manger find him someone to write the book."

"What?"

Collier chuckled. "He didn't tell you? Turns out, he's gotten a few requests for a book. And, since he's a hockey player, he can't read much less put together a sentence."

This time Izzy did smack him with a skate guard. "Stop it, you're being mean!"

"I'm kidding. He told me the other day he didn't want anything to do with the actual writing, so I had my manager connect Quinn with an author he trusts." He arched an eyebrow. "I offered to co-write it, given how Quinn is a close, personal friend."

He dodged Izzy's thrown skate guard.

"My point is, dear Izzy, his story, this book needs an ending. An author will bring up all kinds of dirt, the kind that will sell millions of books, but that's only part of the story. Quinn wants the whole story out there. And everything in his story begins and ends with you on that ice." Collier nodded to the doorway, where they heard the crowd chattering. "We need a happy ending, a big finish. We need you to skate."

Izzy smiled. "Coach couldn't have said it any better, Col. Thanks."

Collier hugged her. "I think, if you look really carefully, you might see him way up in the rafters. You know he's not missing this."

Izzy wiped her eyes and nodded. Behind her, the chatter quieted and the house lights dimmed. *Quinn's coming out to introduce me.*

She stepped to the darkened edge of the ice and waited.

***

Quinn stood in the outer box of the announcer's booth and gave the crowd a weary smile. It had been a long day watching everyone else run the event while he had to content himself with signing autographs and sitting still. He hated having to introduce Izzy from the announcer's booth. He ached to be on center ice, able to see every face when she emerged from the shadows. *I've never sat on the sidelines before.*

He knew why so many people showed up. Serena's name was on everyone's lips. He didn't care. He was, in this moment, the center of attention for nearly four thousand people. A sense of satisfaction washed over him. Because everyone was so distracted with the news, Quinn knew Izzy would be a complete and utter surprise.

A year ago this would have been the high point of my year, having so many people come out for an event. Now, all that matters is Izzy finally reclaiming what's been hers all along.

Nashville, this ice, and my heart.

"Ladies and gentlemen, I want to thank you for what has turned out to be the most amazing day. Nashville has once again gone above and beyond for the Aubri Brown Club! I know, once I reveal the final surprise of the day, we will reach that goal!"

He waited for the applause to subside. "I have to thank my hockey brothers. Everything you've donated today, your time, your memorabilia, it's all been awesome. Watch out, though, because next year I won't be sitting on the sideline for the game, I'll be out there kicking your tails." He nodded to the hockey players who applauded.

Quinn's smile softened. "And all you aspiring figure skaters, I think I see a few future Olympians in this room today." He pointed to the front row of young skaters and there was more polite applause.

"Before I introduce the last celebrity of the day," Quinn looked toward the darkened tunnel, where he knew Izzy waited with Collier, "I wanted to clear up some confusion about a few things."

The crowd murmured in low tones, and Quinn held up his hand. "I know. I've been on TV more than I was in my playing days." He grinned and nodded, allowing the crowd a relieved chuckle. "Some of what you have heard is true, some was not. Some of you fine folks maybe aren't my biggest fans at the moment. Some of you like me anyway." The players chuckled, while the rest of the crowd waited.

"It's going to take a long time for the ugliness to get sorted out." He looked at a group of children, "I've disappointed a lot of you guys. I'm sorry for that."

"What I'm really sorry for, is that, somewhere along the way, I lost it. You all," he nodded to the kids in the front rows, "you know about losing it, don't you? Everything's going along fine, and then something happens, then something else, and suddenly you've lost it. You can't get out, you can't fix what's wrong, and you lose your control, your self-respect. You lose it all because you don't know how to make things right." He took a deep breath.

The quiet tension in the arena hung like a fog.

He waited for the emotion welling inside him to calm. "In hockey...well, in every ice sport really...the very best time to skate is when the ice is fresh. You know how ice gets after a period of hockey, or maybe after a lot of figure skating, it's chipped, it's not smooth...it's ugly. Then the Zamboni comes out and does its job and that ice is smooth, it's clean. There is nothing better than fresh ice, is there?"

The hockey players and skaters cheered.

"Well, it's the same in life. I used to behave very badly. I felt lousy about it, but I didn't see a way to make my life better. I was willing to just skate on busted up ice because I didn't know how to fix it and I thought I didn't deserve any better."

"You don't deserve any better, Quinn Murray! You deserve to go to hell!"

All eyes flashed toward the rafters of the arena, but only Quinn saw the speaker.

Benny raised the house lights immediately, and Quinn's first thought was Izzy. He glanced toward the tunnel.

"Is that Serena?" Benny squinted into the rafters.

"Shut up all of you!"

The shrieking female voice sent shivers down Quinn's spine. "The one and only."

"How the hell did she get in?"

"She must have hidden in Burkes' box. She's part owner of the Preds, she's got all the right keys."

"You'd think they'd search the place, wouldn't you?"

Quinn shook his head. "Yeah, you would."

"It's time everyone knew about you, Quinn Murray!"

Quinn stayed on the outer deck, and struggled to keep his voice calm. "Ladies and gentlemen, please return to your seats. I can assure you, that no one is going to get hurt."

"Can you assure them Quinn? Can you?" Serena's voice, slightly less hyper, drifted over the tense audience.

Is she holding guns? Quinn squinted at her. *How would she have guns in here?*

Quinn closed his eyes and pictured the suite. *Burkes kept a pair of antique pistols mounted on a wall in there. Civil War or something like that.*

Relief washed over him. *There can't be much in the way of ammo.*

"I know what you're thinking."

The crowd kept silent, all eyes bouncing between Quinn and the shadowy rafters where Serena remained out of sight.

"What am I thinking, Serena?"

"You're thinking I'm using Burkes' old pistols, I must not have any bullets, and so I can't possibly hurt anyone. You're thinking I'll be caught, and you'll get to be with your precious Izzy. And then she'll win."

Quinn bit his lip. *How do I respond to any of that?*

"You're wrong. She won't win."

"Okay Serena."

"You understand I have no choice. I have to do this. I can't lose to her again."

Quinn watched the faces of the audience. They watched with a mix of horror and interest. *Live theater. You can't beat it.* "No, I don't understand, Serena."

"Jason had to be punished. He left me for Isabella Landry and he had to be punished. Now it's your turn to be punished for Sally, and for …her."

At the mention of Sally, there was a soft wave of whispers. Quinn ignored it, and kept his gaze locked on Serena. He didn't say a word, waiting for her next move.

"Quinn had nothing to do with Sally Meyers' death and you know it."

All eyes focused on Benny, who now stood next to Quinn. "I drove Quinn home that night and he wasn't the father of her baby. But you knew all that."

"Liar!" This time she fired the ancient pistol in Quinn and Benny's general direction. The acrid stink of gunpowder filled the arena for a moment, and people screamed and ducked in their seats. As the smell faded, Quinn realized she was no longer in the rafters.

Where did she go?

Quinn eyed the panicked crowd. *I have to keep this group from stampeding or Serena will escape.* "Ladies and gentlemen, we are going to find this woman, but I ask that you please, please stay in your seats. For the safety of everyone, stay in your seats."

Out of the corner of his eye, Quinn saw arena security running through the outer corridors of the arena. *They'll find her. They have to find her.*

I have to find Izzy.

Quinn left the pandemonium of the arena, where Benny repeated the call for calm, and headed down darkened halls to the locker rooms. Footsteps echoed around him, but there was no sign of Serena; or of Izzy.

"Quinn!"

Quinn stopped to make out Collier's form in the half light. "Where's Izzy?"

"Don't know. The second we heard Serena's voice, she peeled off her skates and started running." Collier gasped for air. "Clearly, she's in better shape than I am."

"Where were you headed?"

"Not sure. She took a left when I must've taken a right."

"Okay, you go that way," Quinn nodded over his shoulder. "Shout like hell if you find her."

Collier nodded and ran.

Quinn moved from one hall to another, checking locked doors, and listening for any sound that would lead him to Izzy. Another twenty feet, around a corner, and he halted. There Serena was, standing ten feet in front of Izzy, an ancient pistol pointed in both directions. He stared at the pistols, and glimmer of hope sparking in his heart. *Muzzle loaders. She fired one in the arena. At best she has one bullet left.*

Quinn knew his assumption was a gamble, but he also knew it was unlikely Serena could have reloaded in the time it took her to run through the back passageways of the center. "Serena."

Serena stiffened, but did not look at him. "I wouldn't come any closer, Quinn."

"Look at me." He kept his voice low, smooth. Over Serena's shoulder, he watched Izzy. Her face remained stoic. Quinn sensed she wasn't afraid. She looked as if she was waiting for the right moment to pounce and disarm Serena.

Did she go after Serena?

He looked at her face again. There was no question. Izzy intended to fight this battle. They were a team, and she was as ready for whatever happened as he.

"It's over, Serena. You have one shot, if that. Put the guns down."

Serena didn't flinch. "I may have only one shot, but which gun? If I fire, someone will die." Her face broke into a strained smile. "You're going to pay, both of you. One will die, and the other is just going to have to live with that."

Izzy bit her lip, her eyes resolute. Watching her body tense, Quinn realized their weeks of skating practice paid off. He was ready to move in sync with her. He didn't even need to count to three.

He sprang forward and slammed Serena's arm down the same moment Izzy leapt and forced her other hand up. The pistol fired, harmlessly, into the ceiling. The hall filled with the stink of ancient gunpowder and security guards. Quinn pulled Izzy to him in an iron embrace.

Amid the confusion as the guards dragged Serena away, Collier reached them. "Are you guys okay?"

Quinn loosened his grip on Izzy. "I think so. Izzy?"

"I'm fine." Her voice quavered.

"She was pointing the loaded gun at you. You could have been killed." Quinn held her close to him again.

"We didn't know that. It could have been the other one. You're the one who knew she only had one bullet. How?"

"I used to have to listen to Burkes brag about those pistols. I knew they were muzzle loaders. I also knew Serena wouldn't have a clue how to load one."

"So you saved her life, and she almost took a bullet for you. How can I ever compete with that?" Collier's smile held a shadow of loss.

Izzy left Quinn's embrace and hugged Collier. "Col…"

"No Izzy. Don't be sorry."

"But, Collier…"

Collier gave her a tight squeeze and handed her back to Quinn. "A little heartbreak is great for my line of business. I'll be able to write tons of great songs."

"Any chance there could be a happy song in there?" Izzy's concern for Collier echoed in her words.

"Only if there's a happy ending to this. So, you have to skate."

Izzy and Quinn exchanged a glance. "I don't know. Everyone's pretty shaken up out there," Izzy smiled. "We'll do it another day."

Collier shook his head. "Like hell. You have to skate. Right, Quinn?"

Quinn closed his eyes. Above them, he heard the sound of the loudspeaker, as Benny assured the crowd that Serena had, indeed, been caught. There was a thunderous cheer. "It doesn't sound like anyone left. I think we need to give them a finish that's a bit more upbeat, don't you?"

"Right. You'd hate to end a charity event with a shooting." Collier relaxed.

Izzy turned to Quinn. "Are you sure?"

"After everything we've been through to get you on that ice in front of those people I think, if you're up to it, you should do it. But it's your call."

A tear welled in her eye. *What did I say? I'm an idiot.* He brushed the tear away. "Don't cry. If you don't want to do it, you don't have to do it."

"No, it's my call." She beamed. "I'm doing it."

She's never been given a choice. To this moment she's had exactly one choice at every turn of her life. No one gave her more than one choice, one way to go.

He knew the look on her face very well. *She's finally seeing a full sheet of fresh ice in front of her, no expectations, no demands, just the perfect ice.*

"Come on," he held out his hand, "I have an introduction to finish. And I want to do it from center ice wearing my skates, like I always meant to."

***

After putting on his skates, Quinn waited at center ice for the crowd to settle down. *What do I say to an audience that came for a charity event and wound up witnessing an act of insanity?*

"Well, ladies and gentlemen, when I promise a day full of surprises, I mean it."

He smiled and let the ice breaking applause go for a moment, needing the time to calm the nervous energy that flooded through him. "We were talking about skating on lousy ice, weren't we? Well, that's been my life for a long while. Then several months ago, I was blessed to run into a woman whom I have loved from afar for a long time. She's that rare sort of person that makes everyone's life around her better."

He waited for the hum of speculation to die down. "You've all waited quite long enough for my surprise." Quinn skated to the open gate, and stepped off the ice. Benny turned off the house lights and pointed a single spot on Quinn.

"Ladies and gentlemen: Twenty years ago, Nashville called her the First Lady of Pairs' Skating. Today, she's come home. Isabella Landry."

The ice went dark, and when Benny focused a small beam at center ice, Izzy was there, a lone sparkling star against a black sky. The audience gasped, then fell silent, as the first notes of "I Won't Hold You Back," echoed.

Alone on the ice, Izzy was mesmerizing. Quinn sensed the energy, in spite of the eerie hush settling around them, and he knew the crowd was as captivated with her as he was. Every element, every spin was flawless, fluid. She moved as if no more than a moment passed between that long ago night in the Twin Cities and this afternoon in Nashville.

Halfway through the routine, she waved to the tunnel where Quinn stood next to Collier. "Why is she waving?"

"She's trying to get your attention."

Izzy passed by them again, waving. "What? What does she want?"

"You still don't get it, do you?"

She passed by them, third time. "She wants me on the ice?"

"Yes, you idiot. She wants you to do a throw." Collier laughed and elbowed him. "She can't fly herself, can she?"

I would drop her. I'm not strong enough. Her arm is still too tender.

"Get your butt out there or I will. And you won't like where I put my hands."

As Izzy neared, Quinn jumped out and caught her. His hands on her waist and arm, he let her lead him around the arena to thundering applause. "What are we doing?"

"A throw triple Salchow." Izzy skated under his arm. "Ready?"

"Iz…"

"Don't worry." She forced his hand to her flat stomach. "Now!"

He tensed, lifted and let her go. The applause and cheers were deafening as she flew through the air and landed, like a piece of silk, fifteen feet away. Quinn stopped short on the ice, breathless at the sight of her.

The applause and cheers continued as the music ended and they skated toward each other and embraced.

"How did you know I wouldn't drop you?" He shouted.

She pointed down. "We're on fresh ice."

Quinn was certain he'd never seen anything more beautiful. Wrapping his arms around her, he kissed her softly. "I'm glad you got to skate that routine in front of an audience, you know, without being pregnant."

Her eyes twinkled. "Who says?"

"Who says what?" Trying to hear her over the crowd noise, he leaned closer.

"Who says I'm not pregnant?"

Quinn stared at her. *It's not possible.* He shook his head. "But we only…and I…"

She shrugged, "Sometimes stuff fails." She smiled, her eyes shining stars.

"I'm going to be a father?" His words were lost in the din of the arena. *So much better than a jersey with my name on it.*

Overjoyed, he swung Izzy in a circle, set her gently on her feet, and kissed her.

The cheers faded away as he lost himself in her return kiss.

EPILOGUE

The check and the letter lay, side by side, on the table. Everyone sat in a circle, staring at the two pieces of paper as if they were magic.

"So," Cat, sitting on Benny's lap, tried to break the ice. "This is sort of 'It Could Happen to You.' You know, Bridget Fonda, Nic Cage? Cop, waitress, lottery money."

"Yeah, we get it, Cat." Izzy leaned against Quinn and stared at the papers.

"Only this is weird."

"Yeah, we get that, too." Jenna poured herself a cup of coffee.

The check, made out to Izzy, was the life insurance settlement from Jason's estate. With Serena's conviction for assault and attempted murder, Izzy was able to connect enough dots for the insurance company. While no one could officially pin Jason's death on Serena, the insurance company ruled out suicide and paid the claim.

The letter, addressed to Quinn, was a job offer on official WNSH letterhead. WNSH, now lacking a station manager since Serena's conviction, wanted Quinn to fill the position.

"We should start with the easy one first." Quinn draped his left arm around Izzy's shoulders. His simple wedding band, the twin to the one on her finger, glowed in the yellow overhead light.

"Yeah, let's talk about the job offer." Benny nodded agreement, before returning to nuzzling Cat's neck.

"No, the check." Cat said. "The job offer is going to take debate."

"I'm with Cat. What are you doing with that cash?" Mikayla sipped her coffee.

"I'd like to know what Quinn's going to do about the job." Jenna's soft tone barely broke above the noisy conversation.

"Collier could break this tie."

"Yes, Cat, but he's not here." Izzy looked at each face in the circle. Collier was on the road with his band. Izzy knew there was more to it than that. In spite of his convincing words at the fundraiser, Collier needed time to come to terms with losing her again. She hated the gap between them, but was willing to wait until he was ready to come home and be her best friend once more. "We are going to have to figure it out without a tie breaker."

"Okay, Mom, Quinn, who wants to talk first?"

"I'm not taking the job," Quinn said quietly.

Izzy smiled. They hadn't talked about it, but Izzy knew the minute she saw the offer, Quinn would never take Serena's old job.

After the general uproar around the table subsided, Quinn continued. "I'm not management. I like talking about sports."

"So you'll still do color commentary?" Benny asked.

"Not for away games." Quinn shook his head. "I spent too many years on the road. I've got a family now, and I'm not spending one minute away from the baby…or the baby's mother." He hugged Izzy close. "I don't mind giving my opinion on the radio, hanging out at Preds games here in town, but I won't be flying out of town in the middle of the night and I certainly will not sit in the manager's office ever again."

Only Izzy saw the shadow of a dark memory pass over Quinn's face.

"Oh come on! I was going to use your place to impress my lady when you were on the road!" Benny kissed Cat on the cheek. "Seriously, all I've got going for me is the fact that my best friend is a former NHL player with a super cool apartment I can break into. Now you're staying in town all the time? I'm doomed!"

Everyone laughed.

"Benny, you possess the one thing I find irresistible." Cat giggled. "You have the ability to recite every line to 'The Princess Bride.' With the correct accents. As far as I'm concerned, you don't need anything else."

They started kissing, and there was jovial groan of disapproval.

"Okay, so you're not taking the job. But there's still that sweet check, Aunt Iz. What are you going to do with all that?"

Izzy gave Quinn a soft smile. "The day of the charity event, Quinn talked about skating on fresh ice. I think a lot about how easy it would be if Quinn and I just kept the money and lived like rich celebrities."

"So easy," Benny murmured. "I get calls every day at the station, people wanting to book you for interviews, for exhibitions."

"Right. But the thing is, we know what makes us happy, and it has nothing to do with a big time job or having our names in the papers."

"We've been there." Quinn's voice was low.

"So, after talking it over with Jenna, a third of this we'll split between Make-A-Wish and Aubri Brown. A third of it," she patted Jenna's hand, "I'm keeping aside for Jenna. I want you to have everything you need to be exactly what you want to be." Izzy gave Jenna a one-armed embrace.

"And the rest?" Mikayla leaned forward. Cat and Benny followed suit.

"We happen to know the coffee shop could use a new roof." Quinn nodded to Cat.

"And we've arranged with Collier to buy out his partners at the rink." Izzy smiled. "That happiest I ever was when I was a kid were the hours I spent in that place. I'd like to buy it, fix it up a bit, and Quinn and I can give lessons. Not big coaching for future Olympians. I want to give all kinds of kids the same love of the ice that we have. I think it would be a good place for a little one to grow up, too." She patted her stomach. She wasn't showing, yet, but the flutter of life within her was undeniable.

There was a smattering of applause around the table.

Quinn cleared his throat. "Benny, there is one other thing."

"Yeah?"

"Izzy and I are going to be traveling for about a month, maybe two. I'll need you to house sit my place. Starting now."

With a loud whooping cry, Benny pushed Cat off his lap, leaped out of his chair, and, taking her by the hand, ran out the door without saying goodbye.

"Um, are they coming back?" Mikayla watched as Benny's car skidded out of the parking lot.

Quinn laughed out loud. "Probably not. Remind me to burn the mattress and the couch, when we get home."

"So, Mom, where are you going?"

Izzy shrugged. "Here, there. We're going to visit some of Quinn's family."

"Mend some fences."

"We don't know if everything is going to have a happy ending," Izzy closed her eyes, trying to shut out the image of her parents, "but we are going to spend the next several weeks trying."

The girls left the coffee shop an hour later after the conversation and coffee had run out. Izzy locked the front door behind them, and turned out the lights while Quinn waited for her on the stairs.

Backlit by the hall light, Izzy could only see Quinn as a dark outline. She knew he was watching her, as he always did. He watched over her, and that simple thought was enough to make her tingle.

As she crossed the darkened coffee shop to his waiting embrace, Izzy knew she was skating on a sheet of unending, perfect ice, toward a partner who would never let her fall. She didn't need any applause or judge's score to tell her everything was perfect.

Fresh Ice

Acknowledgments

I have to thank Linda Schmalz, my dear critique partner, who made me tear this book down to the foundations and build it back the right way. Thank you to Kelly Moran, for the magnificent cover art!

Thank you to my cousin Jill Frick, who insisted I have a hockey player in one of my books. Thank you to former NHL star Jeremy Roenick, for answering the phone and giving me Quinn Murray. Thank you to my coworker and friend, TJ Noll who only thinks he grossed me out with his tales of shoulder dislocations.

Thank you to the New Minstrel Revue, whose song "Thank You for Asking" inspired more pages of the book than I can count. For more information on this fantastic, talented, group of musicians, http://www.jbradleycollier.com/pages/newminstrel.html.

Thank you also, to my mom, Carolyn Schultz, who is my ever patient editor and biggest cheerleader.

Finally, I'm a writer, but I'm also a mother and the research I did for this book touched my mother's heart. For more information about how you can support the magnificent charities mentioned in this book, here are the web addresses:

Aubri Brown Club http://www.theaubribrownclub.org/

Make-A-Wish http://www.wish.org/

About the Author

Sarah J. Bradley

SARAH is a lifelong Upper Midwest girl who lives with her husband, her two children, and her four rescue cats in Wisconsin. When not writing, Sarah follows both the NFL and the NHL religiously, searches for restaurants with great soup, and attends Rick Springfield concerts. "Fresh Ice" is her third novel.

ALSO BY SARAH J. BRADLEY

Dream in Color

Lies in Chance
A Hero's Spark
Love is…

Also by SJB Books Authors

By S. J. Bradley

Missing in Manitowoc
Super Hero in Superior
Warning in Waukesha (Coming fall 2017)

By Sarah Jayne Brewster

"Not While I'm Chewing!"
Unsafe at Any Speed

Made in the USA
Monee, IL
14 July 2023

38727969R00154